# Volition

A Uniform & Lace Romance

Noah & Tessa's Story
~Book One~

## Tina Maurine

# COPYRIGHT

Trient Press

3375 S Rainbow Blvd

#81710, SMB 13135

Las Vegas,NV 89180


Ordering Information:
Quantity sales. Special discounts are available on quantity purchases
by corporations, associations, and others. For details, contact the
publisher at the address above.
Orders by U.S. trade bookstores and wholesalers. Please contact Trient
Press: Tel: (775) 996-3844;   or visit www.trientpress.com.


Printed in the United States of America


Publisher's Cataloging-in-Publication data
Maurine, Tina.
A title of a book : Volition
ISBN Hard Cover 978-1-953975-13-3
        Paperback   978-1-953975-14-0
        E-book      978-1-953975-15-7

# Dedication

**To my sweet T. & K.**
If you want it badly enough, you can make it happen. Always
push forward in the face of adversity, bullies and naysayers.
Their opinions aren't the ones that truly matter.
Your opinions of yourself are the most important.
Always believe in yourselves.
Always believe in your dreams.
Always make things happen for yourselves.
I believe in your greatness and support your dreams, no matter
what they may be.
I love you bigger than the universe.

**To B.**
Thanks for believing in my greatness and supporting my dream.
I love you forever.

# *Icelandic phrases*

ISL…. Frá krakkar spila á borðið þremur
ENG…. From the guys playing on table three

ISL…. Svo, þú vilt frekar sitja hér hjá mér ha
ENG…. So, you'd rather sit here with me huh

ISL…. Ahh já, en ég mun ekki segja neinum ef þú
ert ekki
ENG…. Ah yes, I will not tell anyone if you don't

ISL…. Komdu
ENG…. Come

ISL…. rekur bar fyrir eiganda'
ENG…. runs the bar for the owner

ISL…. Ég hef sýnt þér meira af mér
ENG…. I have shown you more

ISL…. En ég hef sýnt einhver á löngum tíma
ENG…. than I've shown someone in a long time

ISL…. Þú verður að vera orsök fyrir að hætta við
ENG…. You'll be the reason for my undoing

ISL.... Ég er vakin á þig
ENG.... I am so drawn to you


ISL.... Tessa mín
ENG.... My Tessa


ISL.... sæta mín................(sæta)
ENG.... My cutie..............(cutie)


ISL.... Hvenær munum við ríða aftur
ENG....When will we fuck again


ISL.... Ég hef saknað snertingu þína, lyktina þína,
kossana þína
ENG.... I have missed your touch, your smell, your kisses


ISL.... hrífandi
ENG.... ravishing


ISL.... Þú veist, Tessa mín, myndi ég elska að sjá þig
aftur. Bráðum
ENG.... You know, Tessa, I would love to see you
again, soon


ISL.... Ég myndi elska að grafa mig í fullkomnu litlu
kisa þinn aftur
ENG.... I would love to dig myself into your perfect
little pussy again

"Tessa! Are you ready *yet*? You're taking forever."

I looked in the mirror to put the finishing touches on my curly bob, ran 'Cancan Red' over my lips and smacked them.

Lindy—only my best friend since the second grade—walked up behind me and gave me a disapproving shake of her head. "Well, if that hooker shade doesn't knock a few socks off...I am not sure what will!"

I laughed but knew full well that was her *kind* way of saying the lipstick color I'd chosen made me look cheap. "Hey now, be nice. It's my last night up here in the Pacific Northwest. If I can't let loose and party my last night, then why the fuck are you throwing me this shindig?"

"Alright—I'll give you that." She hooked her arm in mine and began pulling me away from the mirror. "Come-on... you're good enough!"

"Okay," I conceded and followed her back into the throes of the party.

The evening evolved into night, and with it, the progression of my inebriated state. It seemed every time I finished my drink, a new, fuller one appeared in my hand. Thank God the party had started as an intimate BBQ. Without food, I'd have been a total goner.

"So, you're the girl of the hour?" A voice grated from behind me in a husky tenor that dripped with sex appeal.

"That I am." I giggled my drunken reply but gave pause when I turned, as the guy standing before me was, well... I wasn't expecting him at all. "I, I... I mean I leave tomorrow for boot camp."

*Boy, that was smooth, Tessa! I leave for boot camp? Ugh...* Our eyes met the instant I turned around, and a bolt of electricity shot through me... through us. He looked off balance and an expression of surprise crossed his face before it flitted away. His translucent blue eyes captured my gaze. I held his intense stare, swam in it actually, until he cleared his throat and looked away. He cracked his neck and shook out his shoulders a little before looking back at me...

"So, you're leaving for boot camp, huh? Let me introduce myself. Call me 'Ren'—your personal encyclopedia for all things military for the night."

"Oh? That's an interesting service to offer a lady." I winked at him and laid my hand on his muscular forearm before taking a drink of my 151-proof jungle juice. "Ren. *Ren*, Ren, Ren... I like that. I like the way it leaves me breathless when I say it."

Ren narrowed his eyes at me and cocked his head as though he were trying to figure me out. I took another drink.

"Well, Tessa," he took a swig of his whiskey as he advanced

on me, backing me into the wall. "You're going in and I've been *in*, so I figured if there was anything you wanted to know… I'm the exact person you should ask."

"Hmmm… anything I want to know, huh?" I cocked my eyebrow as my mouth curved up into a particularly sly and flirtatious smile.

Ren—this incredibly intriguing, sexy stranger—had me thinking all kinds of 'things' that were crazy, considering I had just met him. *What's wrong with me? Where did this magnetism between us come from? How can it be so instant and consuming?*

"How about you answer this for me?" Ren moved close and now leaned into me, so our bodies were mere inches apart. I felt his breath on my neck, and it sent shivers through me. His smell didn't help me any either… he smelled of whiskey, cedar and his musk… a heady scent that had me on the verge of a good, ol' fashioned swoon.

*Clear your head, Tessa—you just met him.*

*I know… but he's so… everything right. It's my last night here… I won't ever see him again…*

*True…*

I jumped slightly when I felt Ren's thumb on my chin. He tipped it, so his full and insanely kissable lips hovered millimeters from my full, lustful ones. His heated eyes darkened.

"How is it that someone as insanely sexy as you is here all alone?"

Before I could answer, his lips descended on mine in a soft, seeking kiss. I hadn't even had the time to respond, I was so shocked, before he lifted his head. "What is it, Ms. Tessa Christy —that thing about you that I…?" His voice trailed off as though he were working something out in his head. He cleared his throat. "It's too bad I'm just visiting and you're going in for four years."

I reached up, placing my hand on his cheek and rubbing my thumb over his lips. "We have tonight."

"We do—so let's refill your drink and make the rounds!"

We headed off in search of Lindy and some more 151 rum punch. We wove through the crowd, Ren's strong, rough hand never letting go as he led the way. Once we stepped out into the tiki torch-lit backyard, he guided me with his hand on the small of my back over to the kegs and make-shift bar.

"Holy shit, Tessa! I've been looking everywhere for you." Lindy looked as exasperated as she sounded.

"She's been in good hands."

She looked over at me and raised a brow. "Is that so?"

As I downed what was left in probably my fourth or fifth drink, either his hand lingering dangerously close to my ass or the booze… lit me up and made me tingly all over. I smiled coyly at Lindy.

Her eyes widened. *Smart girl. She can see what's going on.* I smiled back.

She looked directly at me. "Tessa, girl, you'd better watch out for him…" she nodded her head at Ren. "…the stories I have heard." She winked at him and halfway scowled at me.

Ren raised his cup to her in a silent toast, all the while keeping his eyes pointedly on me. His intensity unnerved me. Something unsettling about him that inexplicably drew me, not just that he was so fucking hot and fit, more like I craved him somehow.

*What? Like that's even possible…*

*It must be the booze.*

After Lindy took off, an awkward silence hung over us in

spite of the party going on all around. Finally, Ren grabbed my hand and took off in the direction of the mosh pit in the living room. Okay, not really a mosh pit, but everyone had crammed in there, dancing their asses off to House of Pain's "Jump Around."

"Down your drink and give me your cup."

"I will if you say please…" a weak attempt to flirt with him, I'll admit.

"I'm not generally in the business of saying please."

I raised one eyebrow. "Oh? Why's that?"

He flashed me a cocky-ass smile. "I usually don't have to."

"Well, Mr. I'm-so-hot-I-don't-have-to-say-please-because-girls-do-whatever-I-say, with me, please goes a long, *long* way." I winked at him and tipped back my cup—letting the icy, boozy punch slide down my throat.

Finishing, I reached in to grab the piece of pineapple from the bottom. Just as I was about to polish it off, he snagged my hand and took the last small bite into his mouth. He drew and pulled on my sticky fingers, sucking them until my toes curled. Ren studied my reaction intently. Instead of it being weird like it should've been, for some reason I preferred him to be near and paying this much attention to me. Weird. I know.

"You're finished," I found his commanding voice beguiling, "so, can I *please* have this dance?" Sure, he said please, but the sarcasm dripped from his beautiful mouth.

Did I mention his features were to die for? He stood maybe a foot or so taller than me. His worn t-shirt hugged his nicely-shaped delts and pecs. When he'd leaned against me earlier, his firm abs had flattened against mine and had brought about a serious yearning for more in my core. So, of course, I followed him onto the 'dance-floor' where everyone was dirty dancing to R. Kelly's "Bump n' Grind."

We found our spot amongst the grinding couples. I looked up at Ren, and his eyes focused on me as he wrapped his strong arm around my waist. With his right arm, he effortlessly pulled me against his deliciously firm body. He placed his other hand at my side, over my ribs, and began to dip and grind to the music. My hands started on his biceps, but halfway through fucking with our clothes on to that damn song, my other dropped to his hip, where I kept it to hold on for dear life.

He sang to the lyrics in a lust laden voice, choked with desire.

My eyes shot up to Ren's. What I saw instantly—no shit—soaked my panties. His eyes brimmed with passion for me.

*He wants me?!*

I held his intense gaze as we felt every pulse and beat from the music, even after the song switched to R. Kelly's "Your Body's Callin'." I couldn't begin to explain why my level of comfort with him was already so strong; perhaps it was the 151 I'd had… but in any case, it was there. I wasn't going to fight it.

Someone smacked my ass, and I swiveled my head. Lindy threw me the thumbs up sign. I smiled back. I hadn't had this much fun in a *very* long time.

The song's lyrics resounded in my head, but how Ren handled my body, and how he looked at me resonated in my soul.

*Who* is *this guy?*

Ren's hands splayed on my back and ass, snugging me in tightly to his pronounced arousal. My hands made their way up to his neck and played with his nape and shoulders as we danced. The whole affair on the dance floor couldn't have been any more intimate if we'd been sequestered somewhere.

Ren leaned in even closer, placing his mouth at my neck, just below my ear. I could hear him singing the song lyrics. It was so goddamn hot, as though he were singing the lyrics to me, begging me to lie under him.

I was there. I wanted him.

*Fuck it…*

"Ren…?" My voice hitched and came out in a barely audible whisper. I didn't even recognize it.

"Mm hmm…" His mumbled response echoed at my ear and resounded through my body.

I didn't respond. What was I going to say? 'I want you?' My non-response brought Ren to his full height. His eyes met mine and he and I both knew… we only had tonight.

He led me off the dance floor and up the stairs. Pausing at a door, he looked at me again. I flashed him a demure smile. I so wanted this.

No sooner had we pulled the guest-room door tightly shut, then he pinned me against it. His hands cupped my face and ass simultaneously, pulling me harder into his erection. His lips met mine for a kiss that dipped and pulled, scoured and ravished. He explored my mouth completely, leaving me breathless and him fighting for more. He made short work of my delicate shirt, and I struggled to pull his off. He helped me, revealing a perfectly sculpted chest with what looked like a bullet wound in his shoulder and 'Lisa' tattooed over his heart. His body was every bit the sexy specimen I had cooked up in my brain, unscathed by the typical tattoos most 'bad boys' had.

"I. Want. You." A half pained, desire-laden groan escaped from Ren's swollen lips. "God, I want you. I just… I can't get enough of you."

I responded by reaching for his fly and pulling at the fastenings until it splayed wide. I may have been a virgin, but I was not shy, nor was I inexperienced. I reached out, working to release him, and as my fingers touched his stout, engorged cock, he hissed. He ripped open my jeans and made haste to drag them and my thong down and off my legs. No sooner did they tumble to the floor, then his hungry mouth captured mine again, and his fingers went to work preparing me.

I threw my head back as waves of sensation assaulted me. He was way better at this than the frat boys I had been playing around with for the past year. WAY, *way* better.

Then, he stopped.

Cold.

"Tell me you want me, Tessa."

I looked at him like 'What's the fuck wrong with you— can't you tell?' but as soon as my eyes latched on to his, I couldn't care less if he wanted to hear me say it.

Shooting him a wicked smile, I let the words "I want you" fall timidly from my lips.

"Louder."

"I WANT you."

With that, he gripped my hips firmly, capturing my mouth in a searing hot kiss. He hoisted me onto his hips, pushing himself deeply into me, ripping my breath from my lungs and leaving me senseless. He paused, looking at me tenderly for the briefest of moments, letting the realization of what I'd given him register. Then, he began a raw, hungry, animalistic and intoxicating assault that ended in an orgasm that ruined me.

*Oh my God, oh my God...* it took me a minute while my pulse slowed to take a mental breath, so I could think clearly. *Jeezus, Ren's amazing! I'm so glad I used him to break me in before I leave for boot camp, and damn if he isn't the perfect guy to prepare me for all of the rest! Shit, I can't even remember 'what's-his-name'* who *I was seeing last, and Ren won't remember me either—hell, he doesn't even know my name,* I thought slyly, reveling in the anonymity. *And if this isn't the perfect one night stand right before I leave? I. Want. You... Fuck that was so hot!* I thought, damning my most recent weaknesses... Ren and Bacardi 151.

# Chapter One

A t 0600 on the nose, I dropped my pea soup and puke-green sea bag on the flight line with everyone else's.

"… AD2 Burton…, AO3 Miller…, E2 Walker…, E2 Schef…,"

I numbly listened to muster as the squadron personnel I was flying with stood at ease. The frigid 46 degrees in Jacksonville made it hard to pay attention, especially since I'd just come from my last duty station in Puerto Rico a week earlier. I mentally chided myself for choosing JAX as my second duty station when so many billets had been available in California; after all, who would've guessed California would've been warmer than Florida?

"… AT1 Jeoff…AME3 Robins…, Airman Anders…, AE3 Christy…,"

"AE3 Christy…,"

I started at a nudge from the average-looking girl beside me. "AE3 Christy HERE!" I answered much too exuberantly. A few people snickered, and a good many heads turned. I shifted uncomfortably, looked down and shuffled my nicely worn, steel-toed flight line boots; proud of the hard work and experience those scuff marks stood for.

*Sooooorry for being a little excited. Sheesh. Besides, just who do you think you are—laughing at me? I mean, it's not as though I'm a newbie straight from boot camp. I've already done two years' time ... Thank God.*

As I waited for the deployment attendance muster to finish, I found myself nervous as hell. Granted, I wasn't straight out of boot camp, but this deployment was my first ride at the pony show. I was as wet behind the ears as the kids who stepped off the bus at the Recruit Training Center in Great Lakes Illinois for Navy boot camp.

"Hi, my name is Sammie Anders." The girl who mustered right before me spoke in a voice a bit deeper than I expected. With muster ended, we began the typical military 'Hurry up and Wait' game.

I turned to her, smiled and introduced myself. "Hi, Sammie. I'm Tessa Christy. Have you been stationed here long?"

"I checked in about six months ago, give or take."

"How's it been, I mean... have you had a chance to work in your shop yet?"

"Nah, you know how it is—they assigned me to the Geedunk, the squadron snack-food shop."

I nodded. "Yeah, I sure do. I worked in my last squadron's 'Dunk' for at least that long before they assigned me as a parts driver for the maintenance division."

Sammie told her story quite animatedly, gesturing large and speaking with lots of infliction. She was on quite a roll, so I doubt she'd noticed I'd only been answering her with the nonspecific: "Wow... No Way... Hmm," while I'd taken the opportunity to study her.

My new friend stood about 5'7", 135-140 lbs., built like a tomboy, with a mousy brown, style-less bob, parted off center. Her clothes hung on her loosely. She seemed to have no real fashion sense and didn't emphasize her God-given gifts. I noticed she wore no make-up.

*I guess she's a lot like me. I don't feel like it's necessary here at work. Besides, at twenty, she's only two years younger than me. We don't need it anyways.*

At 5'2", I wore my long, loose, red curls, jade-green eyes and sun-kissed, freckled skin on my petite frame as well as she wore her deep blue eyes and olive-toned skin on her athletic one. Neither of us would be described as striking, at least I didn't think so, but I'd wager she, like me, was never short of company either.

"So, Sammie," I nudged her and waited while she took off her headphones. "I'm bored," I said, smiling sheepishly. "Entertain me; tell me about home and your family."

"Shit, Tessa, there isn't too much to tell. Hmmm… well, I come from a pretty dysfunctional family. My dad told my mom he was into his assistant when I was about nine. I think my mom would've taken it better if his assistant hadn't been a guy in his twenties."

My eyes widened. "Wow! No shit? I bet that was a hard pill to swallow."

"Yeah, it wasn't just, 'Hey hun, I've found someone else that I want to be with.' It was also "I'm gay and not into women anymore.' My mom felt like the last two decades had been a lie." She shifted her position. To everyone else, our body language looked as though we were sharing some pretty good secrets.

"Did she ever remarry?" I asked, hoping Sammie's childhood story wasn't all doom and gloom.

"Eventually, but my mom hopped around from guy to guy for a few years. She always had a different date. I hated that she was such a ho, but I've since forgiven her."

"Wow! Good on you! I am not so sure I'd be able to do that," I said sympathetically, patting Sam's leg. "So, then she remarried, and you all lived happily ever after?"

Sammie frowned, eyes tightening in the corners. "Hah! I wish. She remarried when I was about twelve, and a year later Jason was born. He was one of a set of twins; my sister Sarah didn't make it past her second week in the NICU."

"Oh, my gosh! Sam, I am so sorry. I had no idea."

"How could you? It's okay, since she was severely disabled… her cord had pinched off the blood to her brain, and there was a lot of brain damage. Plus, she had the same markers for autism that my brother had."

"Oh, wow…" My voice was tight, and I choked back tears. "The unimaginable pain you and your mom went through." I just couldn't imagine having two babies and one of them dying right away.

"Yup. So… after that Mom pretty much shut down. I basically raised my brother for six of the last seven years

"I bet it was hard leaving Jason."

"Yeah, mostly for him though, 'cause like I said before, he has autism. Right before I left the state for college, I finally had the nerve to tell mom Gary had been making advances. She understood my need to get away from him, and not long after, she divorced him and came out of her depression. She's been a pretty decent mom for the last year, not that it mattered much because I wasn't around, but at least Jason's getting the attention he deserves now."

"You had to grow up pretty fast, huh?" I waited for her to answer.

Sam shrugged.

"I'm over it now. I'm just truly glad Gary got the boot."

"So, he like, came on to you and stuff?" I whispered, fearful that someone nearby would hear, and also half worried I was asking too much too soon in our friendship.

"That's, like, the understatement of the year. I'd be showering when Mom wasn't home and Jason was already down for bed… and he'd try to join me."

"Ewww, that is so disgusting!" I reached out and supportively squeezed her hand.

"Yeah, and that's just one example. He never *did* anything to me, but still, he did enough."

"Holy Shit, Sam! You've been through so much. I feel for you, I do. Abuse just plain sucks. That sicko pedophile shouldn't be allowed to keep his balls!"

Sam's eyes met mine and held them for what felt like minutes. I felt her searching for a reason for my impassioned response, but in truth, I didn't want to share my story. After all, I barely knew her. On the other hand, she was the only friend I had here, and she had just opened up to me.

I took a chance. "Yeah, I seem to be a victim of serial emotional abuse." I looked back up at her, trying to gauge if she counted emotional abuse as 'real' abuse.

*It's probably nothing compared to what she's been through with her mom's neglect and Gary's advances.*

Encouraged by the pure acceptance I saw from her, I continued.

"My dad was very strict. I wasn't allowed to date until I was eighteen, and I was seventeen for my Senior Prom, so I missed it" I shook my head, remembering the night vividly.

"That sucks!" she commiserated. "You'd think he'd have given you a pass for the night." Sammie leaned forward supportively, her wide, guileless eyes trained on me.

"Yeah, you'd think. Instead, I had to babysit two of my younger brothers. My other brother Ansel was sixteen, and that night he was working as a bagger at a grocery store, so he couldn't do it."

"… And your MOM couldn't do it, or your dad?"

I could hear the judgment in her voice. "No. They had plans to attend a benefit dinner. Besides, she's not my mom." I shrugged and looked around the hangar, wondering if any movement would be forthcoming.

*Shit, absolutely nada is happening. Still hurry up and wait.*

I continued, "Then, the summer after high school, I went to Alaska and worked in the fish industry. That's actually the first time I came close to losing my virginity… to Mirek, the nephew of a Czechoslovakian boat captain." I laughed uncomfortably, embarrassed I'd shared that fact. "Then I came home with some money and went to Wazzu—Washington State University. I pretty much ditched school to rush as a Tri-Delt. Lots of dates, sleeping around—frat guys are assholes and the sorority chicks are so superficial and bitchy—in truth, I didn't fit in there, so I joined the Navy. I met Teddy in school, right after boot camp, and he was a sweet, nice guy. Well… I fell hard for him."

"So, let me guess. You married him, and then he either beat you or cheated on you?"

I laughed at her stereotypical ideas of married guys in the military.

*But she's right. God, Teddy is a world-class piece of shit.*

"Yes, he did—cheat on me that is—and with my three best friends no less," I admitted, sadly shaking my head. "There was a whole slew of other stuff that contributed to our not making it, but I eventually couldn't trust a single word he said. We didn't even make it a year. Our divorce was final a few months before I came here."

"Damn, that must have been hard. How old were you, twenty?"

"Yup, I was twenty and he was nineteen. I wasn't a saint either after I found out… I went through my own phase, but I'm okay now."

Sammie laughed, "Yeah, don't we all? I bet the only girls who don't are the tight-ass bookworms who live for school."

"Hey! Now, wait a minute," I protested, pretending to be offended. "I was one of those in high school. I couldn't date, so other than dance, what else was there to do?"

"You danced?" Sammie's eyes bugged out. "You mean, like, seriously learned how to dance at like a school or something, or like just for fun with friends?"

"Yup, I trained in ballet since I was eight. I loved it." I looked off, reminiscing. When I spoke again, my voice was hushed and heavy with emotion. "It was probably the only time in my life I felt pretty and graceful. So then, during my senior year, the San Francisco and Boston Ballet Companies came scouting. They passed me over because they said I didn't have the right body type. Probably another reason I dated so much in college—trying to convince myself I wasn't as bad as they'd said. My ego took a real bruising."

"Shit, Tessa," Sammie said as she reached for my hands and held them out wide, "there isn't *anything* wrong with you. Those companies were stupid for even saying that. I mean, you're even smaller than me, and I've never been considered big."

"Yeah, well, it was still a hard pill to swallow."

I stood up, pushing away from the hangar wall. My ass hurt from sitting on the hard floor for so long. I stretched and gave a final brush off to remove the last of the blueberry muffin crumbs scattered across my lap. Looking around, I noticed that, in the last few minutes, the vibe in the hangar had changed. Now, as though someone had flipped a switch, our shipmates began standing up, grabbing their bags, and listlessly shuffling their feet as though they were being sent off to do hard time.

People were hugging everywhere. Those not embracing stood next to their loved ones in awkward silence. Many held hands limply, overcome by the impending six-month separation.

Then, it was time.

As Sammie and I joined the boarding line, I playfully grabbed her shoulders and gave them a brief shake to let her know I was excited.

"Military life is something, isn't it?" I asked as we made our way across the tarmac towards the plane.

"How do you mean?" Sammie asked, glancing over her shoulder and wrinkling her nose in confusion.

"You know, how everything moves at a different pace. I mean, we just met, and yet, I already feel like you're my sister."

"I know, right?" Sammie agreed. "Here we are, headed off to some godforsaken place, and I was worried about having a good friend."

I nodded, confirming I was in the same situation. "It must be a coping mechanism. I cast the friendship mold..."

"And I filled it." She smiled genuinely at me, and I returned it, excited to be boarding, heading to Iceland, and now with a new best friend.

Outside the cabin door at the top of the rickety rolling stairs placed on the tarmac adjacent the plane, the boarding line came to a complete. I leaned against the plane doorjamb and looked out over the sea of shipmates embracing their loved ones. It was a somber sight: these incredibly intimate good-byes forced to be held in public. Everywhere, I observed an outpouring of emotions. Couples cried while embracing tightly. Many exchanged deep kisses, as if stealing each other's last breath. Even though they knew they'd see one another again in six short months, there was always uncertainty, so the scene unfolded before me more like final goodbyes. Wives felt it. Husbands felt it. Kids, boyfriends, girlfriends, brothers, sisters, parents, friends… they all felt the HARD goodbye. *These six-month deployments are no laughing matter.*

As heartless as it was, I was glad to be completely unattached. The only person that I even had the slightest feelings for was my *person,* Wes, whom I'd left in Puerto Rico.

*Wes*… My thoughts of him led me back to our final days and a single tear slid down my cheek. I truly missed him and his friendship.

The line began to move, and Sammie reached back to hold my hand as the seating arrangement came into view.

"Here we go!" Sammie glanced back at me, gave me a wink and quickly squeezed my hand. I squeezed hers back. I felt awash in nerves and excitement.

There were three rows inside the plane: two seats on either of the airplane cabin and four in the center. Not many seats remained, as this was a government contracted flight and seats our squadron didn't fill would be filled with "non-essential" personnel… those on leave, reservists, retirees, dependents, etc. …

Sammie and I took two seats on the left, way, WAY in the back. I stowed my bag, grabbed my water, and settled in against the bulkhead, closing the shade so the sun-glare coming off the wing wouldn't continue to blind me.

"Are you ready for this?" I teased as I watched her try to get her act together. I made a mental note to add clumsy to the list of adjectives that I had been building to describe her.

She smiled at me as she tried for a third time to get her carry-on and jacket to stay stowed in the overhead compartment. "Ugh!?! Why won't you just go home?" Sammie grumped playfully, making a reference to one of the only movie quotes I knew; Adam Sandler's "Happy Gilmore." It made me smile, and again I realized how lucky I was to have met her just before a long, eight-hour flight that included a two-hour layover in Norfolk.

A Navy attendant rose to his feet at the front of the cabin and began to give us the emergency exit talk. The jet engines screamed, and we taxied down the runway for take-off. Sammie slouched into her seat, placed her headphones on her ears, and hit play.

I settled back and closed my eyes, just as I felt my weight lift off the seat as we screamed into the air.

*God, I love flying!*

I CAME to with Sammie leaning across me to open the shade. "How'd you sleep?"

Realizing my state of disrepair, I immediately became self-conscious and wiped the drool from the corner of my mouth.

*Oh my God, how embarrassing. I must have been out hard to have been drooling as much as I was. God, I pray I wasn't snoring!*

No such luck.

"Damn girl, you were dead to the world," she teased, covering her ears to imply I'd been breathing loudly.

"Yeah, whatever…" I answered, but my attention had been on checking out my surroundings, no longer engaging with Sammie as she made fun of how I slept.

*THIS.*

What I saw around me was utterly bizarre. Weren't these husbands and wives just crying and kissing their loved ones? Weren't they passionately hugging and whispering sweet somethings in their lover's ears?

*WHAT THE FUCK OVER?*

*Why the fuck do I still say that military slang saying? It makes no sense…*

My thoughts shifted immediately to my childhood, and hearing my dad say it. He'd been a Communications Operator on Navy Submarines for three separate tours of duty. Every time I'd ever asked him what it meant, he simply answered it was Navy slang—so I just assumed it was—and apparently, it had stuck with me.

Tuning back into my surroundings, I couldn't believe what I was seeing. It looked like we were on an airplane destined to some tropical, couples-only resort for an intimate retreat. Men and women held hands, talked intimately, laid their heads on each other's shoulders, shared drinks, and gave shoulder and neck massages. It looked like these "couples" had been together for a long time. Granted, many of the men and women worked together in the same aircraft maintenance shops, so obviously some were good friends… but, well, SOME were definitely not just friends.

"Do you see this shit going on?" I whispered to Sam.

She rolled her head to the side on the seat back and regarded me with a raised eyebrow. "To what *shit* are you referring? Could you be a little more specific?"

"What do you mean? Look around! They're married!"

On 'married', Sam gave me a *look* that shut me right up. "What? Were you born under a rock," she asked in a voice barely above a whisper. "These are DFBs…deployment fuck buddies. Some of these couples make the same hook-ups deployment after deployment, squadron after squadron. Unbeknownst to their spouses, many take new orders every two years to be with each other and continue their secret deployment lives. I guess this is pretty common. I heard from AD1 Hickey to prepare myself for this. He said I needed to be discreet when I come to work in the mech shop with him and the crew. I guess some of my AD shopmates video chat in the shop, and he doesn't want me screwing things up."

"Unbelievable." I didn't quite know what else to say. The fact that Petty Officer First Class Hickey felt it was important enough to tell Sammie she had better not rat out the cheating couples when she came to work in the shop kinda made me wish I hadn't taken these orders. I wondered if my shipmates on aircraft carriers behaved the same way.

"At this rate," I commented sourly, "with the bad taste I'm getting in my mouth, I'll never make it out of First Lieutenant. I'll live like a newbie forever. They'll keep me there instead of promoting me to my shop just to keep their secrets safe."

"Good luck with that." Sammie's expression told me I was an idiot. "In First Lieutenant, you can expect to work custodial jobs like stripping, waxing, and buffing the floors."

"Cleaning and mopping the bathrooms, too," I added. "If nobody else wants to do it, First Lieutenant has to."

"That's right, chickee," she confirmed. "When other shops have to send one volunteer to the wash rack for each wash, First Lieutenant had to send four. Let me tell you, washing P-3 Orions…"

"What's that?" I interrupted.

"Enormous four prop airplanes with three wheel-wells… hmmm, how to put this? IT'S A BITCH," she replied, not holding back.

"I would hate to do it. Washing helos and A-4 Jets in Puerto Rico was bad enough." I quickly realized if I wanted to do well in this squadron, if I wanted to make it out of First Louie and into the Line Shack, and then into my Aviation Electrician Shop, I'd have to wise up and grow a thicker skin; all the while not compromising my morals and values.

This, as it turned out, proved harder than I envisioned.

# Chapter Two

"Attention Squadron Sixteen-Oh-Two!"

A hush fell over the concourse where we all waited to find out what was going on.

The intercom speakers crackled. "We are back in business. We've found a replacement for the government contracted plane that broke down here in Brunswick. We will be boarding a C-130 cargo transport plane that will take us to NAS Keflavik, Iceland. Due to its size and ability to carry forty feet of cargo, we'll be transporting some additional items for the base in Nova Scotia. We'll refuel there, and we'll be stopping in Greenland to refuel a second time. Flight-time is projected at sixteen hours."

A resounding moan echoed through the concourse as we all lamented over this unwelcome news. It was going to be ONE HELL OF A LONG FLIGHT...

"Sorry to tell you this, folks," the crackly voice continued, barely comprehensible over the static on his intercom and the buzz of conversation, "but we're not going to be getting off the ground just yet. Stand by for further announcements."

I groaned and settled in against the terminal bulkhead with my notebook. *Figures we'd have to continue suffering through this grueling layover in Brunswick that has already lasted in excess of seven hours.*

A thought, fuzzy and undefined, nagged away in the back of my mind. *What's bugging me?* I frowned as I remembered. *Damn. Writing a letter to my step-mom.* I had been thinking about doing it since I had gotten to JAX, but somehow now, the timing suddenly felt right. *I want to close the chapter where I held my silence. In order to do this and move forward, I need my step-mom to know all the things I kept from her all these years.* Digging out a pen, I began…

*Dear Tulla Dean,*

*I know that I haven't really taken the time to write you since I joined nearly three years ago, and I'm sure you can understand why. Sitting here in the terminal, on my way to Iceland—pretty much alone—has me missing Dad, home, the boys, and thinking about you more than I normally do. I guess, too, I should clarify that I'm not actually alone; I've met a great friend—Sammie— but you know how it is. Someone can feel alone even when they aren't. After all, isn't that something we have in common?*

*I'm not a good letter writer, so to that I just say… deal with it. Also, before I forget, please let Dad know that I am happier than I've been in a long time, now that I'm not with Teddy anymore. Did you know we got a divorce?*

*Let Dad how much I love him and miss the long walks and talks we used to have about Mom, life, love…*

*The reason I am actually writing, though, is that I need you to know something that has been weighing heavily on my heart for a very long time. I guess only now that I am in my twenties, single again and resetting my life so to speak, I feel the need to get this off my chest.*
*So, here goes...*

*Tulla Dean, when Dad met you, I was a very sad, hurt, lonely little girl who had just lost the love of my life. My MOM. I sit here shaking my head, more than a little pissed that you failed to see that and thought I needed to be reformed, changed and forced out of what you perceived was depression. I had just lost my mom for Christ's sake! Why you couldn't understand that is a mystery to me. Even now, I don't think you'll get it...*

*I digress. Back to why I'm writing to you. Well, it's because I am tired of not talking to Dad and sharing my life with him. I miss him. I am glad you somehow make him happy, but Jeezus... live a little. Don't squash him like you did me. Don't smother my brothers with all of your stupid rules, curfews and overly controlling need to run their lives. Let them live.*
*Let them all live!*

*You were so conservative and controlling that as soon as I could leave and go to school... I did. I tried to go against everything my mom and dad had instilled in me about being a good girl—just to spite you—but I couldn't. All those ideas you had about me whoring around, and all the judgements you made and poisoned my dad's mind with... were WRONG.*
*DEAD WRONG.*

*Oh, Tulla Dean, I guess all of this, and all of my bringing up the past is merely an attempt for you to understand who I am and show you that the person you tried to change… wasn't. You couldn't change me because I wasn't acting out or creating drama in your life. It was me. Just who I was… Who I AM.*

*So, we've been sitting around for over nine hours while they tried to fix the plane we flew in on and then to find us another one. We should be leaving soon. I just wanted to get all this out on paper, since I never have told you how I felt; how much I despised the strict rules you enforced that did nothing but clip my wings—nearly killing my desire to fly.*

*Well, guess what, Tulla Dean? I AM flying. I have spread my wings, and I want you to know that with it has come wisdom. I forgive you. I know now you weren't trying to be mean. My beautiful, courageous, full of life mom left shoes too big for you to fill, and that wasn't your fault. I forgive you for only putting forth what I perceive as the minimal effort that you did.*
*I hope you and Dad are okay.*

*Send my love to the boys.*
*Tessa*
*XOXOXO*

I SAT and looked at the letter on my lap for a long time before cramming it into my duffel. Lying down on the terminal floor, I propped my pack under my head and tried to find some sleep.

It hadn't even been an hour before the smell of coffee woke me from my catnap. I opened my eyes and squinted at Sammie, who was holding me a cup of brew from the snack cart. I sat up and gladly took it.

"Now I'm bored," she announced. "We've already played 'getting to know you,' but how would you feel about cards?"

I agreed with a nod, but before she could even finish dealing, a crackle of static and a squeal of feedback dragged my attention away from my hand.

"Squadron Sixteen-Oh-Two, ready yourselves for departure soon," the anonymous male voice mumbled. "All hands stand by."

"Soon? Sure," I snarked.

"I know, right?" She agreed, turning her gaze back to the cards in her hand. She dealt a few more, and then studied her own with an expression of easy determination.

"Where did you get such a fun-loving poker face?" I teased.

"Soccer trips," she replied promptly. "Too much time on the bus leads to dubious skills." She grinned at her cards, but her lips' stretched appearance made me wonder if it was a grimace.

"Soccer, eh?"

She nodded. "Back in high school in San Diego, of course, and then on to Florida State."

My jaw dropped. "I've been following college soccer a bit. Didn't your team do super amazingly well last year?"

"Eighth in the NCAA Women's Division 1." She smirked. "I was a freshman."

*Sounds like a big deal.* "With all that going on, why on earth did you leave?" I inquired.

"Bad relationship," she replied with a shrug, as though that said it all.

Perhaps it did. Looking to turn her life around, she found herself running away and straight into the Navy's loving arms.

Nearly everyone I'd talked to in boot camp and at my last duty station had either joined because they were given an ultimatum; a last chance before serving time; or they'd been running from drugs, bad grades, poverty, toxic relationships and brutal home lives.

*It seems the military promises restitution and a chance to leave all the crap behind. HA! Liars! Every damn one of those recruiting bastards!* I doubt anyone was *thrilled* to be in, but a job is a job. At least we had *that* to console ourselves with.

We'd been lounging around on the tiny airport terminal's hard tile floor, heads propped on our carry-ons, shooting the shit for quite some time. STILL waiting to leave. *The Navy's motto should be 'hurry up and wait.'*

I dozed off, but when I came to again, Sammie still sat beside me, listening to her CD player.

"Looks like it's about that time." She nodded toward the flight line doors, and we could see the lounging crowd rising and shouldering their packs. I must have missed the final announcement while I slept, and I'd bet Sammie had too since she'd had her headphones on when I'd awakened.

Sammie and I gathered up our backpacks and took off for the restroom.

"Think the line will be bad?" I asked.

"It's bound to be," she replied, "but maybe we can beat it."

Sadly, we were too late. The line snaked back dismayingly far.

"Do we wait?" Sammie suggested.

"Let's look for another," I replied, frowning at the women dancing in place.

In our hunt, it didn't take us long to realize that the airport at NAS Brunswick had exactly ONE restroom. We noticed the airport also had a small snack and gift shop, which we were thrilled to see was still open at 0300. We grabbed snacks and some batteries for our cd players, to hold us over on the flight, and headed back to join the line for the restroom. Somehow though, on our way, we'd gotten distracted talking to some of the other kids from First Louie, and before we knew it, the boarding area was nearly empty.

"Hey, where is everyone?" Sammie had a panicked look on her face. I grabbed her and headed to the restroom.

"Don't worry. They have to take muster again before we board to make sure we're all accounted for. Quick, go! I don't think we'll be able to pee on the plane."

*She's not wrong to worry. If we miss muster, there will be hell to pay.* We quickly finished up.

*What if they really have already left us?*

We grabbed our carry-ons and pushed open the heavy restroom door. My stomach fell. *Please,* I prayed, *let everyone just be standing outside waiting!*

Only a handful of people remained in the cold terminal, and as we weren't traveling in uniform, I had no idea who was military or civilian. Sammie started to head over to ask someone, but I grabbed her and pulled her through the exit doors.

Man, if I thought 46 degrees in Jacksonville was cold for February, it was nothing compared to the 18 degrees that hit my face as we stepped outside. It was inky dark and snowing. The bright auxiliary light carts they had on the flight line blinded me.

"You two! Are you with VP 1602?" We heard a shout from the left and headed into the light blindly. I stepped up first.

"AE3 Christy," I said, a little out of breath. I figured we'd heard the mustering officer so easily because her voice was carried by the wind, but running into its resistance, carrying my backpack and airport purchases, with snow whipping my face… well, that was a little tough. Sammie ran up right after me.

"Airman Anders," Sammie choked out before she began a fit of coughing.

"You two should have your foul-weather jackets on," she said, referring to our FWJs—the ugly, sage green, fleece lined, feather-down quilted, fur-lined hooded jackets we were all issued before this adventure started.

"Hurry up and get on the plane. I'm missing two more bodies. Have you seen them?"

"I'm not sure," I informed her. "The terminal isn't completely empty."

*Well, this is it.* I looked at Sam and the MASSIVE plane looming in front of us. As she looked at me, I saw a fear in her eyes matched by only the plane's size. For twenty, she seemed younger; more naive and sweeter than me. At twenty-two, I felt I'd already lived a pretty full life. I had gone to the University of Washington, worked in Alaska processing fish, and joined the military at nineteen. I had also gotten married and divorced already. *I'm not calloused or jaded—not at all—it's just that few things actually scare me anymore. Certainly not a big-ass plane.* What she saw in my eyes was excitement; I couldn't wait to get to where we were going.

*Holy shit that's one big plane!*

The immense cargo bay stood open. We walked up to the belly of the beast and, as the bright, intrusive flight line lighting disappeared, our eyes adjusted to the soft amber emergency lighting inside.

*NO WAY! This is NOT what I expected.*

Before me, there were four rows of seats, if you could call them that. Before actually seeing them, I had no idea what troop seats were. Turns out they consisted of narrow strips of parachute-like material slung like a hammock between the top and bottom tube-like rigging. A three-point seatbelt came off the top rigging, hooked over the passenger's shoulders, and the bottom buckle piece attached between the legs.

A row of these 'troop-seats' hung along the left and right sides of the plane. Two more dangled down the middle, back-to-back, facing the other rows on either side of the plane. Pallets of cargo cluttered the space between the two middle rows.

Sammie and I looked at each other and got down to business trying to find seats. We located one against the left side porthole windows, which I took, and one kitty corner from me in the center. She was close enough to see, but not really close enough to have a conversation. Chatting, clearly, was not in the cards. Once those propellers started turning, it became annoyingly evident that it was just too dang loud to try.

After we had completed our ascent to cruising altitude, I set about trying to get comfortable. They were projecting we'd be in Keflavik, Iceland in about sixteen hours, during which we'd land twice to refuel, and battle the storm between where we were and where we were going. *This is going to be a rocky flight, which will only make the uncomfortable arrangements worse.* We sat literally shoulder-to-shoulder. As in, two other sets of shoulders squeezed mine.

*This really SUCKS!*

"Hey, I'm AE1 Dunnmoth, but you can call me Tim," the guy to my right introduced himself with a smile. Thankfully, he had a mint or gum in his mouth. Since he was about the only one I could hear, I figured it was a good thing that he didn't have cat-shit breath.

"AE3 Tessa Christy, but you can call me Tess." I smiled, but if he had turned to see it, our faces would have only been about four inches from each other.

"An AE too, eh? You must be a new check-in—I haven't seen you on the shop transfer-in list though. Is this your first duty station?" he asked with kind indifference.

"Nah, but I guess we'll be working together after I get out of First Lieutenant and the Line Shack… I am looking forward to that, since I only worked in the Line Shack and Corrosion at my last duty station."

My thoughts took me back to the uncomfortably hot flight line where I launched and recovered A-4 jets and H-3 helos as a line-man attached to the Line Shack. We'd stood out in the unbearable Puerto Rican sun, running the pilots through all the flight pre-checks before signaling a 'GO for launch' with our wands… the kind you see ground crew using to park civilian airplanes at the airport.

And the adrenaline rush! The flash of pure exhilaration I got from standing out in front of the aircraft as they screamed onto the tarmac for a landing. I held my wands held high in the air, waiting to bring them into our squadron flight line area and park them. I actually preferred the hectic schedule of launching and recovering aircraft to the laborious sanding and painting I'd done in the corrosion shop.

Corrosion detail had been pretty grueling. It seemed there was always an inspection to be done on the aircraft. It was our job to keep the birds pretty and the only fun part of the job, if you could call it that, was when we got to re-paint the birds' entire 'skin' in a blue and grey camouflage pattern. Coming up with the pattern, taping off the design, and the detailed painting appealed to the perfectionist in me.

My attention snapped back to what AE1 was saying. "Well,

Christy, it's a pleasure to have you on the team. You really need to take advantage of these deployments and come into the shop when you can—get familiar with the maintenance publications and manuals—see how we do things. Maybe I can sign off on some of your paperwork in the next six months. Get you into the shop sooner rather than later."

"Thanks, I'll definitely try. Does the Line Shack keep you as busy as I've heard?" I felt like I was on the brink of shouting, but he didn't seem to notice. Out of the corner of my eye, I could see Sammie already had large earphones on and her eyes closed. *That sounds like a pretty good idea.*

"… but if you are assigned to my shift, I can pull you in to help out and get training." AE1 Dunnmoth, thankfully, hadn't noticed that I had zoned out and missed the first part of what he'd said.

"Oh, so you're a supervisor?"

"Yup. I run a pretty lax shop… so long as my crews are getting their jobs done and we're meeting the flight schedules. You really should make a point of hanging out with us instead of the kids on the Line."

"Thanks, Dunnmoth, I'll try. It's hard to know what Kef will be like."

Thankfully, he turned to talk to the striking black woman next to him. It was hard to hear what they were talking about, but it sounded like they were making plans about what to do after the AE shop got unpacked. *I wonder if the two of them are DFBs.*

I'VE NEVER BEEN in a time warp, but that's what it felt like on this C-130. With my watch stashed in the back on a pallet in my backpack, and the stormy, overcast, and unchanging sky outside, I had no way to gauge the time.

We'd already stopped in Nova Scotia and Greenland to refuel, so I knew we were on our last leg. I'd had enough of the monotonous droning of the engines, the smell of jet fuel, and the hot air constantly blowing over us. The fact that I had repeatedly slipped in and out of sleep, played numerous hands of War on a coat in Tim's lap, and had snacked on the crap from the snack shop I'd brought along… well, I was just done. There was no other way to put it. I didn't know how much longer I could do this.

Things for me really deteriorated after we reached fifteen flight hours. It had taken all I had to cope with the propeller noise, the stifling heat, the nauseating stench of the plane and its smelly occupants for those first fifteen hours—I was literally counting down the final hour—when bad turned to worse.

A hush fell over the dim cabin as the flight officer came over the radio.

"Hey, gang! I hear you are all surviving in the lap of luxury back there." There was a short pause and I heard chuckles in the background from the flight crew. "So, I have some good news and some bad news. It looks like we will be making it to NAS Keflavik ahead of schedule, if you take into consideration that flight control in Greenland wanted to ground us. However, the not so good news is that we have to circumnavigate a massive weather system that lies between us and Keflavik." We could hear a jovial bull session in the background from the cockpit.

*What was going on in there? A lap dance? A party? I sure hope they're sober…*

He went on, "This means that instead of having the

previously estimated remaining flight time of one hour, we have at least another three to add to that. So, make yourselves comfortable and enjoy the in-flight movie. The flight crew will be coming around a final time with refreshments." At this, the cockpit erupted in high-spirited laughter. *ASSHOLES!*

Darkness invaded me... *Seriously? What the fuck? I am going to die!*

And, die I did. At least, I came damn close.

I hear all the time that anything is possible if you can conquer mind over matter. Well, my response to that is, you've never flown on a C-130 in inclement weather with every foul smell possible assaulting your senses. I'd been hanging on by a thread until I realized I didn't have T-minus sixty minutes left, but four hours instead.

I threw my belts off, forced myself onto my mostly asleep legs, hobbled over and smacked Sammie upon her head—harder than I'd meant to. Her eyes flew open.

"What the fuck?" she exclaimed loudly, visibly startled.

"I need you to get up. I *NEED* to talk to you. NOW!" I pronounced NOW with such staccato clarity that there was no doubt my urgency. She unfastened and followed me back past the seats, to where pallets of cargo had been stacked.

"What's up? Hey, you don't look so good," she said, looking at me with great concern. "You're really green."

"Oh, my word, you have no idea," I replied, glad for something—anything—to take my mind off my misery. *Even talking about my misery. How ironic is that?* "I get severe motion sickness."

"Oh no! That's terrible, Tess; I'm so sorry. This must be brutal for you." She put her arm around me in a conciliatory hug.

"It is. I always have to drive, because I get sick if I'm the passenger, even in the front seat. This flight is so much worse than driving." I shook my head. "I've been counting down the time, practically to the minute, until we reach NAS Kef. I'm hanging by a thread and I do NOT think I can do this any longer."

Sammie nodded patiently, and when my impassioned soliloquy stuttered to a halt, she took my hand. "Come on. Let's go further back, away from prying eyes."

We further veiled ourselves by rounding the back side of the pallet stock-pile.

Ohhhh... it felt so nice back here. No longer crammed in a sardine can, the cold air kept the jet fuel circulating, and preventing its smell from being so nauseatingly strong. We sequestered ourselves well in the shadows cast by the dim amber lighting and piles of luggage, equipment and cargo. The ambiance created an imaginary curtain of privacy that made relaxing and getting more comfortable possible. We actually pulled ourselves up on the last cargo pallet, kicked back on it, and made plans for our future for the next couple of hours.

"Let's room together," I suggested, so blissed out I forgot we'd been friends for hours, not years.

"For sure," she agreed, "and let's go clubbing this weekend too. After this miserable flight, we deserve a drink."

"Or five," I suggested. "How do we set up the room?"

"Hell, I don't know," Sammie replied, pretending to sound annoyed. "We don't even know what it will look like."

"I imagine a plain, beige box," I told her. *I've stayed in so many apartments that look like that.*

"What do you two think you are doing?" A shrill, whiny voice came from nowhere. We looked around, but since shadows cloaked everything, we had a hard time seeing where it had come from.

"First, you need to get down, second, you need to tell me who you are, and third, your butts need to find themselves back in their seats."

Out of the shadows stepped a short, hobbit-like, female officer. She sported the tightest bun on her head that I'd ever seen—so tight that it pulled her eyes up in the corners. It was so harsh, it rendered her appearance even weirder. She had her pen to paper and looked like a state trooper getting ready to give us a citation.

Sammie and I looked at each other and busted out laughing. We took our time sliding off the cargo heap. Still laughing, I let Sam lead the way. To my mortification, instead of stopping to tell the officer her name, Sammie practically shoulder-checked her as she brushed past! That was way ballsier than me, and I quickly followed, making sure *not* to touch her. After all, there was no way for her to know who we were, because we weren't in uniform. I'd say, for Sammie, this was inarguably a stroke of luck; the officer never pursued us.

Apparently, everyone was tired of traveling. It looked like over half of the squadron had unbuckled. A good many played cards, despite flying through a rough storm with significant turbulence.

Not ten minutes after I sat down in the overly hot, overly crowded, overly fumy troop seat, I got the cold sweats. *Oh no. Not this*! I felt sick, again. Just under two hours left of this miserable flight, I was past exhausted, and now had to work hard to hold the contents of my stomach down.

"Move, MOVE!" I shouted as I pushed off my seat and tried

to make my way through the mass of carry-ons and legs, to the bucket in the back.

Off to the side, just before the stacks of cargo was a bucket on a pallet. It had no seat; only was a curtain of sorts that covered most of the three sides. There were at least five-inch gaps where the curtain didn't touch the bulkhead.

As I neared the makeshift facilities, all I could think was, *over a hundred people have been flying for 18 hours, and as far as I know, the bucket hasn't been changed out.* Then the smell hit me. I pulled back the privacy curtain…

*Nope. Not one change. I fucking knew it!*

That alone made me sicker than I already was.

*Crap, this thing is disgusting.* I gagged.

*Kneel, damn it.* A sick vision crossed my mind, of what might splash onto my face if I got too close, but my stomach wouldn't wait any longer. Bracing my hands on my thighs, I puked from about two feet above the bucket.

Then, my belly cramps moved lower; crippling gas pains rippled through my lower gut.

*Oh, God. Not this too?!*

I had no choice but to wipe my mouth, and immediately sit on the same bucket to relieve myself.

I did say that bad turned to worse, but I was in such a miserable place, it wasn't even funny.

After getting so sick, I sat gasping and moaning for several long minutes before I pulled back the curtain. Thankfully, nobody had noticed where I was or what I'd been doing. I'm sure some of my shipmates who were closer must've heard me, but they didn't make me feel self-conscious about it.

The blessed breeze in the cargo area made it cooler than the rest of the plane and felt AUH-MAZING. I didn't even care if the hobbit came back. I just climbed up on a pallet of shop gear and lay back. Fatigue tugged me closer to sleep. The continual hum of the engines and the breeze actually settled both my stomach and my mind. I finally drifted off.

*Mmm... I nuzzled my head into what I can most closely describe as heaven. It was early, perhaps a little after five, and the sun flirted with the horizon, just visible through the 1960 Airstream's window. I smiled and closed my eyes, snuggling my hips and bare torso into the athletic physique and defined chest that had 'Lisa' tattooed on it beside me. I must have woken him slightly, because the faintest "I love you" escaped his mouth on exhaled breath as his tan arm protectively pulled me in. It always amazed me the comfort and security I felt in his embrace, the relaxation that always over-took me in his arms, the unreal truth that he wanted me. That I was what he was looking for.*

*"Thanks be to God," I said a silent prayer. "How did I ever get to where I am now? How did I ever find you?"*

*These thoughts and others ran through my head in lazy circles as the cozy warmth finally overtook me...*

I STARTLED AWAKE, taking a minute to realize where I was. The obnoxious cockpit intercom radio blasted on, interrupting my tender dream. I stretched and rolled over, snuggling deeper into the duffel-bags and mulling over the traces of my dream in my head.

*I deserve to find a guy like the one in my dreams... don't I?*

Wiping the rebellious tears from my face, I pulled the moistened hair off my cheek. I lay there for a few minutes, mindful of my breathing. Willing my heart to slow down, I sat up and saw that absolutely nothing had changed since I'd laid down. I closed my eyes again and let the loud engine hum of the C-130 put me back to sleep.

# Chapter Three

"Tessa, wake up." Sammie's urgent voice cut into my pleasant dream.

I opened my eyes to hear the intercom yakking away. "Repeat, we are in our final approach. Please fasten your seatbelts," there was a pause, "and return your seatback and tray tables to their upright and locked position."

Again, the flight crew yucked it up in the cockpit, though I noticed their laughter sounded weary.

"Assholes," I grumped as I reluctantly climbed from atop my resting spot.

"Let them have their dumb jokes," Sammie scolded as she led the way back to the hated rows of slings that imitated seating. "They just fought through one hell of a storm to bring us here safely."

I pouted and buckled myself back into my three-point harness—my bindings from hell.

"Hold on tight, rookie." I looked up at the sound of Tim's voice next to me. "This will be one helluva bumpy landing. Ari is on our aviation electrician team and a member of the flight crew. He came back while you were… where the hell were you, anyway?" he questioned groggily. I heard him mumble *'sleeping,'* but before I could confirm that's where I'd been, he continued, "Must have been nice." He shot me a friendly smile. "Anyway, Ari told us it's really storming over Kef."

*Crap. More turbulence. Just what I need.* I scowled involuntarily at Tim.

He continued his report, crushing my new resolve with more harsh facts. "It's forty degrees below zero on the last report they had, and there's near white-out conditions with the wind gusting up to 50 mph."

"Do you think we'll land okay?"

"We have to. They don't have enough fuel to circle back. Not to worry, though. We have a good flight officer in the seat. He has made this deployment five times before, so he's used to the weather."

*Sure, mister. I'll just stop worrying because you say so.* Then anger gave way to terror. *Oh please, oh please, oh please, let us be okay. How did I ever get into this stupid predicament?*

Instantly, my mind jumped to how my crazy military adventure all started with me signing away my freedom, followed by my going away party the night before I left for boot camp.

*God, I miss Lindy!*

I'd seen my friends, her brother... *oh fuck that's right... there was that 'Lisa' tattooed guy—what did he call himself? Oh yeah, Ren. At the time, the anonymity felt perfect, but it didn't stop him from getting under my skin. I can't believe this is the second time I've thought about him today. We parted forever and a day ago; but seriously, who hangs onto one-night stands for so long, right?* The plane bounced again violently.

*Oh please, oh please, oh please...*

After that last bout of turbulence, the flight officer came over the cabin speaker. "Make sure you are all securely buckled up. We will be landing shortly…" He cut off as the plane abruptly dropped. I don't know how many feet… but holy shit!

*Please, God, Please,* I prayed silently. *Are we going to make it?!?*

"Sorry about that, folks. This isn't the easiest weather to fly in. Not to worry, though. I'll put us down just fine. Once we land, we'll taxi up in front of our hangar. As soon as we give the word, unbuckle yourselves and put on your foul-weather jackets. Once the cargo deck drops, make haste single-file. It is currently -42 degrees outside plus wind-chill. There will be portable heaters blowing, but I'm sure you'll still feel plenty cold. You'll need to hurry out of the elements. Follow the lead and get right on the buses that will take you to your barracks."

With that, the radio went dead as the plane hit some major turbulence. The best way I can describe it is that it felt as though we were 4x4ing up a granite rock embankment. We lurched from side to side. The plane jumped up and down. I looked around, and a lot of us had gone pretty pale. Sammie was still listening to her CD player and chewing gum. Her large brown eyes had grown even bigger than I remembered, and I saw fear in them. She looked over at me and smiled feebly. I returned it with a broad smile; one I hope conveyed to her that everything was all right, although I wasn't so sure.

*Okay, so I'm lying. God, forgive me. I'm only trying to help.*

*THE HURRICANE FORCE winds hit hard, slamming into our condo building. As they gusted and wailed outside, the windows swelled and buckled—looking as though they were breathing. It was terrifying. There was nothing any of us could do. We sat in a tight circle. Our pasts didn't matter at that moment. We were scared shitless.*

*We huddled tightly, each in our own heads, hands strangling the ones we held onto. The power had gone out hours ago, and the sun had dropped, leaving us in an inky blackness that now consumed us. The darkness smothered us as it negated our sense of sight. The powerful hurricane heightened our hearing, which was all we had to go by.*

*We heard destruction; lots of it. Things flew around outside our dark cave, slamming into whatever crossed their paths. We heard thunderous cracks from branches and glass breaking nearby.*

*"Please, let it not be our car…"*

*"Wait, no. That's dumb. It's a car. If that's all the monster outside takes, we're lucky. Don't forget that the only thing separating us from the devilish hurricane is a sliding-glass wall at the end of our living room, and it's only checkerboard-taped with duct-tape."*

*I didn't pray often, but I found myself doing exactly that— praying my 'family' stayed safe from the monster.*

*My heart raced as though trying to explode out of my chest. I couldn't breathe…*

"Petty Officer Christy?"

I snapped out of my terrified flashback.

"Christy?" I looked at AE1 Dunnmoth, and realized I'd been squeezing his hand until it turned white. "You okay, sailor?"

I barely managed to nod as the terror of the flight brought back the memories of the last time I'd been this scared. The horror in the dark that long-ago night continued to crowd in on me, merging with the rotten flight to engulf me in a state of sheer panic.

I DON'T KNOW how many times I repeated the Hail Mary as the approach worsened and our landing turned chilling. The flight line had been de-iced, but we encountered a sheet of frozen precipitation when we touched down. We slipped and slid, fighting for traction.

I gasped, and a few others let out little yelps of fear as the flying beast fought to stick to the icy tarmac.

"Too many delays," Tim snarled, clutching his rigging until his fingers turned purple. "We waited too long after de-icing."

*Wonderful.*

At last, the pilots straightened out the nose and the wild fishtailing stopped. We taxied in a controlled slide past our hangar and had to circle back around.

When the plane finally stopped moving, I rehearsed a litany of facts to ground myself and calm my pounding heart. *It's February 3, 1998. We flew over sixteen hours in a C-130. We've finally stopped in front of our deployment hangar. We're on the NAS Keflavik flight line.*

I was still fighting to slow my breathing when AE1 Dunnmoth nudged me and said, "Come on, Christy, pull your big girl pants on; it's time to get off this greased pig."

For the first time since before the approach started—hell, since the flight started in Brunswick—time returned to normal. I no longer felt like everything was moving in slow motion. I noticed everyone standing and putting their jackets on, zipping the inner and outer shells and pulling up their fur-lined hoods… I followed suit and got in line behind Tim.

"Here we go. Welcome to Iceland!" Tim's eyes smiled at me, but behind them was also a silent warning. There was so much I couldn't read in his face and from his comment, but I'd take heed, as I clearly had no idea what to expect.

The belly of the beast dropped, and the harsh Arctic wind slapped us in the face. Adding insult to injury, the auxiliary light carts simultaneously blinded us after having spent so many hours in the dim emergency lighting. Physically sore and emotionally worn out, I had no excitement over the fact that we'd landed.

We all hovered within varying degrees of breaking down. Even the most seasoned sailors among us wore haunted expressions and shuffled like zombies out of the innards of the torturous machine. Someone initiated the procession down the 'gangplank' onto the icy tarmac. We paraded, walking so tightly one after the other, our stomachs touched the backs of the people in front of us. Step after step, we trudged on, 'nut-to-butt,' like the penguins huddled in the movie *March of the Penguins*. We shoved our hands deep into our pockets, many of us fighting for our balance against the bullish winds, our heads bent down to keep the icy, cutting gusts from hitting our faces. We marched on, one after the other, without looking up, robotically following the person in front of us.

*I hope this leads us to a much warmer place.*

AT LAST, we reached the buses.

# Chapter Four

I had one last trip—or so I thought—from the flight line to the electrician's shop, but that meant making another several hundred-yard trek out to the plane for the last of the toolboxes. Apparently, we had garnered some sort of attention, because the base's security patrol detail was keeping close tabs on us. I let my attention wander their direction, scanning the men who scanned us so intently. It seemed like they weren't really patrolling the flight line, apart from the few hundred yards around and out in front of our hangar.

*Who knows—maybe this is common procedure for when new squadrons arrive on deployments.*

"Christy, step it up! These boxes aren't going to move themselves!"

God, my annoying supervisor of the minute—Petty Officer What's-her-name—had been up my ass all day as we relocated our equipment from the C-130.

"Christy! I said get a move on—let's go. Now!"

*Screw that! You're not my boss.* "Hey! Come here." I stood by the gear, flagging her over.

"I don't respond to 'Hey,'" she snapped. "You can address me as AE2 Cai."

*Yeah. You're one rank above me. What the fuck over? Whatever! Blow me.* I stuffed down the cutting remark that lingered on the tip of my tongue. "Petty Officer Cai, come here please."

She dragged her ass off the ramp where she'd been standing around barking orders, and over to where I stood just behind the beast. "Look, over there." I pointed to the security detail's Hummer about thirty yards away from me. "Why do you suppose they're watching us so closely? They were practically underfoot a couple of hours ago. I mean, haven't they gotten a good eyeful yet?"

"I don't know, Christy. They're probably providing protective detail until we're set up. Who cares? Get to work." She started to walk off.

"Cai!"

She spun around, and boy did she look pissed. *I'm looking forward to working with such a raging bitch. NOT!*

"What?!"

I walked over to her and pointed to the guy closest to us, at the lead of the detail. "Why do you suppose *he's* watching us so closely? Don't you find it a little… unnerving?"

AE2 Cai threw her hand up in a casual wave. He waved back, and then laid his hand casually on the top on his M4 rifle. "No, I don't. Besides, he's not watching us. When you aren't out here, he couldn't care less."

"What's that supposed to mean?"

"Don't be dense, Petty Officer Christy. It means he's watching you. Who gives a flying fuck? Get back to work. I want to get out of here."

I looked over at him one last time, and this time, he threw his gloved hand up in a wave. I stalled, but eventually waved back before heading into the beast. Stomping through the echoing interior, I slammed my boots onto the floor, childishly pretending to hurt the obnoxious plane that had so distressed me. In the back, near the bucket of my shame, I found one of the last of those damn forty-pound toolboxes. Hefting its bulk while struggling not to strain my back, I staggered back out. My cart sat to the left of the open belly, and I threw it on.

I cannot begin to explain how grueling the rest of the day became. After the toolboxes, I had to unload and set up equipment. As a squadron, we only had today to arrive and set up the remaining shops that the skeleton crew didn't get to when they'd arrived last week. After finishing this monumental task, we had to attend the **Welcome to Iceland: Courtesies and Traditions** class. Last on our mile-long list was getting checked in at our barracks.

*I CAN'T DO THIS ANY MORE! I'm dying...*

Seriously, I felt like I was dying. Time? I couldn't have begun to guess. Iceland is mostly dark out this time of year, then add the snowstorm that soured our flight, well... the bland, overcast grey sky had resembled twilight for hours now. I was so sleep deprived down was up and up was down.

When I climbed on the second to last bus to leave the squadron and head to my new home, I was beyond beat. I had tomorrow off—or as time had it, the rest of the day—before I had to report for duty.

*I can't wait for a bed, followed by a gallon of coffee and a hot shower.*

Someone jostled me awake when we arrived at the barracks. Stumbling semi-comatose off the bus steps, I found my luggage with little effort, as most everyone had already claimed theirs and taken it inside. I exchanged courteous platitudes with the petty officer giving out room assignments, threw my huge duffel over my shoulder and trudged up the three flights of stairs…

*Oh my God I am so out of shape,* I thought, panting. *Now, to find room 308… and my glorious bed.*

I swung open the heavy fire door that connected the stairway to the hall, and instead of the quiet I was expecting, it looked and sounded more like a fraternity party. Lots of people close to my age and a little older meandered along the hall going to and from each other's rooms. Everyone wore either flannel PJ bottoms or sweats, and I had yet to see anyone without a cup or drink in their hands.

*Oh My God. I don't think I can do this. I can't do this. I'm just too tired.*

"Hey, Christy! Drop your bag off and come grab a drink— there's a shitload in the kitchen!" I turned to see an attractive man I recognized from the C-130 flight. How he knew me, I had no idea, but drinking right then didn't sound appealing at all.

"Yeah, sure thing," I responded with as much gusto as I could muster, and then returned to hunt for my room. Just a few doors down, 308 signified peace, quiet, and my sanctuary. I tested the door handle and found it locked. As I reached in my pocket for my key, the door slowly cracked open.

*Oh, Thank You, Jesus! It's quiet inside. So wonderfully, blissfully quiet.*

I entered a mostly dark room with blackout shades drawn. I could see a figure sitting in the sole recliner with her feet up.

"Hiya, hooka," Sammie greeted me in a totally lackluster voice, very unlike herself.

"I had no idea if we were actually assigned to the same

room." My relief reflected in my voice as it washed over my soul. *NOW all's right in the world.*

"Put your bag down, Tess. You're home. I fixed you a Jack and Coke. It's by the sink," Sammie said quietly, the fatigue audible in her voice.

"Thanks," I replied. I dropped my bag, slammed my drink and then collapsed onto my bed, dead to the world.

# Chapter Five

Who knows how long I actually slept, since I'd lost track of time. I had no awareness if it was day or night when I crashed out or when I came to. My brain just couldn't get rid of the idea that maybe it was someone leaving our room that woke me, but when I came to, nobody was there, and Sammie appeared to still be sleeping. It may have been the music coming from her alarm that was, as I later found out, set for four hours earlier that awakened me. Or perhaps it was even a crow flying into our window—they were flocking outside the barracks and it wasn't uncommon for them to hit the glass from time to time. Regardless, whatever woke me startled the shit out of me.

My eyes shot open and my skin prickled, ears perked… my body at attention as I waited to decipher what I thought I'd heard. I sat up, swung my legs cautiously over the edge of my three-drawer, high-lifted bed. I stretched my feet down to reach the floor and walked around the end of the back-to-back wardrobes and caroles—folding desks—Sammie had placed down the middle of our room to act as a privacy divider. Propping my left knee on the cushion of the recliner she had placed on the end and opposite the door, I peered around her wardrobe. Sammie lay sound asleep in her bed.

I looked back towards the door, assessing that it was closed and locked—then stood and leaned my shoulder against it as a precaution—to assure myself that we were safe, and all was well. Then, and only then, did I make my way back into my bed; truly a heavenly comfort that reminded me of a cloud.

In cloud-like fashion, I drifted off to Never Never Land.

"HEY, TESSA? HEY, TE-SSA!" I heard my mom calling my voice.

"Five. More. Minutes," I begged in the same fashion I'd had since I was eleven or twelve years old.

"Get up out of bed, lazy-head."

"Mom, please!"

"Mom? Tessa! Wake the fuck up, dude," Sammie responded with laughter in her voice. "I'm not your mom... you're dreaming, so wake up already."

I finally forced my eyelids apart and took a hooded look at my surroundings. Sammie stood maybe a foot from my face, looking down at me.

"Shit, Sam!" I exclaimed startled. "What's up? Why are you waking me up? Am I late for work? Shit, what time is it?"

"Calm down. It's six in the evening, and I didn't think you wanted to sleep away your entire day off," she responded with an ease that made being around her feel like home. Strange I might add, since I really didn't know her too well... and yet it seemed like we were already sisters.

"Thanks," I said with a half-smile as I sat up. I had gone to bed in my white Hanes work shirt, barely finding the energy to strip off my flight deck boots and coveralls before I'd crashed.

"Ugh, I so, so need a shower." I yawned as I swung my feet over the side of the bed.

"Yes. You. Do," she coughed jokingly as if my stench were choking her. I pushed her aside, opened my wardrobe, and pulled out some clean clothes and shower stuff from my suitcase… seeing as how I hadn't gotten around to unpacking everything yesterday… or rather this morning?

"Ta-ta, beeatch!" Sammie shouted after me as I left the room.

The shower was pure bliss; the hot water washed the impurities of traveling and work off my skin and eased the tightness from my aching muscles. The pelting beads invigorated my still sleep-deprived and weary mind. The public shower stalls didn't bother me a bit, as I had experienced them when I lived in the dorms while attending WSU and again during my stint in boot camp. Hell, at least these showers had curtains on them. The chit-chattering of the gals in the other stalls did nothing to distract me from my heaven on earth.

Ever since I was a teenager, I reveled in long, hot showers. I was able to day-dream in them, relax, and even find clarity in my important thoughts. As the steaming waterfall of hot beads kissed my shoulders and slid down my torso, my thoughts went back to Puerto Rico and the people I'd left behind.

*I miss Wes a bunch. He's such a fine specimen… nineteen, dishwater blonde, 6'3" and about 180, built like a track star with no extra weight on him… anywhere.* After my divorce was final, he asked me to be his 'first.' I really struggled with whether or not I wanted always to hold the title. Although I hemmed and hawed about it, eventually he wore me down and I agreed to it since we were such amazing and close friends.

*I miss the intimacy we shared, our close friendship, and that he was 'my person.' The one that I could talk to... about anything. Everything.*

My memories took me back to a conversation that I'd had with him, one that was etched in my mind forever.

I'd pounded on his barracks room door, tears driving their way down my cheeks like sleet in a blizzard—ferocious, unrelenting.

"Tess, what's wrong," Wes opened the door, took one look at me and pulled me into his arms."

"Oh my God, oh my God…" I choked out through my sobs.

"You're worrying me, what's wrong," he stroked my head and hugged me strongly, surely. "Shh, tell me, Tess. It'll be okay, shh."

I drew in a shaky breath, "They cheated… he cheated on me with all of them."

"Wait, who? What? Tess, you aren't making sense. What happened?"

"Teddy, he slept with my girls." Again my sobs overtook me.

"So, you mean to tell me that the three of them… he slept with all of them?"

I nodded.

He waited until my sobs subsided enough to talk again, "I was just at their apartment and we were doing shots and playing a game of 'Truth'… oh Wes… they all did it. They shared the details. Oh my God, it was so graphic. What am I going to do?"

He'd held me all night, and that was the first time I realized he was irreplaceable. He irrevocably held a position in my heart. Wes had been there for me when I became personally destructive post-divorce and kept me from drinking myself to death; more importantly, from driving while I was that drunk. Finally, after leaving Puerto Rico, he'd been there, a phone call away. Any time. EVERY time, to console my loneliness; spending long hours into the wee mornings whenever I'd needed him to—after I'd moved to NAS Jacksonville.

In many ways, Wes became my sweet angel. I knew he loved me differently than I loved him, which really stirred up deep, sorrowful feelings of guilt. I also knew I couldn't force a different love to form for him. He had needed me to help with his 'problem' virginity... *not that I thought he had a problem*. I had needed him to get through the grieving stage of my divorce. Saying goodbye to Wes was hard since I'd known it was the end of that phase of our relationship, but it was also a little liberating. I'd been loyal to him out of friendship and the fact that I cared so much for him, but it had never been what I had really intended to happen. I hadn't intended to jump from a dysfunctional marriage directly into a serious relationship; so, the opportunity to write a new chapter by moving excited me. I looked forward to my next guy and reveled in the idea of having an inconsequential, carefree and fun encounter. I needed something that was uncomplicated and easy—since being married hadn't worked out so well for me.

The steam swirled around me and transformed my skin to hues of pink and red from the scalding onslaught. I turned and faced the water, letting the hot pin-pricks sensitize the front of my neck.

*Mmm... mmm. This brings back so many memories of Ethan, Teddy, Ryker, Wes, Ignacio... what is it with me and men in the shower?* I giggled.

"Shit, Tessa, are you still in there?" I heard a note of disbelief in Sammie's voice.

"Yes, *Mother*." I laughed. "I still have to shave, and then I'll be out."

"You do that, 'cause I know the guys are getting antsy… they may have already left for the base's sports bar. What's its name?" Sammie's voice trailed off as she focused on trying to remember. "Isn't it Pirate something, or Pirateer? Why can't I remember?"

I just wanted to finish my shower, but after hearing 'pirateer,' the bar name came to me. In a voice laced with victory and dripping with sarcasm I answered, "Sam, I'll tell you if you let me finish my shower."

"Ok… Deal."

"It's The Privateers' Pub. I read about it in the base literature on the first leg of the flight. I think it said they have pool tables, darts, TV; just an all-around hometown type of pub." It sounded more and more like fun now that we'd talked about it.

"Okay, so are you going or what?" I could discern irritation in her voice.

"Yeah, just let me finish up already!"

Sammie guffawed, "Shit, Tessa, you don't have to ask a lady twice!" With that, I heard her squeaking out of the shower room.

"Yeah, right! When you become a lady let me know," I jested loudly as the door squealed closed on its noisy hinges.

I went to work slathering the rich cream on my legs and shaving. As I finished up and ran my hands over my calves, my eyes involuntarily closed, and my mind drifted to how lonely I was for a man's calloused touch. I opened my eyes…

*Maybe day one in Iceland isn't too early to see what this base has to offer.*

A mischievous grin claimed my lips as I pulled back the curtain and stepped out of the shower.

# Chapter Six

"Will you quit looking at yourself in the mirror? It's time to GO," Sammie snapped at me, her jaw tensed in frustration.

*Not that I can tell her this, but just admitting to myself that I'm ready for a new man makes me want to take extra care.* Ignoring her instructions, I gave myself another top-down assessment. *Hair clean and in place. Makeup hot, but not overdone. Outfit coordinated and flattering.* My eyes glowed with excitement and a naughty smile lingered in the corners of my mouth. *That'll do just fine.*

"What in God's name are you wearing those saucers for?" Sammie groused, referring to the hoops I had just put in.

"Whuddaya' mean? I'm just trying to look nice," I said with a bit of a sulk resonating in my voice. *She's being a real mood killer, this lady.*

"It's like -30 or -40 something outside, who's gonna see you?"

I looked up at her and back at the mirror. *Maybe she has a point. I want to look available, not desperate.* I pulled them off and went for a smaller silver drop-style earring. "Better?"

"Sure, whatever. I'm heading down the hall to see who's doing what, and I'll meet you in the guy's room." Sammie grabbed her foul-weather jacket and her Velcro tri-fold wallet.

"Hey," I called after her. "What guys? Where…"

She never waited to hear the rest of my question; hell, she didn't even stop to give herself a final once-over before I heard our door click shut.

*What the fuck crawled up her butt and died?* I thought as I grabbed my own FWJ.

*Damn, this bitch weighs a ton! It must be because of the heavy lining and fur lined hood…*

I surveyed myself a final time and, satisfied I at least looked cute enough to attract the attention of my next conquest, I grabbed my small zippered wallet, turned off the light and went out the door. After the intense quiet of the room, the noisy hallway threatened to shatter my eardrums. The last four or five doors all stood open, playing the same music, "No Diggity" by Dr. Dre and the Backstreet Boys. Everyone carried a cup. I cannot say they were all drinking, since a lot of these shipmates were underage, but… *seriously*… we all know they were.

I went into the first room, and immediately, the smell of that Nag Champa, a strong, musky incense, assaulted my nose. Probably close to a dozen people I had never seen before crowded into the small space. Most were older than me. I received a couple of courtesy smiles and nods. I returned them as I gave a brief look around for Sam. No sign of her, so I moved on to the next room.

Red lights bathed room number two, where a number of couples dirty danced, or should I say stumbled around trying to dance? After a brief scan, I skipped it and went on to the last room on that side. I noticed a couple of familiar faces, so I stepped in a bit farther.

"Hey, Christy, what's your poison?" I turned and across the room saw Tim Dunnmoth, my future shop supervisor and seat-mate on the fateful C-130 flight.

"Jack," I said with a smile.

"What? Did you say in a bottle or can?" He shouted to me over "Return of the Mac," which was now screeching over the speakers. The chorus hit, and everyone started bumping hips and singing along.

Someone thrust a beer into my hand.

*Crap. What am I going to do with this? Damn, he didn't hear me right.*

I thanked a guy I didn't recognize and glanced around the room. A set of intense, blue eyes pointedly watched me from the other side. I couldn't tear my eyes away, until someone thought it was funny to tap the mouth of my bottle with the bottom of theirs, which caused my beer to gush like a geyser.

*Jeezus! Fucking Idiot!*

I ripped my gaze from those baby blues to step out of the puddle and look around for a towel, a rag, napkins… something to clean up the beer on the floor and on my hand.

"Hey, sweets, I've got it." Thankfully, some guy I'd never seen before appeared out of nowhere with a towel for my hand, and then he set about mopping up the mess. I thanked him, but when I looked up to find those eyes again, they weren't there. I searched around for Sammie and found her dancing with a few admirers. *Looks like fun.*

I moved to the make-shift dance floor in the center of the room. We all shouted the last line of the chorus, me as loud and jovial as everyone else.

Strong hands grabbed mine and effortlessly spun me around until I found myself staring up into the eyes of...

*Shit, what was his name? Ensign.... shoot... Daniels!* "Daniels, right?" I said with a smile.

"Yeah, Ian Daniels. We were in the same indoc. group."

Those eyes. Those translucent, violet eyes mesmerized me. Looking into them made me forget that he was an ensign—a Navy officer. Hell, those eyes nearly made me forget about the clear rules regarding officers partying with enlisted.

*What is it with beautiful eyes tonight?*

"Tessa Christy, right?" He reached out and took my unwanted beer from me.

*Wow.* Ok... so I was a little impressed that he remembered my name, since our base and squadron indoctrination had taken place over a week ago.

"Just call me Tess, Officer," I said with a hint of sarcasm and invitation in my voice.

*Whoa, boy! Kill me now.*

The amused look he gave me did little to mask the obvious, underlying masculine—and excitingly dangerous—side of him; it hinted at all kinds of ways he could get me to say '*Officer*'...

"Did you maybe want to get out of..."

"No, she doesn't," Sammie said as she threw herself between us. "Slow your roll, hoss. It's only what... day two of deployment and 1900?" With that, she thrust a Jack and Coke into my one hand, grabbed the other, and led me towards the door. As she pulled me, I turned back to look at *Officer* Ian, who stood there with an arrogant smirk on his face. I lifted my glass to him in a silent toast as I left the room.

"How do you *know* I didn't want to leave with Ian?" I demanded.

"You mean *Officer* Daniels?" She gave me a warning look. "You don't want to go there so early in the deployment… you should know that."

"Rules, I know. Well, society's rules were meant to be broken. I've never been one to play by the book, really." I laughed as we reached the first floor, where some of the mechs from her shop were staying.

"Well, maybe this is a good time to start. I'm betting that I just saved your ass in more ways than one."

"Shit, Sam. Maybe I want to put my butt in a sling. You know it has been awhile since I…"

*Gettin' it. Gettin' it… gettin' it good…*blah, blah, blah," she retorted as though quoting some rapper's lyrics.

"Oh. Shut. Up." I elbowed her as we reached her supervisor's room. According to Sammie, she and Aviation Mechanic Duncan been good at 'dickin' the dog,'—slacking off at work—while assigned to the Geedunk, a division of First Lieutenant, the past six months or so. Instead, she spent lots of her time in the mech shop; which it turns out, benefited not only her, but me as well. *If I hadn't met Sammie and her mech friends, this deployment would surely be a long, lonely one for me.*

Sammie knocked on the door three or four times before someone cracked it open. She leaned her shoulder onto it and pushed her way in.

"Whassup beeatches?" she drawled in her best gangster lingo.

She got a couple of "Woot woots" in response, a few "Hell yeahs", and even a "Hidy-ho" from the redneck of the group. The scene nicely blended casual and comfortable; not a party, but more like Saturday night at a frat house after the game.

I had not expected a bunch of guys to listen to this kind of music—Backstreet Boys—not that I minded a bit, but it *DID* bring back a flood of emotions and memories from Puerto Rico. As soon as we walked in, someone placed a refresher Jack and Coke in our hands.

"Christy? So, where are you from?"

I turned to see whose attention I had. "AME2 Reeser, right?"

I'd noticed the aviation structural mechanic right off, since he was also aircrew and *not* off limits like flight crew officers. From my past experiences, aircrewmen were always cooler, better partiers, and in pretty good shape. I'd yet to complain either, after kissing one. So yeah, Reeser got my attention the first day I'd arrived.

I dropped my FWJ by the door on top of Sammie's and took a seat next to him on the futon.

"Go ahead, and call me Tessa," I said with a smile. "You're Reeser... with no first name. Nice to meet you," I joked playfully.

"Sage Reeser, but you can also call me *Buttercup,* my call sign."

I gave him a flirty giggle, because... *REALLY? Buttercup? Come on... there's no way I'm calling you that!*

"I know, right? Reese's Peanut Butter Cups got shortened to Buttercup, and unfortunately, it stuck." He smiled, explaining without me even having to ask.

*I guess he's been asked it plenty of times before.*

We fell into a comfortable, albeit very dull conversation during which I learned he was twenty-four, from Arlington Iowa, farmed and played football in high school... you know the type. Sage was All-American. I have to admit after learning his first name, I thought I'd find out he was from a hippie family or something, but he was raised by his grandparents in a community of fewer than 800. That surprised me and very few things people say do. Maybe that's why I just sat there nicely smiling, nodding and sharing pleasantries.

"Enough about me. Tell me about you."

I looked up at Sage's eyes, an average hazel that complimented his tan complexion and sandy blond hair. They were by no means striking, but the earnestness I saw in them, his honest interest in what I was about to say, pulled me. I cleared my throat as a sudden nervousness hit.

*Whoa! Where in the world are these nerves coming from? It's not like I even like this guy.*

"Well, I was born in Salem, Oregon. So, like you, I was around a lot of agriculture and farming. My family is still in Oregon, but after I moved to Pullman to attend Wazzu, I pretty much planned on staying there, until I somehow ended up on this Navy ride." I stopped my disjointed and hurried account of my personal history and glanced over at Sage.

He smiled and opened his mouth like he was going to say something, when Sammie shot out of nowhere and plopped her ass between us, toasting both of our cups with hers.

"Mine's empty," she goaded. "You know what that means?"

"Let me guess," I said as I pushed on her back to get her up off the tiny futon. "You're ready for another drink?"

"NOPE!" Sammie laughed, stood up, and headed to the door to grab her jacket. "Who's ready to fly this coop?"

I turned my attention back to Sage. "I'm sure we'll have another opportunity to pick this up some time. You coming to the Privateer too?" I questioned more out of politeness than true interest. If truth be known, I actually didn't really want him to come and then sit beside me all night. Not that there was anything wrong with him—he'd do in a pinch—but I was curious what other prospects the frigid Icelandic winds would blow in.

The commotion of partiers refilling their drinks, joking, grabbing their heavy coats and pushing into the hall drowned Sage's answer.

# Chapter Seven

Whatever logic told the half-dozen of us that walking from our BEQ a good half-mile to the Privateer Pub after 2030 in -30 degrees with winds gusting up to 50 miles-per-hour, could only go by the names: 'I'm Invincible' and 'Excessive Alcohol.' I tried talking to Sammie, but my voice was whipped harshly off my lips as soon as it reached them. We trudged on, faces down, fur-lined hoods covering our heads and zipped up over our chins. We drilled our hands into our pockets, fingers tucked into our palms, making tight, tension-taut fists.

After what felt like an hour, we reached the brightly lit porch of the Privateer Pub. A rush of warm air welcomed us inside as we pushed through the heavy metal door. We stomped off our feet and unzipped our jackets.

"Whoo!" I exclaimed, relieved we were *finally* done with the bitter cold outside. I heard Sammie behind me rubbing her hands together. My nose, cheeks, ears, fingers were all a tingling mess, taking my focus away from the bar scene we'd just stomped loudly into.

"Hey, hun, give me your coat."

I turned and handed it off to Sammie, glad to bestow the awkward, heavy parka.

There were rows of hooks on the wall, and about half were filled with U.S. Marine and Navy Arctic jackets. Royal Army and Icelandic gear too from the looks of the flags stitched onto them. The pub was pretty full, and good beats played on the jukebox. The guys had already moved to claim the one empty pool table of the four. The others hosted lively groups of military personnel. I recognized a couple of squad-mates shooting with guys who appeared to be some U.S. Marine Security stationed at Keflavik. They looked up, and we got a few toasts as they waved to us, their beers in the air, acknowledging our arrival.

I took a seat at the end of the bar under the television. The Armed Forces Radio and Television Service, also known as AFRTS (pronounced A—Farts), provided all service men and women, their families, and DoD civilians "American" television programming, and Gladiator was on. It was nice to sit down, hear American music, watch American TV, and trick myself into thinking I was back home… even if it were just for a couple of hours.

"Rolling Rock please," I said with a smile to the cute, dark-haired Icelandic guy behind the bar.

"Make that two," Sammie added as she plopped down beside me. We turned toward each other and 'scoped' out the bar scene. A couple of cute guys, very few girls, as was very common, so the attention we were already receiving didn't surprise us at all.

"Ey' two shots 'er two lovely ladies."

We looked back at the bartender, and I really began to appreciate *his* beauty. The accent got my attention first; he sounded like a Viking. His heavy brogue had a richness woven in with a deep baritone. He was fair-skinned, more than I'd normally like, but I couldn't ding the guy for the whiteness of his skin when it was -30 outside and the sun had been hiding for most of the last four months. Besides, I'm sure he was considered tanned for an Icelander. He really was striking, with his pitch-black hair—it had a dark, almost blue shimmer to it under those halogen lights. His clear blue eyes radiated a magnetic energy and seemed to twinkle. He gave us a smirk, a cocky-ass bit of a smile that, for some reason, brought a rush of heat between my legs. I don't know what it is but give me a guy who radiates arrogance and confidence and I am a goner.

"Frá krakkar spila á borðið þremur, …from da guys playing on pool table three," he finished with a wink, nodding to the guys. They turned to be sure we were looking, and then each took a shot as though auditioning for our attention.

The bartender turned back to wash a couple of glasses.

"I was hopin' these were from you," I flirted, hoping it might get some attention from the barkeep.

Still drying the glass, he turned around and chuckled, "Now, 'ye know that 'ey cannot buy drinks for da patrons, no matter how cute 'ey might find 'em."

*Kill me now. Could he be any sexier with that accent?*

I kicked Sammie's leg on her stool beside me and winked. She laughed at me as she slid off her stool and went over to thank table three for us.

"'Ye should probably go join 'ye friend over there." He smiled flirtatiously. "With a few more libations from 'em, they'd be payin' all night 'er 'ye."

"Now, what makes you think I want them buying my drinks? Maybe I'd rather sit here at the bar and buy my own and talk to you." I raised an eyebrow and he chuckled as he turned back around.

*REALLY?! What does it take? Maybe he's gay…*

"Svo, þú vilt frekar sitja hér hjá mér ha?" I heard his Icelandic remark under his breath.

"So, what I want to know is, are you going to wash glasses all night?"

At this, he turned around. "I'd planned to, 'ey. They call me Ha'lfdane. Dane 'er short. 'Ye?"

"Tessa Patrice Christy. Tess for short."

We'd barely began our conversation when Sammie came over with one of the guys, interrupting us.

"Shots for Tessa here, and table three!" She hip bumped me, then pulled me off my stool onto the floor, so she could spin me around to Timbaland & Magoo's "Up Jumps da Boogie." She had me laughing so hard that we garnered a lot of looks. Evidently, Sammie's silliness was contagious, because our friends—*yes*—even the guys we came with, wandered over and got in on the fun. We laughed like loons, hip bumping, gyrating and spinning. The song ended far too soon.

Sammie sat down to catch her breath, and I leaned on her to catch mine. Dane had lined up a total of eight shots—six for Sammie and the guys she was flirting with at the pool table, and one for me. I slid my firm derriere onto the stool beside her.

"Hey, Dane."

I waited until he finished pouring somebody else's drinks, and then watched him saunter over to us.

*Yeah, he definitely has game …*

"Who's the eighth shot for?"

"Ey' my lady, it would be 'er me."

"But I thought…"

"Ahh já, en ég mun ekki segja neinum ef þú ert ekki." I

looked at the local civilian on the stool beside me and raised my shoulders in a silent *'What? Please help me.*

He smiled and said, "He won't tell if you don't."

"'Ey, that is what 'ey said." With that, Dane raised his glass and slammed back a first, then a second shot. He held up a third and said, "Toast with me?"

I caught myself giving him a flirtatious giggle and loving how he spoke first in Icelandic as though I understood, and then how he translated for me; It was sexy as all hell. I raised my shot of tequila to toast him.

"Oh my God. Kill me now," Sammie muttered as she stood up. "Hey, when you guys get done, bring the shots over. I'm joining in on the game they're racking before you two make me puke."

I rolled my eyes at her and playfully raised my leg to kick her, which she side-stepped.

"Nice try, hoss…"

I watched her mosey over to the table. She seemed to be getting along with all of them. I didn't mean to stare, but Dane was working the bar, as it had started to get busier, and I was curious which one was Sammie's type. To look a little less obvious, I took inventory of the entire bar, not just table three.

I had noticed our squad-mates at table one when we'd arrived, but they must have left, since I no longer saw them around. The group who had taken their place looked like they were the HOO-RAH type—you know, bulging muscles, high-and-tight haircuts, tattoo sleeves up their arms… Marines maybe… or base security.

*I wonder if one without the tattoo sleeve was that HAWK who watched me earlier.* They obviously came here a lot, as they acted like they owned the bar.

At a nearby high-top round table, two women tried to get their attention by tossing their hair and conspicuously thrusting out their chests. They weren't fooling anyone. The guys, clearly not interested, mocked the women's attempts by gesturing towards them with their heads, and then laughing while tossing their imaginary locks, thrusting out their muscular chests and provocatively rolling their manly shoulders. Their display ended in riotous laughter.

If it hadn't been so blatantly pathetic, I would've felt sorry for the way the guys were acting towards the women.

I turned my attention back to my table, but try as I might, I couldn't catch a conversation wave to surf in on.

Hmmm… *not much going on here.*

I returned my attention to the bar, when the hulks at table one drew my focus again. Right then, one of them looked over at me and then nudged the tall guy beside him. The tall one leaned over while looking at me and said something to the one who had noticed me. They threw a couple of elbow jabs at each other before continuing their game.

*Okay, so is that the same guy or isn't it? What in the fuck is going on at this damn base? Is everyone fucking crazy?* I had to wonder, because if it wasn't the same guy, then that made two sets of weird security dudes scoping me out.

Turning my back on them, I continued my inventory of the bar. When we'd arrived at the Privateer, we'd taken over pool table two. There were six of us, but only four were playing. The other two were at a high-top table shooting the shit, drinking their beers and adding to the overall ruckus of the bar. Every so often, I could hear one of them chime into the conversation on the pool table. Shouted insults and jests resounded above the loud music.

Table three had five guys. Two looked like they were civilians or Icelandic military, perhaps. *Maybe they're Dane's friends?* The others looked older, probably DoD. I took a good look at who had garnered Sammie's interest, and sure enough, saw her flirting with the tall, lanky, dark-haired Icelander.

Lastly, at table four, two couples passed the cues back and forth. I really hadn't paid them any mind, but now, from idle curiosity, I gave them a cursory glance. One couple consisted of a petite Japanese gal and a tall blonde guy; the other, an attractive pair of brunettes. All four of them looked like they had climbed out of an Abercrombie ad.

"'What are 'ye lookin' at?"

My attention immediately refocused on Dane. He had poured another round of shots for Sammie's table and had flagged them over. The two guys that looked like they might be his friends grabbed them.

"So, what's their story?" I asked him once they'd moved out of earshot.

"What do 'ye mean?" He looked totally preoccupied and disinterested in my question—and me now—for whatever it was worth.

"Those guys. Who are they?"

"Triggvi and Kettil. 'Em two are flat-mates of mine." He leaned on his elbows to get closer to me, so I leaned toward to him. "'Em two are nothing but lots of trouble."

*Oh. My. Word. That accent!*

Dane smelled so incredibly spicy, so incredibly yummy, I could munch on his neck. His lips. *M. Mm. Mmm.*

The hour flew by visiting and flirting with Dane. Around midnight, his co-worker showed up, clad in a too-tight tank, despite the cold. Wolf whistles greeted her arrival. The instant she stepped behind the bar, the hoo-rah boys crowded around, ogling her cleavage and demanding beers. She smirked and complied, pocketing tips right and left.

"I guarantee her shift will be lucrative for the bar," I muttered.

Then, recalling I was not alone, I looked up at Dane's eyes, surprised to see that him looking intently at me. "'Ey have a meal break now."

I smiled and nodded, wondering how long he had.

He sauntered over to his co-worker. They spoke briefly, and I could see him gesturing towards me. I lifted my hand in a kind of half-wave, when I realized she was giving him shit for something… probably having to do with me.

*Seriously?! It's over sixty degrees* below *freezing, and you're dressed like you're at Hooters in Miami. Tart. Like you have room to talk about me,* I mentally chided her.

Dane came around from behind the bar, interrupting my incredulous thoughts, and walked up to the jukebox, where he pushed a few buttons. I heard the record drop, and Ginuwine's "Pony" started playing just as Dane reached me.

"Komdu." He gestured to me. I rose to my feet, noticing I stood right at shoulder-height to him. As I looked up at him, his intent eyes smoldered, holding promises not yet whispered to me. He took my wrists and pulled both of my arms up around his neck as he slid his hands down my ribcages and rested them…

NO.

Rested them isn't quite right. He rooted them squarely on my lower back, pulling me intimately to him.

I'd noticed his clothes earlier, but I hadn't *really* noticed how sexy he looked. His cobalt-blue V-neck t-shirt, tucked into the front of his dark wash jeans, revealed a wide leather belt he wore slightly off-center. The buckle drew my attention to right above where his man-V would start if I could see him naked. My imagination did quite the job picturing the taut lines of his firm muscles that I'd caught a glimpse of as they rippled under his tee.

He pulled me onto his thigh, as though I were riding him like a pony, and we stood there grinding, swaying, moving as one while we dirty danced right there at the bar. I cannot tell you what was going on anywhere else in that bar, because Dane had assaulted my senses. I could only feel him. His hands hugged me to him tightly as he wrapped his right arm around my back and palmed my ribs. His other hand at my hip moved me in time and rhythm to him. It was erotic, sensual, and his fragrance—spice, musk and more Dane-spice—entranced me. I couldn't do anything but hang on for dear life until our dance ended.

It took seconds after the music ended for us to quit swaying and pull our bodies apart. My insides still pulsed, and it took me a few breaths to slow my racing heart. Once the lusty fog lifted, the sounds of hoots, hollers and a couple of whoots filled my ears. I had cleared my head, but had to shake it to get Dane out of all my senses.

*Oh my God, he moves better than he sounds.*

"We definitely have to do that again," he whispered huskily in my ear. His lips grazed my ear and sent shivers down my spine.

*No shit, but with our clothes off.*

At last, I brought my gaze up to look into the most lust-filled blue eyes I remember ever having looked into sober… well, semi-sober anyways. As he looked into mine, he brought his lips down to my forehead for the slightest brush of a kiss.

"'Ey get off work at one?" Though the words didn't form a question, one lingered in his eyes and voice.

*Mmm... his voice... off work at one... hmmm.*

Possibilities flooded my head, "We will be at the base club. You and your friends shooting pool with Sam should join us."

I backed up just an inch. I had to get out of Dane's magnetic range and put some distance between our bodies. *What am I thinking? Day one here, slow down; remember—sleeping with someone might be fun, but someone intense like Dane, well, that's NOT what I'm looking for right now... and there's Sage too.*

*Was it what I was looking for?*

*No dummy, you're just horny and missing caresses from a strong, virile man.*

"Holy shit, Tessa! What was that? You guys were fucking with your clothes on!" Sammie stood before me, looking confused. Her raunchy comments fell flat from her lips.

"Thanks for the update," I shrugged off her comedic sarcasm with embarrassed nonchalance.

"What? Like that wasn't what you were doing?"

"Sam, I have no idea what that was. You know we just met. I haven't danced even close to that hot since…," my thoughts took me back to that erotic night with Ignacio in San Juan more than a year ago.

"Since?"

"Never mind. Who's your new friend?" I asked, trying to change the subject.

"Oh no. You don't get off that easy. You haven't danced a hot dance since… when?"

I sighed, "I had a really short-lived, very intense thing with a friend of mine in Puerto Rico. We had an amazingly—and I'm talking soul-shattering, bodies becoming one with each other sexy Latin music kind of erotically hot dance—like I was literally wet afterward."

"No shit. Wow. Was it that virgin guy?"

I laughed, "No. Not that Wes couldn't have moved like that… but Ignacio was all kinds of sexy hot." My memory flashed back to the multileveled club, the strobe lights and the memory of that night. I flushed.

"Hello? Earth to Tessa—you daydreaming about your Columbian or Icelander?"

"He was Argentinean."

"Yeah, okay… whatever," Sammie shrugged with total indifference.

"So, your turn." I smiled and winked at her. "Who's your new friend?"

"Which one?" she asked with a laugh. "Trigg is really arrogant; Ketts is kind of like the guy next door. So, what's the story with that bartender… what's his name?"

"Dane."

"Yeah, so you are planning on fucking him?" She chortled. "I mean with your clothes off next time?" Sammie laughed really good at that one.

*Damn, I thought I had gotten her to drop it already.*

"Who knows, ya know?" I left it at that but turned to see Dane. He had vanished, probably to take the last of his break. *I just want to see his eyes,* I whined internally. *Maybe to get a better idea of what that dance had meant to him… if anything.*

"Hey, the guys from the shop are talking about skipping the base club and heading back to the barracks. They're wimping out, saying we have work tomorrow and squadron muster is at 0800 sharp." She sat down next to me on the same stool, "…but

Trigg and Ketts invited us back to their place—and before you say no—Dane's their roommate, and they live on the other side of the base gate."

"They don't live on base?"

*What to do, what to do?* That is the question that I kept repeating to myself as I tried to find more reasons to not go. That is other than the obvious ones:

*I'm on a new base.*

*I'd be leaving base with strangers and going to their place.*

*I have work in a few hours.*

Nope, I couldn't find any good reason other than I might get so overwrought, so taken with passion that I might enjoy myself in Dane's bed tonight. "I'll make you a deal. Get me the phone number to the VP duty office, and I'll go with you," I said with a mischievous grin.

"Oooh, I like!" She glided off. "Do you have a base phone book?" she asked the busty bartender.

I walked over to Sage and pulled him out of earshot from the other guys, "I hate to ask this of you, since we barely know each other…"

Sage placed his hand on my lower back. "What did you have in mind?" he asked with the same earnestness he'd shown me at the barracks. I looked up at him to see if his expression matched what he was saying… and, well, it did.

*Deal with your conscience later. Just ask him.*

"Ok, so tomorrow is All Hands Squadron Muster at 0800, and well… Sam and I were hoping to get out of it. This is where the favor comes in. We…"

"Oh no you don't! Don't bring me into this," Sammie butted in. "I was only talking about going off base tonight, not skipping muster." She gave me a snort as she handed off the base directory.

"Okay then, I was hoping that you could call the duty office and say that you just left our room and we were really sick, or we called you and are stuck off base, or something?"

"I don't know Tess, it's ALL HANDS. That pretty much means everyone." He rubbed my lower back.

*Okay, you're rubbing me… that's kind of weird… wonder what you think I am going to owe you after this?* At that thought, I changed my mind, because owing someone a favor right out of the gates was NOT a good thing. "You know what, Sage? Never mind."

"I wasn't saying I wouldn't do it, Tessa. It'll just be hard to come up with a valid excuse. Trust me, the officer on duty and mustering officers have pretty much heard every excuse in the book.

Just then, Dane Trigg and Ketts walked up.

"I know. I don't know what I was thinking. Really. Never. Mind," I said it with a smile on my lips, but my timbre left no room for argument. I could tell Dane was sizing up Sage, especially since he still had his hand on my lower back. I made a move to slip out of his embrace, but he wrapped his hand on my hip, further preventing me from moving.

He leaned over. "I've been on this deployment more than once. Those three are not new to this scene. They look at it as fresh meat every six months. Be careful and watch out for yourself." With that, he gave me a little squeeze, let me go and rallied the boys we came with. Without further adieu, they pushed into the frigid Arctic winds.

Gone in fewer than sixty seconds.

Sammie sidled over next to me. I noticed Dane and his

friends hovering around the security 'hoorah' guys. *Chatting up the regulars,* I thought. *Sound business strategy.* Feeling eyes on me, I noticed the tall one checking me out again. *His intensity is a little creepy... but flattering, too.*

"You and Sage? What was that about?" Sammie interrupted my study of the intense, tall guy.

"I'll tell you later." I squeezed her hand.

"Boy, you sure have a long list to catch me up on."

"What's 'ye verdict? 'Ye ladies comin' over?"

*Just shoot me now. I will NEVER get tired of that accent!* "You know, Dane, we really wanted to—tried to make it happen, but we have Squadron All Hands on Deck tomorrow for deployment muster. They're requiring us to be there to go over a couple of things."

"Makes lots of sense, it does. How about if 'ye two come over to my friend's flat? Have a few beers? It's on base."

Sammie pulled me close and dug at my ribs with her elbow, then whispered to me, "He says we can stay on base and go over to his friend's house."

"Thanks, kemosabe, for the on-point translation," I whispered back, scowling playfully at Sammie.

She looked back at me in wide-eyed innocence and sidled over to her Icelandic entourage—Trigg and Ketts. "Let's get this party started!" Navigating her way to the door, she locked her elbows into the crooks of her men's arms. As they grabbed both my jacket and hers, they said something in Icelandic and laughed. I'm sure it was a slam about how ridiculous those dumb coats looked. They headed into the back room through the door behind the bar, in the direction of the rear parking lot. *Must be where someone keeps a car.*

I watched Dane as he talked to 'Too-Tight Tank' by the

register. There was undeniable chemistry between them. She kissed him on both cheeks before she handed him a set of keys and said, "Ciao, Dane," and tossed me a haughty smirk.

*Whoa! She sure doesn't sound Icelandic.*

Dane approached and placed his hand on the small of my back, guiding me toward the stock room. We met up with the others, put on our jackets, pushed through the heavy metal door and leaned into a blast of glacial air that cut across our faces.

I was wrong. No car waited to offer us a reprieve. We walked about two blocks, bent over into the wind to keep from blowing away. Reaching a quad-set of dormitories, we pushed our way into the Plexiglas entrance as Dane got the keys to the inner door out of his pocket.

"Dane, man—hurry up! My balls are ready to shrivel up and fall off; it's so fucking cold out here!"

*Holy Fuck?! Who said that?*

I turned to see Sammie snuggled into Trigg, the tall Icelandic specimen Sammie had said was arrogant.

*I guess her tastes are like mine; tall, dark, handsome and arrogant. Trigg? How can he sound American?*

"Don't make us come over there and show you how to unlock the door, dude!" Ketts elbowed Dane in good-natured fun. He let out a hearty laugh at all the shit he and Trigg were giving Dane.

"So, Ketts, how is it that you guys look like Dane, but sound like one of my former classmates at Wazzu?" I asked the question delicately, giving my manner a playful lilt so he wouldn't get offended.

Ketts smiled knowingly as if he'd answered this question before. "Ahh, dear, sweet, naïve Tess."

*This arrogant shit doesn't know me if he thinks I'm naïve.*

*Maybe a little colloquial in my thinking, but naïve I most certainly am not.* I sighed, a sigh that mourned the loss of who I once was before life shat on my parade.

I waited to hear what other tidbits of wisdom Ketts intended to bestow upon me as Dane unlocked *that girl's* studio apartment. As I stripped off my FWJ, I gave the studio a quick appraisal and found it very college-esque: a full-sized bed and wardrobe, a pull-out couch and TV, and a small kitchen-like area with a hot-plate, microwave, and bar-height round table with two stools. It was tastefully decorated, but so devoid of any personality that it was reminiscent of a mid-range motel in the states. By the time I tuned back into what Ketts and Trigg had been saying, I had no idea what they'd been talking about.

Trigg chimed in, "…Ketts's mam and da' are my aunt and uncle. We all moved to Boulder, Colorado when we were about six because our dads are engineers and hired for some resort work there. We moved back here maybe two years ago to attend the University of Iceland in Reykjavik."

"Fuck, whatever happened to us, Trigg? We never should've taken that semester off. It's now turned into two… what a colossal fucking mistake." I heard in Ketts's timbre and saw evidence in the stress lines across his face, the regret he felt over their decision.

"Ya, you're right, but then, you always are. You've always made me toe the line and walk the straight and narrow. We could still get our degrees, our LL.M. in Natural Resources Law and International Environmental Law. I mean, we did pass the Colorado State Bar."

*At least that explains why they don't have even a hint of an accent.*

"Interesting, isn't it, Tess?" I re-focused my eyes off the

poster of a tree above *her* bed and back to Sammie. Turned out everyone else was staring at me too.

"I'm sorry. It's getting late. What was that?" I asked as I sank to a seat on the couch next to Dane and Ketts. Sammie wandered in the 'kitchen' after Trigg.

I smiled apologetically as Dane repeated for me, "'Ey was saying, 'ey have been working on my English, but Honor 'rekur bar fyrir eiganda'," he cleared his throat. "'Ey have habit of speaking in Icelandic. 'Ey will do my best at translating 'er 'ye when 'ey don't catch myself." He flashed me one of his sexy smiles, "Honor runs da bar 'er da owner and she wants me to focus on sounding Icelandic when 'ye newbies arrive off each new deployment."

"So, you play us for better tips? You lie to us 'newbies'? Real nice. You're a real class act. Nice to know right off you're not who you seem to be." I croaked out the accusation in utter bewilderment.

"Nah, don't 'ye take it that way," Dane said with a sigh. "Trust 'ey—Ég hef sýnt þér meira af mér…" as he trailed off searching for the words in English that evaded him. "En ég hef sýnt einhver á löngum tíma."

I looked to Ketts blankly.

"He said he's shown you who he really is, more than he has shown anyone in a long time." He laughed, "Dane—you'd better be careful, or you'll be a goner over this one." He chuckled and slid off the couch, walking into the kitchen to join Sammie and Trigg.

"Fuck, what 'ey mean to say is that not many have in a long time. 'Ye know, seen da real me." He motioned over to Ketts, "Forget about that one 'ey."

I nodded but was about maxed out at my limit for the night

with bullshit men and their ridiculousness. I stood up and stalked out into the ridiculously small hallway. I knew I was over-reacting, but hell, in the past thirty-six hours or so, I'd only had a few short hours of sleep. I tried to refocus myself by taking a few deep, calming breaths. *What a shitty, fucked up night. I have to be up and at work in like three-ish hours. Fuck this!*

At that revelation, I turned to leave the building. As I reached the entryway, the apartment door swung out, nearly pushing me out of the way.

*What the…? Who the fuck?*

Dane emerged.

"Come on. This isn't funny." My throat tightened at the sight of him, and my voice emerged in a choked complaint.

He quickly and quietly shut the door, as though he had slipped out and didn't want anyone to notice. As it clicked shut, Dane stopped and stood leaning against the doorframe. "Tessa, 'ey didn't want to not tell 'ye what was up… it's why 'ey came clean tonight instead of letting whatever this is or will be play out first." He looked up again, and our eyes connected. Electricity flowed between us, unfiltered and undeniable. "There aren't girls like 'ye but maybe one in a million, I'd wager, and 'ey will be damned if 'ey don't get a chance to get to know 'ye better."

Just then, I discerned, sure as day, his intentions. His intoxicating scent reached me, filling my senses, and I knew I was a goner. I stood at the front entrance and felt him walk forward. Just like a magnet, my body responded to the pull of his energy. I backed up against the icy cold glass, and still, I felt him coming closer. He stole my hand as he leaned in close to my ear.

"Komdu."

He pulled me down the hall and around the corner, around a

second corner, and a third—weaving me through the corridors. He practically pulled me, forcing me to keep up, until at last, he reached a closed door labeled 'Staff'.

He turned the knob in the darkened hallway, and we slid through the widening crack, to find a nicely appointed storage room with a small couch and shelves of supplies lining the walls. A night-light cast a dim and otherwise eerie luminescence in the small space. Dane let go of my hand, and the dim light disappeared as he unplugged it.

As suddenly as the energy advanced on me, it stopped.

*He's close.*

*He's very close.*

*I can sense it.*

Every cell in my body could feel it. His energy pressed in on mine, so that even though our bodies did not touch, every molecule of me was *touched*.

I felt his breath at my ear.

*Oh, sweet Jeezus...*

"Deliciously sweet Tess *mín*," he said with a rough, throaty growl. "Ye', argh! 'Ye affect me. How can 'ey express to 'ye what magic ye' cast over me? Þú verður að vera orsök fyrir að hætta við."

I didn't even care that I had no idea what he'd said, his accent alone made me wet. I felt him take a step back. As my eyes adjusted to the dim shadows cast by the light under the door, I drew in a tortured breath.

"About earlier, 'ey didn't play 'ye. It's part of my job; it's how 'ey make a living. 'Ye can understand that... right? Tessa?"

I could sense him starting to squirm a little, and I wasn't going to make it any easier for him. "There aren't many like 'ye... all bold and shit."

I could feel his breath on my neck while he sought for the English words to describe what he felt.

I knew what I felt and refused to lie to myself; to pretend this was anything more than exactly what it was… the luxuriously hot, primal one night stand I needed to fill the carnal desire that had been building in me since I'd left Puerto Rico. To put it quite simply, I needed a stout, rigid cock pounding into me. I needed a good fucking.

"Tess, ever since da dance—all 'ey can think of is kissing 'ye."

Dane's nearly inaudible words sounded a personal revelation whispered aloud, rather than an intentional expression of his feelings. My cogs quit turning the moment Ha'lfdane Freyson placed his thumb under my chin and tilted it so my soft, full lips could meet his in an unbridled, lust-driven kiss. It started with his lips dancing across mine, sending an invitation. Once my lips accepted, our tongues sparred and jousted, getting to know the other.

His mouth broke free of mine just long enough for him to say, "Ég er vakin á þig," which sounded to me like a garbled mess. As Dane's impassioned eyes met mine in the dim light, he said it again, this time though in his accented English that dripped with sex. "'Ey am so drawn to 'ye." The restrained promise tumbled easily from his lips.

"Shut up and kiss me," I said, my voice raw and unfamiliar even to my own ears.

Dane did just that. His right hand held my jaw at my ear, tilted my head and controlled my movements, his left vied for the best position between my right hip and the small of my back. I simply could not get enough of him, and my hands slid up his firm, athletic torso, finding his nape and tangling in his thick, dark hair.

I pulled his mouth to mine fervently, tasting and drinking of him; his neck, his lips, his mouth. Dane's need for me trumped my own as his kiss sought all of me. I reveled in giving myself over to him and to this experience. He fucked my mouth with his tongue. He tugged and bit at my lips and nibbled along my jawline to my neck. The lustful growls he emitted from the back of his throat nearly unhinged me, and his hands up my shirt sought to unbalance me. I could feel every ROCK HARD MUSCLE against my firm, yet pliable ones. I melted to putty in his hands.

Dane flattened me against the concrete storage-room wall and molded himself against me. The two of us passionately fought to become one. He palmed my thigh, lifting it up over his hip; his hips gyrated and ground between my legs. I was beyond fucking wet and all I wanted was him. There. Here. In me. Now.

"Oh, my fucking God, Dane. I want you in me so badly. Fucking… fuck me. *NOW*." My invitation rasped in an impassioned, barely audible whisper.

He dropped my thigh, setting to work stripping off the cotton barrier between us, as I made equal haste to get out of my tight jeans. Shadows danced on the walls every time someone walked down the hallway. I could hear laughing and party music emanating from the rooms nearby; the background soundtrack to our lascivious liaison.

"Dane, we're so getting caught…" my voice trailed off, so I could hear his whisper.

"'Ey sweet Tessa *mín*. It's da danger that will make our first time unforgettable."

Dane ran his lips from my earlobe, down my jawline, so they

just grazed my lips. Then, I heard him drop his last garment on the floor. I shuddered in anticipation.

I sensed Dane before I felt him, rock solid and bare before me. I ran my hands over his chest, down his torso and rested them on his hips. I pulled him to me and felt his cock against my upper belly. We simultaneously drew in a sharp breath.

"You'll be da death of me." His gravelly whisper broke the dam at my apex, and I felt my slick wetness roll down my thigh.

"Touch me, Dane. See how ready I am for you. See how badly I want you."

I elicited an indecent and steamy sound from him; lewd, yet incredibly genteel, raw and hot all at the same time. He came across as sinful and properly moral, truly sensual and wholly male, rugged masculinity seeping from his pores. His left hand reached up to cup my jawline at my ear, and he kissed me deeply as he slid two of his long fingers between my folds. I fought to breathe through our erotic kiss and fought even harder to hold back the shockwaves his exploration of my swollen pussy evoked.

I hadn't yet touched him… there. I slid my palms down his chiseled back, over his rock-hard ass and cupped him for a second, while I bit at his neck and shoulders. Each bite extracted a brazen and near pornographic rasp from deep within him, but that was nothing compared to the sound Dane made when I knelt down and took his impressive, pulsating cock into my mouth. He inhaled with a harsh intensity that spurred me on. I took both hands and, along with my mouth, worked him from tip to root. I was pumping him, urging him towards abandon.

"Tess—ah."

He fisted my hair and held me captive as he pumped slowly

in and out of my mouth, reaching the back of my throat before pulling me up to my full standing height.

When his hands left me, I felt cold and abandoned. I felt licentious, immoral, uncontrolled. I heard the tear of a foil packet, and then Dane's hands were on me again.

Between me, again.

*IN*, me again.

Facing me away from him, he bent me over, spreading me against the storage shelves, and as I felt him position himself at my entrance. A breathy question seared my ears, triggering goosebumps down my neck and spine. My anticipation skyrocketed.

"Tell me 'ye want me to fill 'ye past full. Fuckin' say it."

Desperation echoed in his voice, his command strained as he fought to maintain control. I felt him lose his last shred when I rasped four words. "Fuck my wet pussy."

It took just those four little words to completely unhinge him. He smacked my ass.

"Grab 'ye ankles." His order left no room for hesitation, and I did as I was told. No sooner had I bent over, then I heard him drop to his knees, and his mouth burrowed against my pussy, lapping at me and suckling my wetness. I swayed. One strong hand at my hip steadied me, as the fingers of other assisted his tongue in their goal to get me to climax.

Just as my knees began buckling from sheer ecstasy, he stood me up and spun me to face him. The swollen head of his engorged cock pressed against me firmly, as his mouth came down hard on mine. I reveled in the taste of my pussy on his tongue and savored my sweet honey on his lips. He threw my right thigh up over his hip, grabbed my ass and left hip, and bulleted his hips into me, thrusting with a ferocity that surely would've ripped me, if I hadn't been so ready for him. Dane stilled after that first push, so I could adjust to the fullness. It didn't seem like I could get him any deeper, yet I wiggled and gyrated, trying to slide more of him into me.

I don't know why, but how Dane was fucking me—with respect, reverence and unbridled need—made me trust him more. While still buried in me, he lifted me by my ass, and I wrapped both legs around him. He reached up, grabbed a newly laundered shower mat off the maid cart and tossed it onto the floor, where he tenderly placed me on my back. He hovered above me, poised to fuck me raw. My legs no longer wrapped around his hips, but I still pulled them high to allow for maximum Dane fulfillment.

It was as though I were the poison and the remedy he needed, I was his murmured undoing, holding the key to a not-so-distant future full of salacious gratification.

"Dane," I provocatively purred, "You're not in nearly deep enough. I need your 'beast-cock' in me, balls-deep."

My purr commanded him, just as a siren used to entice captains into her treacherous, dark waters. Slowly, sensuously, he pulled out of me, before cramming me full to the hilt. I cried out in ecstasy and at the sheer length and size of him.

He stilled. "Are 'ye okay?" I could tell he was worried that he'd hurt me; Dane was fucking huge. He knew he was at least a full twelve inches, and so thick I had to work him with both hands. He had a monster cock, and it was stuffing me full.

"Never better." My voice hissed confirmation as my mind screamed for *more*. More friction, more Dane… fuck, I just wanted MORE *now*.

"Ey Tessa. Tessa, Tessa, Tessa *mín*. 'Ey am going to fuck 'ye so completely that 'ye will still feel me tomorrow and da day after. 'Ey will own 'ye after this…"

*Oh, my fucking… please make good on your promise.* I begged to myself. "Dane," I purred, "I want to make you come so hard it will be *you* still feeling *me* tomorrow and into next week."

"Ey promises." With that, he began to work his hips in circles, grinding deeper before pulling nearly out and deeply thrusting his stout cock back in.

*Holy shit! This man knows how to fuck!*

Dane set a pace that began like an easy stroll but soon built in urgency, strength, and intensity. He drove it home and built me up to an orgasm so powerful, I thought I would surely break if I didn't find my release. He drilled into me while holding my shoulders, forcing me down onto him with each powerful thrust upward.

"Komdu!" Dane commanded through clenched teeth. It was my undoing, and I shattered into a million pieces. I cried out as my pussy spasmed and milked the orgasm from his thunderous cock.

An incoherent, ragged growl escaped right before he came. "'Ey *fuck, sæta mín*!" a guttural cry escaped his lips.

We both lay on the floor in a spent heap. I could feel my pussy still running waves along his cock, milking the last of his release from him. I felt Dane twitching inside me. It was a good thing he wasn't any larger, because there was no way ANY more was fitting into my hungry little cunt. He nuzzled my neck for a brief second, before he propped up on his forearms above me.

"'Ey we have definitely got to do that again," he said with a smile in his voice.

I would've given anything to see his face when he came and

to see it now… I imagined his eyes were wondrous blue gems. I could envision them sparkling.

"I agree." I smiled although I knew it was too dark for him to see. "…definitely in agreement with you. Thanks for that stellar orgasm. Fucking… WOW."

In spite of the intimacy we'd just shared, I felt a little awkward. He was still in me; I just wanted to get cleaned up. As though he read my mind, he pulled out of me, keeping a knee between my thighs as he rolled his condom off. He then reached over and grabbed a hand towel off a stack of clean, laundry and began to stroke it over me. This gesture surprised me. Although I'd had men clean me up after sex, they'd always been boyfriends, not one-night stands, or casual sex… or whatever this was.

"Thanks," I breathed.

I finished the deed, and he pulled me up. We felt around for our clothing, cracking the door to allow in some illumination. It seemed an unspoken agreement that the overhead light would've been too bright, too harsh. The fresh draft that careened into the heady scent of sex in this storage closet helped bring me to my senses. The sex fog that ensnared my brain slowly released its hold on me. Once we were done dressing and had finished looking at ourselves in the small locker-mirror, Dane pulled me to him in a tight, sensual hug, as he stroked his fingertips languorously up and down my back. He nuzzled my neck and kissed my ear before grazing my forehead with the slightest of kisses.

"Are 'ye ready?"

"Yup, let's do this thing." We stepped out into the worn hallway, navigating the maze of corridors until we stood in front of Honor's apartment. We looked at each other as if to say, "Here we go!"

I had to blink to adjust to the brightness of the studio. I made sure I wore a smile to cover the nervousness I felt walking into the room after… hell, who knows how long. To my chagrin, all eyes locked on us. As Sam turned back to Trigg—and I might add she may as well have been sitting on his lap she was so damn close to him—I could feel her questioning disapproval, or at least something close to that. Honor turned back to her tiny kitchen and pretended to be busy arranging the impressive collection of empty beer bottles on the counter and washing the one shot glass in the sink. Warren G played loudly on the stereo. It appeared a good time was being had by all.

Dane guided me toward the living room with his hand on the small of my back. As we passed the kitchenette, Honor turned around, and, smiling at Dane, asked, "Would you like a glass of wine or a beer."

He looked at me and I shrugged. He stood there waiting for Honor to get our drinks, but before I could grab a seat next to Sammie on the futon, she pushed off of Trigg's thighs, grabbed my arm and led me out the front door into the hallway.

"What are you doing?" I asked incredulously. The last thing I fucking needed was for her to chastise me when I already felt like Dane and I had been more on the inappropriate side of the fence. I mean, who disappears immediately after arriving at someone's place? The only comfort I had was in knowing most everyone, except Sammie, Dane and myself, were shitfaced.

"What am I doing? Seriously? You have the gall to fucking ask *me* what *I* am doing? Where'd you guys go off to?" She sighed, and her demeanor changed when she saw how mischievous I looked.

"Nowhere. We just walked around a bit and talked. There's no privacy in the small studio, and we wanted to chat without eavesdropping ears."

"Sure you did." She sidled into me for a comforting bear hug and I threw my arms around her. "It's not like we *have* to see them again. They're not from our squadron or anything."

"True," I said with a hint of resignation, "but what if I'd really like to?"

"Tess, there are other fish in the sea, and we'll worry about this fish as we need to; but right now, we really should head back to our room. It's got to be after three."

It was looking, and reassuringly so, that Sammie would be a strong moral and personal compass to help me to walk the respectable side of the fence. I nodded in agreement and a sigh of relief gushed out of me.

*She's not going to hold this over my head. It's already water under the bridge. She doesn't care that I just had a hot roll in the hay with a stranger.*

We hugged one last time and opened the door to Honor's flat.

Dane and Trigg were standing there. Trigg pulled Sammie aside as soon as we walked back in. "How's Tessa doing? Dane didn't get out of hand, did he?"

"No, no… it's nothing like that. They were just visiting."

"Okay, cause I'd hate to have to kick his ass again."

Sammie looked at me, "No, Trigg, really, she's fine."

He put his arm around her and dropped his voice, "Would you maybe like to come back to my place; I've had a great time with you tonight."

I saw Sammie give Trigg a brisk hug, and pat his back, "We are really beat, and after the crazy night we've had, I think it's time to head home, but why don't you give me a call after work tomorrow?"

Dane had stood there with his hands shoved into his tight jeans, occasionally pulling one out to comb his fingers through his mussed hair while the two of them set up plans for tomorrow.

"Tessa, let's talk, 'ey."

Dane guided me his usual way with his hand at the small of my back, out the door.

"Hvenær munum við ríða aftur," He paused "'Ey, in English, Dane," he chided himself. "I'd like to see ye' again."

"Mmm hmm." I cocked an eyebrow, giving him a skeptical look. "Is that what you said the first time?"

"'Ey, Tess, not exactly. 'Ye got me." He flashed his million-dollar smile. Before I could ask him what he'd said, he interrupted my line of questioning, "I asked 'ye, *sæta*, when we'd *fuck* again. But 'ey have to say, thanks for an amazing evening; I'd truly like to see 'ye again."

I smiled and shrugged, touched that he even cared about trying to make plans.

I, however, had chosen to listen to my carnal desires and not to reason. "I'm not sure. The deployment is new; work hasn't even really gotten into the swing yet," I said with a laugh. "Let's just play it by ear. We'll either make something work or there's no love lost, right?"

*You chose to have this one night stand before you even met Dane, remember?* I reprimanded myself. *Don't be so heartless and rude. You should make more of an effort to see him again.*

I looked up into his eyes. It's not as if it were easy to act so cavalier about all of this, but the reassurance that I saw there somehow made me feel better.

He came in for a hug and was grabbing my ass as the studio door opened and Sammie came out.

"Let's go," she said, and looked back inside to shout goodbye to everyone.

I squeezed Dane one last time, gave him a sensual kiss that inevitably deepened more than I'd intended… just for good measure. For him to remember me by. He tapped my ass as I looked inside and also bid everyone adieu.

"I'll talk to you tomorrow." The words fell listlessly from my lips as leaves do when they turn brown and fall off their branches. They held no promise.

"Until then, *sæta mín.*" His clear blue eyes shone back at me, and I knew that this was either the most interesting one-night stand I'd ever had, or I'd been in Iceland barely forty-eight hours and was now in a casual fuck-buddy relationship. Either way, I needed to absorb what I was feeling. Getting home and resting for a couple of hours before work was just what I needed.

# Chapter Eight

"Ugghh. Oh. My. God. I am so tired!" I couldn't help complaining when the alarm went off. I rolled over, and 0710 glared back at me. And no wonder. *By the time Sam and I walked back to our barracks, showered, very briefly debriefed one another on our evening and slid between the sheets, the clock read 0445. We didn't even get two and a half hours of sleep, and now we have, I presume, a full twelve-hour shift.*

"Sammie, get up. It's time."

I only elicited a moan from her. We had until 0730 to be downstairs waiting for the squadron bus to pick us up. I turned on the TV and the weather read -33 degrees Fahrenheit with 30-40 mph winds. I sighed. *Today's going to be a long, long day.*

We made it downstairs at 0729; a true feat if I do say so myself, considering I literally had to pull Sammie out of her bed. We somehow managed to throw our hair up into proper chignons, dress in our crisp, long-sleeved shirts, black sweaters, dungaree bell-bottoms, and even whip the instant buff polish across our scuffed flight deck boots. Not bad considering we were negotiating the world in an exceedingly fucked up, zombified state.

The bus rolled up and we crowded on, all zipped up and huddled into our FMJs. I couldn't tell if the bus heater even worked, but it had to be only ten degrees warmer on the bus, so instead, I just meditated and try to keep blood in my extremities. The bus made one more stop at the officers' barracks, and then circled back around to the squadron hangar located on the flight line.

Once we rolled up on the flight line side of the hangar, we filed out. The doors were mostly closed, and huge heating fans bellowed massive amounts of warmer air into the hangar's open-air spaces and smaller shop areas. I gave points to the khaki-clad administrative officers for trying to warm up the hangar before muster, but it still had to be about forty inside the enormous space. Here, two P-3s could easily fit side by side, with ladder carts parked in between. Along the left and back sides were the shop doors and beyond them, the different workspaces. All the ordinance racks were parked on the right. This hangar; however, was maybe two-thirds the size of the one back in JAX.

I shook my head. *Here we go again!*

Sammie patted my shoulder in support.

Operation officers stood in their working-blue uniforms, or flight suits if there were on the flight schedule. They held their clipboards with quiet authority, checking off our names as we reached the front of the lines we had voluntarily formed, and telling us which shop to check in with for our deployment assignments, which would last the next several months.

From the looks of it, we weren't the only two, Sammie and I, who had partied too hard last night. The somber faces surrounding us didn't help improve ours when we got our assignments: First Lieutenant… again. As we walked off in the direction of what we assumed was the Geedunk, Sammie spoke first.

"Are you fucking kidding me? First Louie again? I am so *over* cleaning up piss the guys cannot seem to get in the toilets, as well as stripping and waxing shitty tile floors that should be retiled. Ugh! You cannot turn a pig's ear into a silk purse, so when are they gonna stop trying to make us do it?"

I patted her back through the heavy jacket, completely understanding her frustration. *My second duty station, and here I am again at the bottom of the pecking order.*

Once in the squadron hallway, Sammie seemed to relax. We walked by the Aviation Mechanic's (AD) shop and dropped her jacket off. As we passed the Aviation Electrician's (AE) shop, I slung mine in, and it landed on the vinyl couch. Then, we headed toward the delicious smells emanating from the end of the hall. The Geedunk supervisor already had her crew slamming out breakfast burritos and sandwiches nearly as fast as they were ordered. We stood in line and ordered our own burritos and coffee. Trust me, we definitely needed coffee after the night we'd had.

*Shit, I need it, because I'm still in a fog from all the crap that's occurred since I've stepped onto that deployment plane in Jacksonville two… three… four days ago? Honestly, who knows how long it's been.*

My mind, along with our deployment thus far, had been AFU, and coffee was definitely what the doctor ordered. We sat down, and it took less than ten seconds for Petty Officer Reeser to walk up to us. He placed his hand on my shoulder, ever so briefly.

"Hi, Petty Officer Christy. It's good to see you today. Did

you have a good evening?" There was an upward lilt in his voice.

*Unbelievable. He's actually asking me if I fucked the bartender after he left the pub last night.* "I did. Thanks for asking." I left it at that and gave him a flirtatious smile. *It's none of his business anyways.*

"Glad to hear it." His response came off probably harsher than he had intended, so I let it roll off my shoulders. "Just glad to see you made it to work on time."

We traded courteous smiles and I turned back to Sammie as Sage walked over to a table filled with some guys wearing flight suits.

"What the fuck was that all about? He acts like he owns me, or something."

"I didn't take it that way at all. I think you must've gotten under his skin and he was just glad to be done worrying about last night. You know, he only warned you about Dane 'cause he likes you."

I flipped her a look that may as well have been a 'bird'.

"Don't look at me that way! He truly seems to care, which I can't for the life of me understand; especially considering that you don't seem to at all."

I cursed because I knew Sammie was right. I resolved to myself not to go 'hooching' around on this deployment. I hadn't at my last squadron and I DID NOT want a reputation. Those were terrible and impossible to get rid of.

Before we knew it, all shifts were in the hangar-bay, our division officers had taken muster and we stood in our assigned shops, a shoulder-width apart in parade rest.

"All hands, ATTEN-TION!"

Our feet snapped together, our bodies upright with an

assertive and correct posture—in boot camp they'd taught us 'chin up, chest out, shoulders back, stomach in.' We saluted the Commanding Officer until he reached the podium.

"Parade, REST."

The C.O. waited while the shuffle subsided, "You have all attended the deployment prerequisite class on the proper behavior while you are attached to this squadron, on this base, while the eyes of the world are focused on us. You have been made aware of cultural differences between yourselves and the Icelanders, so as not to offend them when you are addressing them or working with them.

This is a NATO base, and in addition to the twenty-five US military commands, Canada, The Netherlands, Norway and Denmark have representatives stationed here as well. NAS Keflavik also supports deployments from the German Navy and Royal Air Force." He paused and took a swig from his coffee mug, "Why is all of this important? Because, I WILL NOT TOLERATE behaviors that are not in line with the Uniform Code of Military Justice. You are to respect yourselves and others while you are here, and this includes the more than 900 Icelandic civilians employed by this base. ANY mistreatment of others will result in punitive action."

He droned on and on about squadron deployment rules and regulations regarding officer and enlisted relations—they're not allowed socially. He discussed cohabitation between the opposite sexes in the BEQ—also not allowed. He addressed where and when we were allowed to smoke—and not to purchase duty-free cigarettes and alcohol for the Icelanders.

Parade rest is a terribly uncomfortable position; we stood with our feet about ten inches apart, our legs straight—hard to do without locking your knees—and with our hands behind our backs, placed straight, overlapped across the other at the small of our back, palms out. Our heads and eyes remained at attention, and our bodies silent and unmoving. I cracked my neck and bent my knees a bit, tuning into what the CO was saying.

"...Only defense force members over the age of twenty years may purchase, possess and/or consume alcoholic beverages aboard NASKEF and in Iceland," he read from the base regulation manual. "So, that while the drinking age on NASKEF is twenty, that does not mean that it gives all of you under the age of twenty-one, or anyone else for that matter, free license to make asses of yourselves. Anyone from this squadron who violates this instruction, or the regulations contained in the base manual, is subject to administrative actions and or punishment under the Uniform Code of Military Justice."

We continued to stand at parade rest for the rest of the hour while they made sure we all understood the NAS Keflavik laws, rules and regulations. Then, the C.O. went over his expectations and regs; ending with, "I know this time away from your friends and family is a trying time. Please try to leave work at work and use your time off to decompress responsibly. Take the time with your loved ones when you visit to truly share, that's what keeps relationships strong in our absence. Squadron, DISMISSED."

It was a long squadron command, but a much needed one, since I'd already broken two rules and had almost broken four. I'd already had relations with the locals, which he strongly discouraged, and had gotten home long after his unofficial curfew of 0200. If we had gone off base, that would've been three, and not making morning muster would have been four rules broken. I know if Sammie had been standing closer to me, I would've felt her elbow in my ribs.

After they dismissed us from the squadron command, some

of the guys in our respective shops snagged us. It took Sammie and me a bit to show up at the Geedunk for check in with our supervising petty officer, much longer than it had taken the others.

No sooner had we walked through the door than she was on our asses. "So glad you two could finally join us." The sarcasm dripped from her voice, thick and edged.

"Sorry, we both were pulled aside by our shop supervisors," Sammie responded snarkily before I'd the chance to belay her comment.

*God, Sam! You never challenge your new supervisor!*

"You must be Airman Anders? It would seem Petty Officer Christy–" she looked at me. "You are Christy, correct?"

I nodded, "Yes, AE3 Tessa Christy."

"Well, Christy, try to keep your friend in line. Teach her the lay of the land so to speak before she falls off a cliff."

"Sure thing, Petty Officer…"

She interrupted me, "Nuniez. Petty Officer Second Class Nuniez."

I nodded, and smiled—showing her I knew my place, and that I understood her veiled threat. This was *not* how I had reacted at my first duty station back in Puerto Rico; I'd learned my lesson though, check my tongue at the proverbial door.

"As I was saying before these two showed up, I am Petty Officer Nuniez, and I run a tight ship. My Geedunk is always spotless, and the food always comes out fresh and quickly. Is that understood?" Again, we all nodded. "A though M, go with Petty Officer Rodriguez for your job assignments, N through Z, come with me—it's time you see how I do things."

We all lined up according to the first letter of our last names, behind our respective supervisors.

"Airman Bach, Airman Monte, Airman Glass—you have the admin offices upstairs, personnel, C.O. and X.O.'s offices as well as the duty office. Starting today, take care of trash in all spaces, and on a three-day rotation, mop and buff the floor, mop and top dress the floor with new wax and buff, then on the third day strip the floor, mop and wax it. Bathrooms and locker rooms need to be spotless. Understood?"

They nodded then she turned to me, "Petty Officer Christy, Petty Officer Julliet, Airman Anders, you have bathrooms and first floor walkways—same three-day rotation applies for you." She went on and addressed the remaining three who were stand-by; basically, they were assigned as permanent wash-rack volunteers, filled in in the Geedunk or wherever else she needed an extra body. I didn't really catch the other jobs they'd have, since I tuned her out once I heard I had the fucking shitters and floors.

*Again? Unbelievable. Who'd I piss off already?* I had to wonder, since I had time under my belt and really shouldn't be assigned to First Louie at all. I'd figured *maybe* the Line Shack, or even the possibility of an assignment to my AE shop, but *toilets? AGAIN?!*

After she'd assigned us to squadron spaces, she went on dangling the 'Line Shack' carrot over our heads if we "did our jobs and did them well." Perhaps in the next couple of weeks, when a new set of newbies checked in, if all went according to her plans.

For those of us in the inner circle, the Line Shack wasn't just a shop placed far out on the flight line that housed young plane captains, the 'runts' who launched and recovered the aircraft. Oh no! The Line also served as a clubhouse hangout, which was part of its allure. Everyone was young, even the supervisors. The only time older Petty Officers showed up out there was either if they had been part of the crew in their time, or they were considered cool by the rest of us. There were a few who had been accepted and they usually came out to the Line Shack when they needed a break from the squadron bullshit and found themselves in search of somewhere lax to hang out.

The shack, a small cinder block building, sat maybe 200 yards from the squadron hangar. It was not far from the wash rack and where all the tractors were parked. It made more sense to be out on the flight line when all the work the linemen had to do was out there. Smaller equipment needed to be inspected once a month, and every three months for bigger equipment. Doing the math, this made for a lot of down time.

Working on the Line was a pretty cush job, depending on the day and the flight schedule. If all or most of the birds were up flying, everyone just sat around, chilled and shot the shit until they came back in. If the birds weren't in the air, if they were downed for repairs, or when the weather was inclement, linemen usually supervised the aircraft washes. They made sure all the 'chipper' volunteers that came from the other shops were pulling their weight; inside if it was cold and outside if it was above freezing. Even during washes, there was room to fuck around A LOT.

The scene when I'd visited this shack, or even my prior squadron Line Shack, was the line crew sitting back, feet up, music cranked, and either playing cards or shooting the shit. Seriously. All the time. When the intercom or 'walkies' went off, the CD player was paused, everyone shut up, and the supervisor would take the call from the maintenance chief. Fuck, I doubt seriously if even *he* knew what went on out in the Line.

*God, getting to the Shack can't happen soon enough!*

Scowling, we busted out the mop buckets and got to work on the floors for the next seven hours, until night check showed up at 1800 for their shift.

When 1800 rolled around, I was OUT. THE. DOOR. Fast. Lightning Fast. I did not want to stick around at all and get roped into doing something else.

I know, I know. I should be busting my ass and making myself stand out, right? *Wrong.* There is no way to shine and make oneself noticed while mopping floors and cleaning toilets. It was a totally unappreciated job, and we were invisible while working. I cannot tell you how many times people walked on our floors in spite of the cones I had put out, nor how many times I was shoulder-checked as people passed by. I didn't exist, and as far as I could tell, nobody knew me from the next mop-monkey. So yeah, I was out the door at 1800 and on the bus minutes later.

Two weeks later, I found myself frowning in disgust at the pee stained floor around yet another toilet. *What's wrong with these guys? Aren't they potty-trained yet? How can they miss so often?* Grumbling under my breath, I swished my mop in the sudsy bucket and slopped it onto the floor, spilling bubbles everywhere.

*Why the hell did Sammie have to go to the other side of the hanger today?* I asked myself for the thousandth time as I scrubbed at the sticky, yellow puddle. *Her company might have made this duty more bearable. Yet here I stand alone, mopping up piss and dreaming of my real job.* I sighed. *At least there's the bonfire tonight. It will be a nice change from all the time the four of us have spent at the base club, at dinner and watching movies. If I can get this mess cleaned up, that is.*

I moved on to the next toilet and closed my eyes. *This is worse than the other one.* To take my mind off the mess of urine… and other, even less palatable substances smearing the tile, I tried to draw up in my mind an exact image of the last time the four of us had gathered—my roommate and our two new friends—in their room. Under their beds, they fashioned an inviting nook with a make-shift couch of pallets and tons of pillows so they had great views of the TV. The four of us cuddled there like young siblings.

*Ace sat with Sammie*, I recalled, picturing the two of them leaning on each other. He resembled my mental picture of a strong, hardy southern ranch hand or Appalachian mountain man. A bit on the smaller side, with longish, dark hair, he had a stocky build, but was also lean as fuck thanks to his small-town varsity high school football career. *He's nice to look at*, I admitted to myself as I scrubbed absently at a stubborn smear, *and although I am NOT a fan of Wranglers, I'd wager Ace looks plenty fine in his with a pair of shit-kickers and a flannel shirt unbuttoned 2/3 of the way. He's single and younger than me. I wonder why I never tried to hit on him… guess he must be more of a brother type; easy to talk to and so, so much fun to dance with at the base club.*

Two more toilets remained, and the next wasn't as bad.

*I don't hit on Lucas, of course, because he's happily married. That'd be trashy of me, though he's sexy as an NFL quarterback and built like an Academy Award.* Like the Oscar statue, Lucas had wide shoulders and quite a narrow waist on his six foot, lean and fit 170-pound frame. He had an attractive, olive complexion and his haircut was so high and tight he practically looked shaven. I'd even go so far as to say Lucas had a regal appearance, with a pronounced brow and square jaw. Despite thin lips and modest features, he came together in an attractive package.

*Damn. Two hot buddies, and no one to flirt with. This two-week absence of worthwhile opportunity since the one time we went to the Privateer Pub is getting tiresome...* as was cleaning this bathroom. At last, I swished mop water around the last porcelain throne, gave a final look at the shining sinks and gleaming tile, and dragged my bucket out of the latrine.

As I walked down the passageway, I ruminated on these past couple of weeks; Sammie, Lucas, Ace, and our other new friends, Ari and Kari. We had hit the base club and Arctic Bowl in our off-time more times than reasonably made sense, and we'd gone to a few parties at the Officer's Barracks and get-togethers over in the permanent housing quads.

I recalled again our good fortune. As fate would have it, real excitement, something new seemed to find us as tonight we'd been invited to a bonfire tonight somewhere on base. Evidently, the word on the street was nobody would get the final location until night-check had finished their shift at 2230, a good four hours from now. *Just enough time to get ready, and do I ever need a shower.*

# Chapter Nine

"Tess, baabeee…" Sammie drawled out in her best southern accent, as she tugged on a clean shirt, "head with me to the Servmart?"

I squeezed my hair with a towel and turned my head just enough to acknowledge her with a goofy face, the kind of face I always delivered when I felt the answer was obvious. In spite of the saying, "There are no dumb questions," there actually were, because she already knew the answer before she asked it.

"Buuut of course, dahhling," I drawled back.

We stepped from the safety our warm barracks provided and the strong, stiff-blowing Arctic wind nearly knocked us off our feet.

"Can you believe," I shouted as I steadied myself, "how much the weather has improved since we arrived? It must be in the mid-twenties."

"I know, right?" Sammie agreed as she and I pushed the barracks door closed behind us. "I can hardly believe it was negative forty-something that day. Windy or not, this is so much better."

"It's windy all right," I replied as I caught sight of the wide canvas straps bolted to both doors. "I've heard it's common for the wind in Iceland to catch a car door and whip it open so far, it gets bent and won't align or shut correctly after."

"Burns like hell, too," she concurred, wiping at the tears that had been ripped from her eyes.

I nodded. Blinking hard only squeezed out more tears, which were blown immediately from my eyes too, leaving them painful and desert dry. I walked behind Sammie. She didn't quite make a windbreak, but it was nicer to follow than to be the lead guy.

As I made my way, I noticed from behind her, that Sammie wore her ill-fitting, boy-styled Levi jeans slung low on her waist, her well-worn flannel and down vest over-sized, and her hair in a ponytail tucked under a baseball cap (whipping hair stings one's face like a bitch-slap). Her brown Doc Martins trudged forward on the slick, icy sidewalk.

*Really, you can't tell she's a girl until you saw see her from the front... and then there's no question.*

We ducked into the outside breezeway between two barracks to get a reprieve from the wind. I took this opportunity to pull my brimmed Oakley beanie off my head, gather all the loose curls and tendrils that had escaped my hair 'claw' and re-twisted my mass of curly, wavy red hair back up onto my head. I pulled my cherry Chapstick from my royal blue down vest, which contrasted nicely with the mustard-yellow wind parka I'd worn underneath, and complimented my antique dyed, slightly boot-cut, well-worn and loved Diesel jeans. I rewrapped my chunky scarf around my neck, tucking it up over my ears and down my neckline, before I stepped back out into the windy onslaught. I assumed the lead and thankfully, it wasn't much farther until we'd reach the base Servmart.

Servmart was the closest thing we had to a 7-11 convenience store. It served much of the base with deeply stocked shelves of quick and easy to prepare foods, awesome selection of frozen pizzas and dinners, and a MASSIVE collection of beers and spirits—equal to and outdoing any stateside liquor store. Here, we could find most any kind of toiletry to get through the weekend until the base grocery store, the 'commissary' reopened on Monday.

I bent my head forward and pushed on against the wind until I reached our destination. The automatic slider sighed and parted for us. We stepped out of the biting wind and headed straight to the liquor section to grab a fifth of Captain Morgan's Spiced Rum for Sammie and my usual Bourbon—Woodford Reserve —for me.

"Tell me again why you go for that fancy shit?" Sammie asked.

"Because it's so much smoother than Crown… just in case you're taking notes," I replied.

She pursed her lips and then changed the subject. "Tessa, let's try to hit the commissary up for ice cream. They have the *Haagen-Dazs* bars I like, and we have ten minutes before they close."

*Grabbing a box of my favorite ice cream bars isn't a bad idea.* I looked at my watch and saw she was right, we hardly had any time to walk there before they closed. "I'm game, if you take over the lead."

I tossed her one of my Hollywood smiles; a genuine grin that showed off my undeniably beautiful, straight, white teeth.

It felt like it took the full ten minutes to get there, with how hard the wind was blowing against us. We literally jogged the next long block and a half until we reached the front of the aged commissary. No longer white, the pull through covered area that enhanced the front entrance of the building had been worn by time and beaten by the weather. A long line of European vehicles waited their turn to pull up out of the crazy weather that was brewing outside and load groceries.

We hurried inside the first set of sliding doors, past full, abandoned carts, and people waiting with their groceries for their turn to pull up their cars outside.

Things here in Iceland were just different, but already now seeming less and less so. After all, I'd never seen this kind of organized chaos until I'd gotten here, not even in Puerto Rico where two lanes of traffic become four during rush-hour.

I noticed I was still bent over, uncomfortably so, from fighting that damn wind, so I straightened up. I huffed a warm breath into my frozen hands and made a mental note that I'd need warmer gloves if I was going to keep braving this bullshit Arctic weather. I glanced up at the weather report on the community board that hung just inside the door. The commissary manager updated it hourly, and it read eighteen degrees with wind-chill.

*Even a few degrees' drop makes such a difference with this wind. Well, that explains why I can't feel my fingers or toes.*

As I continued blowing into my hands, I searched the crowd for Sammie. I wasn't sure exactly where she was—probably already at the frozen section, not wasting any time getting her chocolate chip cookie dough ice cream and vanilla, dark-chocolate bars. If I knew her, she was also grabbing mine, since the commissary was closing in just a couple of minutes. It seemed like EVERYONE wanted out as I slowly pushed in. I felt like a salmon swimming upstream during spawning season. *How did Sammie make it through this mass of bodies so quickly?*

That's when it happened. My eyes caught his. I was searching, looking left, right, behind me, up close in front of me and then farther out into the crowd, when my gaze stopped hunting and locked onto his. His eyes riveted me and speared into me, enchanted me and searched me. Startled to catch myself staring, I turned my eyes as far away from his as I could, and even in that briefness, I felt vulnerable.

*WHAT THE FUCK?*

The crowd pushed me backward, and my back actually hit the glass adjacent and to the left of the automatic door. I was not squished; the crowd had just moved me out of their way now that the store was closing and everyone was waiting either to get out, get bundled up, or head for their car.

From the time I looked away, was pushed back, and turned my eyes back upward to find his… well, this only took a couple of seconds. Maybe seconds. Maybe even less, but it felt endless. The distance seemed even larger.

When I looked back, up he was still a good twenty feet from me, but I just knew. I didn't know what was happening, but I was rapt, captivated by glinting light blue eyes draped in thick velvet eyelashes. My mystery man sported dark-chocolate hair in a longer than average crew cut—military style. He had perfectly arched, wide, pronounced eyebrows that couldn't possibly look that good au natural… he had to groom himself unless he was the baby of an angel. *Which I wouldn't doubt.*

His olive brown skin looked like he spent his days on the beach playing volleyball and surfing which, obviously, he hadn't been. My stranger had a strong jaw and a sexy five o'clock shadow that framed one of the most perfect mouths I had ever laid eyes on. His eyes shimmered, his bronze skin exuded life and energy, and his frame—well, it could NOT look like that unless there were some defined and sculpted muscles under there.

Purely virile.

Wholly male.

Totally unexpected.

My eyes found his again as he moved, gliding through the crowd as it parted for him like Moses parted the Red Sea in the Book of Exodus. As he approached me, I gave him a good once-over, which he evidently noticed because he flashed me the quirkiest, most sarcastic smile I think I'd ever seen. His eyes twinkled, smiling at me.

*Holy Hell, I am such a goner.*

"There you are!" Sam emerged from somewhere on my right, grabbed my arm and started to pull me backward. I stumbled, righted myself and we scooted out the door, back into the Arctic cold and stormy wind. This time, I welcomed the gusts, which now only felt like breezes, as I had gone searing hot, my breath coming in erratic pants.

"Fuck, you look like you've seen a ghost." Sammie nudged me.

I had no words for her. Hell, I had no idea what had actually happened and was still trying to process it. The wind claimed the rest of what she was shouting. With our ice cream and booze tucked tightly under our arms, we headed off toward the permanent barracks to wait for word from Ari about the bonfire with his friends.

Once back in our room, I felt the need to share, to get this weird and totally amazing feeling I had just experienced off my chest. I needed to talk to someone, but Sammie wandered down to Lucas and Ace's room to wait for Ari. *I wish I could just call Wes up and talk to him.*

*Fuck, maybe I should just give him a call. What's the worst that could happen?*

I searched through my papers on my carole until I found my Puerto Rico notebook, flipping through the pages until I got to the one on which Wes had written his going-away note to me. As I read through it, his words shocked me by tearing at my heart, even after all these weeks.

*My poor Wes. I never meant to hurt you like that. Surely though you're over me by now.*

I cracked my neck and picked up the landline, dialing the numbers to the duty office for VC-12, my old squadron.

"VC-12 Fighting Eagles duty office, Petty officer Martin speaking. How may I help you?"

"Yes, could I please speak with Petty Officer Wes Porter?"

"One moment, please, while I check which shop he's attached to." I waited patiently while I heard the person on the other side ruffle through papers. "Here it is; I'm putting you through now. One moment please."

"Certainly."

"Corrosion, Porter speaking."

"I can't believe my luck." I sharply drew in a chest-full of air.

"Excuse me? How can I help you?"

"Sorry. Wes, it's me—Tessa." Silence followed. An incredibly long silence. I pulled the phone away from my ear to look at it, as if that would tell me anything. "Are you still there? Wes?"

I heard him clearing his throat on the other side, "Sorry. Tess, you just really surprised me—I mean it's been so long—what I mean to say is, how are you?"

I could hear the confusion in his voice and wondered if I should be calling at all. *Jeezus, I'm being selfish calling him... I suddenly realized. I didn't even think this would affect him. STILL?*

"I'm doing good actually. Really good. How are you?"

"You know how it is here. Craner is up my ass, same as he was when you were here too…" I nodded, not that he could see it. "… and Shewner is dating Ryker. You know, pretty much the same-o, same-o."

"Yeah, but how are *you* doing, Wes?" I waited in anticipation, hoping he'd say he was ok.

"It's been rough, I'm not going to lie." He paused, "Tessa, you know how I feel about you, felt about you, I mean." He stumbled over his words, obviously flustered. "It's been hard without you here. I miss you, ya know?"

"I miss you too, Wes… it's just probably different for me."

"Yeah, you've moved on and I'm still stuck here. So, like, every time I want to go do something, I remember the great times we've already had there."

"That's true, but not really what I meant about how my missing you is different than how you miss me."

"Yeah, Tess, I KNOW. I don't really want to hear again how you love me differently than I love you."

"Sorry, Wes. I never meant…"

He interrupted me before I could finish my apology. "I didn't mean to steer us down this road." His voice suddenly took on a more upbeat tenor. "So, what's up?"

*Shit. I can't share this with him now. Fuck. This was such a big mistake.*

"Actually, why I called doesn't make sense anymore… I didn't really think this through. I just wanted someone I trusted to talk to, and you came to mind."

"Okay… so, share. I can take it. Really. I've been doing better; it's just your call caught me off guard is all." I heard him shouting to someone off in the distance. "Hey, Craner says I need to wrap it up. We have inspections to finish before the birds can be signed off for flight, but they're already on the schedule —so you know how it is—they work us to death."

"Okay, well we can just say bye then…"

"Damn it, Tessa, out with it already. What? Did you meet someone? I can take it; besides, hearing about it might make it easier to get over you." He laughed uncomfortably.

"Okay, Wes, okay." I sighed in resignation. "So, have you ever noticed someone out of the corner of your eye—maybe not even such a little notice—but, you know… from your peripherals, from out of the crowd in front of you? You detect them, though and… They. Discover. You?" I paused. "Wes?"

"Yeah, Tess?"

"You okay? Maybe it isn't fair for me to go on?"

"No, go on. I *TOTALLY* get what you're talking about." He sighed deeply.

"Well, it sizzles," I pressed on, doubting this call more than ever. "There's a heated cosmic exchange that takes place in the atmosphere that coexists, in that time, between the two of you."

"Sure do. That's how it was for me when I met you, but you were married to Teddy."

*Jeezus, I had no idea he felt like THIS about me! And now… now I'm going to tell him…* Another shout sounded in the background. *Wrap it up and be done with it. If he's right, and it will help him move on, it's well worth it. He can't pine for me like this. It's unfair. Rip off the Band-Aid, Tess.*

"Well, that's what happened to me today at the commissary. This open exchange left me feeling exposed, bared, naked and even a little emotionally raw. I just cannot get him out of my head. It was like… I don't know… it was like he reached into my soul with his eyes and carved out a spot in my heart." I laughed, "Okay, well maybe not *quite* like that, but it was fucking intense, Wes." I could hear him getting even more flack in the background about still being on the phone, and he took it, like he always has. "Sounds like Craner is really being an asshole—maybe I should let you go?"

"Yeah, he is. It's just there's all these inspections to get signed off and we're still down a person here in the shop… so we're hustling double-time."

"Well, thanks for listening…"

Again, Wes interrupted me. "Heya, Tess? Thanks for sharing with me, I mean, it wasn't the best to hear, but I'm glad you thought of calling me. It's nice to know I still cross your mind. For what it's worth, you should go after this guy. That kind of connection doesn't happen very often. Trust me, I know."

"I know, Wes. Sorry."

"Enough with the sorries! Hey, Craner's ready to go off. I can see it in his eyes, even from this far. I'd better go."

"Okay, and thanks again." I cleared my throat, "Oh, and, Wes, it was really nice being able to talk like this with you. I've missed you and our hours of great conversation."

"Yeah, me too. Bye, Tess."

"BYE."

I hung up the phone, his saddened voice still vivid in my ear.

I'VE no idea whose beater pick-up we climbed into, and I didn't care either. It was just a means to an end… the bonfire.

"Jeezus, Tessa! Could it be any fucking colder?" I could hear most of what Sammie was saying, as we jostled and bumped along, but didn't feel inclined to pull my face from the nest I'd created in my chunky scarf. It was dark and cold whenever I lifted my face from its warm cave, so I just huddled in the corner of the pickup bed and tried as best as I could to keep from getting tossed around. At last, we slowed, and I felt us turning. We came to a complete stop shortly after.

"Hey, baby girl, can I give you a hand?"

I looked up, wiping at my nose, and noticed we had arrived in some sort of aircraft graveyard; the place where all the decommissioned planes ended up. Let's call it what it really was —a military junkyard.

I gave Ari my hand, and he pulled me to my feet. "Ready to go throw down?"

I looked up and smiled at him.

*5'11", maybe 160, half Italian, half African-American— simply gorgeous. I wonder what it means that he just doesn't float my boat in THAT way. Still, in the time I've worked with AE2 Ari Benson—had him sign off on my shop qualifications when I hung out in the AE shop—I've found him genuine, laid back and fun. He's such an easy person to get to know; I consider him a true friend, which is better than a crush any day.*

"Hey, beeatches!"

I turned my head to where I'd heard Sammie's voice, but found it too dark to see more than a few yards out. Sure enough, she bounded from that direction. "I didn't know you'd leave me!"

"Hey, I looked *everywhere* for you and thought maybe you'd gotten on a truck in front of me."

"Is that so?" She raised her eyebrow skeptically.

"It's my story, and I'm sticking to it!" I laughed and jumped down from the truck. "Let's go find us a drink!"

Just then, a huge explosion lit up the blackness in a bright flash, and then dimmed to a steady glow.

"HOLLA!!" Sammie blurted out rambunctiously. "Sounds like they just lit the bonfire—see the glow over there? Come on! Let's go, hooka!" She was already drunk, but then again, so was I. Fuck, pretty much everyone had arrived already loaded. Ari joined us, and the three of us walked off in the direction of the bonfire.

"Sounds like someone threw a gas can on the fire."

"It does, huh?" I smiled again, surprised Ari would know that kind of thing. He always seemed so… well… proper. He walked with us but kept his eyes on me.

"Watch out!" I shouted, just in time to keep him from smacking his face on an ordinance rack hung low from a wing of one of the haphazardly parked, decommissioned airplanes. If we hadn't had our arms linked like the Three Musketeers, and I hadn't jerked him, the rack would've pegged him right in the face.

"Shit, that was close! Thanks, baby girl."

I squeezed his arm.

Suddenly, a weird feeling like I was being watched came over me. I stopped abruptly and jerked Sammie and Ari to a full stop as well.

"Hey!" Sammie complained. "What's up, Tess? I. Must. Get.

To. The. Rum." She lowered her voice an octave, and started to walk like a zombie saying, "Redrum... Redrum..."

"Knock it off, dork. You're creeping me out; come here."

She dropped her arms and came back to where Ari and I still stood. "What's up?" she asked.

"Do you feel that?"

"Feel what?" Ari focused on me, trying to see what I was talking about.

"I don't know. It just feels like someone's watching us," I whispered. We all looked around, but the bright glow given off by the nearby bonfire cast even deeper shadows over the parked planes, and the inky blackness behind them somehow grew even darker.

"I don't see anything," Sammie observed.

"Yeah, Tess, I don't either." Ari squeezed my arm, but this time it somehow felt... *different*. More... *intimate,* so I dropped it.

"Okay, never mind. I guess maybe I'm just drunker than I thought. You know me and my paranoia." I laughed nervously.

"Oh boy, do I. This one time at band camp..." She and Ari laughed at the movie reference and took off toward the pickup parked closest to the fire, in search of more booze to further waste ourselves on. I heard her telling him all about how ridiculous I'd been earlier this week, when I'd been too drunk for my own good.

As they walked away, I reflected on how I'd had this feeling that I was being watched a lot lately. It had me on edge; it was creepy. Perhaps the creepiest part was I never felt unsafe despite drowning in this paranoia. I just wanted to know *who* was watching me, and *why* they hadn't come up to me.

The night wore on. I joined Ari and Sammie, claiming the

Jack and Coke they'd poured for me; it was about six ounces of Jack and one ounce of Coke, if I had to guess. The first cup went down painfully slow. The second was halfway done, and now I was thoroughly enjoying it.

Probably a good forty or fifty of us stood around bullshitting. Someone had turned on the radio to Icelandic techno-beats, and a handful of people danced with light-sticks under the wing of a dead C-130. I stayed away, and it wasn't the slightest bit hard either. *If I never saw another one of those it will be too soon.*

I'd just brought my cup up to my lips for another swig, when the feeling of being watched overcame me... AGAIN.

*Seriously! What the fuck?*

I held the cup up to my mouth, pretending to drink from it, but really using it to hide behind while I slowly turned back to face the fire.

There.

Looking through the fire were those deep blue eyes. He stood, his gaze pointedly focused on me as he held his beer. His intensity drew me in like a black hole, swallowing my paranoia.

*Oh my God! It's the guy from the commissary... the GUY with the eyes!"*

Now I knew. It was *him*. He'd been watching me all this time. Instead of unease, a warm heat flowed up me from the ground, pooling in my belly. Butterflies swirled, and something akin to nausea threatened to overtake me.

The flames licked and danced before us. Their heat and brilliance amplified the chemistry that flowed between me and Mr. Intense Blue Eyes. The music faded to the background; the people talking around me became a blur. It seemed there was only him and me. Me and him.

"Tessa! Hey!"

I startled, jumping at Sammie's voice. Looking at her, I wiped the slosh of Jack off my chin. "Been drinking long?"

I smiled absently at her, looking back to where he'd been standing. He was gone.

"Earth to Tessa…"

"Yeah, I'm here. Question is, are you?" A drunken giggle escaped past my lips. "What's up?"

She motioned up towards the sky, "Some of us are gonna climb up on the wings and watch the northern lights. Wanna join us?" Slurring drunkenly, she took a final slug, downing the bottom of her beer.

"Yeah, sure. Sounds fun—cold but fun."

She hooked her arm in mine and led me toward the group she'd been carousing with.

REALLY, I can't tell you much of what happened the rest of the weekend. We partied with some security and Icelandic officers and at our BEQ, we ate A LOT, and I found my thoughts going back to the mystery man I had imagined on Friday.

Part of me knew I'd seen who had been watching me—this sexy, mysterious and solitary man. Another part of me felt sure he was a figment of my imagination.

I glanced out the window and could easily see the barracks across the street in the early dawn-like light. I stole a glimpse at the alarm clock I had perched on the window sill. It read 23:49. I had about four hours before I had to be at work, but the poetry I was writing felt like it just had to get out. I loved to write, but this was different. The words would not stop flowing. I wrote into the early morning. I wrote until my hand cramped; I felt like

my hand was possessed. Eventually, I closed my eyes when they
wouldn't focus any longer on the last words I wrote…

*…gnawing, throbbing, abusing me.*
*where did it come from?*
*It blisters & scalds me—*
*this desire that possesses me.*
*Go! I do not want you to take hold of me.*

*Or is it too late?*
*I am completely possessed, deeply intrigued,*
*wholly consumed by desire.*
*Safe in the knowledge that it's you.*
*It will always be…*
*Just You.*

# Chapter Ten

So, the next five weeks wore on.

Mundane, uneventful and unattached, my usual schedule had me getting up at 0330 so I could be at work at 0400. This allowed me a good two hours or so before I had to check in for muster with my First Lieutenant shop at 0600.

So, when my alarm went off this morning at 0330 on the dot, I did what I always do… swing my legs over the side of the bed and force my weary body to move.

"Sam? Sammie—are you up? You asked me to get you up to come in with me this morning."

"Noooo," she whined in a terribly sleep-deprived voice, "I'm so sorry, but I'm not going to make it."

"Sam, you asked me to make you get up. Come on, let's go!" I tried to be adamant, forcefully firm, but I totally understood. *Just like her, I'm beat.*

A loud sigh came from her side of the room, "Tessa, it's not going to happen today—we have to scale it back a bit. I just can't keep hitting it hard like we've been doing; it's seriously killing me." A groggy giggle sounded. "Seriously, Tess, if we don't stop staying up half the night with the guys on our floor, pounding booze pretty much drinking every night, and then getting up at the butt crack of dawn to do extra work so we can get to our shops sooner, you'll be writing my eulogy."

*God, I love her... this is the best way to wake up this morning! She's too damn funny.*

I checked my laughter. "10-4. Rodger that, Sam." I shook my head, totally bummed that I wasn't giving myself the extra two hours I needed desperately, as she crawled out of bed and went about getting ready.

*But she is right. Day in and day out Sammie and I go to work, get off work, make dinner in the barrack's kitchen and then drink. We drink every day—sometimes because it compliments dinner, sometimes because we're bored. Sometimes we drink because work made us mad, but mostly we drink for fun and to pass the time. We drink in our room, in Sammie's mech friends' rooms, Sage Reeser's and Ari's rooms, the other guys' rooms from my AE shop.* I took a look in the mirror, *Fuck, come to think of it... where don't we drink?*

Since we'd run into Ketts and Trigg not long after my night with Dane, they'd been coming over to our room and hanging with our friends Ace and Lucas... A LOT. They often crashed in our chair, which we'd named the 'Blue Beast', when they weren't sacked out on the floor or sharing our beds—strictly in a platonic sense, at least with me. I'm not sure how much longer Sammie would have luck fending off Trigg's advances though.

In spite of my reflection on our whole 'to the excesses' issue, it took me all of maybe fifteen minutes to have my coveralls and flight-deck boots on, my hair up in a bun, face washed, and teeth brushed, and an 'Everything' bagel toasted. I looked at my clock, 0348...

*Damn, it's been eighteen minutes! I have to hurry.*

I had two minutes to be downstairs to catch the duty van I had called ahead to pick me up. I threw my FWJ over my arm, grabbed my backpack and bagel and scooted out the door.

I hastily ran down the hallway, hit the fire-door at the end and flew down the three flights of stairs, taking them two at a time. *There's no way I'm going outside to wait.* It had been ridiculously windy the past week, even though the weather has just started to warm up, closer to 36 degrees Fahrenheit during the day, with about ten hours of daylight. We'd gained about four onto the six we'd started with when we arrived that frigid day back in February… not so long, but forever ago.

I glanced at my watch—0351. *Fuck!* Depending on the duty driver, I might have already missed it… especially if it is Airman Onnie. She loved being the duty driver because it afforded her some small amount of power, and she actually loved taking off if you weren't on time. Even a minute late.

*Talk about a serious fucking abuse of power.*

Shaking my head, I opened the door, and sure as fuck, there went the goddamn duty van.

*Fuck, fuckity, FUCK!*

Just like I'd expected, the wind was howling, bringing the temperature down to probably about fifteen or twenty degrees. I looked around, hoping to maybe hitch a ride with someone; I really didn't feel like walking, but of course, who's outside at four in the morning?

I tugged on the heavy metal BEQ door, and nearly fell over when it gave way easily.

"Ey, careful there." His hand shot out to steady me, catching me before I fell back on the icy pavement.

My head snapped up while I found my balance and stared

into those familiar lusty blue eyes. "Dane? What are you doing here?"

*I'd bet I already know the answer... wonder who she is?*

"'Ey, sweet Tessa, it is 'ye. 'Ey wasn't sure since 'ey haven't seen 'ye in a while."

"Yeah, hey... I'd really love to stay and chat, but I'm supposed to be at work right now, and the duty van took off because I was a minute late." I spat out hurriedly.

"'Ey, that fuckin' sucks," he slurred and patted my back through my parka. "If 'ye need a ride, 'ey can give 'ye one."

"Thanks, Dane. That would be awesome." I looked around the lot, hoping I'd see someone a little less inebriated. "Which one is yours?"

"Ah, it's da Audi over there," he motioned with beer, "'Ey shit," he said laughing, "I'd better get rid of this! 'Ye boys Ace and Lucas gave it to me." He tossed the bottom of the beer in the smoke-pit trash can, not twenty feet from where he'd been standing, then jogged over to where I was shuffling through the lot to his car. We walked in silence. Upon reaching his car, he unlocked it with a chirp.

He gently nudged me out of the way, so he could open the door for me, taking my backpack from me before I slid into the car. He opened the trunk and tossed it inside before getting in.

"Thanks for taking me, Dane. It's already after four, and that's when I'd told my shop to expect me."

He turned on the heater, and we waited for the car to warm up and windows to defrost. "Tessa, anything 'er 'ye. 'Ye know that 'ye and 'ey are friends." He shifted his weight so that he now faced me. "Believe it or not, 'ey have missed 'ye."

I chuckled, "Dane, we've been around; it's not like we don't share the same friends. I was actually just talking to Sam about this, and she and I agreed we need to quit hanging out so much in everyone else's rooms, pound back fewer beers a night, and maybe we'd get the rest that we need, instead of slogging through each day at work like zombies. Honestly? I have no idea how we've been partying this hard for as many weeks as we have without totally crashing—but I can feel it coming soon if we don't slow down."

"'Ey, sweet Tess.'Ey can see that. 'Ye are there a lot, but that's not what 'ey meant when 'ey said 'ey missed 'ye." With that, he reached up, placing his strong hand at my jaw, his thumb grazing my bottom lip. Instantly, my core fluttered. "Ég hef saknað snertingu þína, lyktina þína, kossana þína...

"In English please." My request fell breathily from my wanton lips.

"'Ey, *sæta mín*." He looked searchingly at me, his blue eyes questioning mine, penetrating their depths, "'Ey have missed 'ye touch, 'ye smell, and 'ye kisses."

No sooner had he said that, than he brought his mouth to mine. His lips were soft, seeking, against my ill-prepared ones. His hand slid to the nape of my neck and encouraged me to fall deeper into the kiss, an understated suggestion. My mouth relaxed, inviting him in as he explored and sparred with my tongue, and I savored my favorite beer on his tongue. He nipped at my lips, passionately sought all I had to give until he pulled away, leaving me breathless.

*Jeezus, fuck! Damn, he can kiss! What am I doing?*

"Like 'ey said," he repeated, eyes glinting mischievously, "'ey have missed 'ye, Tessa. There's no reason why we can't be enjoying each other more..."

I went to open my lips to respond, but he placed his index finger over them, effectively shushing me.

"Just think about it 'ey?" I nodded, before he shifted in his seat, smacked on the wipers, and took off in the direction of the hangar.


"HIYA, HOOKA!" I jumped at the sound of Sammie's voice.

I must have been in that weird zone between being fully aware and asleep; you know, kind of like napping with my eyes open. "Jeezus, you startled me. What time is it?"

She sat down beside me on the ugly vinyl shop couch. "After nine."

"Holy fuck!" I started to get up, but she grabbed my belt and pulled me back down.

"Best as I can tell, AE1 Dunnmoth was letting you rest. I heard him in the 'Dunk' talking to that chick in your shop and Ari, about how impressed he's been at the effort you've shown—coming in early every day for the past few weeks just to get shop sign-offs and learn." I smiled weakly. "You should've seen it though. Rodriguez…"

I interrupted her before she could finish, "Roz is looking for me?"

Again, Sammie pulled me back down on the couch. "Chill out. Rodriguez went over to AE1's table to ask if he'd seen you, since you'd missed the 0600 shop muster and passdown. I'd been standing at the table next to them, talking to the guys from my shop, so I was able to hear it all. He said that you'd been in the AE shop for the shift passdown, and that he'd mustered you with the shop. That Chief knew, and for her not to worry."

I shook my head. *I'm going to be in so much trouble the next time I see her. She made it explicitly clear that I was to check in with her for the day, NO MATTER what.* "So, what's she think I'm doing?"

"AE1 said you were out on a generator change. She threw a bit of a fuss, and he said he'd have you back no later than ten."

I smiled at her and relaxed back into the couch a bit. I truly appreciated what AE1 had done for me. He had become a lot like my 'shop daddy'… not like 'who's your daddy', but more like someone I could count on to watch my back and for sound advice. When I'd first seen Tim Dunnmoth on the hellish plane ride to this godforsaken base, I'd no idea that this dark-skinned, dark-haired, and even darker eyed individual would end up impressing me more than his short, unimpressive stature would suggest. AE1 was fun to work for and had taken personal interest in getting me assigned to the shop. *I'm truly grateful to know him.*

"I'd better get going. All I need is for Petty Officer Cai to come in and give me shit—I'm surprised she hasn't already."

"Yeah, well about her…"

I looked at Sammie, raised an eyebrow and waited. And waited. "What the fuck, Sam? What about her?"

She laughed at my angst. "I'm not too terribly sure, but I guess the Line was short a supervisor for the day, and Dunnmoth volunteered her. She's supervising a wash!" Her voice cracked from holding back laughter at Cai's misfortune.

"No shit? Who'd she piss off?"

"You know, she asked that very question, and AE1 said something about lightening up on the shop newbies and future newbies who were making an effort to learn. He told her that maybe…" she paused, taking in a breath and fighting back more laughter, "and now get this… he told her that maybe she needed to remember what it was like to be a 'newb,' and it might do her some good to go work with them for the day."

We both cracked up. The laughter bubbled out of us. *It's so great to hear that that bitch has been checked.* We sat around drinking coffee for another fifteen minutes or so, before Ari came in.

"Hey, Sam, Tessa." He nodded to us. "You know, Petty Officer Rodriguez was looking for you guys a while ago?" He motioned towards the door that led to the passageway. "AE1 covered for you, but I'd get going if I were you." He smiled at us kindly. "I'd hate for you to have to pull extra duty…"

"Thanks, Ari," I accepted his extended hand for a boost up. When he tugged, I stumbled from the force of his pull and fell into him. His eyes locked onto mine, but his usually warm, friendly gaze looked different—more heated, shining with an unspoken fire. Quite frankly, it startled me.

"Anytime, baby girl."

I stuttered while I thanked him again and, backing up, grabbed Sammie's hand and pulled her out of my shop.

"What do we do now?" she asked.

"Get the mop bucket," I replied. "No reason to put off the inevitable. The fucking floors have to be done just like they've had to be done every damn day prior, and every next day for the foreseeable future." In my discomfort over Ari's sudden change in demeanor, my voice came out snappier than I'd intended.

"Jeezus, Tessa, did you see the way that Ari was looking at you?" Sammie commented.

*Damn. She noticed. I'd hoped I was imagining things.* Our feet echoed in the long, worn tile passageway, and her voice echoed off the bulkheads.

"Shh! That's all I need, Sam! People will hear that and then all of a sudden I'll be fucking him," I exclaimed in an agitated whisper.

"Sorry, I forget gossip here travels like the damn Telephone game."

I nodded in agreement with her, then shook my head. *People can be so stupid.*

Hours into the day, we had already mopped the entire downstairs passageway, placed our cones out, and were now laying fresh wax over the clean tile… not that you could tell; half of them were cracked, broken or stained. It was a thankless job, and didn't make the slightest bit of difference in how they looked. I'd busted my coveralls down to my waist, knotting the arms like an old sweatshirt, and my t-shirt was damp with sweat when I heard my name.

"Petty Officer Christy?"

I looked up, saw it was, AE2 Simone Cai, my shop nemesis, and decidedly blew her off.

"Christy!" I looked up at her again, and if looks could kill, I'd have died, right there, on the spot.

"What, Cai?" I demanded with clear disdain. I frowned, one eyebrow raised as I eyed the half French-Creole and African-American standing not far from me. Beautiful, creamy, café-colored skin, a petite nose, exotic green cat eyes and curly, short, dark brown hair. She purred in a soft southern accent like the actress Jasmine Guy.

*How can such an angelic looking creature be such a raging bitch?*

"Excuse me for stating the obvious, but…" she paused for dramatic effect, "…how the eff am I supposed to get by with these cones in the way?"

I shifted my weight and put my hand on my hip. *As if you*

*can't see we were laying fresh wax down and waiting for it to dry so it could be buffed to a shine. What the fuck is your problem?! Jeezus, crawl back into the miserable hole you crawled out of!* "Well, Petty Officer Cai, you *aren't* supposed to get by."

Sammie chimed in. "That's what the cones mean. You can easily get past us in the hangar and cut through a shop farther down..."

Sammie's response was cut short as Cai began walking with her wash-rack wet coveralls and heavy-footed flight-line boots, through our freshly laid wax.

*That BITCH! She's leaving footprints!*

She shoulder-checked me and then turned around with that bitchy face of hers. "Oops. Did I do that?" She laughed snarkily. "Maybe next time you'll only do the hallway one side at a time, LIKE YOU'RE *SUPPOSED* TO?"

"That's it!" I seethed, thinking about all the work she had just created. We'd have to strip the floor now... the whole fucking thing, re-mop it and then lay new wax down before it was even ready to buff. I'd be lucky if we were even halfway done before night check arrived. I swear I would've taken her down—and I'm not even the fighting type—if AE1 Dunnmoth hadn't heard the commotion and stuck his head through the shop door.

"What's going on here? What's the commotion about?" He turned first to me, then to Cai for an answer.

"I feel so terrible," she drawled on in that sickeningly sweet accent of hers, "I wasn't paying any attention and accidentally walked through Christy's new wax."

"Accidentally?"

She interrupted me before I could go on. "You know me,

Tim. I can get flighty sometimes… especially after such a long night." She smiled at him angelically, suggestively.

I wasn't an idiot. The hunch I'd had on the plane that they were DFBs… didn't look that far off.

"Well, Christy, it's an honest mistake. I'll take a look at the shop and flight schedules, and if we're caught up, I'll see if I can't get a body out here to help you guys get done."

I felt defeated. I'd gone from pissed and ready to throw down to just plain beaten. I nodded. "Thanks, AE1." I must have sounded as downtrodden as I felt, because he went on.

"Don't let this small set-back get you down. It happens to the best of us and will happen. It's not what happens to you in life, it's how you take it that counts."

All I could do was nod. *What the fuck? Seriously? That's it? She added at least another four hours of work onto our day!*

Cai sauntered off. As soon as the door to the shop closed, and Sammie had checked to make sure we were alone, she erupted. "What the fuck is wrong with that bitch? Didn't she see the cones?"

I shrugged and headed off toward the utility locker for the floor stripper.

She trotted after me. "I don't get it…"

"What's that, Sam?" Annoyance laced my every word. I wasn't annoyed with her, but just generally with the whole situation.

"I've heard Cai is as easy to spread as Country Crock on a hot summer day. How can anyone want to get with that?"

"I don't know." I pissily grabbed the supplies and gear we'd need out of the closet at the far end of the passageway. "Ari's been in there, so has that young married guy, Towers, and who knows who else… I mean, it sure seems Dunnmoth is getting a piece of the action too, since he's divorced."

"I just don't get it, Tess. I mean, if it weren't for her personality, her demeanor, how miserably she treats people, I wouldn't fault the guys, but her attitude sucks!"

"It's not how she treats *people*." I closed the utility closet and started back down the hall, lugging the supplies. "It's just me." I exhaled heavily, out of breath. "She seems to think I'm some sort of competition."

"Well, you guys both have cute bodies and have to be within maybe six or seven years of each other. Maybe she feels threatened? Younger competition and all that?"

"Yeah, I just don't know. You saw her. She's a roaring bitch to me anytime we're alone, and then sweet as a newborn kitten when any of the guys from the shop are around." I stacked the cones out of the way and dumped stripper onto the floor, splashing it on my boots, not even caring that they'd need a good polish after this. "You know what sucks the most?" I paused, looking up at Sammie.

"What? Let me guess, that she's been with Ari?"

I shot her a look like she was crazy, "No! I don't care about that. What sucks the most is that I could've really used an ally in the shop—a woman who knows how to hold her own in the sea of testosterone and pass on some pointers."

"Yeah." She smiled at me. "Sorry, Tessa. That definitely would've been better than all the shit she's giving you."

"Oh well. Why beat a dead horse?" I slumped against the wet mop as I dragged it against the floor. "What the fuck else can I do? What the fuck over…"

# Chapter Eleven

"Yay! We're off, we're off, WE ARE OFF! Three day weekend, here we come!" Sammie exclaimed exuberantly as she opened our door. I followed her in. I could hear her incessant chatter behind the wardrobe as she grabbed her robe and shower stuff, but all I could think of was getting my dirty coveralls and sweaty t-shirt off.

*I love how Cai royally fucked the day up with her little stunt earlier.* Thank God AE1 sent over two shop newbies to help. They hadn't seemed too thrilled at first, and who would've been? At least it got them out of the wash scheduled for this afternoon. I laughed to myself. Their whole demeanor changed once they realized he was doing them a favor. *I am* SO *glad we were able to get it all done!* Funniest part though, was that Cai was left two bodies short on her last wash of the day; we actually left before she could.

I closed my eyes and lay half-crashed on my bed, pulled my feet under me as I drew in a deep, calming breath.

*A three-day weekend after working eleven 12-hour shifts straight. I sure hate duty weekends, but the three day weekend that follows almost makes them worth it.*

It suddenly dawned on me that Sammie had continued speaking while my mind wandered. "Sorry, Hon. What were you saying?"

"Get showered. We're going out tonight."

I responded with a grunt. "Ugh. I. Don't. Want. To. Move." I stood in an honest effort to get the ball rolling, but my ass only moved two feet from my bed before it found the welcoming cushion of the Blue Beast, and I collapsed.

"Get up, lazy butt! The guys from my shop and our friends from the Privateer are meeting us in less than an hour. Get up!" She tugged on my arm in a futile attempt to get me moving.

"I'll be there soon." I closed my eyes, indicating that I was done arguing.

"Oh no, you don't!" Sammie full-on collided with the side of the recliner I was curled up in and tipped it over.

"What the fuck?!" I said more out of surprise than anger. I got up, righted the chair she'd just bull-rushed, and grabbed my shower stuff. "This had better be worth it," I mumbled.

"I promise, it's just what we need," she said as she bounced out the door and headed off in the direction of the showers.

Slumping limply again, I pondered my options...

*Doing nothing but work and coming back to the BEQ was boring, but it kept me out of trouble.* I sighed. *She's not going to take no for an answer, so I guess I'm going out. I can see the potential for two things happening tonight. I could have a great time keeping it real with Sammie and my boys, Ace, Lucas, and the rest of them. Or, I could get raunchy-dirty and dust the cobwebs out of my VaJayJay.* The idea had definite merit. *I've been craving some good loving, ever since that amazing night with Dane.* Decision made, I heaved myself to my feet.

I PUSHED OPEN the bathroom door. As I entered the hall wrapped in only my towel, I bumped into Officer Ian Daniels. He stopped. The stunned look on his face and red creeping up his neck to his ears deepened as he slowly dragged his eyes from my bare calves up my legs to where my short towel grazed my upper thighs. He paused before he drew his gaze up my towel and over my chest. I'd hadn't planned on running into anyone, since this *was* a 'strictly' female floor.

"Ian, a picture would last you longer," I laughed teasingly, and in no way meant any bad-will by it.

His eyes snapped up to mine, and he had to clear his throat before he could speak. "Tessa." He cleared his throat again and gave me a weak smile. "Trust me, if I had my camera, I would take you up on that." he chuckled.

I made sure to brush into him as I walked past, turning to check him out, and as I expected, he was looking… so, I winked. I sauntered down the hall to our door, knocked, and as soon it closed behind me, I dropped my shower basket and began giggling.

"What's so damn funny?" Sammie urged, clearly curious what had brought on my serious fit of giggles. She stopped getting ready and sat on the edge of her bed, smiling, eyes prying.

"Oh my God." I paused, trying to regain my breath and stop laughing before I continued. "Oh man, I just ran into Ian in the hallway, and you'd think I was a playmate the way he was gawking. Shit, you'd think he hadn't gotten any since we'd been here, he was drooling so damn bad!" I began laughing again.

"Well, look at you. Pretty hot and bothered yourself by his sincere attentions, huh?" Sammie smirked, only half serious. "Maybe you can remedy that for him tonight? You know, I'm pretty sure he'll be there, and after seeing you ninety percent naked, if you wanted to take advantage of him, it probably wouldn't take much." She roared with laughter, knowing full well I was *not* planning on taking advantage of him at all. Not tonight, not tomorrow or any time in the foreseeable future.

"You're such an ass. I love you so much." I blew her kisses before I slipped over to my side of the room, out of her view, and began getting ready. Not too long after, Sammie knocked on my wardrobe before she popped around on my side.

"Can I ask your honest opinion?"

I could tell by the rare seriousness that etched her face something was weighing heavily on her mind.

"Sure, give it to me. I'll try my best," I replied, and continued getting dressed.

"So, you know it has been about seven weeks, and I've seen Trigg quite a bit… and well, I was thinking about maybe…" Sammie paused, and I looked up at her. She was biting her lip, studying her toenail polish.

"You want to do him, huh?"

"Well, I don't know. I mean, yes. Or maybe… shit, Tessa, I don't know. I like him and all, but don't want to ruin our friendship."

"How serious is it, Sam? Are you guys more friends, or is there that pulse of passion that creeps up and burns in your veins? You know, the way you get when you're around someone and feel like you're going to explode? That passionate coil that builds inside you, and you know you're simply gonna blow if you don't find your release in him, with him? You know… the 'I've got to fuck you, or I'll die' feeling?"

Sammie stood, dumbfounded. Her jaw went a little slack, and a blank glaze clouded her eyes. "You mean like the way you were with Dane at the bar?"

I nodded. "Sam, does he do that to you? You know, make you feel unhinged when you touch?"

I could tell she was processing, reconciling my words with what she had witnessed of Dane and me at the Privateer and later at the flat.

"Huh? Well, no." She plopped down on the arm of our recliner. "Fuck, Tessa. I don't think that I've *ever* felt like that for a guy… ever." The awkward silence that followed spoke volumes about her experience in the love/fucking department.

"You've fucked before, right?" I asked softly, not wanting to insult her innocence if she hadn't, and not wanting to piss her off if she had.

"Well, I'm not a virgin, if that's what you're asking."

"It's not." I smiled at her encouragingly.

*We're becoming more and more like sisters; the chapters of our past slowly opening for each other to read.*

"Fuck, Tessa—NO, I've never had a guy take me the way Dane took you."

"Sammie, this is not about me. It's no competition either. I was just asking if you and Trigg had that magic spark that turns your friendship into a relationship, or an exciting passion for each other… 'cause if neither is present, it might be safer to just keep it on the friendship level." I shrugged apologetically. "I didn't mean anything by what I said—you know I love you and am not trying to make you feel badly." Again, I smiled, trying to ease the tension her last defensive outburst had sparked in the room.

Sammie emitted a growl of frustration. "Ugh. I know. I'm sorry. I've just always been the goofy friend. Guys don't think of me the way they think of you. Guys—everyone: Ari, Dane, Ian, Sage… fuck, and a number of idiots in my shop and on the Line, think you're hot and would do you in an instant."

"Oh, and that's great, right? Is that what you really think? Sammie, that just means that they want in my pants, not that they like me or want me for their friend. You don't think it would be nice for me to have someone like Trigg around; someone to hang with, cuddle with, really get to know and feel valued by? Why do you think I always talk about Puerto Rico? It's the last goddamn place I actually felt valued for me, and not for my tits and ass!" That admission startled even me. I sank to a seat on my bed, feeling pretty sacked myself. Smiling at her, I shrugged. "Maybe we should just stay in and call it a movie night?"

"Funny, isn't it? We always want what's on the other side of the fence," she mused. "What I wouldn't give to have some random guy looking at me the way Dane did you. Dance with me the way he did with you as if you two were the only two people in the world. Fuck me until I came so hard I was heard in the hallway and rooms next door over their loud music and parties." She stopped, embarrassed, and chuckled nervously as she looked up at me. "Guess I didn't realize how jealous I was of your romp until now…"

It was my turn to be a little embarrassed. "I had no idea until now, that you'd even heard us." I stood up and walked over to where she sat, looking defeated and forlorn. I pulled her to me and gave her a hug. "Sammie hon, why don't you just play it by ear? If it's meant to happen with Trigg, it will, and you won't have to overthink it 'cause it will just feel right. *Not* that everything that feels right, is right. Take me, for example," I laughed, and she looked up, fully engaged in our growing mutual understanding for the first time, and laughed with me.

"You can say that again." Still laughing, she hugged me back. "Thanks, Tess. I had no idea when I met you how much you'd mean to me, girly."

"I know, right? Isn't life curious?"

AFTER A GOOD HOUR OR SO, I looked back in the mirror at something I could work with. I had applied a pretty dose of makeup to my already flushed face to emphasize my eyes and lips. My hair was drying nicely into curly waves that graced my shoulders and cascaded mid-way down my back. I had chosen a simple, form-fitting, faded green t-shirt, and had paired it with my favorite pair of low-waist jeans and a wide brown leather belt. I really liked how the shirt made my tits look hot and totally out there. They were like, "Hi! Here we are. Come ask us to dance!"

As I turned to check out my ass, my shirt rose just a bit, enough so I bared some midriff without looking trashy. I didn't have much to choose from as far as shoes went, so I opted for a well-worn pair of heeled leather ankle boots. I threw on a beaded wooden necklace for good measure, plumped my hair at the roots and focused on what Sammie was saying to me.

"Yeah, sure."

"Don't yeah, sure me. You haven't heard a word I've said, have you?"

I looked at Sammie and could tell I was busted, again. "No, sorry. Tell me again."

"I was saying I couldn't wait to dance with Trigg, and maybe you might feel like dancing with Sage or Ketts? I bet Ensign Ian will be there too." She smiled at me in the mirror. "I love your hair, Tessa. I wish I could do something different with mine, but this is pretty much as good as it gets." She flounced next to me, waving her hair back and forth as she swayed from side to side.

"It looks good."

"Beeatch, quit lyin' to me, or I won't be able to call you my bestie anymore!" She smacked my ass and sat down in our terribly over-stuffed, faded recliner, to tug on her brown leather Doc Martin boots.

I turned, and what I saw was pure Sammie. She never wore any makeup unless she let me put some on her, and tonight was no exception. I mean, I didn't wear much either, but she somehow seemed to wear even less. She had on her men's Silver Tab jeans with no belt and a form-fitting shirt. *I have got to take her bra shopping; those babies should be riding much higher.*

Sammie had brushed her hair, glossed her lips, and well… that was pretty much it. I have to say, though, she was a natural beauty. Her eyes—sparkly and alive—tied for her best feature with her lips (not counting her 'girls'). She laughed with them, spoke with them. Her quirky mouth turned downward when she smiled, but was full and voluptuous when she was pensive, angry or working. I hadn't kissed another girl on a dare since Puerto Rico, and didn't plan to, but, well, get me drunk enough sometime and I just might.

"Should I bring my coat?" Sammie asked as she stood at the door, holding her Velcro wallet.

"Should you bring your coat? Seriously?" I laughed, threw

her leather jacket to her and grabbed my Colombia. It wasn't trendy but would keep me warm to and from the base club. I gave the room a quick once-over and, satisfied I had everything, grabbed the beer Sammie held out to me, my purse, and we scooted out the door.

# Chapter Twelve

I angled my watch into the flashing strobe lights that were ricocheting off the club's ceiling and walls. I had no idea what time it was. Finally, the light hit my watch and it read 0152.

*Holy Shit. We've been here a long time.*

We'd arrived at the Top of the Rock's Enlisted Dance Club around 2000, shot some pool and had a few beers over pizza, before heading into the crowded dance side that had been beckoning to us for the past hour. The music had started as Country, and we'd all united on the floor for some flavorful line dancing. I say flavorful in only the best way. It was OUR interpretation; a comical, sexy effort. Sometime around midnight, the beats switched to dance music, and the place really began to bump.

As MC Lyte's "Cold Rock a Party" boomed over the system, Ace—a friend of ours from the mech shop—pulled me onto the dance floor. Our friends joined us and, it was as if we were a massive organism; moving, bouncing, jumping and swaying as one. Song after song, dance beat after dance the beat thumped and vibrated off every surface in the club. I felt like *goop* being held together by the energy in the room. Every cell in my body became hyper-aware, high as I was off the five or six Jack and Cokes I'd had along with the intense bass that coursed through me. The dance floor had to have been a broiling 90 plus degrees causing my skin to glisten with sweat and my shirt to stick to me in *all* the right places.

The bass vibrated in my chest as I danced with Sage in front of me and some random guy behind me. Neither could dance worth a fuck. I was gearing up to leave the dance floor just as masculine hands landed on my hips, and then gripped them strongly. This mystery man's strong, virile hands rested squarely on my hip bones, now revealed as my jeans slung dangerously low from my relentless affair with the dance floor. He guided my hips as we danced to Freaknasty's "Da Dip", amidst the circus of pulsing insanity that swallowed us like an irate, foaming sea.

Ginuwine's "Pony" came on next, and when the music slowed, the hands behind me snaked around my torso and guided me into an erotic, sensual game of Simon Says. It seemed that for every response I gave, he countered, and we easily anticipated each other's next play. I swept my hips from side to side, grinding and gyrating into the rock-hard firmness behind me. Between the Jack and Cokes and whiskey shots I'd taken, the scent of his cologne, and the general fuzzy glow I had from the energy in the bar, I started to feel a certain sensation creeping into my core; a small glow he'd ignited. I guarantee he was the best chance I had at having it put out.

The floor was so crowded, the club so dark, and the lighting so intensely bright as it spiraled around the room, that when those hands turned me around and I looked up, the details of his face were lost in the shadows, painted in the club's camouflage.

I squinted hard to see through the strobes and shadows. He towered close to a foot over me, his strong, lean build molded into mine as though we were meant to be connected. He was roughly hewn, strong, raw and incredibly masculine. His black t-shirt and dark jeans hugged his sculptured body, clinging to the sweat-dampened planes of his form.

I thought I saw some scruff on his strong, determined jaw and high cheekbones that complemented the combat soldier demeanor he radiated, although it was so dark, and I was so delirious from the Jack and beats, that I wouldn't have bet my life on it.

His full lips parted slightly as he danced. The faint scent of whiskey mixed with his cedar and sweet musk cologne in an intoxicating zephyr. He drew me inexplicably as though he were the nectar and I the bee.

The music paused, and another slow bump and grind R&B song played its opening riff. The strong bass pulsed through my body, and my core answered back, countering each beat. His commanding movement ordered me to follow his lead. He took my hands and drew them up my taut stomach, to my ribs, past my breasts and back down. He led us in an erotic tango. Our bodies conversed in a language all their own, and with each dip and grind, every sway and roll of our hips, our bodies' non-verbal conversation deepened, as did my draw towards him.

I don't know how many songs we danced to. At some point, we began moving to our own beat. He kept running his fingers through his dark, wavy hair, mussing it... but brown or black, who was to say? All I knew was I could've danced with him all night.

"Hey, Tessa, me and the guys are gonna head back. It's

already twenty minutes after last call," Sammie shouted over the loud, 'fuck-me' music that was beginning to wind down. I nodded, indicating I'd heard her.

The song ended and with it my ride on this carousel. The night had come to an end. Hot lips brushed my forehead as he leaned toward my ear, and I heard in a rough-hewn, sexy growl, "Thank you." His feverish lips nipped at my neck by my ear and then… he squeezed me and was gone.

It was as if the sea parted for him.

The lights came on not long after the final song ended, and with the music off, the club was emptying pretty quickly. A wisp of a girl came up to me. "You guys looked pretty hot out there."

I raised an eyebrow, but in my inebriated state, really didn't give a shit, "Thanks." I replied flatly.

"He was pretty hot. I was going to ask him to dance with me —he usually dances with me."

"Oh, that's nice," I mumbled, and seeing my friends at a table near the door, excused myself, and sauntered over to them. There were a few hangers-on like us, but they were grabbing our shit and getting ready to blow the joint too.

"What was that about?" Sammie put her arm around my shoulders.

"I have no idea—some loon was staking a claim to the guy I've been dancing with. It was weird," I said shrugging.

"Hey, Tessa just got some chic's digits!"

"Tess, don't you know there's a don't ask, don't tell policy?"

My dipshit friends pretty well raked me over the coals, when the only person I felt like talking to was nearly four thousand miles away. *If only Wes was closer than several time zones, all those miles, and a phone call away. I could really use his ears, his chest to lean my head on and arms to hold me tight.*

I sighed just as Sammie opened her mouth. "Don't start on me. I'm too tired and feeling homesick for some reason."

She dropped her arm from around my shoulders, "Whoa, slugger!? Comin' out of those gates sluggin' eh?" She jostled me with her elbow, and I nudged her back. Then she looked at me, really looked at me. "Hey, Tess, what's wrong? You're usually super spiked after a night of dancing."

"Ugh. I know, right? Not sure what's wrong with me. Just listening to the jackasses we choose to spend our time with—"

"…Get it, Get it. Get it!"

"Flip her over and cram her doggy-style…"

Sam raised her hands once she focused on the crap behind me, "ENOUGH! Effin' change the topic already, she's had enough."

"Awww, we're just jokin'."

"Yeah, tell her to lighten up…"

Once again, Sam came to my defense. "I'll lighten you up once I knock a few teeth out of your perverted mouth!"

They sparred back and forth as we grabbed the last of our jackets, the drunkies we'd come with, and headed out the club doors to the front entranceway. Top of the Rock was like a super small mini-mall with a few phones in cubbies and around corners, in hallways. At last, Ace found one that worked and put the call in for the duty van to come get us; now my watch read 0254.

We stepped out into the glassy, ice-covered world to wait for our ride. I blinked a few times, trying to clear the haze from my sight, but it was no use; I'd had too much damn whiskey. The orange streetlights cast a warm glow, but just above, the inky darkness pressed in. In my inebriated state, it felt like I'd stepped into a Twilight Zone episode in which I existed inside a snowglobe universe. It was so fucking cold that my breath came out in a frosty fog. The night had worn on too long as it was, and I was relieved when the duty van arrived to take us back to the BEQ.

# Chapter Thirteen

We opened and then closed our bedroom door and I tossed my keys on the sink counter just inside. I worked to get my shoes and clothes off, struggling with my tight jeans. Sighing deeply, I released myself to all the emotions and brain fatigue that were now setting in after my electrically charged night at the club.

"Talk to me, Tessa."

I could hear the genuine concern in Sam's voice. I wouldn't say that I was mopey waiting for the duty van, or grumpy on my ride home to the barracks. I had tried to jest with the boys who had continued to heckle me, but my heart just wasn't into it. I knew that my Jack buzz was coming down, and that was part of it, but after being away from my last duty station for so many weeks—a place I had called home for just over two years—I was simply homesick. What I really wanted to do was call Wes. I needed the familiarity and comfort of my 'person'.

"I don't even know where to begin, Sam," I said with a sigh that totally deflated me… hell, it deflated the room.

"Just start where it makes sense. Tell me where your head's at."

I laughed. Her simple statement was so loaded that I struggled not to comment on the irony; instead, I began. "Sam, it's... well, it's just that I'm so exhausted. Not really from the long hours at work, or even from hanging out dancing tonight, not even from the obscene amount of drinking I've been doing... which is even a lot for me." I finished removing my makeup at the sink and settled myself on the end of my bed, just a foot or so from where Sam's feet hung over the armrest of our dilapidated recliner.

"Mm hmm..." Sammie encouraged me as she stood to turn off our lights, and then plopped back down in the same position she'd been in. She rested the side of her head on the back of the *Blue Beast*.

"Okay, so nothing seems like it could stay tangible forever. First, there was Ethan for a college summer; second was Teddy. Hell, I even married him, and that didn't last. Then, there was Ryker and his power-hips; fun to ride but dumber than a doornail to talk to. Ignacio and his magnetic eyes, whispered Spanish sweet nothings and electric merengue hips; fun, but couldn't last; a story I will have to tell you another time." I took a sip of my water.

"So, basically you're bummed you're still single."

I ignored her. "Then, there was sweet Wes, our liaison cut short by my inability to love him like he loved me, and my new orders to JAX. Then, we come straight here... and let's just look at my prospects so far. Ari—not bad; in fact, in so far as looks and personality go, far from bad."

"Ari might be too nice for you, and he works in your shop."

"Gee, thanks. So?" I stuck my tongue out at her. "I don't think of him like that anyway, for some reason; we're truly *just* friends, so he's really not even a prospect."

"Yeah, I can totally see that, *and* he works in your shop," she reminded me jokingly.

I continued, "Ian's pretty fine…"

Sammie interrupted me. "He's an officer! Albeit a young, dumb and full of cum one, but still definitely not a good idea… even if his pecker seems to think so."

I laughed. *She always was good for lightening the mood.*

"Don't forget Sage. He seems pretty into you too," Sammie volunteered. "Did you even notice the way he danced with you tonight? Plus, he's nice. I've worked with him in the mech shop."

"Yeah, I'm not too sure about him. He's from a town that's barely bigger than my graduating class. Besides, I *did* notice how he danced with me… he flat out sucked!" I laughed spiritedly.

"You can't hold his hick roots against him," she pointed out, "but he'd sure like to hold you against him!" Sammie dodged as I whipped a pillow off my bed at her head. "Careful, Tess, you don't want to write a check your ass can't cash!"

At this point, Sammie and I were laughing hysterically. It felt wonderful, this cathartic release.

"And then…" she urged me on.

"Well, there was Dane."

"Yes," she half laughed, half choked, "…there certainly was him. What was it… all ten inches of him?"

"Closer to twelve."

"Holy shit!"

"No. Holy Dane!" I joshed back.

"You're effin' kidding me, right?"

"Nope. Anyway… Then there was that guy tonight. Damn, that was electric."

"Wait, I'm still stuck on the bartender, Dane. How'd you fit that in you? At least NOW I understand why you walked so funny when you guys got back."

I flung my last pillow at her, and she fended it off with her leg, no problem.

"One, I didn't walk funny, *ass*. Two, trust me, you'd have fit it in you too if he'd done to you what he did to me!"

Sammie smirked and changed the subject. "So, that guy tonight was some dancer, huh? Seemed he really enjoyed you rubbing your ass all over his Woody Woodpecker."

"Woody... really? That's crass."

"Yeah, but that's all you were doing. Sage was dancing up front with you, but you were so into this... what's his name?"

I rolled my eyes, not that she could see me in our dark room. "I don't know."

"You didn't get his name? *Wow.* Ok, so anyways, you were so into this guy that even Sage knew it."

"Bullshit."

"No, really. When the "Pony" song ended, and Mr. Mysterious was all grab-ass and whispering to you, Sage came back and said something to Lucas, Ace and the rest of us about how it was time to look elsewhere."

"Oh, crap." I hadn't had any intention of going out with Sage, but I didn't want him to find out this way. I had hoped I could somehow tell him differently or avoid it all together by focusing on being *just* friends.

"Yup. Guard that rep of yours with your life, 'cause it will make or break you while you're here. I keep tellin' ya." She stood up and gave me a hug, then plopped back down in the folds of the Blue Beast.

"That's not even what I was trying to do. Ugh, see? See what

I mean? All these guys, and it all just turns to crap. No happiness. Just crap."

"Well, crappy girl; let's get some sleep."

I nodded.

"By the way, you should know I covered for you when we left the dance floor and you were still with that guy while he was all whispering in your ear."

"Oh?"

"Yeah, they were all talking about how you'd fuck him, blah, blah, blah. I just told them to shove it. I told them to quit acting jealous."

"Thanks. Did it work?"

"Yeah, I think so. Lucas pretty much shut right up. Ace kept his eyes on you even though he pretended not to, but Sage was the toughest… he's the one who felt the most slighted, I think."

"Thanks, Sammie," I breathed, relieved to be putting this night to rest. She stood, peeling herself from the Beast. We hugged, and I glanced at my alarm clock, which now read: 0347.

"We really need to get to bed," she said, reiterating her previous suggestion.

I wearily dipped my chin, nodding. *Best idea of the night.*

# Chapter Fourteen

*What the fuck?*

"Sammie! Stop knocking already!"

"It isn't me." I could hear her moving on the other side of the wardrobes. "Fuck off already! Quit knocking!" I could tell by Sammie's tone of voice that she was pretty pissed.

The incessant knocking continued. I could hear Sam grumbling and thrashing around on her bed—I thought to get up and take care of the asshole on the other side of our door—but no such luck. With a pissy sigh of resignation, I threw my legs out from under my comfortable cocoon of blankets and down comforter, and trudged to the door.

"Alright. Alright! I'm coming. Quit your knocking!" I flipped the locks and opened the door, letting in the brightest light I think I'd ever seen. At least, it sure seemed that way considering how badly my head was hurting from romancing Jack and his buddy Coke last night.

"Rise and shine, baby girl," Ari exclaimed as he let himself into our room and gratefully shut out the grievous hall lights. I crawled back into my cloud-like bed haven. I was so, so tired, and my head hurt, and I just wasn't ready to get up.

"Who is it?" Sam mumbled from her mountain of covers.

"Just Ari."

"Huh?"

"Ari Benson. AE2, you know, from my shop. Sheesh, you've only been hanging out with him since week one."

"Shut the fuck up. I know who he is," she said as she sat up.

"Shit, I thought I was more memorable than that." Ari let out a good-hearted laugh.

One great thing about Ari; he never seemed to take things personally. He was either confident or arrogant, I hadn't decided which, but I was betting on confident because he had everything he needed to back it, especially those exotic good looks.

"Oh. Hey, motherfucker, next time you wake me up beating on my door, I'm gonna open it and pound *you*," Sam said groggily.

With a chuckle Ari slapped her bed. "Just try, Airman Anders. Just try."

I heard Sammie try to kick him. Thankfully, before it turned into an all-out war, Ari plopped himself down in our Blue Beast and kicked out the foot-rest. I glanced at my alarm, which read 1005, and quietly sighed, counting that I'd had just under six hours of sleep. I *so* loved our black-out curtains. I prepared to settle into another bout of well-deserved sleep.

"I know you don't smoke weed; I know this. But I'm gonna get you high today, 'cause it's Friday; you ain't got no job... and you ain't got shit to do."

*Oh Brother! Really? He's quoting Smokey from the movie* Friday*? Where do I find my friends?*

"Ari, it's Friday. I have a job, and the shit I have to do is called nurse a hangover." With that, I rolled over to face the wall.

He was quiet.

He was still quiet.

*He's being too quiet. Maybe he took the hint and is taking a nap too?* I rolled back over and saw Ari still kicked back in our recliner, just staring. I couldn't tell if he was stalker-staring at me or just zoning.

"Hey! Go do that in your own room," I said with a yawn.

He cleared his throat, "Hey, so, remember when I'd told you that volunteering as a body on the bus washes would pay off?"

I mumbled something that resembled a yes.

"Well, the guys at the at the Keflavik motor-pool remember you and Sam pretty well, and when I called up to see if there was a van available for this weekend, we got to talking, and they extended us an open invitation to use their vans anytime there's one available."

I didn't say anything. I heard him, but I could feel myself fading.

"I've already picked-up a van for today. Fenton, Towers, Finn, Montgomery, Reeser, Daniels, Garren, Archibladt… they're all going…"

I interrupted him, "Who's going? I was halfway gone between here and getting *there*, and none of those names sound familiar."

I heard him mutter under his breath, "Jeezus Tess, least you could do is stay awake! I'm trying to get you in on a fun day," as I watched him crack his neck and then massage it. "Anyways," he went on with a sigh, "the van is an eleven-seater, and there's room for at least two more… so, here I am."

"Going where?" I asked with another yawn. I couldn't chase the hangover fog from my head, and now a vicious headache threatened.

"Wait. Who did you say was going?" Clearly, Sammie had cleared her haze.

"You know, your friends Lucas, Ace and Kari, an electrician from Tess's and my shop, Sage, Ian, and two security guys…"

"How can Ian Daniels go? He's an officer. And who are the last two? New check-ins?" Sammie's voice had changed its location, indicating Ari had at least piqued her interest, as she no longer burrowed under the covers.

"First of all, Ian and I fly together, so it isn't weird for us to hang out. And, no, Garren and Archibladt aren't new check-ins, they're base security. In fact, we met them at the base gate on our way back in a couple of weekends ago."

"Whoa there, hoss! You mean to tell me you've been off base again already and didn't get us? You suck." I could just imagine Sammie's pouty face.

"Trust me, what we were out for wasn't your type of fun, if you know what I mean," Ari snickered suggestively, giving us a clue to just what they *had* been up to.

"You still suck," Sammie said, pulling back my covers and crawling in next to me. I shifted over to the wall to make plenty of room for the girl who already felt like my sister.

"So, hey—we're gonna pony up around 1100. It would be great to get some more estrogen in the van. I'm sure your friend Kari Fenton would appreciate the company."

"Ugh. Okay, Ari," I said with a moan. "I can't let Kari brave you all alone. I just hate having to get to know new guys, ya know? I don't even know if I'm up for it, as bad as I feel." I groaned again.

"What do you mean? I thought you guys met them last night. I heard all about it from the gang," he laughed. I could hear him putting the footrest down on the Beast before standing.

I sat up.

"What exactly did you hear, Ari?"

"Never mind, baby girl, just get ready. You only have about thirty minutes before we're supposed to roll out of here." He started to open the door...

"BRIGHT LIGHT! BRIGHT LIGHT!" I squealed.

"Gremlins—right?" He shut the door to just the barest crack. "We're headed to Blue Lagoon, so pack accordingly." Ari blew us sarcastic kisses, pausing to catch my eyes, and scooted out the door.

"What did he mean by we met them last night?" I asked Sammie, my interest definitely piqued. I'd spoken with so many guys and danced with a good handful. Who could guess which was base security?

Sam had already gotten up and flopped into the Blue Beast, flipping through the AFARTS. She stopped on the weather.

"Hey, it's supposed to be nice today. Forty degrees and winds only about fifteen miles per hour. Says here about eleven hours of light."I climbed out of bed and set to work looking for my swim stuff and something to wear that might at least make me feel presentable. Sure, they were my friends, but I had to at least look somewhat decent. *Right?*

I HAD my forest-green and leather Jansen backpack from high school all packed with my bikini, towel, make-up, etc. on my bed, and was putting the finishing touches on my messy, curled up-do, when a knock sounded at our door.

*I just can't seem to get my tendrils right... damn it!*

"Sam, can you get that please?" I know I was literally an

arm's reach from the door, where I stood looking in the mirror over our sink, but I still had to sweep lip-gloss, bronzer and blush on.

Sammie complied and let Ari in as I was finishing my face. I smoothed my hands over my sage-green, long sleeved V-neck t-shirt, admiring how it contrasted nicely against the bright white cami I had layered under it. I finished my look with a kick-ass pair of black stretch pants, which I'd tucked into a cute pair of Uggs. I grabbed my black down vest, pack and sat down to wait for Sammie which, I might add, NEVER happens. I am always the last one primping.

Sammie looked outdoorsy herself. She'd taken extra care getting dressed and had on a pretty tight pair of black jeans and a chunky ivory cable-knit sweater. She wore her leather Docs and was actually putting her hair up in a high, tight ponytail; a fun style that really accentuated her cheekbones, which were always hidden under her short hair. As she ran Chapstick over her lips and pinched her cheeks, Ari grabbed her brown leather bomber jacket and pack.

"We really need to get a move on. The guys on my floor were headed outside when I came up here to get you, and I still have to get Fenton."

*I'm never going to get used to calling people by their last names. It's a military thing, but so formal to me.* "I'll go get Kari."

"I'm ready, too," Sammie said as she grabbed her signature Velcro wallet and room key.

We jumped out the door, and seconds later, knocked on Kari's, just two rooms down from ours. She was ready, and we all headed down the three flights of stairs to where our chariot— the government motor-pool van—awaited.

The guys were all in good spirits as we drove across the extensive parking lot to pick up Garren and Archibladt. It resembled an expansive stadium parking lot, so not just a stone's throw away.

I had sobered me up a little, and if it weren't for this damn headache, I'd have been doing pretty ok for the most part. If I'd woken up any drunker, my hangover would've been unbearable. It hurt enough already.

The van stopped, and my stomach lurched. Ari jumped out from behind the wheel and hurried into their building.

"These aren't the squadron officer barracks, are they?" Sammie asked anyone in the van who might know the answer.

"Pretty sure they aren't. I know Trigg and Ketts have friends over there though," Lucas commented off-handedly as Ace nodded in agreement.

*Do they ever do anything without each other?*

"Yeah, those are not our squadron barracks, but they do house officers, security, and other NASKEF personnel on regular billets," Ian volunteered. "I've been in those apartments. Not only do they host the best parties, but their pads are pretty fucking amazing. Did you know they're like mini-apartments?"

"Aren't they more like quads?" Everyone turned to look at me. I shrugged, squinting against my queasy headache and forcing my mind to the conversation. "It's not like I've been in one, I've just heard talk in the shop. There's like a common living space. Some have kitchens, and then the rooms are off the common area?" I threw my hands up in the air. "Come on guys, you've seen quads at college, right?"

Silence.

I could've heard crickets chirping.

*Okay... so who fucking cares apparently?* I shifted uncomfortably, wishing I was back in my cozy bed.

And then, it started…

"So, Tessa," Sage spoke first, "what was up with last night anyways?"

I scowled at him. "What do you mean, exactly?"

"He wants to know what was up with you and that guy from last night, but what I want to know is, what was up with that girl you were dancing with before him?" Ace jested, but I knew he actually wanted to know—he was a bit of a freak like that.

"Which one?" I asked, playing stupid. One girl had come on to me, and it had been blatantly obvious… but that just wasn't my cup of tea.

Ari climbed back into the van. "They'll be down in a sec. So, whatcha all talking about?"

"Hey, Tessa I didn't know you like girls!"

"I don't. We just danced." I looked Ace squarely in the eyes, but then Lucas took a turn…

"Tess, don't you know that's against the UCMJ?"

*Jeezus. The Uniform Code of Military Justice… Really?*

I sighed, reaching up to hold my head. Sammie turned towards me. "Don't start on me." I eyed her wearily. "I'm tired, hung-over, and my head hurts. I refuse to deal with their stupid shit today."

"Whoa, Tess, you don't look so hot… here take this," she reached out handing me her Power Aide bottle and two 800mg Ibuprofen. "That should do the trick."

"Thanks," I said taking the hangover treatment she offered. "Ugh, I'm not sure what's wrong with me. I'm usually never this hungover."

In the background the guys were still razzing me about my night of debauchery… if you could even call it that.

*Don't they have anything better to hack away at?*

My eyes connected with Ari's in the rear-view mirror, and he mouthed 'sorry'. I smiled and rolled my eyes, but this wasn't the first time I'd dealt with a bunch of 'boys'. Working amongst them made this pretty common territory, and I'd developed a tough skin.

Thankfully, they moved on from me and on to discuss what had become *THE* food to try here in Iceland—sheep dogs.

"…I don't know, but they sound down-right horrendous to me." Kari faked a gag-me-out expression that got all of us rolling; that is, except me. I nursed my aching head, resting it on Sammie's shoulder.

"Oh. My. God, they are the absolute best after a night drinking in Reykjavik!" Ian and Ari high-fived in the front seats of the van.

"What are they exactly?" I'm sure my voice sounded weak, as miserable as I was feeling.

Ari saw me in the mirror, "Jeezus, Tessa, are you okay?"

Everyone turned around in their seats to look at me, "I'm workin' on it," I said with as much gusto as I could muster. "I just took something for my hangover headache."

I got a resounding 'Hope you feel better' from the peanut gallery, before they went back to discussing the sheep dogs.

"They're not *that* bad, they're actually really good," Ari volunteered, "They're some sort of hotdog made from mutton. They're really popular around Kef and Reyk."

"Yeah, and those of us in the van that have made it off base to whore around have already tried them." Sage laughed, and Ace leaned forward to give him knucks.

"Well, that leaves us out." Kari winced.

"It certainly does," Sammie agreed.

I eyed Ari in the mirror and shook my head. *These boys.*

*I don't much care what anyone else thinks about sheep dogs, but a fat, pale hotdog made of lamb, beef and pork smothered in a tangy mustard and remoulade mayo sauce, heaped with onions and even bacon or chili...well, EWWW!* I shuddered as the nausea from my hangover tightened down.

"Tessa, you've no idea what you are missing; these sheep dogs are THE BEST things ever when you have the 'drunk munchies'… am I right, guys?" Ari turned around eyeing the passengers in the van.

"Dude, bro! You're totally right, they're *heaven.*" Sage pretended to eat a dog out of mid-air.

"Well, I'm glad you all love them so much," I said, laughing now in spite of my sour stomach. This had gotten seriously ridiculous, "but there's no way you'll ever get me to try one! Now can we quit talking about them, *please?*"

I nuzzled my head even deeper into Sammie's shoulder. "Hey, hon, please wake me in about fifteen minutes. I think a power nap is all I'll need to feel human again."

She reached across to pat my forehead, taking care not to shove me off the shoulder I was resting on. "Sure thing, Tess."

*I'm so glad I met you, if it weren't for you, I'd only have Ari.*

I closed my eyes, and as I was fading, heard the van doors open and close. We'd been on the road about ten minutes I'd guess, when I voluntarily opened my eyes and, blinking at the bright light reflecting off the windows, noticed my headache had substantially subsided. *Thank God.*

"You're up, about time," she kidded.

I nodded and sat up. It wasn't until then that I really took notice of the two new guys in the first row. Sammie, Kari and I had chosen the rear bench seat so we wouldn't have the numb-nuts talking over us, but it probably wasn't the wisest choice since I already felt like shit and suffered from motion sickness. Memories of my hellish experience on the C-130 flooded over me.

I tried hard to hear the conversation the middle bench in front of us was having with the security guys in the first row. The one on the left had coal-black hair, thick eyebrows and a sexy beard, which lent themselves to his ruggedly attractive appearance. He looked to be a broad man, definitely built, as I could see even from where I sat, on the right side of the van. His shoulder muscles rippled as he moved. He totally looked like Special Ops to me. They called this one Dirk Archibladt.

The other sat on the same side of the van as me, so I didn't have the best view of him. From what I could tell, he also looked like lean and sculpted; not as built as the other one, but his sinewy muscles were clearly etched under the white shirt he wore. He had wavy dark hair long enough for any woman to grab a hold of. That is, should she ever get the impulse to. He had a manscaped scruff, a nice profile and cute ears. What struck me the most, though, was his laugh; throaty, masculine, fun and sexy as hell. *Something about him resonates with me, but why does he seem so familiar?*

The three of us in the back carried on our own conversation, as it was pretty hard to hear over the music three rows up.

"As your trip commander, I am pleased to announce we will be arriving momentarily at the Blue Lagoon Geo Thermal Hot Springs." Ari laughed and cranked the music back up. Dirk turned around to say something to Ace, who was sitting in the seat in front of me. While they talked, Dirk caught my eyes and held them.

He raised his right eyebrow ever so slightly, grabbed the other new guy by the neck, and pulled him forward so he could say something to him in his ear. He then slapped his shoulder and they both laughed.

*What the fuck was that about? Great. A day with more assholes, as if there weren't enough of those at work! Seriously? On my day off? Fucking wonderful. I'll have to remember to thank Ari for this one.*

Ari navigated us into a parking spot. Cars already nearly filled the lot, as it was a top tourist destination in Iceland. I wish I knew then, what I knew now: just how lucky we were to be stationed so close to one of the recognized wonders of the world —literally out our back door. Sadly, hindsight is always like that. Had we known, we would've probably 'soaked' it in more…no pun intended. Then, all I knew that they had only just opened the public bathing facilities last year, and I had in my mind it was going to be some kind of amazing spa.

As I clambered out of the van in my usual 'graceful' manner, I realized just how wrong I was in my assumptions.

The gang had all gotten out ahead of us, and most were doing their 'bro-thing' as they walked. Only Ari came around to give us a hand down and lock up the doors. He was, after all, in charge of the van. The four of us bought our tickets, and as Ari disappeared into the men's locker room, we heard him shout, "See ya inside, baby girl!"

"You have *got* to be kidding me!" Sammie turned around and looked at me immediately after walking into the locker room. The fairly small, white tile room had no lockers; wooden cubicles had been mounted on two of the walls, and most were taken. Numerous canvas bags lay scattered around the floor and on the wooden benches. A wall of dressing-room style closets each had a white curtain hanging three-quarters of the way to the floor. The other side of the locker room had the showers. These were like boot camp; just shower heads jutting out of the tiled walls, pelting thick streams of water over mostly naked, overweight granny-types.

*What? Did the geriatric tour bus just arrive from the local nursing home?* I mentally shushed myself for being so rude, but the thought actually made me laugh out loud.

"I guess there is an element of comedy about all of this." Sammie smiled at me and started changing for the pool. She'd brought her black Speedo racer-back one-piece... not too different from the one-piece we'd worn in boot camp.

Kari went into one of the dressing rooms and came out in a cute one-piece that only had a thin strip of suit up the middle connecting her top to her bottoms; the entire sides and back were open like a bikini. It was actually sexy as hell.

"Awesome suit, Kari!"

"Thanks! Saw it last summer and just had to have it. Never thought I would go from wearing it in Florida to wearing it here in Iceland, though. Funny where life takes us, huh?"

*Boy, did she have that right!*

I finished tying the itsy-bitsy bikini around my neck and at my hips. I'd chosen a plum purple Roxy suit that looked awesome with my red hair and green eyes. I, too, had figured it would make waves on the beaches in Florida, more specifically in Daytona during spring break; instead, I was wearing it here for the first time.

We stowed our bags and made our way to the *very* public showers to rinse off. We grabbed our towels and headed outside onto decking still smattered with snow on the edges farthest from the water. We looked for the guys and, not seeing them anywhere, decided to walk over to the far side, where we laid our towels on the deck and walked gingerly into the water up to our calves.

"Holy fuck! Shit!" Sammie exclaimed a little louder than I would've liked as several heads pivoted our way. I didn't really blame her though, because I was thinking pretty much the same thing. I cannot really describe it to you how the scene unfolded before me.

There were lots of elderly people, along with younger blondes, brunettes, men, women, topless women. A group of college kids—could've been military too—loudly gossiped, laughing and gesturing. Decks snaked out to a wooden island, and people sat around the edges, even lay in the white volcanic silica mud on the shore of the natural pool. *I think it's supposed to be so good for the body—to cleanse and exfoliate or some shit.*

People had it smeared to cover their faces and bodies. I saw people drinking blue drinks from small wine-type glasses. Pitch black volcanic rock provided a backdrop. Steam lay heavy like a blanket of fog on the Oregon Coast, easily hiding faces. It was pretty incredible, even with the overwhelming Sulphur odor that stunk like rotten eggs. I would say that after a good five or ten minutes though, all our noses got used to it.

About this same time, Ari walked up with drinks for the three of us. He sat down on the shore with his. I took mine, leaned back on my elbows and closed my eyes, taking a long drink.

"Perfect," I purred. "Thank you, Ari. It's just what I needed… a drink to get over my hangover." I smiled at him sincerely and winked before dreamily closing my eyes. Even holding my glass, and with my elbows in the soft silica mud, my legs floated effortlessly on top of the hot mineral water. No trace of my headache lingered.

"So, baby girl, did you ever figure out who Noah Garren and Dirk Archibladt were?"

I peeked at him under hooded eyes as he jounced his eyebrows playfully up and down.

"Dirk, no, but there's something about Noah…"

"Are you effin' kidding me?" Sam shot me a look like I was slow as I moved back away from the group a bit into even shallower water. I didn't want to have to worry about getting the seawater in my drink as I half reclined with one elbow in the mud, my legs floating out in front of me. I closed my eyes, cogitating on her snide comment and judgmental look, but they did nothing to my mood—I was healing from my hangover—as I absorbed the heat, steam, mud, my elixir… everything. I wasn't going to let her ruin my good mood. It had taken me all morning to get it.

I listened now to the banter going on between Kari and a new voice. I opened my eyes briefly to see it was Dirk Archibladt—I still wasn't going to call people by last names— standing between Sammie and Ari.

A strong hand glided up my left calf. My eyes flew open and Mr. Familiar-For-Some-Reason Noah sprawled on his elbows in the mud floating beside me. He smiled, and I noticed how straight and pretty his white teeth were; a good sign that he didn't chew or smoke. He walked himself up on his elbows until he reached shoulder to shoulder with me. I took my time *once again* admiring his tanned, rugged good looks, thick hair, strong shoulders and back, nice firm ass and killer legs. His legs extended a good ten to twelve inches or so past mine, so he was about a foot taller than me, easily over six feet. I'd have to see him standing to be sure.

He smiled a shit-eating grin at my blatant perusal, before turning over onto his back. As my gaze combed back up his body, I noticed his strong thighs, taut six-pack, and an amazing chest that had a hint of ink hiding under the silica mud that covered most of his body. His chuckle brought me back from my lollipop walk down his yummy body.

"Like what you see?" Noah gave me a notably arrogant smirk. Then it dawned on me… his voice. It was the same husky baritone that had whispered in my ear last night after the last dance. Those amazing hands had been on my hips. The real kicker though—those full, sensual lips and already nipped at my neck. My nipples grew hard at the thought. Now, it was my turn to blush.

*What were the fucking chances Ari would invite him? A million to one? How could he know? He wasn't even at the club. If he had known, would he have invited him?*

"I could ask you the same thing," I countered back flirtatiously, successfully playing off an arrogant indifference just for the fun of it.

"I knew you'd look good, but had no idea… I mean, damn." His honest admission caused crimson to creep across his cheeks and ears in a blush I wouldn't have expected from this hunk of a man. He was, after all, security, and many of them had been Special Ops or skilled Artillerymen who had seen action on previous tours, and *I* had made *him* blush. It brought a genuine smile of victory to my lips.

"You never did answer me," he prodded back.

"Well shit, Noah—what do you think?" With that, I arched

my back, dipping my hair in the water and thrusting my chest into the air. I closed my eyes and inhaled deeply. *God, the water feels amazing.* Its heat eased the tension in my achy, hung-over muscles and felt luxurious as it gently swathed my throbbing head. *Right now, there's no place I'd rather be. I'm so glad I came. I'll have to make sure to thank Ari for such an incredible hangover cure.*

I felt Noah's confidence radiating from every pore in his body; our chemistry undeniable, mutual sexual tension so thick you could cut it. He sidled up, saucily—hip to hip with me and turned on his side, his package firm against my hip, and draped his forearm across my taut abs. His hand rested on my hip farthest from him as his fingers gripped me in a possessive gesture. "Maybe you'll give me the chance to take you out on a real date?"

I opened my eyes and saw intense, hopeful ones looking back at me.

"Smoochy, smoochy, lovebirds over there! Hey!" We both turned to see Ace and Lucas coming our way with Sage, Ian and Stuart—the electrician from my shop.

WE'D HUNG out for the last several hours visiting and drinking, eating and sunbathing, if you could call it that. It was more like lying on the shore in a heavy mist, soaking our bodies and souls in the spa-like waters of the Blue Lagoon. The gang, as we were now calling Ari, Ace, Lucas, Sage, Stu and Ian, had met an equally attractive group of young college girls and had been hanging with them pretty exclusively the last thirty minutes or so. Kari had branched off after lunch with a hot businessman with silver hair and very tan skin. Sammie and Dirk were hitting it off not far from where Noah and I lounged. Pretty much everyone seemed to be having an amazing day.

*Mmmm... I could so listen to his voice all day.* I caught myself staring at him like an awe-struck schoolgirl and discreetly looked away. *What am I doing? I never get this way around a cute guy!*

"...and so, after I got out of The Corps, I continued to need breathing treatments to recover from the damage caused by all the oil fire smoke I'd been exposed to in Kuwait. Recovery was long, but after I healed—*hell*—I just up and decided I wanted to start my life over. It was as though I had been handed an opportunity for a do-over..." His voice trailed off as though he were lost in the memory.

I lay on my tummy in about a foot of water. The luxurious white silica mud cushioned my elbows and stomach as I lounged just deep enough that I could stay warm in spite of the light rain, but shallow enough that I could still rest my head in my hands.

"I cannot imagine what it must've been like over there. It must've looked like hell... and you were so young," I said, the last bit barely a whisper, more to myself than to him. One of my flaws, if you could call it that, was my extreme empathy, especially for soldiers. It just tore me up when I really took time to think about young men and women—kids really—out there running from themselves, something else, or even just trying to find themselves... seeking to define what it was that made them who they are.

"It really was tough; there's so much I'm ashamed of. I wrestle with the guilt daily." Noah's voice cracked at his eerily hushed confession, intended more for his own ears than mine. "I left a confused eighteen-year-old kid and came back a pretty fucked-up man. I was barely twenty, but I didn't view anything the same anymore," he ran his troubled hands through his damp hair, sending renegade waves falling onto his forehead.

I rolled to my side and watched him as he scrubbed his face, like he was trying to remove the vivid images from his eyes. I reached out toward him, my hand unsure, before it stopped short and dropped back to my side. I turned onto my back and submerged my head and face into the insanely hot water, trying to release the depressing thoughts and images filling my head. I came up for air and wrung the last thoughts away with a good swipe across my face. As I slicked back my hair, I lay there with my elbows fixed in the mud, floating in the seawater that came from 2000 meters below the Earth's surface.

"Tessa?"

"Mm hmm?" I replied huskily, weary with heat-induced grogginess. The hot water and emotional overload had taken their toll. It almost felt as though he had drawn from my energy to tell his story. The combination left me drained.

"Come here."

I opened my eyes as I turned toward him. Noah's appearance struck me. The pain I could see in his eyes, the guilt scarring his face, gave him a severe countenance. Dominant. Confident. Powerful. Raw and insanely handsome. I slid deeper into the water so when I sat on my knees, my chin flirted with the surface. Noah followed me.

"Come here." He rasped the command and I obeyed. Something about Noah attracted me—purely animal, un-caged and wild—visceral even. I was irresistibly and dangerously attracted to him.

*Moths and flames,* I mused. *One remains in place, bright, hot, and beckoning, while the other flutters toward it with abandon, desperate to bask its warmth and radiance. "Be the flame, not the moth," advised Casanova...* The thought slammed into me with a shudder that raked through my body.

"Come here," he urged. "Are you cold?"

I looked up, taking Noah in. Confusion twisted my expression; his reflected concern... or intrigue maybe? I struggled not to touch him, to reach out and find the steadiness I knew he would provide.

*What is wrong with me? Why am I so unbalanced? I've only ever felt like this once and have been searching for it since. Maybe this guy would be worth getting to know better...*

My eyes broke from the electric connection they'd had with his, a magnetism so strong that it shook me at my core. My gaze dropped to his flawless nose and full, kissable lips. They continued their journey across his strong, arrogant jawline to his neck and collar bones.

"Holy Fuck!"

"Jeezus, Tessa—what?" Noah startled at my exclamation— one that I thought I'd said only to myself, but there it was.

*There it was.*

*THERE. RIGHT. THERE...*

*'Lisa' tattooed across his heart.*

*Oh, my God. OH. MY. GOD.*

*How? It just doesn't make sense. HOW?*

*Noah was Garren, and Garren was 'Ren'. Noah Garren was the boy I gave my virginity to!*

We knelt in three feet of water; three feet of liquid fire made even hotter by our desire. We shared the same space, the same breaths. Every one he exhaled, I inhaled. The only touch we allowed ourselves was where our knees met in the mud. His skin against mine felt hotter than the hot spring's water. I don't know how long we knelt, our bodies facing each other; only a diminutive barrier comprised of electrified molecules, charged by our mutual magnetism, separated us. We vibrated with the energy our bodies created. We controlled our mesmerism, in spite of the fact that we had already explored each other's bodies, taking greedy liberties the night before on the dance floor.

*How do I tell him who I am? Am I right? God—what if I'm not? If I am, why would I be pretentious enough to assume he'd remember me? What happened between us nearly three years ago was only a big deal to me because of what I had lost that night. I mean, fuck, I didn't even tell him who I was, because I'd wanted to remain anonymous.*

"Tessa," his voice came out raw and gravelly. He palmed his face and ran his hands roughly over it and up through his hair before finally placing them on my upper arms—the barrier between us breached at last. When his hands touched me, energy flowed between us. Noah touched my soul and mine touched his, not just figuratively, but in a concrete, literal and very real way. This man did something to me that no one else ever had. He reached deep into me and pulled from my twisted, sarcastic, 'keep-my-head-high-nothing-ever-can-hurt-me' self and teased the real me. He tempted me to let him see who I really was…

"Tessa, I… well, there's something about you," He dropped his hands, his mouth hovering a mere inch from mine. I felt his heated breath sweep across my damp lips, where I had unconsciously licked them in anticipation of the kiss I felt sure would send me to the moon and back. *Not that I have the most concrete memory of Noah or how he kissed—truly—the night he took my virginity.* Again, I found myself cursing Bacardi 151, and probably not for the last time.

Noah reached up again, pulling me to him, his right forearm around my lower back. The firmness I felt my soft curves collide with, sent shivers as explosive as the energy it took to split an atom.

"Are you cold?" His warm breath grazed my lips.

I shook my head. "No... I, I can't explain it..." my voice trailed off.

He placed his left hand just under my ear, tilting my head so that he had full access to my addled eyes as he glided his lips across mine, whispering, "I can't either." He dropped his hand and rested his palm on my chest plate. My thundering heart left no reason to pretend I wasn't rattled. He held me to him, gently stroking my back until he felt my heart settle.

"Let's go get another drink, shall we?"

I nodded, because although my heart had calmed down, I still hadn't found my tongue.

We came back and joined Sammie and Dirk briefly, giving them a larger breadth as they seemed to be hitting it off, sharing intimate details made for their ears only... well, sort of...

"Can I ask you something?"

"Sure, shoot."

"You served with Dirk prior to this set of orders?"

He nodded and smiled, "Yes, we served together my first tour in Kuwait, before the whole thing went to shit and we pulled out in 1991... of course, that's probably not what you heard back here at home."

"What did you do after you left Kuwait? Take new orders overseas?"

"Why would you say that?" He cocked an eyebrow at me as he rested his hand on the hip that skirted the surface from just below.

"I don't know; I mean, I've heard some guys once they go over, need to stay in it… that civilian life is too hard?"

"I mean, that's what happened, but it wasn't like that. When I got out, I came home but it was no longer my *home*. It had become just a house with shit in it that I didn't need any more. That I didn't WANT any more."

It was as though I could see a movie playing behind his eyes; those faraway eyes moved me, so I reached out and rested my hand on his side. I wanted him to feel it was okay to talk to me.

"I tried," he said finally. "I tried to make it work. I finished my treatments, made it to all of my military psychologist appointments. Hell, I even got a job as a bartender at Joe's Bar & Grille." He laughed. "Don't get me wrong, it wasn't *all* bad, but I felt more like I was on leave, and when it was no longer a nice reprieve from the action I'd seen… and I realized it was all I had to look forward to, well, hell. That's when I re-upped."

"Wasn't it hard on your family… your girlfriend? I mean, to lose you again after just having you home?"

He chuckled to himself, "Shit Tess, they never got *me* home. My heart stayed in Kuwait."

My eyes reassured him, my mouth parted, searching for the right words to say, but in the end, all I did was stroke his side.

"Can you believe it took me nearly four years of fucking off, traveling, living in various countries, and immersing myself in different cultures, to decide that the tapestry my life was being written on wasn't one I'd be proud to share later…"

I interrupted him. "So you reenlisted."

He smiled. "I did. I came here last year on a security billet."

"How did you give up the travels, the gypsy lifestyle?" I asked, secretly jealous of the opportunity to live in so many places.

"You know, it wasn't that hard… I mean, don't get me wrong; I LOVED living in different countries—forty in four years—couch surfing on locals' couches or staying at the youth hostels when there were vacancies."

I couldn't help but raise my eyebrow at that one… *He wasn't staying with the flavor of the month? I mean, Jeezus, just look at him!*

Noah's mouth formed an arrogant grin. "Your level of consciousness is so insightful, so wise." He chuckled. "To answer the question you directed to me with your eyes… yeah, I did that too." We both chuckled, him for reading me so well, and me out of nervous embarrassment.

*How is any of this happening?*

Our conversation ebbed and flowed miraculously well. *He really is an interesting person.* We found ourselves getting along sexy-good, so to speak. He gave me a lavish leg massage with the majestic white mud. I hadn't expected the Noah I was getting to know—the one sharing surprisingly intimate details about his time in the Marines—would be so much deeper than the playboy dance king I'd met.

Time passed fabulously, and as I looked around after only God knows how many hours, I realized it was just Noah and me. Sure, lots of strangers paddled around in the warm water, but where were our friends? I checked my watch: 2034.

*Eight thirty? Holy shit, where did the time go?*

"…and when the snow melted, the roads opened back up and we were able to make it down out of the mountains."

"Noah, that truly sounds amazing, and I really hate to interrupt, but have you noticed where our friends went… or that it's almost nine?"

He blinked and lowered his eyebrows, looking a little

unsettled. "Wow, Tessa. I can't remember the last time—shit, if ever—I've felt so comfortable talking to someone that I lost track of time." He raked his long, slender fingers through his wavy hair and grinned at me.

Few things in my life made me want to fall to my knees in awestruck worship; his smile topped that list. His grin alone made the ladies want him and the gents want to be him; it truly was a panty-dropper. *FUCK. I'm SO in trouble.*

Noah gave me his hand to help me as I stood. "Well, let's go see about finding them." He flashed me that million-dollar smile again. We both stood on slightly wobbly legs. We'd been in the water for hours, and it felt as though my bones had turned to jelly. With the sun hanging low in the sky, the wind had picked up, dropping the temperature to positively freezing. The gently dusting mist now blew hard, hitting us as a heavy blanket of water.

"It's amazing how fast the weather's turned; let's grab our towels. Could you tell it had gotten this bad when we were in the lagoon?" I shouted into the wind.

He shook his head and held up a finger, indicating I should stay. He took off in a trot to where we'd placed our towels, not that they'd be worth a shit since the sky had been dumping on them for hours.

Wrapped in our wet towels that acted only as damp windbreak, we kept our heads low as we fought the stiff wind on the way to the main side of Blue Lagoon. We looked in the café, locker rooms, and even walked the decks around the water but couldn't see our friends anywhere.

"Screw it," I suggested, nearly choking on a mouthful of fine, driven spray. "Let's shower and warm up. Get dressed."

"Agreed. Sooner or later, our group will turn up out front."

"THE VAN IS STILL HERE, but no one is there." Noah frowned, full lips turned down and eyes squinched, a look of great perplexity.

"It's not like they could've gone far—and they would've at least said goodbye," I said, confused and worried. "At least Sam would've…" my voice trailed off as I voiced a last-ditch reassurance that Sammie wouldn't have left me here. *Alone. With Noah. Would she? And without the van no less? No, that doesn't make sense. They're here somewhere.*

"Hey, beeatches! Where the hell have you been?"

I spun around and saw her hanging out the door of a large luxury motorhome, a crooked smile on her face and a Pabst Blue Ribbon beer in her hand. I could see our guys, a.k.a. the gang, behind her. I shouted over my shoulder at Noah and motioned for him to come over, ploughing across the icy parking lot slowly, so he'd have a chance to catch up, and so I wouldn't fall on my ass. Navigating the ice with the wind blowing against me strained my abilities.

"Shit, Tess," Noah panted as he reached me, "I was getting worried. How'd you know they were in there?"

"I didn't. Sam must've seen me, 'cause she hung out the door and called."

We reached the motorhome, tapped the snow and ice from our shoes on the bottom step, and climbed past Sammie into the warmth. Lucas, Ace, Stu, Ian, Sage, Ari, Dirk, Kari and some guy were all kicked back on the sectional, the captain's chair, and assorted stools from the mini bar.

"Shit, assholes, nice of you to send me the memo," I verbally tossed into the proverbial air, waiting to see who had the catcher's mitt big enough—so to speak—to catch it.

"Now, now, pretty thing."

I averted my gaze from Ari, who I thought would respond, to the tan, fit man wearing low-slung surf shorts in the same silver shade as his hair. His silver-blue eyes added to his extremely unusual look. If I didn't disregard all things supernatural so completely, I would've thought he was a vamp or something. He was so intensely handsome in such an extraordinary way, I actually found myself staring as I tried to make the southern drawl that oozed like molasses over his lips mesh with the bad-boy surf model I saw before me.

"Don't you go getting them bees in your bonnet all riled up. I believe it was all my doing."

Kari interrupted, "Sorry you were worried, Tessa, but we're fine, and judging by how long it took you to notice we were gone, you were doing just fine yourselves. Forgive me. Please meet our new friend, Dax Fletcher. He's in bonds and securities." Kari said this last part with a hint of oh-là-là in her voice. The gang picked up on it.

"Oooh, he's in the stock market! Why didn't you tell us he was a big man on Wall Street?"

"Yeah, dumb shit, like you couldn't tell by his rig?"

"Any idiot could tell he was somebody! Look at this place!"

As the banter among the guys continued, Kari and Sammie made their way over to me.

"Sorry we made you worry. I really didn't know we'd be drinking with Dax for this long." Kari gave me a squeeze around the shoulders.

"Yeah, I should've at least tried to find you. I'm sorry too," Sammie said as she gave me a playful slug on the arm.

"No worries, guys. Just glad everyone is okay. So, 'fine-man' Dax is a *fine man on Wall Street*. Way to go Kari!" I lifted my eyebrows provocatively at her and winked.

"Shh, it is so not like that. Not like that at all… *yet*." She gave me a playful nudge as she sauntered back to her exotic, alien-handsome man.

*I know. It's not like that between Noah and me YET either.*

I looked over at Noah, and he smiled that smile that does things to me. His eyes, those stalker eyes that had been watching me for the past few weeks, remained trained on me, recording my every move. I found it both sexy and a little unnerving… so I laughed it off to myself.

"Sam, who are you vibing on?"

That really opened the flood-gates as she began sharing about Dirk. She thought she'd been all covert about her crush on him up until now; she wasn't even close.

I'd already had at least three shots since I had stepped into the motorhome; it seemed someone kept shoving them into my hand, and at this point, I'd had just enough that I was buzzed and selectively listening to her. The cacophony surrounded me as a backdrop to my own thoughts—the guys sparring, razzing and joking with each other alongside Kari and Dax's conversation, topped off by Sammie's soliloquy—save me plenty of time to take it all in without having to join.

The motorhome was *PIMP*, nicer than any Las Vegas suite I'd ever stayed in. Industrial Modern finishes in dark wood tones, stainless steel and natural granite stone showed that Dax obviously had good taste. The carpets of his—let's call it what it really was—luxury touring bus, were plush. The furniture was exquisitely done in deep, dark leather, and the wood paneling in mahogany. *AMAZING.*

"Hey, Tessa. Did you know that Dax rented this rig right after Prodigy left?" It took me a second to realize it was Ari who had directed this at me.

"You mean the same Prodigy we saw in concert last weekend on March 28th? *That* Prodigy?"

He nodded and turned back to Dax to learn more of his 'greatness'.

*Oh! So, he RENTED it. I gave him too much credit for his good design taste.* I knocked him down a couple of pegs on my personal score chart.

After I took inventory of the bus and gave myself a tour of the upstairs, with its Jacuzzi, bedrooms and media room, I turned my attention inexorably back to Noah. First, I took notice of his height. He stood above average compared to my buds. A deep tan, one that looked like he had just returned from surfing somewhere exotic like off the coast of Thailand, darkened his skin. His unruly mass of finger combed waves hung over his collar. A rough five o'clock shadow etched deeper tones above his full upper lip and along his strong jawline. High cheekbones gave structure and highlight to his almond-shaped eyes.

After swimming, he had changed into a navy Henley and dark jeans. His shirt, open at the neck, showed his defined upper pecks and collar bones and were pushed up his strong forearms. He had a long torso, and the hem of his shirt just touched the top of his low-slung pants, so that every time he tasted his beer or raised his hand to pat someone on the shoulder, I could see his chiseled lower abdomen and "V" that disappeared into his waistband.

*Holy shit, he's beautiful.*

As he shifted his stance and turned his back more to me, I watched his mannerisms. He acted respectful with the guys but mixed the 'bro' comradery with just enough raunch to be deemed cool. He had a genuinely infectious laugh; a warm, hardy, full-bellied sound that seemed to make everyone on the bus join in, even if they were involved in other conversations. He worked the room with ease and dominated the conversation, but it never came across as disingenuous or condescending. I could tell everyone liked him. Shifting my attention to the physical, I admired his back's network of sinewy muscles that rippled and bunched under his cotton shirt every time he lifted his arms or moved. And in true Tessa fashion, I saved the best for last. His ass.

Ever since the ninth grade when I fell in "like" with a JV soccer player, I have loved small, tight, firm asses. Noah's ranked with the best of them. Noah's waist narrowed, and his fine ass followed the precise lines God had intended when he created him. What a masterpiece, even up to littlest detail—those two cute upper-butt 'dimples'.

*Oh, Lawdy! Help me now!* It had to be illegal to be as ruggedly good-looking as Noah without knowing or even trying.

I GLANCED AT MY WATCH, 2253.

*Holy Shit, it's almost 11? Where did the time go?*

Since a little before nine, after Noah and I joined everyone in the tour bus, we'd continued to drink, listen to the beats through the impressive sound system, and kick back. I cannot speak for everyone, but I really enjoyed myself. I especially enjoyed getting to know Dax.

He and Kari had instant chemistry—*a lot like Noah and I do* —and I was so bummed to hear he was only here for four more days. I could tell Kari was too, but her whole demeanor changed for the better as soon as he offhandedly announced that tomorrow he'd call his office and let them know he would be extending his vacation. Now, of course, being the boss-man, he got to hang out here until the first week in May, just under four more weeks.

It's amazing how chance encounters can change life plans. Take for instance Dax meeting Kari. He was extending his trip another three weeks, so he could spend more time with her, in spite of the fact they'd just met. Kari was crossing her fingers that when she returned to work on Monday she'd be allowed leave, so the two of them could tour around together.

*Take it easy! Breathe...* I stood up and rolled my shoulders, trying to ease the tension in my neck.

Maybe it was the stale, cigarette-clouded air in the bus, or perhaps I'd just had too much to drink, but I'd been seriously overthinking things, and when I did that, I tended to get myself tied into knots. Whatever the reason... I. NEEDED. AIR.

I was suddenly on the verge of getting sick, so I pushed past the bodies in front of me, muttering, "excuse me" and "please move" with an occasional NOW thrown in.

*God, this bus is long!*

I reached the door, flung it open, and threw myself haphazardly down the steps. The stars twinkled, and the crisp air felt *wonderful*, exactly what I needed. The lump in my throat subsided almost immediately. My vertigo lessened, and the cold sweats eased as I leaned back against the cool side of the bus. It really wasn't uncomfortably cold with the bus acting like a wind break, so I inhaled the frigid air and looked up at the awesome display of northern lights. Greens and reds streaked in colorful layers like frosting spread over a cake. At this point, in my life, I didn't think all that much about God, but that night, with all the magnificent arrays of colors streaking the sky… well, I definitely felt like *HE* was present.

"Here, put this on."

I started at his voice. I hadn't even heard him open the door and come outside. I took the men's size XL hoodie he handed me and bundled up in it.

"Ohhhh, that feels amazing." *I guess I was colder than I thought I was.* "Thanks, bab…," I caught myself before I let the word *babe* slip from my lips. Instantly, my mouth went dry and my back stiffened at the thought that he may have heard me.

*Way to go, dumb ass.*

Noah wedged himself behind me, between the bus and my body, snaking his arms around me. I found myself enveloped in marvelous warmth. He nuzzled his chin into my nape; his warm breath at my ear stoked the fire I had kindled. Just like that, the tension from my slip-up vanished.

*This guy is good for me.*

*This guy is dangerously good for me.*

"Mmm. You smell amazing," Noah whispered, sending chills down my spine. "I could stay here with you all night." His half-sighed, half-moaned combination of contentment and sexual frustration made an intoxicating concoction. I found myself leaning back into him and pulling his arms around me tighter.

I sighed contentedly. "That would be nice." I knew I was inviting trouble by agreeing, but that didn't mean that it was going to happen anytime soon. I felt something good brewing with Noah, but there was something in the way that I couldn't pinpoint. Maybe I was just being a nervous ninny, but something told me to take it slowly with him.

"I just wish we'd met in another time and place. A better time. A better place. You know?"

*No. What an odd thing for him to say, especially since I already feel like there's something I can't pinpoint, edging in the way of an us.* "What's wrong with the here and now?" I asked, hoping to draw some explanation out of him.

"Oh, nothing. Life's just complicated, you know?"

"Noah, is there something I need to know? I mean, we only just met."

"No. Really, everything's fine. I shouldn't have said anything. I'm just thinking out loud."

"'Cause like I was saying, we only just met. This doesn't *have* to go any further," I whispered, choking on the lie. *This DOES need to go further.*

"Shh. Shh. It's all good. I want to take in the magical scenery, the show in the sky. I just want to burrow my face into your neck with my arms around you. To only think about you—your smell, your warmth, how you feel—nothing else. Nothing else matters except here, where I want to be right now."

I liked what I was hearing, but the red flags I'd felt before now waved in front of me. We stood leaning against the bus for a good long while before Kari and Dax came out and joined us. Not even a minute later, an unruly and visibly intoxicated Sammie stumbled out on Dirk's arm.

"Hiya, hooka! Did you have time to finish?" She obviously thought she was hil-ar-i-ous because she busted out laughing. I know I was feeling pretty good from all the shots I'd drunk, but I have to admit, her comment stung a little. She booted me right out of my happy place with that one.

*Seriously? Is that what everyone thinks about me... that I fuck every guy I like on day one?*

Noah could see I'd finally had enough of the night, and before I could say anything, he did it for me. "Hey, Kari, do you know what you, Sam and The Gang are planning on doing for the night? I know Dirk and I don't have duty, and from what Ari said, he didn't see any of y'all on the duty roster either."

"Oh fuck, Noah. I have absolutely no idea if anyone else has to be back to work for tomorrow. Hold up, wait… it's coming back to me. I did check for me and the girls. Since Sammie and Tessa just pulled eleven days straight, they're off for sure, and I checked mine too, so I know sections two and four are in the clear."

I looked over at Kari in the moonlight; she was beaming… proud of herself for remembering, or because of Dax, I wasn't sure. The genuine bliss eased the stress lines on her forehead. The way her eyes caught the moonlight rendered her beautiful, and I hoped more than anything that Dax wouldn't break her heart.

"I think section three has duty," I said. "That would mean Ace and Lucas."

Noah spoke up from behind me. "I'll and let them know Dirk and I are ready to head back and see if they want to come now with us or find their own rides." He gave me a quick squeeze and headed back into the bus.

"What are your plans, Kari?" She didn't seem to have heard me, as she was busy hanging onto Dax's every word.

Finally, she answered, "I have the weekend off, so he's going to park right off base tonight and I'll stay with him. Tomorrow, he was talking about going on a road trip. You're all invited if you want." She looked expectantly at Sammie and me. "You could go back and pack tonight and meet us at daybreak."

Sammie cocked her head like a puppy trying to figure out

something important. "Why wouldn't you need to go back to pack too?" I swear I could see a puppy in her—in the way that she stood there, ears perked, head cocked at an angle, waiting for some sort of answer or action from Kari.

"Well, earlier we talked about how we were going to just take off, and I figured I could wear some of Dax's things…" a blush deep enough to see in the moonlight darkened her cheeks.

"Why don't we send the van back with Lucas and Ace, and the four of us can just bunk with you two tonight? We can borrow a pair of his pants too, or shop for stuff." Sammie smiled, pretty excited she had come up with such a clever idea.

"Hey, so the latest news from The Gang is that they're making plans with some of the girls they met today at the lagoon," Noah said as he stepped out of the bus. "Guess they're all planning to cram into some girls' cars when they get here. It seems they're on their way now."

Just then, the bus door swung wide and a blast of warm air, the smell of booze, and loud rap music assaulted our senses. Sage and Stu pulled Ari back from the doorway. He laughed and finally broke free. It seemed the guys didn't want him to go, but he made it outside in style by taking a fantastic parkour leap off the top step. Wild cheers erupted from inside, and even Sammie exclaimed a loud, "Whoa Buddy!" followed by enthusiastic clapping.

Ari dusted off his wet knees before he said, "Hey, so I was thinking, why don't I drive Ace and Lucas back tonight. I told some of the guys we'd go to the Viking Village tomorrow anyways." He directed the decision to me. "The rest of the motley crew is planning on taking their brouhaha to those college chicks' place about ten minutes from here." I shifted in place, knowing where this was going. "You and Sam should hang out with Kari and your new friends."

I knew he was hoping I'd say something to contradict his suggestion, since he'd been mini-crushing on me for a while. Sammie was semi-crushing on him too; that is, when she wasn't crushing on Dirk or Trigg. *Super awkward.*

*What a fucking mess this is turning out to be. Poor Ari, I feel so badly for him.*

"Hey, that's a fuckin' awesome idea!" Sammie couldn't have been any more enthusiastic. "See. Wasn't that what I was saying?"

"Sam, I was thinking maybe we should get back home and sleep off what promises to be the worst hangover since the ones we woke up with this morning." I gunned her down with a look that *strongly* suggested we should NOT stay. *Come on, Sam! You know what happened last time we hung out drunk with guys. Back me up here!*

"Nah. Bad, bad idea. VETO! I veto that very bad idea!" She giggled as Dirk tickled her ribcage in a flirtatious way. "Besides, I know I need you to stay and you know I need you to stay... so, you're staying." Still giggling, she struggled with an authoritative voice. "Ari! Tessa's staying with me and Kari this weekend. We've decided for her."

Ari nodded and squeezed my arm as he walked by. Pausing before me, his eyes said a million things his voice couldn't, didn't dare, utter. Even in the dark, I could hear them loud and clear. I watched him walk away from me. Turning, I looked at the girls and Noah before taking off in a sprint after him.

"Ari! Hey, wait a sec!" I caught up to him and we walked across the icy parking lot to the van. Stopping beside the door, we stood in awkward silence as he fumbled around for his keys. Finding them, he bent to unlock the driver's door.

"Ari?" I paused, clearing my throat. "Are you...? Are we okay?" I reached out and touched his shoulder.

"Yeah. We're fine." He turned away from me and pulled the door open, climbing in. I approached, standing beside him and blocking him from closing the door.

"You know what I mean? I just, well... we've become pretty good friends, and I don't want you mad at me is all."

"I'm not mad. Maybe a little frustrated, but ya know...? What can I do that I haven't already? I've always been there for ya baby girl."

"Ari, I know you have. You're honestly one of the best friends I've had in a really long time—you know, other than Sammie."

"Hey, I can't make you feel something for me that you obviously feel for that new guy, and that you felt for what's his name? That Icelander... Drake?"

"Dane, but I haven't even seen him again since."

"See? That's exactly it, Tessa." He blew out an exaggerated sigh. "So, what exactly was the fucking point of you and him anyways? And this guy; what's the point? We're almost halfway through the deployment, and none of these guys you are investing in are going to have a damn thing to do with you after you leave in August." Ari slouched in his seat and ran his rough hands back and forth over his short hair. "Fuck, where are Lucas and Ace? I want to get the fuck out of here and move past tonight."

I leaned forward and placed my forehead on his shoulder, then rolled my head so that I rested my cheek on it. I patted his chest.

"Thanks, Ari, for always being so good to me; for always being there for me. I wish I could be there for you the way you want. It's just… I don't know, it's harder to find a good friend than a guy, and I don't want to lose you." I looked up into the greenest, most dejected eyes I could recall seeing. Ari leaned down and rested his mouth on my forehead. We could hear Ace and Lucas walking toward us, creating quite a ruckus in their obnoxious, drunken state.

He pressed a tender kiss on my forehead. "Just be smart, okay? Sure, he's good-looking—even as a guy I can admit that —but he's not long-term, so just take care of you. Promise me, okay?"

"Aww, look at these two love-birds!" Lucas busted out laughing.

"Sookie, sookie now!" Ace slapped Lucas on the back, and the two of them clambered drunkenly into the back seat.

I stepped back and shut the door, smiling at Ari and turning to go.

"Baby girl! Promise me, okay?"

I looked back and nodded. "I promise, Ari. I'll be smart, okay? Thanks for everything. Drive back safely, and thanks too for getting those idiots home tonight." I stepped back to give him room. He saluted me as he pulled out. I slapped the hood of the van and waved as they took off.

# Chapter Fifteen

It had taken the college girls all of five minutes to arrive after Ari took off with Lucas and Ace. *I'm sure Ari was glad he'd already left with those two clowns before two carloads of hot chicks showed up.*

Once they drove off, I followed Sammie and Dirk inside the bus with Noah at my heels. We all readied the bus, put the loose bottles away and cleaned up as Dax un-chocked the tires. Before I knew it, we'd pulled out, headed toward base. It couldn't have been more than fifteen or twenty minutes, before Dax had us parked in a lot across the street from the base's gate; he'd made REALLY good time. He and Kari hopped off to secure the bus for the night.

"Hey-ya, Tess?" I turned and looked at Noah. He had an expression on his face that I'd yet to decode. "Since we are staying here tonight, did you plan on staying with me, or Sammie?"

I didn't know how to answer him. I'd gotten the spins as soon as the bus had started moving, and honestly didn't want to deal with any potential weirdness, drama or bullshit on top of it.

My conversation with Ari continued to bug me, further

complicating my decision. I felt badly because I couldn't picture a world where Ari and I were more than just the best of buds, nor a world without him as my bestie. It was so much easier ignoring the situation than having to hear it come out of Ari's mouth and seeing the look in his eyes.

*I hope he'll still want to continue being a part of my family here in Iceland, now that the truth has revealed itself.*

Between all the drama with Ari and how carsick I felt, all I really wanted was for the world to quit spinning, so I could get a good night's rest. Clearly, that was NOT going to happen. Even if it *did*, it didn't mean Noah would understand and chill. *And by the way, where the hell did this question come from? Where did the chill guy who was in the moment and perfectly content to stand by my side disappear to? Did we accidentally leave him back at the Lagoon?*

"Noah, I'm a wreck. I don't feel so good all of a sudden. Ugh, this feeling just came on like a bat out of hell and hit me square between the eyes and in the gut. Maybe we should just get some rest." I looked down at my feet and the beautiful dark wood that covered the kitchen floor as I moved to find a spot to relax. I sank into a leather recliner and closed my eyes, focusing on settling my stomach and quieting the pounding at my temples. A smile formed on my lips as I focused in on the cacophony that surrounded me.

Noah moved to the fridge to make some kind of drink, and from upstairs, I heard Kari and Dax's playful banter coming from the master jacuzzi suite. Sam and Dirk were teasingly chasing each other in the back of the bus by the bunks. I grinned to myself, enjoying all the laughter around me and knowing my friends were really having a good time. I was so focused on the peace in which I had ensconced myself that I started when Noah appeared quite suddenly behind me.

"Whoa, beautiful. Sorry. Didn't mean to make you jump. Here, I made you a ginger ale and lime; it should help settle your stomach a little." He handed me the drink and leaned on the counter, not far from where I sat.

I looked up at Noah's hopeful eyes and rubbed my neck. "Thanks. I'm sure this'll fix me all up. To answer your question from earlier, sure. Yes, I guess I was hoping before I got sick that we could spend some more time getting to know each other better."

"Awesome. What a relief. I thought maybe I'd misread your signs and you weren't that into me after all. Hey, I couldn't ask for a better way to spend the night." Noah's voice smiled practically as big as his perfect lips.

NOAH LET me use the bathroom and shower first.

*Now what?* I wondered to myself as I stepped out onto the mat and wrapped myself in a towel. *I didn't come to the Lagoon with the intention of spending the night. Kari volunteered Dax's clothes—or was that Sam?—but I barely know him. Still, with nothing of my own to put on but a damp bathing suit, and the casual, dirty clothes I've been wearing all day, I guess I have no choice but to borrow something from Dax.*

I tiptoed out of the bathroom and knocked on the banister leading up to the master suite.

"Come on up," Kari's voice called from the top of the stairs.

I climbed the stairs, butting in on Kari and Dax involved in an intimate conversation while they snuggled. Talk about uncomfortable.

"Sorry," I mumbled. "I was hoping I could borrow something to sleep in…" I trailed off, realizing how stupid I sounded.

"Tee shirts in the middle drawer," Dax replied without batting an eyelash.

I slunk past them and claimed one without another word. *Good thing they're really cool about it, but how embarrassing. I think I'm also a little jealous. How awesome is it that they're just getting to know each other? I honestly thought they'd be fucking in the Jacuzzi…*

*I want that… intimacy without being physically intimate.*

Making my way down the stairs, I considered my options. Let Sammie and Dirk monopolize the bunk room. *There's NO WAY in hell I'm going to hang out in there with Noah while listening to them suck face.* That only left me on the leather pull-out.

*Really, this is a way better option anyhow,* I tried to convince myself.

The couch folded out into a rather nice and roomy queen-sized bed. I set to work making it up with fresh linens I found in the closet, and then turned off the lights so that only the aurora borealis and moon lit the bus. I'd just slid under the covers when Noah came down the hall, freshly showered, and from the looks of it, freshly shaven too. His rugged five o'clock shadow had been manscaped and urban-city trimmed, losing some of the ruggedness he'd had about him earlier. His hair hung in a damp, unruly mass. It appeared he had towel-dried it and *maybe* run his fingers through. He had thrown on a pair of Dax's loose-fitting, fleece sweats. They hung perfectly low on his hips—dangerously low. *It looks like everything's hanging perfectly.* I actually blushed at that thought. I could feel the color creep up my cheeks.

"Boy, beautiful. What I wouldn't pay to know what ran through your mind just now." The smile in his voice hinted at one of his shit-eating grins, but in the moonlight, only his silhouette remained visible.

*How can he see me blushing when I can't even see if he's smiling?*

He slid into bed next to me. Lying on his slide, he propped up on his elbow, and I could easily see his ruggedly-hewn face, his azure eyes twinkling as they intently watched my every move.

"So, Tessa, and I'm just throwing this out there… but for me, there is *no pressure* in any way to do anything more than get to know one another tonight. I don't want you to think I expect anything from you. Really, I just want to continue what we started in the Lagoon."

His unexpected and surprisingly genuine comment made me smile.

"Now, see. That's what I want to make you do all night long." His sincerity made me smile even bigger.

"So, Noah, how about if we play a little game of 'Tit for Tat'? It kind of breaks the ice and makes it a little easier to pose the hard questions." I smirked and raised my eyebrows challengingly.

"How's it work exactly?"

"I ask you tit, you respond with tat—hence its name—'Tit for Tat'."

"You ask me tit, huh? I think I'll like this game."

I elbowed him playfully in the ribs. He reached out, wrapping his arms around me and effectively pinned me down.

The energy in the air suddenly changed; it vibrated faster. His closeness mesmerized me, and those damn blue eyes held me in their twinkling gaze. My breath caught in my throat as I inhaled. His amazing eyes glistened; pools that reflected his soul… and boy, did I want to see in.

"Shoot," Noah challenged, pulling me from my reverie.

"Huh?" I'd forgotten it was my turn.

"Shoot—remember? The game? Ask me your first tit." He chuckled softly; the fresh smell of Listerine floated past my nose.

I cleared my head of the Noah fog. "What is your favorite memory?"

"Do you mean while I was in the Marines, or here, or just in general?" he inquired.

"Any. Answer it however you'd like. What is your favorite memory?"

"Well, there are some things you need to discover about me on your own. I can't give you all of my secrets, but this moment is one. This memory's climbing the charts quickly."

*Lame. Kind of sweet, but mostly LAME. He didn't even answer… wonder why? Red flag, red flag!*

"Okay, my turn. So, Tessa, why is an amazing girl like you still single?"

I felt my lungs deflate as the air slowly escaped. "Well, without sounding too clichéd, I haven't found the right guy."

"But how do you know who the right guy is?"

"Come on, Noah. The same way you know when you find the right girl." I smiled, trying to keep the mood light. It had suddenly become heavy, and even a little accusatory. There was a testy, not-so-fun vibe in the air.

"I honestly don't know, which is why I asked you. Do you have a shopping list you check off each time you meet a guy?"

"Not really a list, but there are some things I look for. Obviously, I have to be attracted to them both physically and mentally. I think my biggest pet-peeve is stupid people or people who act like they can't do anything on their own. You know, the super co-dependent type?"

I could see Noah nodding his head in agreement, so I continued. "Genuinely thoughtful is important to me. This is different from just being nice. Nice is great; amicable and very… vanilla, but I like thoughtful better. A thoughtful person doesn't just say things to try to make you feel better when you have a bad day, they know you well enough to anticipate what it is you need; be it space, a back rub, or an ear. They're intentionally thoughtful, and I value that so much more than pleasantries and insipid niceness."

"I hadn't thought about it like that before. Shit, Tessa, you sure make a guy think."

"Oh yeah? What about?" My emerald green eyes looked squarely into his deep blue ones for an answer.

"I don't know, just about stuff. You know, I spent a great deal of time in the hot zone, and a great deal of time in my own head. You pose some interesting ideas. You have a pretty unique way of looking at things is all." He smiled and gave me a little wink.

I was glad the only light in the bus was from the moon and the spectacular light show through the windshield and skylights. Cloaked in this semi-darkness, it felt as though we were in a safe little cocoon. Safe enough to share… everything?

*It just doesn't seem right to reveal that our paths have crossed before—not until he shares something deeper.*

I felt his foot reach out, searching for mine, but I discreetly pulled it back. *Why is he being so vague? He's saying shit, but not like at the Blue Lagoon. Tonight, he's dancing all over the place, and I'm not learning anything new about him.* Maybe I was just tired, but the more I thought about it, he began to really piss me off.

"Okay, I have one," I said, probably a little snippier than I should have.

"Oh?" I could tell he was bracing himself as he pursed his lips, tension lines appearing across his forehead and at the corners of his mouth.

"Do you want me to go on?" I asked in all earnestness, because if he were feeling uncomfortable, I could just as easily go to sleep at this point.

"Sure, shoot," he said, and gave me another half-grin.

"This evening, you said something about wishing we'd met in another time or place, or you wish it was a better time and that life was less complicated. What was that all about?"

Man, you would've thought that I'd stuck him with a pin the way the air hissed out of him in an exaggerated sigh.

Noah removed his arm from my side, rolled on his back, and put his hands behind his head. He just lay there for what seemed like a long time. When he finally spoke, it startled me. I jumped, now wide awake again.

"It's pretty amazing, this thing called life. It truly is a magically fucked up maze that has so many dead ends. When you reach one, you have to retrace your life, just so you can try to move forward to reach the goal—the end, and inevitably just reach another dead-end. Then it's a do-over all over again."

I listened in silence.

"I've found those who are the most courageous are the ones

without a destination. Real courage is having an affair with the unknown. Do you get what I'm saying?" he asked.

I didn't really, but gave a nod, so he went on. "After I joined the Marines I met a woman, Pallavi Amrav. She was from a Persian family. We fell in love while I was stationed in Kuwait. I saw her every day on patrol. We only had a handful or two of stolen moments, but we were made for each other. We both felt it. We exchanged information, so we could covertly contact one another. Of course, her family would not allow her to marry an American.

Fast forward a couple of years to shortly after I got out of the Marines. I get a call from her; she's in New York. I was in Havelock, North Carolina. It was close to MCAS Cherry Point, so I could receive lung treatments and undergo a weekly psych eval. Anyway, after her cryptic call, of course I went to see her. We had an impassioned, completely amazing month together."

On 'together', Noah's voice cracked, and I propped myself up. I wanted to see him for who he was. Really see *HIM*. His eyes appeared to glisten. He averted his gaze, choosing to look at the northern lights through the large windshield on which we'd neglected to slide the privacy screen. I was leaning back when he shot his eyes directly to mine. They were dark. Hurt. Seeking.

"Tessa?" It was a question, a simple one. A question that didn't trigger my bitchiness like the ones before it. Still on his back, he propped himself up on his elbows. Our faces were now mere inches from each other's.

"Tess... I...," his voice broke again, and his eyes began to fill with emotion. "Tessa, I woke up early one Sunday morning. I remember the rising sun streaming through all of the large twelve and sixteen pane windows of the industrial flat Vi had. I threw on my sweats and a hoodie and ran down around the corner to the neighborhood baker for some fresh pastries and coffee to surprise her with when she awoke. I was in such a good mood. I hadn't felt like I needed my treatments or therapy sessions. I really felt like we'd found our groove and that life was looking up. We had talked in depth about a future together. This reality, this future with Vi… Well, it all came crashing down around me when I stepped off her lift. Vi and her… her…," Noah's voice trembled precariously close to the point of no return; that place where the dam breaks and one can no longer keep the harsh sobs from escaping.

As I lay there listening to Noah, my earlier pissiness melted away, and my heart thawed. I dreaded where his story was headed, even if I felt I already knew how it would end.

*Noah. My poor wounded Noah…*

Noah cleared his throat and once again placed his hands behind his head. "When I got off the lift, Vi and her husband were arguing. His suitcase sat by the landing, and he was still in his suit and trench coat at one of the large windows. I remember looking at Vi and her looking directly at me. She was crying, in hysterics actually, and all she did was hug herself tightly as though she were trying to hold a million little pieces together. She just shook her head at me. That was it…" His voice faded into darkness.

I turned to look at Noah. He had fallen silent, and I could see he needed a minute. I got up, excusing myself. On the way to the bathroom, I could hear giggles and other outbursts coming from the back of the bus. *They're definitely having a merrier time than we are.*

All I could think was how unfair life had been for this brave soldier, one who had received no recognition for his patriotism, and found life after war discriminated against him, as it did with so many other soldiers.

*Poor, poor Noah.*

*At the Lagoon earlier today, he told me he wandered aimlessly after getting out, looking to fill the void left when he no longer was part of something bigger than himself. Eventually, he re-enlisted and joined the only family of brothers who loved and understood him. What a tragic story that I now have a chapter in.*

I made my way back to bed to see if I could gauge anything from Noah. He sat on the edge of the bed, his legs splayed. His tan skin reflected the moonlight and occasionally the brightest of the northern lights that danced across the sky. He looked ethereal, ghostly even. I turned to sit down.

"Tessa. Tess, please come here," He demanded simply, his voice barely audible. I paused, and instead of joining him, walked from my side of the bed to his.

When I arrived beside him, his hands reached for my hips and pulled me between his legs. I looked down at him.

*Sweet Noah. My poor, hurting Noah... if only you were mine...*

The lump in my throat made it hard for me to swallow, let alone say anything. His eyes were swollen and red, still filled with moisture and emotion. I ran my fingers through his hair and guided his head to my stomach. I held him to me, embracing him, trying to take away some of his hurt. His arms immediately wrapped around my waist, imprisoning me. He held me captive to him, as his memory of Pallavi and that fateful morning held him.

"I turned around, got on the lift and our gaze never broke

until it dropped me from her sight. We never exchanged a word. Nothing. It just… ended."

I wasn't sure I had heard Noah at first, as he had started talking in such a gravelly whisper. His voice gained strength as he went on. "Vi contacted me roughly nine months later to tell me I had a daughter, Suri Noa-Garren Amrav. She didn't say where they were; I assumed they were in her posh flat in New York City with her rich husband." He swallowed hard.

"After that, and up until this morning, I hadn't heard from her in six years. Right before I left my apartment, Vi called to tell me that she left her husband. She wants me to come meet my daughter, and to give her another chance." He blurted out the last sentence fast, as though afraid of it. Shaking off the sudden rush, he continued, more slowly.

"That's actually why I came today. When Ari called and said he was putting together a trip to the Lagoon, I was hoping maybe I'd meet some nice girl. We'd all party and drink… I just wanted to feel numb. I just wanted to feel something other than pain. And then, *it was you.*"

I felt Noah lift his head, so I looked down.

His eyes met mine. "I met you for a second time. You're so special. Different. I can tell you're rare." He reached up and placed his hand along my jaw, grazing my lip with his thumb. "I'm damaged goods, Tessa. I don't mesh well with many people, especially not with women. I don't really do feelings and shit that women always expect." He shrugged, looking me squarely in the eyes, and dropped his hand. He nuzzled his head deeper against my abdomen and let out a deep sigh, his hot tortured breath burning my stomach.

In a hushed tenor, he continued, "But with you, I did. We got along, and it came easily. With you, I could be myself, and just…

be. Today, at the Lagoon, there were times when I was so in the moment with you, I didn't feel damaged or hurt; times when I didn't think of Vi and Suri. You helped me to just be me. Not me and my shitload of problems."

Noah stood up, never breaking the bond he had around my waist. The friction of his body sliding against mine as he stood, hitched my shirt up. His bare torso pressed against mine, his chest against my chest. His arms tightened around me as he nuzzled into my neck and continued in a throaty whisper.

"When I said I wished we'd met at another time, in another place; when I said I wished the timing were better and that life was less complicated, now you can understand why. I feel I have unfinished business with Vi. I love my daughter Suri, even though I've never met her, and I know that my future has Vi and Suri in it. Just what role they will play, I'm not sure. And gods be damned, I am undeniably and uncontrollably drawn to you. Quite frankly, it scares the shit out of me."

Our eyes met, and Noah's lips came down and paused a hair's breadth above mine, waiting for me to answer the silent question that had been hanging in the air the entire day, and all evening. I answered as I barely lifted my chin to close the gap between our two souls. His lips melded with mine, our tongues slowly tasting each other's before becoming more ravenous and demanding. Noah's right hand left the small of my back and grazed it up my side before reaching my full, heavy breast.

It craved his touch. He cupped me strongly and massaged before sliding up my chest, to rest at my nape. His hand wove into my hair, using it to guide our kiss. Our tongues sparred and licked, our lips meshed and glided, composing a synchronous ballad. Our bodies swayed into one another, our spirits seeking an even closer intimacy. Our kiss... so ardent, so intense and heartfelt, left me raw, exposed… and dazed. Before we parted, our passion ebbed, and our tongues became tamer. What mere moments before had been an exciting and ravenous, deeply soul-searching kiss now felt sad. It was soft and deliberate; careful and slow. As we drew apart, our lips chilled and grew lonely. Time stood still as we looked deeply into each other's eyes, and our foreheads burned as they rested together. This, right now, was goodbye. I could feel it. It was goodbye to the possibility of an 'us'. I knew it, and Noah did too.

"Tessa?"

"Noah?"

"Now can you understand why I didn't want to tell you right away? Telling you ended this before it had a chance to begin."

"But it did begin, Noah. It began last night when we met at the club. It began even before that, when you came by the squadron on your patrols and watched me. Shoot, so much began before you found out about Vi." My voice cracked as I shook. "Just know I'd rather find out now, rather than four months from now when my deployment ends and you tell me—or just never tell me. I'd hate to think I did something wrong. I would much rather know where *this* stands from the get-go."

We stood comfortably hugging for a long, *long* time. Noah stepped out of the embrace and climbed onto the bed, pulling me with him. We lay down on our sides, so that while Noah's arms encircled me, I rested my head on his bicep. I fell asleep, totally and completely enraptured by him.

# Chapter Sixteen

*ear God, will you PLEASE turn the lights down?*

*D*My eyes hadn't even opened, and I felt blinded by the early morning sun piercing the mega-sized windshield and open wooden blinds across from where I lay. I rolled away from the intrusive sun, right into Noah's strong, devastatingly perfect, and unexpectedly still-desirable chest. A slight, breathy moan escaped his lips as I brushed a single feather-light kiss to the base of his throat.

*What are you doing? Jeezus, Tessa. What DID you DO last night?*

I pried my eyes open, so I could assess the damages.

*Oh, THANK GOD! I still have my clothes on!*

Noah had lost his sweats, and I'm pretty damn sure that what I was feeling against my t-shirt clad stomach was NOT his hand. I tried to relax, so I closed my eyes and breathed in Noah's scent. As I settled back into a peaceful half-slumber, I forced out the thought that we'd never be together. Yesterday's conversations at the Lagoon and last night flooded back to me.

*"...when I pull up, Copper bounds towards me, like there's never been any distance or time between us."*

*"Noah, that sounds like an amazing homecoming." My eyes softened, as I heard how much sweeter his voice became talking about home. "Copper sounds like an amazing dog."*

*"She really is. You know, my mom and dad got her for me on my fifteenth adoption anniversary. Hell, I was..." He paused a minute to reflect, "...I was only nineteen then. That ol' dog is eight years old and still chases after me like she's a pup."*

*I could hear the love for her in his voice. "Adopted? Noah, I'm so sorry you went through such a hard time; I had no idea."*

*An endearing smile flitted across his sensual mouth, "Shit, Tess, no reason to be sorry. Yeah, so I lost my birth day." His eyes met mine and a rush surged through me. "Shit happens, and if you make it out, you're all the better for it."*

*His cavalier attitude impressed me—and put me at ease. "You got Copper on your fifteenth anniversary, so you were adopted at age four?" My voice hitched, and the thought of a little Noah left scared and alone about broke me. "How did you meet your adoptive parents? Did you already know them?"*

*"My parents were the foster parents I went to when the state took me from my piece of shit father—he was a loser junkie. You know, I can't think of a time when he wasn't either drunk, abusive, or loaded." He huffed disgustedly. "The parole officer had gotten a call from our park landlord that my dad was two months late on the rent, and every time he came by and rapped on the trailer door, he heard a kid crying inside."*

*"And you were the kid..." my voice wavered, full of emotion.*

*"I was." He ran his hands over his face, scrubbing at it as though he could erase the memories. "Fuck, Tess! I covered my dad up with blankets, I talked to him... Hell, I even made him a goddamn bowl of cereal!"*

*He rolled over onto his back and lay blanketed in the*

*dancing lights of the Aurora Borealis. I heard him mutter how stupid he'd been under his breath.*

*"The police declared the cause of death an OD, and placed the time a good day and a half before they entered and found me. My social worker brought me to Laura and Dave, who became my parents. They'd been trying to have kids with no luck, so they fostered instead. Their home had just re-opened, and they welcomed me with loving arms."*

*I reached out and placed my hand on his chest, sliding it down his abdomen, tracing his six-pack with my finger tip—I heard his sharp intake of breath, which caused my intimate parts to pulse. He stilled my hand. So far, Noah had played the perfect gentleman all day. He hadn't gotten too close to me, nor had he tried to score a home run... although I'd allowed him to make a base or two.*

*"You know," he began again after a comfortable silence, "if it hadn't been for my parents, there's no way I'd be lying here with you. It's because of them that I've made something of myself. They made me believe that I was loved, at least for a time."*

*"For a time?" Instinctively, I went to console him with my hand, but he held it quiet on his stomach, sighing in the process.*

*"Yes. My parents were movers and shakers. They made things happen. Can you believe I was adopted only months after they moved me in?"*

*I inhaled in preparation to respond, but he inadvertently cut me off. "Once they realized there was no coming back from the rough spot they were in, they divorced, just as quickly."*

*"No shit..."*

*"Yeah. Like I said, when they wanted something, they made it happen."*

Even though he hadn't had the perfect childhood, *I reflected,* it was clear how much he still loved and respected his parents— *hell, the intelligence and courteous manner he'd displayed while we shared all day impressed me. "Noah…?"*

*He absentmindedly interjected, "You know, Tessa, I can't remember the last time—shit, if ever—that I felt so comfortable talking to someone that I lost track of time…" He paused to reflect, "Oh yeah," he smiled, "this happened earlier today with you too. What is it with you, Tessa?" He interlaced his fingers with mine, giving them a gentle squeeze.*

*As dark as Noah's eyes had been when he had been retelling the various parts of his dark history; they shone bright and full of life now. It was as though sharing these things with me had unburdened his soul and freed him; free to shine. My soul welcomed the connection and reciprocated.*

Noah's strong arm drew me in tightly to him, pulling me from my thoughts of last night.

*Noah is truly a class act, and I REALLY like him and all he seems to be.*

I distinctly recalled, as I lay there with my skin warming in the full light of the morning sun, the precise moment when I realized just how close we'd gotten—more than I'd thought possible in such a short amount of time. He'd brushed a tendril off my cheek.

My recollection of the sweetness of the moment carved a smile across my lips, which faded as soon as I remembered that it didn't matter how strong our chemistry was or how much I liked him. He had no room in his heart for me.

Noah shifted, tucking me in even tighter to him; grabbing my ass and fitting me to him like a puzzle piece. Our legs entwined and our hips molded into each other's instinctively. My shirt had hitched its way up, leaving nothing between me and Noah's hand on my ass except my skimpy panties. I wiggled just a little, trying to shift his morning wood away from my specials.

"Mmm… Good morning, beautiful," he growled in a husky voice.

"Good morning, Noah. Dream well?" Insecurity laced my voice. I cleared my throat, drawing attention to the stiffness that jabbed against my very aware body.

"As a matter of fact, I did. But then, how could I not?" With that, Noah playfully thrust his hips toward me. He chuckled, and I could tell he was smiling; a good thing after how last night's conversation ended.

I couldn't seem to get comfortable. I wiggled in effort to find that cozy zone, not because he pressed so impressively against me, but because I felt he shouldn't, or rather that I should at least feel a little more uncomfortable that he was naked and sporting morning wood. After all, this sexy, virile almost-stranger who was now decidedly ONLY my friend lay too intimately close to me.

Swiftly, his right hand, which had been holding my ass, snapped up to quiet my squirming hip. I whipped my head around, opened my eyes and found myself staring into deep, visibly aroused indigo blue depths.

*How strange that his eyes were nearly clear yesterday, and today they're azure. Stop thinking about his raging hard-on! Oh man, he smells so, soooo good. Jeezus... We ended it, remember? You are JUST, and ONLY friends because it can NEVER go anywhere, dummy!* My thoughts were all over the place, and how could they not be, with Noah there… like he was!

Noah kept his eyes locked onto mine, his hand firmly placed

on my hip. I swear I could feel his heartbeat in his stretched, full member.

"You're going to be the cause of my undoing," he said in a husky, lust-laden voice. "You really should get up, but I cannot have you do any kind of moving… just yet. I need a minute to… unwind."

I couldn't help myself and flashed an ear-to-ear smile.

"Yeah, yeah go ahead and be proud of yourself. I haven't been wound this tightly in a long, LONG while."

# Chapter Seventeen

I'd say everyone was up and moving about the bus by ten. Even if Sammie and Dirk hadn't made an appearance, I could hear they were awake. It was a much later start than I would have preferred, especially since I'd been up for close to three hours already.

After Noah and I had progressed past the intimate awkwardness, and I'd been allowed to move, get up, and get the day going, things really started clicking. Not just the routine of showering, getting dressed and starting coffee, but Noah and I seemed back on track comfort wise. Honestly, we were hanging out a lot like Ari and I do—as besties. I felt the sexual tension between Noah and me that Ari and I also felt, but truth be told, when do two good-looking people of the opposite sex *NOT* feel some sort of attraction to one another, even if they're just calling themselves friends? *NEVER*, that's when. I was okay with that; harmless flirting, sexual insinuations, and innocent touching were all part of the fun when you can call a *single* guy a best friend.

"Hiya, hookas!" Sammie bounded down the hall and stepped down into the kitchen. She made a bee-line straight for the coffee pot. Clad in only a partially buttoned down long-sleeved shirt cuffed to just below her elbow, her hair all kinds of mussed up, she definitely had the 'freshly fucked' appearance. I couldn't outright assume anything, though, until she gave me the 411 later.

"Enjoy yourselves last night?" I questioned simply enough. Sammie filled her cup to the brim, turned and raised her left eyebrow while smirking a Cheshire Cat half grin.

"That good, huh?" I quipped and threw her one of my famous Hubba Hubba eyebrow raises.

Sammie looked at Noah, now wearing a pair of expensive, name-brand sweats, and sauntered over to me. She leaned toward my ear so only I could hear "Tessa. Oh. My. God. You have no idea." She leaned back and grinned at me, took another look at Noah's half-clad body and his delicious pecs and abs. "Then again," she added loud enough for everyone to hear, "maybe you do." She winked and turned to head back down the hall, laughing as she disappeared behind closed doors for what ended up being another couple of hours.

I looked over at Noah, who sat in the captain's chair looking like the cat who swallowed the canary.

"Knock that ridiculous grin off your face. You know, everyone is going to think something went on between us."

"So? Let them think."

"Easy for you to say. You don't end up with a reputation." I rolled my eyes at him, wishing he were a little less cavalier about the whole thing.

Sure, I was pissed, but couldn't help but notice how well he filled out the front of his sweats as he lounged there. I licked my lips, dragging my eyes up from his 'V', knowing he was commando under them.

"Tessa."

I dragged my attention away from what he looked like, and back to what he was saying.

"You and I know what really happened. Dirk knows about Pallavi and me. You'll set Sammie straight. As for Kari and Dax, do you really think they're going to give us much thought at all? I mean, they're acting like they're on their honeymoon. So, trust me. This is NOT a big deal."

I went over to Noah and pulled him up out of his chair. My eyes fluttered across his sculpted chest, pausing on his 'Lisa' tattoo.

*Lisa? Lisa...* I felt the briefest stab of jealousy that he had cared so much for another woman, even more than Pallavi, that he tattooed her name over his heart.

"I need a hug," I said timidly.

I'd borrowed one of Dax's shirts this morning after my shower to wear over my bikini. To my dismay, Noah unbuttoned it and wrapped his strong arms around my barely-clad body. He pulled me to him tightly, nuzzling into my neck.

*God, I love the feeling of his bare skin against mine.*

I relaxed into his embrace. We stood snuggling in each other's warmth, pulling energy from the other. A quiet moan of contentment escaped Noah, as I became keenly aware that the third party in his pants had joined us.

"Noah?" I sighed. "Noah. We're *just* friends." I did everything I could to keep myself from taking a peek.

He gave a frustrated growl, "I *know,* but... shit, Tessa, there is just *something* about you. I can't—*He* can't help himself."

*Trust me, handsome; the frustration's mutual.*

When Noah lifted his head and his pale blue eyes anchored onto my jade ones, my knees actually buckled. He gave me the same kind of look a lover gives; the kind that says a million things he feels but cannot express verbally.

"Ahem." At the sound of someone clearing their throat, we finally tore our heady gazes apart, and I peeled my body from his. Keenly aware of how uncomfortably cold the room had suddenly gotten, I immediately pulled my shirt closed and began buttoning it.

The two lovebirds stood in the kitchen, Dax in his expensive sweats and Kari in a Chambray shirt. He had his arms wrapped around her waist from behind, holding her tightly to him.

"It looks like a sweats and chambray kind of day," I said jokingly, gesturing to what we were all wearing. I was trying to quickly move past what they had seen, had time to process, and most definitely had questions about.

"Looks like!" Dax said enthusiastically as he squeezed Kari and winked at Noah. Kari tipped her head back. He placed a sweet kiss on her lips before she set about making their coffee.

"So, what's the plan for the day?" I asked as I positioned myself in the leather recliner, kitty-corner from Noah and across from the honeymooners. I crossed my legs, now feeling very aware of how naked I was. "You know, it might be really nice before we leave to swing by our room to pack some clothes."

"Pack, schmack. I vote we go shopping in Reyk!"

Dax grinned like an idiot at Kari's suggestion, as his hand indiscreetly made its way up her naked thigh.

The morning's laid-back cadence continued until about twelve, when we all decided to get a move on. Dax prepped the outside while Kari and I cleaned up what little mess we'd made. Noah made our bed and folded it away.

On the way, Dax and Kari spent the majority of the time planning out ideas for their eminent road trip. Noah and I...

well, to put it frankly, we fucked each other with our eyes pretty much the entire time. It started out flirtatious, friendly even. Dax cranked up the music, so there was no point in shouting over the tunes from our seats opposite one another. We gestured at first like clubhouse sign-language, the comical kind you create when you are a kid to keep others from understanding what you were talking about. I can pinpoint the exact moment when our innocent, friendly flirtation changed to something more; his eyes went from a light-Caribbean blue to deep cerulean.

After this, and for the rest of the drive, I became aware of his every movement. I watched how he licked his full lips, and how he ran his long, strong fingers through his hair. I even took note of how his breathing changed instantly when R. Kelly's "Your Body's Callin'" came on the radio.

*Could he possibly remember? That night. That song. THAT dance we had? No, impossible. He's a guy, after all, and one who did that kind of thing all the time.*

I pulled myself out of my head in time to see that Noah's countenance had changed; his face had grown more troubled. He shifted uncomfortably, readjusting what looked like a semi in his pants. I glanced up toward the front of the bus, then back at Noah. He was devouring me with his stalker eyes—those ones I now appreciated, that stole the breath from my lungs.

From here on out, our eyes FUCKED. We were in our own world where nothing else mattered. His breathing quickened, his desire hardened, his eyes darkened and grew more intense and demanding, challenging even. My pulse quickened, my mouth became dry and my lips swelled. I couldn't look away from this intriguing, sexy-as-fuck man that sat before me, nor could he look away from me. My body vibrated with need, and not just sexual need. It was far greater. I craved him; to be near him, to be with him. My soul ached for fulfillment. The desire I felt consumed me. My volition held me prisoner to the unattainable 'what if'.

The loud music that flooded the bus suddenly muted. "Tessa," Dax shouted, shocking me out of my headspace. Two things happened instantaneously: I thought of Pallavi and Suri, and just as I pulled my eyes from Noah's hypnotic ones, my gaze focused on his Lisa tattoo.

*Reason ONE. Reason TWO.... just friends. Enough said.*

"Tessa." Dax was still trying to get my attention, and everyone was looking at me since the music was still off. "Can you pour me up a cup of the good stuff, Suga?"

I grabbed Dax the coffee he requested, and then settled in for the remainder of the ride, along smooth roads surrounded by fun scenery... not something I usually enjoy, since I am *not* a huge fan of road trips. We flew past land still mostly covered in snow, but as we got closer to town, the Icelandic grasses and tundra landscape emerged. Lucky for us, Dax was driving, since some of the road signs in town made absolutely NO sense to me whatsoever.

"Well, here we are! There are over 100 shops and businesses and three floors to cover. What do you say we meet back here no later than 1800? I'll go ahead and leave the key on the inside right rear tire, so if you get back before us, you can get in."

"Sounds good!" I glanced at Noah and found him staring at me with an arrogant smirk affixed on his face. *Today's going to be an interesting test of how well we can be 'just friends'.*

"Hidey-ho!" Sammie made her appearance from the bunk room, grabbed Dirk and bounced off the steps. *She's* definitely *in the mood to shop.*

MY GROWLING STOMACH reminded me I needed to eat. I hadn't had more than a couple of cups of coffee on the bus earlier, and my watch read 1645. I'd found a couple of pairs of nice jeans, a few shirts and a few sexy boudoir pieces that, believe it or not, Noah picked out for me. I wasn't sure how I felt about wearing the sexy panties, but they were cute and fit well, so I figured it would be a little rude to put them back and pick out my own.

"Hey, Tess? Where's your head at?" Noah playfully nudged me. "Are you really okay with the whole Vi thing?"

*Okay, yeah. Like, right? Right now? He wants to ask me this now? Like I could even say "Fuck NO, I'm not okay. I was really starting to like you and now you feel about as far off limits as a married guy with a family. Oh, that's right?! You DO have an instant family." Sure…yeah. Like he wants to hear the truth.*

"Jeezus, Tessa. Where are you?"

I looked up at Noah. We'd taken a seat at the indoor food court, and I was supposed to try to decide what kind of crappy fast food I wanted to poison my body with. *He's right,* I realized. *I am a bit in my head, not very talkative today, but I've been plenty pleasant, just not overtly into him. After all, why should I be?*

"Sorry, Noah. It's not you. What do you want me to say? Sure, then. For you, I am A-Okay with Vi and Suri; why shouldn't I be?" The sarcasm oozed off my lips like dark molasses. "We only *just* met two days ago. That's what you want me to say, isn't it?"

*Fucker—it was three years ago! It's such bullshit that I obviously feel more for you than you do me.*

I know I sounded far more put out than I should've, but I

didn't feel like being nice just for the sake of being nice. If I didn't feel it, why should I act it, right? After I snapped at him so rudely, Noah frowned at me. I saw his shoulders slump, and he sat there quietly, awkwardly.

*I know, I know. Don't lay into me... I chose this weekend road trip, but in my defense, it was before you became completely unavailable.*

"Tessa, I'm sorry. I guess I just didn't realize how difficult this whole hanging out together thing would be. I was just hoping that because we'd made such a genuine connection, maybe you were supposed to be in my life in some way." He rubbed his hands roughly over his face, as though trying to erase the scene that unfolded before him, before he continued. "I guess it isn't fair for me to ask you to be *just* my friend. Maybe that's not what you're looking for." He sighed, his penetrating blue eyes growing shades darker than they were this morning, when we were playfully cuddled in bed.

I felt like crying—and why? I just kept coming back to the same argument.

*I've only known him for two, TWO days. I mean, really, that's all that counts. I got over our past long ago, and there is no future. Man, I'm such a dumbass. Why do I even care so much?*

*It's because you're alone in Iceland. You don't have Wes or Ari to talk to, and Sammie is on Cloud Nine and totally inaccessible. And Jeezus, Tessa... it's 'cause... well, FUCK, he's the ONE! Who are you kidding... you've never gotten over him or THAT night, even after all this time.*

I felt a little guilty after everything I'd said. He was being so mature, unlike most guys who would've taken this opportunity to be rude. I squared my shoulders and bit my lip as I looked up, noticing his eyes were dark—haunted.

"You know, you are so sexy when you do that thing with your lip."

"See? *That*. That, right there is why being *just* friends with you is hard. If you acted like just my bud *all* the time instead of throwing in comments like that…" I trailed off because I knew I sounded like a hypocrite.

"Fuck, Tessa! I've said I'm sorry to you more in the past twenty-four hours than I have in some of my past relationships. I don't get it. I've seen you with Ari and Sage and a bunch of other guys. If they had said that to you, you would've giggled and flirted back. So, what's the fucking deal?"

I ruminated in silence about what he'd just said. "You know, you're right, Noah. I would've been that way, but this thing you and I have…" My voice trailed off. "For some reason, with you, it's *harder*." I shrugged, now really punishing my lower lip.

"Noah?" The tremor in my voice reminded me of a little girl who had just been scorned by her father.

He looked at me with those intense indigo eyes of his, his hands crammed into his down-vest pockets as he sat slouched nearly to the edge of the food-court chair. He was the picture definition of conflict, like he had given up for good, awash in palpable dejection.

"Noah?"

"Yeah, what?"

*Brrr.* Noah's demeanor had turned icy cold. What exactly had I done? Damn it, I *did* want to be his friend—not *just* his friend—but I'd settle for that because he was genuinely an incredible guy. And really? Was I giving him this hard a time for wanting to be with the girl of his dreams and their daughter? For doing the right thing… Fuck, I was so dumb.

I pushed back from the table, picked up our bags and stood

beside him. He didn't even look up at me. He just sat there sulking or in complete and total disgust, I couldn't tell. Although, if I were a betting gal, I'd bet on the latter. I reached out my hand to him. It hung there in the air, denied. I squatted down beside his chair and placed my hands on his thigh. Finally, he looked at me.

"You know why I am being such a bitch?"

Noah cocked his head to the side a little, waiting to hear what I had to say.

"You want to know the truth? It REALLY sucks that…" *I just met you again,* "…that we get along. Not just get along okay, but like, really, really well. And, shit… it just sucks that because you are the guy you are; a *really* good guy, you want to be with your daughter. It's not fair." I hovered on the verge of crying, and I could tell my rawness touched him.

"Come on," he commanded in a soft, sure voice. We stood up and he wrapped his arm around my petite waist, pretty much guiding me out of the mall to the bus. We walked in total silence. I stood before the door, quietly weeping as he retrieved the key from the tire. We were in luck; nobody else had made it back yet.

We entered the bus, and Noah took the bags from me, tossing them aside. His hands went to remove my jacket, pausing on my shoulders briefly as though he were asking permission. He felt me give it, and he set to work peeling his Henley off and stripping me of my new violet tee.

He locked the bus door and looked back at me, his eyes dark with raging desire. He approached me with the driven desire of Adam ready to devour the forbidden fruit. He wrapped his right arm around the small of my back and ran his left hand up my abdomen, between my breasts to my clavicle. His palm slowly slid up my neck to my jawline, his thumb tipping my head back ever so slightly.

"Tessa, life isn't fair, but we met for a reason. We have the connection we do for a reason. I don't believe in happenstance or coincidences." He gently stroked my jaw as he held me on my toes, our bodies pressed tightly together. "God, you're exquisite."

The intensity in his eyes penetrated straight through me, reaching that little spot in my brain called logic, and drugging it. I was under his spell; inured, completely hardened and broken, and I realized I wanted Noah to want me more than Vi. That's what I really wanted; which, truth be told, probably became truer once he'd chosen *her* over me. He'd made that choice for both of us when he'd told me about her contacting him. He knew I couldn't stand in his way; he'd constructed the roadblocks directly in front of us.

*So much for 'our' future.*

I managed barely a whisper, "I just want you to want *me.*"

"Oh God, Tess I *do* want you!" He looked shocked that I was second-guessing his desire for me. "I want you more than you even know. I have wanted you since I..." He caught himself, clearing his throat uncomfortably. "Tessa, ever since I saw you at the commissary. Shit... ever since day one, when I saw you on patrol... I've wanted you since we danced two nights ago, and I let you leave a virtuous woman. Shit, Tess, you really have *no* idea?" His husky voice broke. "If there wasn't Vi and Suri... Damn, there's so much chemistry between us it unnerves me, and THAT doesn't happen. Not to me."

At his disclosure, Noah's lips careened into mine fully and with fervor. An honest, straightforward need I hadn't felt in a long, long time welled up in me. His hand cupped the back of my head and guided the choreography of our kiss. The kiss was warm, full and ever so slightly wet. He pulled my tongue into his mouth, rough and wanton, his hand pulling me to him, grabbing my hip and ass. I definitely felt his desire for me. I felt… *wanted,* like the first time he'd taken me. The first time I'd been taken. *This is what I need.* His need for me made me feel brazen, shameless. My hands went down to release him from the confines of his jeans.

A knock sounded at the door. As quickly as the fire between us ignited, the interruption smothered it.

"Open the damn door. It's cold out here!"

Noah threw me my shirt and waited while I pulled it on. He adjusted himself and was still pulling his shirt on when he flipped the lock to reveal Sammie and Dirk, and behind them Kari and Dax. Sammie held up the line while she surmised what had been going on. The bags were tossed aside, my hair mussed, our coats thrown over the furniture and Noah was straightening himself. It wouldn't have taken much to figure it out.

"Well, well, well," Sammie said as she pushed past me. "Saw you in the food court, but it looks like everybody's made up!" She jabbed me with her elbow as she brushed past me and snickered. "Hooka."

I know it was all in good jest, but I grabbed a pillow off the couch and threw it at her head just for good measure. It clocked her squarely. She turned her head, smiled and winked as she pulled Dirk into the bunk room. *Again.*

Kari and Dax went up to their room with their impressive quantity of bags, leaving just Noah and me again.

*Awkward!*

Noah dominated the small space we occupied; his energy demanded attention as he walked over to me. "Tessa. Tessa, look at me." He placed his hands on my hips. "I just want you to know that *you* mean something to me. You already mean a lot, actually, and it's intimidating, frustrating, and very, *very* sexy. I thought Vi was the only one for me, but now? Well, now I just don't know. But I can tell you this, I *do* want you, and if they hadn't turned up, I would've shown you just how badly."

"Hell, yeah! You want to ride her around the track like a purebred taking its victory lap!" Dirk laughed as he stepped down from the hallway into the kitchen.

"Crap," Noah muttered. He turned and slugged Dirk in the shoulder.

"No offense, Tessa!" Dirk muttered, rubbing his injury.

"None taken," I shook my head.

The two of them traded insults all while pulling beers from the fridge and opening a round for all of us.

"Hey, Tess?" Kari had followed Dirk into the galley. "Dax and I were thinking about hitting a market up for food and supplies, and then heading out of town for an Aurora Borealis bonfire and picnic. Are ya game? 'Cause I just asked Sam, and she and Dickhead are." Kari winked at me, knowing full well the response she'd get from me.

I threw her the thumbs up sign.

"Hey! I heard that. Who are you calling dickhead, Scary Kari?" Dirk demanded, laughing.

"Oh, Burn!" Sammie arrived on the scene. "Kari, you gonna let Dickhead call you scary?" Rolling with laughter, she jumped up on Dirk, trying to bring him to the floor. *Yup, Sammie's not a girly girl by any stretch of the imagination.*

When Dax arrived, it must've looked like all hell had broken loose. I tapped the mouth of Noah's beer with the bottom of mine, trying to get his to overflow, but he side-stepped me, and I ended up in the chair with him on top of me, tickling me relentlessly.

"Hey, y'all, pony up. We're outta here." Dax sure had a way with words. "Heya' Suga', help me outside?"

He gave Kari what I considered a lewd look and an indiscreet roll of his hips; incredibly obvious with his invitation. Don't get me wrong, I liked Dax well enough, but he definitely handled himself differently than Noah did, or even Dirk for that matter.

*To make an even stronger case against him, if that's what I want to do, didn't someone say he works with bonds and securities? So, he's involved in the high-end business world of investments and banking? I'm saying I would've NEVER, EVER thought he'd be involved in all of that.* He reminded me of a silver-haired, surfer-style Matthew McConaughey. He was every kind of oxymoron you could imagine, all rolled into one.

# Chapter Eighteen

"Damn it! We forgot to buy the BBQ sauce." Sammie pouted as she pulled the lamb ribs from the full-sized oven. They smelled amazing, but I wasn't fond of lamb back in the States, and the idea of eating Icelandic sheep ribs didn't appeal to me in the slightest. I had promised Noah I would at least try them when we all ran into the city supermarket and picked out dinner—lamb ribs, corn on the cob, a large French baguette, and a shit-ton of beer, but now I wasn't so sure I could keep that promise. The thought of them quite frankly, made my stomach turn.

"Here, babe. It was behind the case of beer," Dirk said wrapping his arms around her waist and giving her a little squeeze before adding a swift smack on her ass. It was fun to see them getting along so well.

"Are the ribs done? I need to get the garlic bread in." I had prepped the baguette with no help from the guys. Noah and Dax had pretty much stayed outside since we'd pulled off and found a deserted spot on some side road in BFE. They had cleared an area for the bonfire, stacked and built the pit, put out chairs and gotten the fire going.

Dax had insisted on stopping a second time at a hardware store, where he picked up three double-sized inflatable camp mattresses and six down-filled sleeping bags with accompanying fleece camp blankets. They had already inflated them in preparation for the northern lights show we all planned to enjoy later.

Make no mistake, it's NOT like it was already summer. We were smack dab in the middle of the sub-arctic spring, which only lasted April and May. This meant we were lucky if it would warm up tomorrow to forty-five degrees Fahrenheit, after hovering right around freezing tonight.

Any way you slice the cake, it was gonna be fun in spite of the cold temperatures. *Besides, I do have Noah to keep me warm tonight.* A smile spread across my face, thinking back to our kiss and his confession that he felt the same chemistry between us that I did.

"That look you're wearing suits you," Noah commented, having caught a glimpse of the smile I couldn't seem to hide, thanks to him, and had been wearing off and on for most of the evening.

"Thanks. Yours looks good on you too." We weren't like the other couples, all grab-assy and cuddly, but we were finding our groove. It was starting to feel like there was potential for friends-with-benefits; that way, I didn't have to lose him completely to Vi, and still got him as a friend, one who also satisfied my carnal desires. *BINGO!* It was kind of like I got my cake and could eat some of Vi's too. The wicked side of me really liked this aspect of the Noah and me that we were becoming.

Dax busted in the door with as much enthusiasm as he always did. I was beginning to wonder if he ever did anything small. *Don't they have a saying about everything being bigger in*

*Texas?* Kari had confirmed, with a mischievous wink, when I'd asked her earlier, that at least that particular saying *IS* true.

"Bonfire's roaring and ready," he announced.

"Good, cuz the ribs are done," Sammy stated.

"I checked, and she's right," Dirk seconded, earning himself a female kick to his ankle.

I had already pulled the bread out and sliced it into chunks. "We were just waiting on the cobs to cook," I announced. Glancing at the timer, I saw we had just under three minutes left. I glanced at my watch—*holy crap*, it read 2135, and I was starving. I hadn't eaten at the food court, nor had I really snacked. I had, however, consumed five or six beers on an empty stomach. Let's say I seriously wanted to chow down.

Everyone bustled around, getting their jackets on and bundling up. The guys had already put some beers outside to get cold.

It didn't take long before we all sat around the fire, scarfing down some gigantic portions. Thankfully, I was drunk enough that all I wanted to do was sober up, or I doubt I would've had more than just a tiny bite of those ribs. They were, after all, baby sheep ribs. Yuck and fucking serious yuck, but the food helped, and I felt like a new woman by the time my plate was empty. I even had an appetite for more beer!

The conversation through dinner and after remained jovial and light. Everyone had a great time teasing one another good-humoredly. Nobody took themselves too seriously. The weather also cooperated, and we only felt the occasional breeze, which, between the alcohol I'd consumed, and the fire burning so hot, felt amazing.

Noah leaned over from behind me. "Hey. I *cannot* get our kiss out of my mind," he quietly confessed in my ear. His hot breath burned my neck. I wasn't sure if it was the memory of that kiss, the anticipation for the next, or the feel of his lips so close to my neck, but my nipples instantly drew taut, and I got goosebumps all over my arms. I shivered ever so slightly.

"You're cold?"

"Nope. Actually warm. It's just a side effect of what you do to me." I turned my head, poised so that our lips lingered a hairbreadth from each other. Our bodies weren't touching, but he still had a way of lighting me on fire just by being so close to me.

"Yeah? Well, want to feel what side effects you have on me?" Noah ever so slightly shifted his gaze down to his pants and by turning, I could see, even in the dim firelight, that the front of his jeans had drawn tight.

"You're awful," I blurted with a laugh.

I was going to say more, but Kari started in. "Alright, let's get this party started! Let's play a round of Bullshit."

"Aw, come on, Suga'," Dax said, nuzzling her neck. "We could go snuggle instead." He was doing his best to dissuade Kari from partying. He hadn't realized he didn't stand a chance.

"Alright." Noah's voice startled me. "How do you play?"

I turned back to look at him, and he flashed me one of his million-dollar smiles as Kari began…

"Well, everyone has to have a full beer. Someone starts with a sentence about their past. The next person tries to add a true sentence about their past that creates a storyline. If it's too outlandish, someone can call 'bullshit'. If you tried to sneak a lie in—you drink; otherwise, they have to."

Noah raised an eyebrow, "Alright. Who goes first?"

"I can start. I just figured we go around the circle… me, Dax, Sammie, Dirk, you and Tessa?"

He shrugged noncommittally and turned toward me, lifting his cold beer in a silent toast. I provocatively winked and took a long draw from my own drink. I hated these games, but really, what the fuck else was there to do?

Kari began. "When I was a kid, I played ball with the neighborhood boys."

Dax started laughing, "Yeah, I *bet* you did!" She glared at him before he took his turn.

"I played football in the Bayou Swamp Division." I looked at Dax and found it believable enough.

Sammie added, "I loved to play in the dirt; I hated acting all girly and shit."

This time, Dirk chimed in... "Fuck, Sammie, you don't say?" He drunkenly elbowed her—as if to say Hubba Hubba. We all laughed.

"I loved to play dirty with all the neighborhood girls."

"Ewwww, Dirk!" Sammie looked appalled, "You sound like a pervert!"

"What? I did!"

This really got us rolling, we couldn't stop laughing. He was drunk, so we let it slide.

I looked at Noah. He seemed to be lost somewhere in his head before he volunteered his line in a monotone, deadpan voice; "I played a lot with Lisa until she...," he paused. Everyone but me figured he was trying to come up with a lie. I wasn't convinced. He cleared his throat and took a swig from his beer. "I played a lot with Lisa until she went missing."

*Wait, what? Lisa? WHO the fuck is Lisa?*

I'd been studying Noah, but couldn't tell by his face if he'd fed us a line. Everyone else, except Dirk, who was focused at that moment on studying the label on his beer, chorused 'Bullshit'!

Noah's eyes met mine and held them for an intense second before he looked away, held up his beer in a toast and took a long, cleansing pull from it.

It was my turn. I fed everyone a line about how I had run away, which to my chagrin, nobody 'bullshitted' me on. *REALLY?*

We played round after round sharing, lying, drinking and exuberantly calling 'bullshit' at the top of our lungs into the Icelandic wilderness. Fuck, by the end of the game, everyone was calling 'bullshit' on everyone, just to get them either to drink or to have a reason to drink their own beers.

"Hey, everyone! So, now that we're all totally tossed, how about a good old-fashioned game of Truth or Dare?" Sammie proffered drunkenly.

Dirk, Dax, AND Noah all whistled and whooped. Kari and I groaned good-naturedly.

Kari looked over at me and shrugged her shoulders. "Sure, why not?"

"Yeah," I acquiesced. "I'll play as long as it doesn't get too serious or vengeful, and the dares are harmless."

"Sounds fair. So, guess that means you volunteer, roomie!" Sammie pretended to pass me the gauntlet. She was a nut, with all the grace and acting flair of a hippo trying to walk a tightrope.

*Drunk Ass!*

"So, Tessa… Truth or Dare?" Dirk asked me.

"Dare."

"Oh, Yeah! Okay. Hmm… give me a sec while I come up with a good one."

Dax leaned over and whispered something in his ear.

"Hey, that's no fair!" I pretended to pout.

From behind me, I felt Noah's presence before his cool hand snaked under my jacket and rested on my hip bone, pulling me firmly backward into his hard body. A shudder rippled through me.

"Okay, I dare you to three-way kiss with Sammie and Kari, and I'm not talking about a peck. I want you to see some tongue action… for at least few seconds."

"What? Seriously? Come on, that's the best you could do?" The idea didn't appeal to me at all, but it was my dare. I started to pull away from Noah, but he held me tightly.

"Boy, aren't you enthusiastic? Why don't you give it your perfectionist best?" he razzed.

I teasingly glared at him. "*You're* next," I threatened.

Pulling Kari out of her chair, we walked to where Sammie stood by the fire.

"Face us! You've got to face us!" The peep chorus chimed in.

I placed my hands on the necks of both of my friends, "Ready?" I asked in a hushed whisper, making sure they were game for the lame dare Sammie's dickhead boyfriend had put me up to. I closed my eyes and went in for the kiss. I kissed Kari first. Her lips were smaller then Sammie's. Sammie and Kari kissed, and pretty soon, all our lips were mashed together with some tongue mixed in here and there. I'd say we gave it a good effort, but I broke the kiss off when I had counted to twelve in my head.

"Fuck, yeah! That was awesome!" Dirk exclaimed, smacking Dax on the back as they both rejoiced in sharing the same pervo likes. I looked over at Noah, who seemed to have enjoyed it as well.

"Okay, hmm." I walked around the lingering embers of the bonfire. I purposely stopped in front of each of my friends, looked them in their eyes and raised an eyebrow or cocked my head before moving on. I had fun building up the suspense.

Finally, I reached Noah—my back to the fire and the Peanut Gallery. I unzipped my jacket as I straddled his lap, where evidence of his arousal had been before. The gang hooted and hollered as I rocked and wiggled on his lap, feigning an effort to get comfortable. I leaned in and pulled ever so slightly on his earlobe with my teeth, giving it a gentle kiss and slight lick before sucking on it for a second.

"So, big boy," I said squirming and wiggling again just for good measure. My plan was working because I could feel him growing hard at my apex. I leaned back in so that my hot breath teased his neck… "I did tell you that you'd be next. Truth. Or. Dare?"

Noah choked getting the word 'Dare' out of his mouth.

"He chose dare!" I announced. Everyone shouted and whistled in rambunctious encouragement. Still perched on his lap, I leaned in, so I applied a good amount of pressure to his now HARD cock. My full breasts, exposed from when I'd unzipped my jacket, now bounced directly below his chin.

"So," I whispered seductively. His cock jerked along his thigh, as my hot lips brushed his earlobe. "I dare you to show me your…" again, his dick twitched. I leaned back and said loud enough for the others to hear, "That's right. He knows what I am going to say." I leaned back in and fisted my hand in his hair. He no longer operated of his own volition. I pulled his head back, so I could look into his eyes. They were dark, raging with pure desire. My lips hovered so close to his, they burned from the proximity. His breath came in short, uneven pants.

In a voice meant only for him, I whispered, "Noah, I *dare* you to show me your *junk*." I grabbed his lower lip with my teeth and gently drew it into my mouth. Noah simultaneously gasped and moaned into my mouth. I felt myself dampen. His deep blue pools locked onto my bright green ones. Without looking, he lifted my weight off his lap as he shifted his cock on his thigh and repositioned me so I more directly straddled his lap. Or rather, his cock.

"What did she dare you to do?"

"What's she want to do?"

"What's she want to see?"

The peanut gallery fired catcalls and incessant questions at us.

Noah answered them without breaking his impenetrable and intoxicating gaze from mine. "My cock."

"What did he say?" I could hear Kari asking Dax, but it was Sammie who answered.

"She dared Noah to show her his boner."

A chorus of laughter, tittering and razzing resounded in the background.

"So, beautiful, if you want to see him for the first time, you need to take him out."

I don't know now if the dare was more for him or for me. It certainly felt like the tables had been turned; now, I was the nervous one facing the dare.

I could hear that the game had gone on, as others were choosing new dares for each other. The background noise faded, leaving us in our own little world... again. My focus fixed solely on Noah, or more precisely, on the unveiling of his cock, which now seemed to dance and jerk with every slight touch of my hands; first on his buckle, then his button. He stopped me halfway down his fly; all that lay between me and his glory. Noah reached up, putting his hand on the nape of my neck and pulled me forward.

"So, you wanted to see it? Look," he commanded huskily. His voice, deep with emotion and pent-up desire, soaked my panties.

With his hand still on my neck, I obeyed him and looked down. My heart raced. I watched him take my left hand in his right, and the two of us pulled down his zipper. It wasn't until he further opened his fly, and simultaneously reached in to shift his position, that his substantial cock sprang free.

Upon its release, it escaped with such fury that it smacked his six-pack abs with a distinct slap. I caught myself sucking in my breath. There it stood, blanketed in dark shadows and lit by the flickering firelight. I had never in my life seen such a handsome dick.

Noah sat there, bare to me, bare to our friends, bare on the tundra. He hadn't taken his eyes off of me, not even while mine had broken free to explore the fruits of my dare. The carnal tension between us grew thick; molecules so sexually charged that I'm shocked we didn't spontaneously combust.

I could faintly hear our friends heckling us. "Put it away already!"

"Fuck, go get a room!"

"Let go of me! I can't see shit while you're holding onto me!"

"You can join the party anytime!"

Noah's firm hand remained at my nape, pulling my ear

toward his mouth. "Tessa. Don't *ever* doubt that I want you." It fell out in a hoarse, throaty whisper. *"EVER."*

"Are you guys ever going to finish that lame-ass dare?"

"Come on, already!"

"Use the master upstairs. Just get it over with already!"

Noah's eyes finally broke from our long, heated stare. "I'm going to pick you up, and I want you to swing your legs around so that you're standing in front of me. Stay there until I get situated."

I placed my hands on his shoulders and helped brace myself while he lifted me, still seated I might add, until I stood in front of him. I watched him try a couple of times to get his cock back in his pants. Finally, he lifted his hips and pulled at his jeans, finding eventual success at resituating himself before zipping his fly. "Woman…" was all he said before he smacked my ass. I was so fucking wet that I had no choice but to stand—uncomfortably —beside the bonfire.

It appeared as though the Truth or Dare game had fragmented. Kari and Dax walked off a short distance from the fire and were pointing and looking up into the sky. Sam and Dirk were sucking face, pretty much like always.

I went inside to go to the bathroom. When I came out, Noah stood in the hallway, blocking me.

"What made you choose that dare?" His stance and the tone of his voice made me a little uncomfortable. "What made you want to share my cock with everyone else? I wanted to share it with you in a different way. My way."

I surged forward, and he stepped down the first stair into the kitchen, so that we were nearly eye-to-eye.

I narrowed my eyes, "I didn't share *you* and I won't share

what I *saw* with anyone else. As far as I'm concerned, it was just you and me out there."

I felt compelled to place my hand on the side of his face, caressing it gently as I laid out my feelings for him to either accept or chastise. He listened, and when I was done, he buried his face in my chest as his arms snaked around me in a bear hug. I squeezed him back tightly. We stayed like that for what seemed like forever, until we both heard the bus door opening. We gave each other a final squeeze and let go.

In a hushed whisper, I heard Noah say, "Why couldn't it be a different time in a different place? A better time? A better place?"

I hadn't expected to hear emotion in Noah's voice. Lust, for sure. But emotion? All I could think was… *Vi? Suri?*

"Lover's spat going on in here?" Dirk asked as he and Sammie nudged past us into the hallway that led to their bedroom, not pausing for an answer.

Once their door closed, I spoke. "So, we're okay, right? I didn't mean any disrespect by my dare. I just...," I sighed. "I just really wanted to see *you and* thought it would be fun."

"Sure, we're fine. Grab your jacket. It's cold outside, and I want tonight to be perfect."

*Chapter*
*Nineteen*

I pulled the sleeve of my cold parka up just enough to see that my watch read 0047. I placed my hands over the tired bonfire. Kari and Dax had already snuggled into their sleeping bags and fleece blankets. I watched them cuddling and occasionally pointing up at the Aurora Borealis. It warmed my heart when I heard them laughing and getting along well. I knew a little about Kari's past, and knew that she of all people deserved to find a guy who knew how to respect her. I just prayed Dax was as genuine as he seemed.

I jumped when strong arms encircled my waist; I hadn't heard Noah walk up behind me. "Sorry, beautiful. I didn't mean to startle you." He nuzzled into my neck and I heard a quiet sigh escape past his lips.

"I just can't believe how insanely gorgeous it is."

"You truly are." His comment caught me off guard, warmed my core, and pulled at my heartstrings.

I reached down and ran my hands down his thighs, squeezing him in sweet appreciation. Looking back up at the sky's wonder, I paused. "The sad thing is that no matter how much detail I use to describe the brightness of the reds and greens, and how they shift and dance across the sky… I'll never convey their beauty to anyone. Unless they're here tonight, nobody will actually understand how majestic the northern lights are."

"Well, Tessa," he said, giving me a comforting squeeze, "I couldn't be more honored knowing I'm one of those people sharing this moment with you." We stood, cozy and warm, staring back at the embers as they died down. An iridescent and completely God-created light-show took place above our heads.

*This is an evening I'll never forget.*

I was so caught up in nature's brilliance and the steady breathing by my ear, a comforting rhythm that set the cadence for the evening to march on to, that I didn't hear Sammie and Dirk approach; they just appeared beside us. In fact, I couldn't tell how long they'd been standing there taking in the magnificence of the Icelandic night sky.

"Ready to go snuggle in?" Noah asked.

I was getting used to the husky rasp in Noah's voice when it was laden with lust and emotion. I stepped out of his embrace; an unspoken 'yes' to his question. I grabbed his cold hand in mine, squeezed Sam's arm goodnight, and led him to the mattress farthest from the bus. I chose this one because I knew the northern lights would be most brilliant where there was the least amount of light.

All around us, tundra grasses grew in low-lying clumps. Chunky glacier rocks spotted the landscape. The barren earth and dark sky felt otherworldly to me, like we had somehow landed on an alien planet where only Noah and I existed.

*This is our time, our place…*

I slipped off my boots, placing them at the base of the make-shift bed, and my jacket I tucked under the top of the sleeping bag, so I could use it as a pillow. I noticed Noah's silhouette seemed to be doing the same.

Glancing back towards the embers, I saw Sammie and Dirk climbing into their bed too. That explained the singular outburst of giggling and frolicking I heard coming from that general direction.

I climbed onto the air mattress, careful not to pop it, and snuggled under the covers, lying on my back to drink in the dramatic show taking place on the sky's stage.

"Hurry! Come and keep me warm."

The chilly tension in my muscles eased once Noah joined me and snuggled in close. A welcome burst of heat warmed the double-sized sleeping bag and my chilled bones. He lay on his side with one arm over my abdomen and the other bent under his head as a makeshift pillow.

We watched the neon green, sea-foam green, and mint green swirl and streak across an inky-black night sky sprinkled with millions of bright white stars. The pink, purple and red streaks elicited ohhs and ahhs from all six of us; the only time any of us were aware that we weren't alone.

As the night hour deepened, I still couldn't get it out of my mind… I hated to break the mood, but I had to know if I was right.

"Noah?" I whispered it so as to not disturb the others. He shifted his head to focus on me and not the sky.

"Tessa."

"Hey, so if you don't want to tell me, you don't have to, okay?"

I watched him, and my comment didn't elicit even the faintest action. No movement. No response. Nothing. I drew in a tight breath of Arctic air. Its chill made it hard to pull it in far enough to get the strength I needed to continue. "Earlier tonight, about Lisa…"

At the mention of her name, his body stiffened and his eyes became pained.

I hesitated. The silence enveloped us. "Never mind. I can tell it's too personal." I dropped the subject, rolling my head so I could better see the display in the sky. The pained energy that emanated from Noah made it hard not to want to reach out and hold him; something I knew would seem out of place and uncomfortable if I did.

We lay like that for a long while; me looking at the lights, Noah watching—no, make that studying—me. He radiated the same intensity I'd felt that night at the aircraft boneyard, when he'd watched me from across the bonfire.

Finally, Noah broke the silence. "Tessa?" I turned toward his wounded voice. "It's not you. It's just…"

"Shh… it's okay. Really. I shouldn't have pried. It's too soon." I smiled reassuringly, hoping he could see that I *was* trying to be a good friend to him.

He raised up on his elbow, leaning over me. His grief-stricken eyes targeted my empathetic ones before his mouth descended, searing mine. His lips burned me everywhere they touched, his kisses so intense, they nearly hurt. He wasn't being overly aggressive, though his kisses did lean more towards that; however, these weren't meant to be hurtful or punishing. Instead, his spirit, his soul poured pain into the kisses until they left me branded. Then, as abruptly as his heart-wrenching kiss began, he ended it.

"Lisa," he said in a voice woven with suffering, "was my little sister." I heard him take a deep cleansing breath.

"Was?" My question seemed to fall on deaf ears, but he finally answered me.

"Yeah. My parents adopted me when I was four, only seven months after my father's parole officer received that call from the park landlord about our rent. I think I told you last night that he came for a home visit and saw the neglect and squalor I was living in?"

I strained to remember through last night's and tonight's boozy fog; vaguely, I recalled he'd mentioned something about it...*Oh yeah! I was thinking about it this morning after I woke up.* "Yes, I remember you mentioned it; you said your foster parents were movers and shakers—that they made things happen."

"Right, well when the parole officer found me I was half starved—*fuck I was skinny*," he said it more to himself than to me. He reached out, laying his hand on my hip. "Tessa, I was gross. I had scabies and head lice..."

I interrupted him, "Noah, it wasn't your fault. What's gross is how badly your real father neglected you."

He mindlessly traced imaginary circles on my hip with his finger. "Anyways, none of that mattered since they found my father with a needle in his arm; he'd OD'd a day and a half earlier on heroin. Social Services pulled me from his shitty trailer and immediately placed me with Dave and Laura. *What a piece of shit... they say the apple doesn't fall far from the tree.*"

His sarcasm hit me hard, "Noah, don't say that. You're nothing like your real father."

"*I still hurt the ones I love,*" he whispered his testimony, looking far off over my shoulder before his aggrieved eyes met mine. "Mom and Dad were really loving at first, I was six when Lisa was born, just two years after my adoption. I was the solution when they'd been told they'd never have a kid of their own. *She* was their miracle baby. The baby that they were told they'd never be able to have. Lisa was our family's dream come true that could do no wrong, she was a sweet angel." He reminisced softly, lovingly. "She was an angel child. Everyone loved her, especially me. Lisa was my miracle best friend…" his voice cracked "…and I lost her."

I listened, reaching out to comfort him, rapt as he continued. "About a week after my twelfth birthday, Mom left me to watch after Lisa." He drew in a ragged breath and slowly exhaled. "She'd begged me to take her to play Hide and Seek in the rural woods that bordered our house. She just wouldn't leave me alone," he ran his fingers through his hair and took in another labored breath, obviously back at his childhood home in his mind. "I was so damn frustrated Tessa. I mean, I had just gotten my Nintendo for my birthday and she just wouldn't quit begging… so I sent her outside to hide and told her I'd be right out to count. I finished my Nintendo game; I hadn't kept track of the time, so it had been awhile, and headed to the big tree we always counted from. I looked around and didn't see her but closed my eyes and counted to fifty like I had done a hundred times before."

Noah's voice cracked from choking back the sobs. "When I opened them, I couldn't find her… *I looked EVERYWHERE.* I couldn't find her *anywhere*. I kept listening for her giggles, waiting for her to jump out at me. I called to her for hours, crying as I panicked. She was *nowhere,* Tessa. I'd lost her."

I couldn't take it anymore, and reached out, pulling him firmly to me and held him tightly while his whole body shook with silent grief. After a gut-wrenching couple of minutes, Noah wiped the tears from his cheeks.

"So after hours of looking for her and calling, I decided I'd better go home once it started to get dark. You should've seen their faces, Tess, they were so scared, but that first look was nothing compared to the looks they became when they realized Lisa wasn't with me." He shuddered involuntarily, "When I recounted for them what happened, my mom collapsed, and my dad immediately called the police."

He sighed, "The next few years were long. Mom went off the deep end, obsessed that Lisa was still alive; she kept the missing-persons campaign open until the city mayor—a good family friend—suggested that they hold a burial for her. I'd just turned sixteen, nearly four years to the day. My mom had all but neglected both me and Dad for years."

Noah shifted, pulling me, fitting me like a puzzle to him. "Unfortunately, my dad took off after the first two leaving me alone, unloved, feeling to blame, and feeling worthy of all the verbal and psychological poison Mom slung at me for the next two. It was hell. Pure, unequivocal hell," his voice cracked, choked with emotion. The minutes of silence that followed stretched on while Noah was lost in his memories.

"Well, so,… basically right after that I started living out in the backyard shed. It was also around that same time I started bringing girls home from school, soccer moms, other women I'd meet on the street, even my friends' moms," his voice wavered and I felt him shrug. "I don't know, maybe I was trying to prove my mom wrong—that I was a decent person. Hell, all I know is that was a rough time. Mom blamed me, and all of her abuse left me naked, raw and emotionally hungry—so starved that I guess was just trying to find love wherever I could."

*My sweet, tortured Noah. How many people has he shared this story with? Did he share with Pallavi?*

'*Lisa.*' For the first time since seeing it tattooed across his heart, I embraced it as a part of who he was. Now, knowing who it stood for and why he'd gotten it, I loved that he'd placed it on his heart, even if it was a painful daily reminder of his great loss. The night hadn't ended all sunshine and roses, but I felt closer to Noah, inexplicably and undeniably so. How could I ever be okay with *just* being his friend?

"MMM." It was all I could think as a strong, calloused, and tender hand alternately massaged my rib cage and the swell of my heavy breast and caressed of my upper thigh and my most intimate parts. His firm, muscular body lay beside me, his impressive length snuggled against my hip. The warmth and heat I felt at his experienced hands, and the well-orchestrated rhythm and pressure of his touch felt luxurious.

"Tessa? Are you awake?"

As the awareness of how cold my nose and ears were washed over me, I realized rather quickly that I must have fallen asleep, and Noah was waking me up.

"Tess, are you awake?"

My eyes fluttered open ever so slightly, as I turned my head in the direction from which the husky voice originated. His lavish exploration stopped when I opened my eyes. His hand rested squarely on my hip and bare stomach. Even there, it turned me on, promising great things in the not so far future… at least I hoped.

An alien neon-green light bathed everything. When I looked up, what I saw stole my breath away. A collage of greens—mint, neon, sea-foam and chartreuse blanketed the sky. Pops of pink, purple, yellow, blue and violet ebbed and flowed, dancing across the sky before disappearing. Swirls of the rarer orange and white lights appeared out of nowhere, only to disappear as quickly as they had come. The sky-canvas looked close enough that if I were to touch it, the colors would transfer to my fingertips. I reached up and it looked like I was finger painting. This night, and our gift of being able to witness this phenomenon, were magical.

I tore my eyes away from the mystic display and sought Noah's. I found him studying me with an intensity that curled my toes.

"You're exquisite, Tessa." He propped up on his elbow and brushed the renegade tendrils off my face, before leaning down and giving me the softest and most tender kiss to date.

"You fell asleep. You're so peaceful to watch." His voice trailed off. "Please forgive me for taking liberties, but I couldn't contain my feelings for you, and with everything I shared about Lisa…" his voice grew heavy as he sighed. "I know it sounds dumb, but I wanted to bring you pleasure as a small thank you for being exactly what I needed when I shared… and I can't explain my deep attraction to you. The comfort I find being next to and with you." He smiled sheepishly for having felt me up in my sleep. *I didn't mind. Not that I'd ever tell him so.*

His admission that I brought him comfort shocked to my senses. I reached up and pulled his head down until our lips met. The kiss started slow and languid at first. It didn't take long before he shifted his weight over me, his knee between my thighs so he had the height he needed to dominate the kiss. I reached up to entwine my hands in his hair, but he stopped me, took me by the wrists and imprisoned them above my head, where he held them with only his right hand. His left hand made quick work of lifting my shirt up and freeing my breasts from the confines of my lace bra.

His desire felt divine. Our tongues sparred, teased and retreated. Our lips meshed, and teeth nipped. He made short work of getting to my neck, finding all my sensitive places. The moans escaping my mouth further guided him. He made the presence of his hard erection known as he ground his hips into the most sensitive parts of my sex, churning and thrusting in a cadence my wanton body provoked and gladly marched along with.

"God, Tessa, I…" he raised his head and his voice trailed off as though searching for words that eluded him.

The break from our passionate kiss gave me just long enough to realize what I was doing, what we were doing. I tried to pull my hands out from his, but he held them firmly.

"Noah, we've got to stop. Please, *please* let me go." The desperate coldness in my own voice startled me.

The look of reverence that had glowed in his eyes and been etched across his face vanished as though I had slapped him. He instantly released me and moved off, lying on his back—not even touching me. The iciness I felt wasn't just from the Arctic winds screaming across the field; the frosty blast radiating from across the imaginary center-line of the mattress that had been a love-nest only seconds before.

"Will you listen to me?" I whispered in a weak but heartfelt plea.

Noah wasn't having any of it. "Honestly, Tessa? I can't read you. I'm getting tired of trying to, and at this point, every cell in my body just doesn't give a fuck."

"OH, REALLY!" I snarled, so ready to give him a harsh tongue lashing. *How dare he come on to me that strong, and then not even a minute later, blow me off like that?* "So, you're pissed because you wanted a piece of ass?" The stutter of disbelief fell like a dead body out of my mouth. Lifeless. Cold.

"No, but fucking believe whatever makes you happy, sweetheart."

"Don't sweetheart me. Don't ever fucking sweetheart me. I stopped you because we're moving too fast, because… because…" my voice broke and trailed off, turning away from him so he wouldn't see the tears that fell rebelliously from my traitorous eyes.

A stark silence enveloped us. The northern lights lost their wonder and now felt malevolent.

My hot, angry tears quickly subsided, and I turned back. Noah stared directly at me. He appeared inquisitive but gave nothing else away with his body language. He reached out, "Tessa…"

"No, wait. Let me get this out." I wrapped my arms around my body and snuggled deeper into the covers. "Noah, you confuse me. In fact, everything you make me feel confounds me."

"Tess…"

"Noah, please. Let me finish before I can't get it out." I drew in a deep breath and continued. "Rational me knows that when you met me three days ago, you had no idea the love of your life would contact you the very next morning. I get that—truly, I do. I know from what you've told me that you've moved on but have always had that huge 'what if' resonating around in your head. You haven't seen, let alone met, your daughter since you found out about her more than six years ago. I get all of that. I really do. I understand the intense and compelling feelings you must have that drive you to explore the possibility of how the three of you could be a family."

"However, the emotional side of me foolishly wants you to discard the possibility of a future with them and explore one with me. It sounds so idiotic and selfish as I hear myself say it that I cannot even fathom why I thought you were on the same page as me. I guess when you made me feel so desired and wanted, it made me think—even if just for yesterday and today, that maybe you wanted me instead of Vi." I released an uncomfortable and humorless laugh. "God, I even hate saying her name. Isn't that laughable?"

Expunging the weight of all these feelings from my slender shoulders felt cathartic. I lay naked in spite of the sleeping bag and clothes I wore. Noah's face had changed from one of inquiry to one of resolve. What that meant for me, for us, I wasn't sure, so I just kept to my side and looked steadily back at him. *It truly amazes me how much better I feel now that I've told him all the crap that's been weighing me down the last couple of days.*

As Noah drew in a deep breath, I knew I needed to brace myself for whatever he was about to say. "Tessa, I'm sorry for being so disrespectful. It really isn't a habit I'm proud of. I am working on not saying things I don't mean when I get mad, but in my defense... well, I thought this was *IT*. Yeah sure, it was about sinking my cock into what I can only imagine would feel like pussy jackpot—pardon my frankness—but for me it was more than that. I can't explain how I feel about you. I know you're right when you say I entertain the idea of a future with Suri and with Pallavi as my wife. I've thought about it more times than I can even count since I left her flat that day in New York, and since I got that call about my daughter." Noah stopped and growled in exasperation while he scrubbed his hands over his face; an act I had grown accustomed to seeing him do.

"You're right. Everything you've said is true. Tessa, I know I met you at the *worst* possible time. I was just trying for a hook-up to get them and that mess out of my life, to give myself a clean break so I could finally move on. I admit it. I was hoping you'd give me a sign tonight, now that we've moved past having *just* met, so I could 'charm' you into riding my cock. Sure. What kind of guy in my place wouldn't?"

His admission stunned me. I had no words. I could only stare at him, unable to shake the blank look frozen on my face. *I just bared my soul, and this prick responds by telling me he hoped I'd be a good lay? Who does that?*

Foolish optimism swelled in me, the more I considered his situation. *He didn't set out to hurt me; I'm just collateral damage.* I found I started to seek excuses for his behavior. The nurturer in me wanted to wrap my arms around him and console him. I'm sure if it were hard for me to get my feelings off my chest, that for a guy, it must be even harder.

He continued his tirade, voice growing angrier with every word. "But, damn it. Then *you* stormed into my life. There's no logic or sense to explain how or what the feelings that I've developed for you are, but there they are. Boom. You've totally upended me."

A deafening silence fell for a single, breathless moment. Then, I heard him inhale deeply once, twice. "So, my plan, if you were wondering, is to take leave and see where Vi and I are. Regardless of how that goes, I want to meet Suri more than anything. I want to see if she looks like me, or like both of us, or more like her beauti..." Noah cut himself short, but not before I caught he was about to call his ex 'beautiful'.

*Well, FUCK. That sucked. There's only so much I can take. I mean, is he hurt and confused, or just a total egomaniacal asshole?*

"Noah, I know we have this amazing connection. I also know our ship has taken on too much water already, and I don't even think we've left the dock yet. Not really."

"But we can do this. We can make it work." He tried to sound convincing but fell short.

*This is moving so fast. Do I want to make it work?*

"Noah, it only works if you go see Vi and decide that after all the years you've spent wanting and dreaming of her, you decide to discard it all and gamble on an 'us' that hasn't even started yet. That is a HUGE gamble. Not only that, but it would require me to accept that I'm second fiddle. That being with me is *not* your first choice, which is true since you are exploring your possibilities with her before you explore what we have."

I watched Noah, and I could tell he was squirming.

"Don't misread what I am saying. I DO NOT expect you to make that gamble, nor do I foresee you being able to come right out and hurt my feelings, so I'll do it for you. We cannot, will not, have sex. I cannot kiss you anymore because it draws up feelings I don't want to have for you, not when you're in love with Vi." I sighed deeply, squirming uncomfortably myself.

"Noah, I deserve to have someone feel about me the way that you feel about her. I want someone to think about me for years, even if life keeps us apart, and then drop everything to take leave to come see me. *That* is what I want, and certainly what I deserve. So, this is it. It's the way it has to be." My voice shook, and a trail of tears flowed down my cheeks. "I *hate* it, but it's what I have to do because it's best for me, and ultimately best for you."

Resigned, Noah slid over and pulled me into his arms. "God, you are an amazing woman. I'd be… anyone would be so lucky to have you."

"This. Sucks," I said with so much emotion in my voice that I choked on the words. Then, heavier tears came. Noah held me, rocking gently. "I believe everything happens for a reason…," a sob racked me before I could finish.

Noah held me, waiting patiently until I composed myself.

*What a shitty night.*

"I knew from our first meeting that there were so many things I would be looking for in the guy who ended up being right for me. I don't want to freak you out, and I am afraid that what I say might, but I love you."

I felt Noah squeeze me tighter, and the slightest moan slipped from his delicious lips.

"I'm not saying I am in love with you, Noah. It wouldn't take much, but there are so many things about you that I do love. I can't imagine us losing track of each other. I know I want you in my life."

"Tessa, I love you too. You're one of the most intriguing and amazing souls I've ever met. Maybe, if the stars weren't crossed, we'd be right for each other, but you're right. There are too many obstacles to jump, and we've only begun the course. Man, I *do* love you. It feels like we're some kind of soulmates, maybe best friends in another life."

I interrupted, "I know, right? Doesn't it feel like we've known one another forever?"

I wanted to tell him since yesterday that we'd met three years ago, before I joined the Navy. That he'd taken my virginity. That he was the one I compared all others to, because I'd felt such an immediate and intense chemistry with him. I wanted him to recognize me just like I figured out he was 'Ren'. Now the door for this opportunity had closed, and there was just no point.

*Even if he felt the same as me—which he's alluded to daily, it isn't enough with Vi on the sidelines.*

I was crushed.

Noah's lips came down on mine with such caged passion that I had no option but to let him. *Not*, that I would've tried to stop him if he'd come at me any other way.

We spent the remainder of the night kissing passionately, groping, caressing, cuddling, and clinging to the flickering hope that we both knew would die at the first hint of daylight. We lay in each other's arms as the suggestion of dawn crept into the night. I knew, and felt that Noah knew, that this was the final goodbye to 'us'. Goodbye to the possibility of anything that reached beyond '*friends*'.

SAMMIE PLOPPED down on my air mattress and bounced me right off it. I hit the ground with a resounding thud.

"Son of a…," I exclaimed loudly at the rude awakening. I sat up, still in my sleeping bag, and surveyed the camp. Dax lingered in bed. Dirk and Noah had disappeared. Now, Sammie lay down on my bed—waiting for the right time to fish for information.

"So…?"

"So *what,* Sammie?" My patience, already thin since I had landed on my ass not even two seconds after waking, snapped like a twig.

"You know… What happened between you and Noah?"

I sighed. *Not even a sip of coffee or an aspirin to take the edge off.* "There really isn't much to tell. We've decided, in spite of our connection and budding feelings for each other, that he has a prospective wife and a child with her, so that's what he needs to explore—not something new with me."

"Holy Shit?! You don't say? I knew something about it from what Dirk told me, but sorta figured that everything was ok because of how you guys are around each other."

"Yeah, well… maybe that's how it would've turned out if it were meant to be. Hey, I'm kind of done with all this. It was a really rough night, very emotionally charged, and in spite of all the rest I made up by sleeping in, I'm still beat. I just really want a shower and a good cup of coffee."

"Oh no… you don't get off that easily. What did he say?"

"Sam, he said he wanted to be with another woman—not even seconds after he made me wet with a passionate kiss."

"Fuck. That's not cool."

"No. It isn't. Oh, and get this—before he told me he wanted to explore a future with Vi, he told me that his little sister was kidnapped."

"Shit! No fuckin' way." Sammie's slack-jawed appearance must have resembled mine when Noah told me last night. "Is that why her name is on his chest?"

"Yeah, it is. After she was kidnapped, his mom lost it and his dad left," my voice wavered as tears slipped out of my eyes. "Sorry, it's been a really emotional night."

"I bet," she sounded shocked and reached to put an arm around me.

"Sam, it sounded terrible the way his mom treated him… she blamed him for letting it happen. It sounded like she closed off into a shell of herself, withholding her love and slinging verbal and psychological poison at him until he moved out at sixteen."

"Oh. My. God," her voice left no question about her feeling sorry for Noah. "I'd have never guessed that. I mean, sure I could see that something somewhere in his past probably made him a womanizer, but I'd never have thought that the reasons ran so deep."

"Right? He moved out, Sam, into his backyard shed of all places… and then it got really bad."

"Jeezus, how much worse could it get?"

"Well, the way he told it he started looking for love in all the wrong places and with pretty much everyone—girls from school, soccer moms, friend's moms, pretty much any woman he met on the street."

"It breaks my heart." Sammie sat on my bed with her knees drawn up, gently rocking. She reached up to swipe a tear from her cheek. "So, now that he's found you, a real chance for something good, I don't get why he's running."

"I don't know either. Maybe it's his M.O., or maybe it's always been about Vi for him?" My voice shook, and she leaned over and pulled me into a hug.

"Tessa, it'll be alright. Things happen for unexplainable reasons. Maybe this isn't the end like you think it is. Maybe Vi won't want him."

I sobbed and chuckled at the same time. "That's not very likely—have you seen him? Better yet, have you kissed him? How about the depth I've seen in him after hours of just talking? How about the depth I've seen in him after hours of just talking? There's so much about him that is amazing, I cannot bring myself to believe I've lost him as soon as I've found him."

"Tessa, you didn't lose him. You never had him to begin with."

I looked up at her through teary eyes and just shook my

head. *She's right. Two days and a night three years ago does not a future make.*

"Come on, girly," Sam said, getting up and pulling me to my feet. Once I had my boots on, she wrapped her arm around my waist and gave me a tight hug from the side. "You've got this. Everything will work out just fine somehow. You'll see. Now let's go, Kari's already inside working on breakfast. I'm sure she can hook you up with a good cup-o-brew." She chuckled and gave me another hug as we walked side-by-side toward the bus.

# Chapter Twenty

I'd already made it into my second cup of coffee when the bus door opened and in stepped Dirk with Noah. I discreetly glanced at my watch and realized that, based on what Sammie had said, they'd been gone for over four hours.

"Good morning." I smiled at Dirk, my smile broadened as I directed it toward Noah. I noticed how tired Noah looked. He had deep lines etched into his forehead that hadn't been there yesterday, and dark circles were forming under his eyes. He looked every bit his age… this weekend had been rough on him.

"Morning, ladies," they simultaneously replied, and everyone laughed.

*Thank God, today looks like it's going to be easy. It's just what I need. NO MORE DRAMA.* I unconsciously released the breath I'd been holding in a liberating sigh.

Thanks to Kari, there were sage sausage patties, hash browns and fresh fruit for breakfast. In an attempt to be on the same schedule as Dax, who wanted to get an early start, Sammie, Kari and I had already showered and dressed. This was a complete turn-around from yesterday, when it had taken us more than two hours longer just to be ready by noon.

I felt a weird tension in the room; an uncomfortable vibe I couldn't really put my finger on. It may have been because Sammie and Dirk had finally done the deed, or because of Kari's nerves about taking a week off and leaving today with Dax. I'm sure I was contributing to the whole peculiar vibe myself by how strange Noah's and my evening had gone, especially since he'd been gone when I'd awakened. I had been nervous at first, not knowing if he was okay, but Sammie had said that he and Dirk had taken off around 0500 for a walk.

Dirk spoke first. "So, what's the plan? Looks like everyone knows 'cept Noah and me."

"Well, nothing definite has been decided yet," Kari offered, turning around from the sink where she was cleaning up the breakfast pots and pans, "but Dax was telling me he wanted to get camp packed up, so we could roll out of here no later than 1000."

"That's right, Suga." Dax emerged from the hallway, silver hair styled in a mussed do and wearing an expensive pair of jeans and what looked like an angora/wool sweater in greys and blue. They sold that type of sweater all over Iceland. He looked stunning with a pair of dark blue rimmed glasses that set off the color of his blue eyes. "I was thinkin' y'all could head back to base and my woman and I could get some miles in today before we needed to pull over for camp."

I let my mind wander for just the briefest second to imagine when he and Kari got it on, how good of a lover he'd be. He just looked like he knew what to do. It made me a little envious that I *did* already know what Noah was capable of and couldn't take full advantage of him.

*Fucking Vi.*

"Jeezus, Tess! Where are you?" Sammie's voice snapped me back from my perverted contemplation.

"Right here. What's up?"

"I wanted to know what you wanted on your plate, that's all." She sounded a little more put out that she should have.

"Just fruit, I think. Not really in the mood to eat, but thanks."

"Tessa, can we talk?"

I looked at Noah, and he gave me a shamefaced look.

"Hah! Well, I guess I can't use the excuse that I want to eat first, now can I?" I glanced over at him as I felt an emotionless mask fit itself firmly on my face. I turned when he walked past me and followed him to the stairs that led to Dax and Kari's bedroom. I paused out of sight and within earshot, hoping to hear what the gang was saying about us. *Maybe I can find out what Dirk and Noah talked about for over four hours this morning.*

"Wow! What in the hell is going on with them?" Kari posed the question quietly to the gang in the kitchen.

Dax also voiced his confusion. "Yeah, I thought they'd end up mated by the end of this weekend."

"Dirk, what's going on?" Sammie inquired, knowing he had the answers they were searching for.

"It's really not my place. What I can say is they're crazy, and I mean crazy, about each other, but the universe is doing its best to keep them apart." I heard someone walking and plates being placed on the table. I could only assume it was Dax.

"Thanks. So, what you're saying is they're star-crossed lovers?" Sammie said in an 'oh that makes all the sense in the world' voice.

"Yeah, basically. They really see themselves together, but

there are some loose ends Noah needs to tie up—and they may permanently keep him tied up, if you know what I mean."

"I don't, but I'm sure I'll get the 411 from Tessa soon enough."

"Well, I can tell y'all this; if they're that crazy about one another, then they'll make it work. Look at the lengths Kari and I are goin' through so that we can see each other after I leave here."

Sammie started a much lighter conversation revolving around possible plans Kari and Dax might be up to for the week.

*He's crazy about me? He told Dax we were crazy about each other and that we were star-crossed lovers? So, wait, he said he felt the same way about me that I felt about him? Why didn't he just tell me instead of making it sound like I'd been nothing but a distraction to get his mind of Vi? Fuck! How did all of this shit get so fucked up?* I just shook my head as I climbed the stairs, glad I'd eavesdropped, but now more confused than ever.

At the top, I paused, taking note that the bed had been freshly fucked in. I grabbed the comforter off the floor and straightened it over the bed, taking a seat as I watched Noah. He stood at the far side of the small master suite with his back to me, looking out the window. I turned away, contemplating how uncomfortable I felt, up here with Noah and with this whole mess.

*This is so out of control! How did it get this bad?*

*How can I remember him, and he NOT remember me? Didn't that night at Wazzu mean anything to him? I KNOW he knew what he took from me...*

*How could this weekend and all of the conversations we've had mean nothing? I know it can't just be me who feels the electricity between us when we kiss or touch? Hell, I can feel when he walks into the room!*

*This is so, SO fucked up. I've had it!*

*I deserve to be having fun like everyone else…*

In the midst of my own little personal pity party in my head, I didn't notice at first that Noah had walked around the edge of the bed. I looked up to see him kneel down before me.

He placed his hands delicately on my knees and cleared his throat. "Thanks for following me up here. I just…" Noah's voice wavered, and I watched as he physically crumpled—his shoulders slumped, his head hung, and he scrubbed his palms over his face. He ran his strong fingers through his thick, wavy hair before limply placing them on his lap. He was the picture of defeat. I never imagined such a self-assured and comfortably arrogant guy could come to care so deeply in such a short period of time.

I sighed. I was just, well… done. I wanted him, couldn't have him and was fed up with the drama and emotional roller coaster.

He cleared the emotion from his throat. "I just wanted to say that I've really thought about everything I said last night. I told you the truth but was dishonest by not telling you everything. I'm sorry I was so disrespectful. After talking to Dirk all morning, I've decided to take the trip to see Pallavi and Suri. I don't know if I can manage this quickly, but she has a modeling gig in Saint John's next week. I plan to be there if I can get my leave approved." He paused, waiting for me to say something.

I just sat there and looked at him, so he continued. "So, what I was thinking… we could be friends. I… I really need you. Damn, that's hard for me to say… *I don't need anyone…* but everything's alright when I'm with you. You're like a piece of my fucked up puzzle and I want us to be friends."

I squared my shoulders, "You know what? You're a piece of shit. You want me, I want you, but you're being selfish by insisting on chasing after a dream you've held onto for far too many years. It's so completely unfair for you to keep me bouncing up and down like a goddamn yo-yo. Figure out what you want! If it's me, and I haven't moved on, then we'll see; but, as of now, I am truly done. I cannot take the bullshit vacillating, and the keeping me on a short leash bullshit. I really wish we'd never met. Fucking leave me alone already."

I stormed down the stairs, past everyone in the kitchen, ignoring their stares and stormed off the bus. I. NEEDED. AIR.

# Chapter Twenty-One

The rest of the morning went by in a blur. I must've had 'Fuck Off' on my forehead because everyone, including Sammie, gave me *lots* of space. While outside I rolled all the sleeping bags and folded the fleece blankets. I deflated the mats, pretty much packing up the outside campsites before anyone came out. Dax tested the waters first.

I watched him move with refinement; he was so much more polished than the guys who worked with me at the squadron. I figured it had to be a side-benefit of having lots of money.

"Hon? Tessa, Suga? Do we need to be worried? 'Cause you're out here and Noah hasn't come downstairs yet."

"Nope, no need to worry. I am *FINE,*" I said with such finality that he couldn't have questioned it if he were inclined to do so.

When Dirk joined him outside to pack everything up in the storage compartments and remove the chocks, I went back in to help get the bus travel-ready.

"Hey guys, need my help anywhere?" I looked around and it really didn't appear so, but I actually hoped they'd put me to work. We had a good two to two-and-a-half hour drive ahead of us. I guessed we'd traveled a little over 90 minutes from Reyk, and it took about 45 from there to get to base. I really needed to stay busy until the absolute last minute, because it was going to be hard enough having to be so close to Noah for the entire ride home.

"Yeah, you can help. Go upstairs and tidy up," Kari challenged. She stood in the living room space with her hands on her hips.

"Oh *hell* no. There's no way I am headed up there if *he's* still there."

"What the hell happened to the two of you? Even if you can't be together, you still need to be cordial… this is affecting more than just the two of you. After all, Dirk and Noah are friends, and so are you and Sam. Not to mention your sour mood is making it terribly uncomfortable for everyone else here. For all our sakes, get your shit together and make up, or at least fucking fake it." Kari turned to Sammie and gave her a high-five.

"One of you is going to have to swallow your pride first—may as well be you." Sammie smiled at me, "It gives you the upper hand."

"Goddamn it. Fine! *Fuck!*" I spat, as I turned on my heel and headed up the stairs. The closer I got, the more nervous I felt. I can't really explain why, but every joint in my body grew stiff, and trudging up the stairs felt like climbing through thick oatmeal… slow and tedious.

At the top, there was a pony-wall about four feet high that kept people from falling down the stairs. I peeked around the corner and saw he wasn't on the couch or any of the chairs, thankfully. I took a seat on the overstuffed leather couch and looked out the window to try to calm my nerves.

The late morning sun beamed in the open blinds, warming

my skin. The light caught the highlights in my hair and greatly improved of the reflection I saw in the tinted window. On these rare moments, I truly saw my hair as beautiful and not just cute like I'd heard my entire life. I closed my eyes and laid the side of my head against the back of the couch. It felt so warm and soft, and I was so spent from the whirlwind of the weekend that I just let the peace consume me.

"Even now, knowing you hate me, I still find you enchanting."

Before I heard the familiar rasp and smelled his sweet masculine spice, I felt his energy. The reminder of our connection stabbed my heart like a dagger. I opened my eyes and turned to look out the window, resting my chin on the couch.

"We're taking off," Dax called up. "If there's anything else y'all want to do outside, now's the time."

I let the announcement drop, like the feeling in the pit of my stomach.

Noah took my silence to mean I was good, so he answered back to Dax, "We're ready to take off whenever you are."

I could hear the jovial conversation downstairs and wished like hell I had the heart to participate in it, but couldn't bring myself to let go of the resentment I'd felt since last night.

Reflected in the window, I could see Noah still standing there, looking at me. He laid his hands on his face, and I watched him scrub them up and down in an attempt to lessen his stress. This, if nothing else, showed he was frustrated, agitated and tense.

A final call came across the intercom. "Find your seats." I felt the emergency brake release, and the luxury bus began the trip back to base.

As the vehicle swayed, Noah stood with his feet wide to keep his balance, one hand on the recliner, and the other jammed into the front pocket of his low-slung jeans. I mentally chastised myself for taking the opportunity to admire his muscular build in the window's reflection, along with his mussed hair, and slightly too tight thermal Henley, which he'd left unbuttoned at the neck. Its graphite grey color looked great with his tan skin.

I was so tired of feeling dead. I needed my joy to return. *Dear God, please help me.* I sent out a silent prayer, and once I did, an incredible peace came over me. I couldn't explain it then, but I've come to learn there's power in prayer. Peace welled up within me, and with it, an almost overwhelming need came over me to make things right with Noah.

About this same time, Noah made a move toward the couch. I watched him approach in the window, catching the occasional glimpse of his 'V'. I turned once he reached me and took him in. Barefoot and all, he was stunning, especially having had little to no sleep in close to twenty-five hours.

He motioned to the couch, and I nodded. I had my feet pulled up and easily took up half the couch. He sat with his back against the opposite arm and slid his leg along the back of the seat, tucking it in beside my hip. The other bent to a stop at the middle cushion. He reached out, pulled my feet onto his lap and began to massage them. My head dropped heavily onto the couch back, and I let him pamper me. We sat quietly this way for at least a half-hour before I broke the silence. I'd waited to say anything because I didn't want it to go badly and saying nothing was safer.

"Noah?"

He turned expectantly, looking at me and waited.

"I feel terrible for calling you all of those names and for telling you that your dream of a family with Vi and Suri was bullshit. It's not up to me to decide if it is or was… it's none of my business. And…," I gave pause because, although I felt bad, saying I felt sorry wasn't entirely true. However, the small part of me that wanted a reconciliation continued, "I'm sorry for saying I wish we'd never met." I choked on the words a bit. I actually hated saying I was sorry, but there it was. Mostly though, I hated that I'd let it get so out of hand that I felt like I had to say something today to make things right—because, well, damn it—it was his fault as much as mine. *Fuck,* more so.

Noah hadn't said anything yet, but the expression on his face combined with the fact that his touch was sure, steady, and comforting… said a lot. It said he wasn't an asshole when he was mad. It said that he put his feelings after mine because what mattered to him right now was letting me know he cared—in spite of the hurt I am sure my words had caused. I still remembered the look on his face from the pain I had inflicted just a short hour ago. His caresses said that in the past, when he said I mattered, that he wanted *me*, that he loved me and wanted me for a friend, he genuinely meant it. There's no other explanation for why he still wanted to have anything to do with me.

"Tessa," he said, still massaging my feet, "you really don't need to apologize… I get it. I know I don't say what I mean, and when I do, it usually comes out all fucked up," he paused, cracked his neck, and took a deep breath, "but I'll try. What you said struck a chord. I get that my decision to go see Vi makes no sense. I get that." His hands stopped their slow kneading of my feet, as his gaze fell on the window and the passing scenery beyond.

"Tess, it's been really unfair of me to keep stringing you along until I made up my mind. You're right about everything you called me out on…fuck, you're probably even right that being with Vi is a dream that should've died years ago…" his voice dropped so soft I could barely hear him. I wondered if he was still talking to me or thinking out loud, "…but I have to know."

"Noah," I leaned forward and took his wrists in my hands, "I was a raging bitch this morning and I should've handled myself better, I suppose. It's just that you made me so damn mad! I wish you could see what I can… but, anyways, sorry for being such a bitch—even if you deserved it."

*Okay, that was probably the worst apology I've ever, and I mean EVER given.*

I tried again. "I know, thinking back on this morning and what I want from you and our relationship—if we're going to have anything—that I should've given you the support and friendship you needed. If I'd behaved more like a true friend, it wouldn't have mattered how hard this has been on me, I still would have supported you. Following your dreams, or anyone following theirs for that matter, is a hard thing to do, and I have given you nothing but grief. I called you selfish when in fact the only feelings I took into consideration were my own; I was being selfish too. So, on that count, I'm sorry." I gave his hands, which were now holding mine, a squeeze. "Go do this. Go find Vi. Go meet Suri and take back your family. You, of all people, deserve happiness."

"Why me of all people?" His eyes bored into my soul, questioning, "I went out Thursday night to the club hoping to get laid. I was *hoping* for a one night stand. Friday, the only reason I accepted Ari's invitation was because I was hoping for a hookup, and then it turned out to be you. So, like the bullshit gentleman I am, I earned your trust and won you over in the hopes that last night we'd fuck. I selfishly thought it would help me forget, make me feel better." He hung his head, "Tessa, nothing I did yesterday made me worthy of happiness. I was only thinking of myself."

"All I was to you from the beginning was a conquest? A piece of ass?" I felt my friendly demeanor falter as my heart slammed into my chest.

"No!" I could hear angry frustration in his voice. "Listen, from the moment I spotted you I had to get to know you. You've always intrigued me, and the person you are way surpassed my memory—I mean my idea of who I thought you'd be."

I looked at him, taking in what he said.

*Did he mean memory of me, or did he accidentally say it when the word he was searching for was the idea of me? Who am I kidding? If he remembered me he would've said something by now... wouldn't he?*

He interrupted my inner monologue. "Tessa, the truth is, you're beautiful, stunning actually. Like most assholes, I was looking to dip my dick—at least originally—it was just about someone to make me feel better." He looked down, tracing circles on my feet. "I'm a guy and I don't have the words to really... to express myself right."

I gave him that, but he sure as hell had better try. I sat quietly.

He began again. "Okay, so, Tess it's like this. You and I shared amazing chemistry on the dance floor, but you were too damn sweet to take advantage of, so I let you go. When I saw it was you Friday, I was only bummed out for a second, because I thought 'Here's a girl who's already into me, and I like her, so let's just see what happens.' Jeezus, Tess! Friday at the Lagoon *talking* with you... it was one of the best fucking conversations I've ever had. It was awesome."

He smiled, remembering it. "I was a good boy again, leaving you virtuous that night, which I might add was hard as fuck with nothing but those thin panties you were wearing between us. Those were sexy as hell, I might add." His intense indigo eyes caught my green depths as he squeezed my feet. "Saturday redeemed itself once we ditched the mall and I got you back to the bus." He winked at me and I swear he had little devil horns. His mischievous grin earned one from me.

"You see, in spite of my best efforts to find a body—I found a heart. I discovered you had so many qualities I've been looking to find... so many qualities you checked off my list of ideal traits. It's so unrealistic, I *never* thought I'd find someone, and yet, somewhere amidst all this mess, I found an amazing friend. Tessa, I connect to you like NO ONE I have *ever* met... And then you pulled that dare on me! Jeezus, I had resigned myself to keep you sweet, but fuck—your tight little ass on my lap, your tits under my chin, and your eyes. YOUR EYES when you saw my cock. Well, let's just say that between the moist heat I felt radiating through my jeans and your eyes that screamed 'Fuck Me'... That's exactly what I went into the night hoping would happen. But for me, honestly? It's never just been about that with you. I have *every* confidence that we'd have no problem in that department." He winked lasciviously at me.

"And while I'm being so honest, you should know that the reason you feel like I'm flip-flopping between you and Vi, well, it's because I have been. Am. Hell... I don't know anymore. What you said about letting her go after all of these years... it stung."

Noah reached forward and placed his hands on either side of

my hips. In one swift move, my ass landed between his thighs and my legs slipped up over his hips. We sat there staring in each other's eyes; deep azure pools connecting with emerald green ones, the energy palpable between us.

The laughter and music drifting up the stairs didn't faze us; the striking scenery flying by our window didn't either. He kept his hands on my hips and I had mine hands slung over his shoulders, fingers entwined in his hair that flirted with his collar. It seemed at this moment like nothing could come between us. It truly felt like we were two parts of the same person… two parts that needed each other, but also two parts that threw us into discord.

I knew it was going to happen and was okay about it. When he pulled my hips sharply forward so my intimates pressed hotly against his, and his right thumb brushed over my lips, I felt no surprise. I rested my jaw and the side of my face in the palm of his hand and closed my eyes, while he adoringly caressed my lips with his thumb. I drew it into my mouth with my tongue and teased its tip with little nips and long languorous draws. The soft moan I elicited from him heated me through. He glided his moistened digit over my pouting bottom lip. It wasn't long before I felt a tension against my clit that hadn't been there before.

*Oh, sweet Jeezus, it always comes to this. What are we doing?*

Noah easily covered the mere inches that spanned us and brought our souls into alignment when he placed his heated lips on my own. It was hot; don't get me wrong, but also affable. It took the pace of two friends holding hands, taking an afternoon stroll in the park; pleasant, and oddly just what I needed. I now felt more relaxed and at one with myself. Admittedly, I was having an *extremely* hard time ignoring the substantial bulge in his pants that was pressing on my pussy, and the ache it was creating.

"You'd better move to the other side of the couch, beautiful, or I will *not* be responsible for what happens next." Noah warned in a voice filled with the same heat I was feeling. I sat a few seconds longer and dropped one of my hands from his neck onto his thigh.

"*Tessa*. Please," he said through clenched teeth, and I knew his restraint was waning.

*What's the worst that could happen? He could fuck me silly... Jeezus he'd ruin me for every other guy... again.*

I regretfully acquiesced by moving back to my side, afraid that if I didn't, we'd have THE most amazing sex of my life. Our souls would connect us on an even deeper level that we already were. I would surely be ruined after that.

As soon as I moved, Noah popped off the cushion like his ass was on fire. I watched him adjust himself, allowing his cock room to breathe by facing it up. The only problem with that was, when he adjusted his hard-on, so it stood vertically against his abdomen, the head popped out above the waist of his low-slung jeans. He caught me watching.

"I guess that's not going to work, is it?" He laughed awkwardly.

I couldn't knock the silly smirk off my face, "Nope, it sure won't." It was comical even if it sucked for him.

"I can think of a way you can help me get rid of it." Noah looked at me, cocking an eyebrow.

"Yeah. I bet you can." I laughed at his tempting invitation. Thankfully, he didn't know how tempting it was.

"Tessa, what the fuck am I gonna do with this thing? Last

time we made out—you know, last night? This little fucker didn't go away until about six this morning."

"No shit? That really sucks."

"Yeah, understatement of the year."

He walked over to me, his cock right in my face before he knelt down. "You know, we probably won't get another opportunity like this, and the things that I would do to *you* and for *you*. You just have NO idea. NONE." His voice sounded like liquid sex and I was a thirsty girl.

"Yeah, Noah. I *do* know; and don't you DARE ask me again, because it is taking every breath in my body not to fucking rip your cock out of your jeans and milk it with my mouth right now. I can imagine how large you would feel in my tight pussy. I know the response my body has to you; I am fucking drenched right now and just this one time with you wouldn't be enough. I fear I'd be devastated if you didn't come back to me. So, it's going to HAVE to wait. Wait until you pick me."

"Take a look at this." He drew the hem of his shirt, so I could see a bead of pre-cum dancing on the head of his cock before it slipped and rolled off, and a new bead appeared.

I closed my eyes, my mouth watered, and it was my turn to rub my palms over my face, trying to erase some of the sexual tension smothering me. When I opened my eyes, I nearly came right there. Noah had opened his fly and was working his fist slowly down the length of his incredibly handsome cock and back up to the head, over the top and rubbing the slick bead over its length again. My core instantly pulsed, and I felt a surge of juices flowing, as my pussy physically begged for Noah.

"Let. Me. See. You," he commanded with a labored breath, and I readily obeyed. I turned to face him on the couch and slid my ass to the edge of the cushion. I undid the button and fly, and he made short work of pulling my jeans off for me. When he saw my tiny, lacy G-string, he nearly lost it, and at the moan it ripped from his lips, so did I. His eyes locked onto mine, and he took his hand off his cock, moved between my legs and pulled the sheer barrier aside. The look of pure awe that shone in his eyes made me want to fuck him even more.

"You're so fucking sexy… your pussy… I had no idea you'd be bare."

The compliment made me feel even more desirable, perhaps the most I'd ever felt. He brought his eyes back up to mine, questioning… never taking without asking. My eyes fucked his, giving him the answer he was seeking, and his mouth lowered into my sex.

My head shot back in pure elation as his tongue made the first few laps through my tight gash. His lips and mouth took special care over my sensual bud, humming and suckling until I writhed beneath him. My hands fisted his hair, and I begged far louder than I should've, considering we were on a bus with four other people downstairs.

Noah didn't stop there. He inserted one, then two of his fingers into my mouth. I mouth fucked and blew them as if they were his cock, while watching him pump his steely rod.

Begrudgingly, he pulled them from my wanton lips and slid them both into my hungry cunt in such a way that his thumb could still tease circles around my clit. I was so fucking hot for him, all I wanted was him in me. I was so furious, so enraged he wasn't there yet, and so goddamn hot at the same time, that I couldn't think clearly. I wanted him in my mouth, in my cunt, fucking. I wanted so badly to taste him, feel him, that the void from not having him was unbearable.

I watched as his hand expertly worked me while his other

worked himself. When my eyes found his, they weren't focused on what he was doing, they were watching me. Watching me! His eyes bored into mine and sought my soul. I tried to look away but couldn't tear my gaze from the intense connection we had. I couldn't take it anymore, I just couldn't. It wasn't fair to either of us. I placed my hand on his, begging for it to still. Noah cocked his head and stopped his assault on my most intimate parts, but I wasn't done.

"I want you." My voice sounded small, shrill, and nearly incoherent. "Noah. I want you in me. Let me just feel you. Just once..." I repeated myself, so I could be sure he heard me, although from the sharp intake of breath he drew, he'd heard me the first time.

"Tessa, are you sure?" his voice rasped, raw from fighting to restrain himself. "I don't have a condom, and you..." I placed my finger on his lips to silence him. He had removed his hand from his cock, which now bounced on its own, waiting for more attention. He gingerly removed the last barrier I still wore, and he stood and removed the articles of clothing he still had on. I'd never seen him completely naked. I drank him in like an alcoholic on my final binge. I stripped off my top so that I sat on the edge of the loveseat in only my steel-blue lace Dolce & Gabbana bra.

"You're exquisite. Truly beautiful." Noah walked back over to me and knelt between my bent legs. His hungry cock rested against my smooth and fully bared sex. He wrapped his arms around my waist and ribcage, fully imprisoning me in his embrace as he nuzzled into my neck. He held me.

*God, start something, do something, get me going again before I change my mind!*

Somehow, he heard my thoughts, and thus it began. His lips

set my skin on fire with their riotous onslaught of suckling at my neck, collarbones and shoulders. He palmed my wet pussy, just holding it—but it drove me wild.

Before I could recover my senses, he launched his second assault. He unfastened my bra and his hot mouth caressed first one and then both lust-heavy breasts, while his right hand pumped himself before spreading me and coating his fingers with my juices. He spread me all over him, blending it with the pre-cum now weeping heavily from the head of his fully aroused and impressively hard erection. All I could do was bury my hand in his hair and grab onto his shoulder for dear life. I arched my back, pressing my tits into his sculpted chest, as his nipping and biting drove me even closer to the brink of no return.

"Let me taste you. I have…" my voice shook, sensations and emotions threatening to overtake me. "Let me taste you. I *have, HAVE*… let me taste. You." I begged. I know I wasn't making any sense. Hell, I could barely keep my wits about me, so many sensations had taken over.

"Fuck. Yes," he ground out.

That was all I needed. I slid off the couch on my knees and pushed Noah back onto the floor. I straddled his left leg as I drew his handsome member into my mouth like I had wanted to since I'd seen it last night. It was delightful; rigid and unyielding, chiseled and unrelenting. His cock tasted every bit as good as it looked. I was in heaven with him in my mouth and worked him from tip to root while I rode his thigh. Noah fisted my hair and watched me intently as I devoured him like I would a melting ice cream cone on a hot summer day. I just. Couldn't. Get. Enough.

"Stop," he growled lustily. He pulled gently on my hair,

arresting me from starting another wave of my attack—sucking and swirling. "Give me a minute."

My eyes met his and I could see his restraint wavering. His forehead furrowed in concentration. He gently tugged my hair before releasing it, indicating he wanted me against his abdomen. I rose off of his thigh to lie in between his legs. Before I could settle in, he issued his next command.

"Straddle me, beautiful."

I obeyed and straddled him so when I lay on him, his heavy cock aligned against my abdomen, incredibly hot and hard. My juices pooled at his root as my clit lay against his tight nut sack.

"Fuck, Noah. I want you in me. I want you. In me now. I need it." I barely recognized my own voice, it was laced with so much desperation. His hand went to my chin and lifted it, so our eyes met once again. His usually clear blue eyes had turned obsidian black with passion and desire, barely recognizable but absolutely sexy. Our eyes never left each other as I felt him reach down to check my readiness. There was no doubting my voracious need, nor my complete desire for him—I was so fucking wet. He lifted me by the hips, and I reached down and positioned his cock at my entrance.

"Are you sure? Just one feel, right?" The animalistic edge to his voice only fueled my fire more.

"Yes, I need to know," I managed to say before the anticipation silenced me.

I could feel his head teasingly graze my opening, a feeling so intense it was as frustrating as it was amazing. I pushed against his chest, straining to lower myself, but he held on to my hips, keeping me just out of reach from being able to envelop him wholly.

"Goddamn it, Noah! Please?"

The playful smile he beamed me made me want him all the more. "I'm all yours." The tension in his arms lessened, and I felt my knees catch my weight. I was in control! I placed one hand on his chest to steady myself, as I reached down and slid his rigid cock through my dripping wet pussy with the other. I started at my entrance and slid it all the way up to my most sensitive bud. I shuddered, and Noah emitted a guttural groan.

I dragged his fiercely sensitive helmet back through my softness until it lined up with my hungry little cunt and slowly, deliberately eased myself down his full length. It felt like I slid down it, and down it, and down it some more until I had swallowed him all the way—fully sheathed by my pussy's ravenous desire. I arched my back in ecstasy and I moaned in unison with Noah when he made the slightest rounding grind of his hips. He stilled.

*I knew it would feel this good; I fucking knew it! So incredibly big. Hard. Oh my God. Oh my...*

He sat up, settling even deeper into me, and interrupted my train of thought. Oh, how I wanted to move, but I reminded myself this was 'just a feel'. Noah's right hand buried itself in my hair at the nape of my neck. His left drew my back closer to him as it crossed to reach over and held my right shoulder pinned down. I was unable to rise up; wiggling was next to impossible and the look Noah gave me when I tried, suggested strongly that I stop. His right hand pulled my hair back and exposed my throat to his assault. Here, I was replete, unable to move, being driven even past the edge of sanity by his mouth. He kissed my mouth sensually, amorously, taking care that I first felt his passion before he roughly fucked my mouth with his tongue. He bit my neck, shoulder, and my breast hard enough that the pleasure mixed with the pain, creating an unfamiliar sensation that drove me even higher. My hands buried themselves in his hair, held his throat, as I caressed and gave back as much as I took. I moaned, he groaned, our souls joined. Still coupled, still just 'feeling', he hadn't moved, not even once since I had fully seated myself on him.

When he pulled back, I felt startled, puzzled. "Is everything okay?"

"Beautiful, I... This has to stop, or it's going to go further than you wanted. I can't... I'm so close, it's killing me."

"Just once more, please, Noah, just once more. I want you to take me this time."

With me still seated on him, he took the hand from my hair, wrapped it around my waist, and flipped me onto my back. He tossed my shapely calves up over his shoulders as he painstakingly withdrew himself from my stingy depths. He leaned over me and kissed me deeply, before bracing his hands on either side of my shoulders and pistoning into me so hard and passionately-rough that it took my breath away. He immediately pulled out.

"I want to see you, Tessa." it wasn't a command this time, but a plea. Noah had his fist around his cock, squeezing its head painfully hard and then slowly, *very* slowly slid it from its head to its root. He still had my wetness coating him. God, he looked so damn sexy on his knees before me, slowly stroking his cock. I reached down and spread my lips with one hand. Inserting two fingers, I began a lavish assault on my own clit while I pumped into myself. I writhed in elation as my climax built. I couldn't keep my eyes off Noah, watching his beautiful body draw taut as he worked his stout and steely rod.

"I want some..." He widened his knees enough so that his cock dropped to the same height as my pussy, and he slid it through my wetness before drawing back up onto his knees and pumping his tortured cock again.

I felt the waves building, and all I could think of was how he had felt in me, and how amazing he looked fist-fucking his cock in front of me with my pussy juices all over him. That's all it took. I squeaked out a small, "Come for me!"

Noah's eyes locked with mine until I had to shut them as I came hard, wave after tumultuous wave hitting me, sending me crashing over the edge. I lay shuddering, still orgasming as I heard Noah emit a throaty growl. I threw my eyes open, not wanting to miss his climax. He gave his cock a couple of final pumps, and even his growl fell short on his lips as his hips thrust forward and hot, thick ejaculate pumped out of his rigid length all over my stomach. He pumped himself a final time or two, squeezing the last of his crème from his cock's tip before he rocked back on his heels, sated and completely wasted. His peacefulness drew me, and I fought the urge to hold him. Getting up, he walked into the master bath and came back with tissue, so I could clean up enough to make it there myself.

I had just entered the bathroom and shut the door, when I heard a knock.

Noah stood there in all his glory, still fully erect, at my mercy.

I motioned toward the shower, "Want to rinse off?"

"Sure, that sounds wonderful. Want to turn it on?"

I knew we weren't supposed to be running the shower while Dax drove, but there was no way, now that he'd mentioned it, that I wasn't going to rise that smear off my belly.

Noah got in first and I joined him a half-second later. It was scorching hot, too hot at first, but also incredibly relaxing. We briskly soaped up and then stood there hugging in the water, half sleeping, half delirious from the intense orgasms we had shared.

"Tessa?"

"Mmm mm."

"You amaze me."

I laughed awkwardly at his compliment. "Thank you, Noah for respecting me, for not taking it farther than I wanted.

"Mmm… well, about that. You do know *that* was considered 'going all the way,' right? I mean, I don't care what you call it, but I was definitely making love to you, beautiful."

I just squeezed him. I wouldn't allow myself to let it feel that way. I still needed something left to give if he returned and chose me later.

"Well, whatever you want to call it," he winked at me, "it was fan-fucking-tastic. Just what I needed, and between you and me… what I've wanted to do since the first time we kissed."

I smacked his ass at his admission and kissed his shoulder. "Me too. Now rest. I am so incredibly tired."

We finished up, straightened the bathroom and sitting area, dressed and lay down to rest the couple of hours until we pulled onto the NAS Keflavik base.

"Hey you two… hey, wake up. We're here."

I groggily struggled to open my eyes.

"You *slept* the whole way?" Sammie mock scolded me while digging for info. "We're on base. Get up."

"Where are we?" I demanded, still feeling slow, like waking from a deep coma.

"We're here, outside the barracks. Get up!" Sammie held her

hand out to us. I patted Noah awake and helped him stand as they grabbed what little we had on the bus.

We got a half-asleep Noah up to my room and onto my bed. I hugged Kari and asked her to thank Dax for a great weekend before we shut the door. Sammie lay down next to Dirk as I shed my clothes, set the alarm for an hour before work, and climbed into bed next to Noah. His arms wrapped around me as he snuggled in close. I soaked it in, knowing this was if not the last, then very nearly the last time we'd ever lie like this again. I fell asleep craving the fulfillment I'd felt when his handsome cock had finally filled me to the brim.

# Chapter Twenty-Two

"Tessa! Get the fuck up… NOW!" Sammie whipped back my covers and pulled on my arm to get me up. I glanced at the clock and it showed we had ten minutes before the last shuttle that would get us to work on time. My feet hit the floor running. I raced down to the community bathroom and was back in less than five minutes. I threw on my wool socks, thermals and my coveralls, belted it and turned in the mirror.

*Ehh… Anyways.*

I whipped my unruly hair into a quick chignon and bobby-pinned the crazies that were sticking out here and there.

*Good. Done.*

I plopped down in the worn recliner with my flight deck boots and went to work lacing them up.

"Tess—let's go, are you ready?" Sammie popped her head in the room just long enough to toss her morning kit on the sink counter. I could see she already had her jacket on and looked ready to meet the bus.

I stood up, grabbed my FWJ and ball cap, slamming the door behind me.

*Oh Crap! I didn't even say goodbye to Noah. I wonder if he'll be there when I get off.*

I tossed this thought back as I dashed down the flights, two stairs at a time. We reached the bottom and threw open the BEQ doors, just as the shuttle bus was closing its door, a signal it was about to take off. We ran toward the bus and boarded it… Right. On. Time. I had a little pep to my step as I found my seat. Sammie plopped next to me.

"Boo-ya. BOOM—and that's how you do it!" I looked at her and threw her the 'West Coast' gang sign.

She laughed. "Did something happen last night? Why are you in such a good mood?" She nudged me with her elbow.

"Yeah, right. Noah was still comatose while we were getting ready with the lights on this morning. Nope, definitely not." I looked out the window at all the windsocks blowing fiercely horizontal, whipping from side to side. *Fucking great. Another wind-burn kind of day,* I thought miserably.

We had about a ten-minute ride to the hangar on a bus packed with a lot of people who had evidently partied hard and slept in until the last minute. The driver had on some Euro Club Mix, and the bass was pretty loud for this early in the morning. It made me think harder than I wanted to.

"So? This weekend; are you going to tell me anything?' Sammie feigned a pout, complete with sad puppy-dog eyes.

"Oh my God. I have absolutely no idea where to begin."

"Well, give me the abbreviated version… the good stuff, since we only have a few minutes."

I considered for a moment. *Not* that I'd actually entertained not telling her; I was ready to burst from an overload of hormones, emotions, sexual tension, and too much information too soon. It was tell Sammie or risk spontaneous human combustion.

*Good thing Sammie only gossips to me about others, not to others about me.*

I took a deep breath. "I've never connected to someone in my life the way I did with Noah at the Blue Lagoon. It felt like we'd known each other forever," I blurted.

Her jaw dropped. "That fast, eh? Wow. And here I thought you were just looking for a weekend hook-up, like with that Dane guy."

I frowned at her. "Do you want to hear my story or give me shit? Shut up."

She schooled her face into a false-serious expression that threatened to dissolve into laughter at any moment. *Good enough, I guess.*

"Anyway, while he might feel connected with me, and find me easy to talk to, it's complicated."

"That's what they always say," Sammie groused.

This time my scowl shut her up by itself. "So, if I may continue," I said primly. "He has an ex and a little girl—I think I've told you that part—but, the clincher is that he's never seen her." I talked fast over Sammie's gasp, filling in words before she could interject again. "His ex wants him back, wants to be a family, and he thought that was what he wanted, until he met me, and then… now… Shit, now we have all of these bullshit feelings involved, and he kissed me. Oh, God. That kiss." I shook my head. "I've never had a kiss like that in my life." Just remembering it made my body soften and moisten.

"Oh, Tessa, the look on your face. You want him bad, don't you? In spite of everything…" I nodded, opening my mouth to say something, as she interjected, "You still haven't gotten to the good stuff—the dare—you have to tell me about his junk. You could see it even in the dark by the fire, right?"

I laughed bitterly. "It may have been—no shit—the prettiest dick I had ever seen." *Too bad it's wrong of me to want—so badly—to taste it, feel it again.*

I could hear her sharp intake of breath at that little detail. Her humor faded into empathy. *That's a true friend for you. Juicy gossip, sure. But she actually cares. Thank God for Sammie.*

"The morning was truthfully amazing. We stayed up all night together talking and just… I don't know, just being."

She tilted her head to the side, looking puzzled. I don't think she really understood all the insanely deep feelings my soul had with his, apart from my actual feelings for him. In fact, I'm pretty sure, from the look on her face, that she thought I was plumb crazy… but, whatever.

She raised her eyebrow skeptically, looking deeply into my eyes—staring me down, actually.

"Seriously, it was magical."

"Sheesh—calm down, I'm just messin' with ya. What crawled up your ass and died?"

"Ugh. Sorry, Sam. It's just been a really emotional forty-eight hours. I've reached amazing heights and destructive lows… all this weekend."

As the hangar came into view, Sammie said, "So, I know we have no time, but what the fuck was wrong with you two yesterday morning? I mean, why'd he take off? Then, we could hear you fighting, then an hour later fucking. I mean, what was with all that?"

"Shit, you could hear us?" I knew my face showed my mortification. I mean, I knew we had been kind of loud, but the music was up, and they had been so rowdy that I just assumed they couldn't hear. "Well, you pretty much know what happened. The feelings behind our… whatever we have, well—they're complicated, to say the least."

The bus came to a stop, and shipmates stood and started filing off the bus into work. I glanced at my watch and saw we had only five minutes before morning muster and morning pass down began. We hurried forward, and I squeezed her arm as she headed in the opposite direction to the Line Shack while I hurried on to First Louie.

I showed up for muster and daily assignments just in time.

"Thank you, for joining us," Petty Officer Rodriguez nodded to me as she glanced at her watch, "just in time," she said with a smile and went back to checking me off on her muster list attached her clipboard.

"Night check had a slow night, so we didn't have to give any bodies for washes. We put people on extra head and passageway duty. That means," she looked directly at me, "Christy, your work was done for you. You're heading over to the morning cook line right now to help over there."

I shot her a questioning look, which she reciprocated with a genuine grin—one I don't think I'd ever seen.

*Does this mean maybe I'm finally moving up? Are my days waxing floors and polishing shitters over? Oh, please, Jesus. Let's hope so.*

Being on the line in the Geedunk meant most everyone I talked to was in a great mood. They were either getting coffee on a break or getting a snack to take back to their shops. In all instances, they were not working at that moment and their positive attitudes rubbed off on me.

"Hey, Christy, how the heck are ya?' I glanced up from the omelet I was gently loosening on the grill and saw Sage.

"Hey, Petty Officer Reeser, you look chipper this blustery morning!"

He laughed, "What? Trying to be Earnest Hemingway?"

"Yup, you know it!" I winked. "So, how was your weekend with all those college girls you guys met at the Lagoon?"

"Well, would you believe you don't have to be eighteen to attend college here? Apparently, you can get your first year of college out of the way while still in high school."

My eyes widened. "NO shit?" I lowered my voice, "So they were all underage?"

"Yeah. So, the jail-bait dropped us off at the gate and we had to walk on base at about 3 am."

"Wow, man, that really sucks. Hope the rest of the weekend went better."

"Ha! Not exactly. Our buddy Ensign Daniels…"

I interrupted, "Oh no! What did Ian do?"

Sage placed his hands on the counter and leaned in so that others would have a harder time making out what he had to say. "Well, we went out Saturday night and met some 'girls', if you know what I mean. By this morning, he couldn't keep his hands out of his pants and he's pissing fire."

For the second time, my eyes grew wide, "You mean he got…?"

Sage interrupted, "Shh… nobody knows 'cept me and the guys and his immediate supervisor. He had the duty van drop him at the infirmary this morning; he actually was on the flight schedule. This could turn out really bad for him if the wrong people find out."

"My lips are sealed."

He winked at me as I handed off his breakfast sandwich.

"Thanks, Tess—have a great day. I'll tell Ian you said *'fire'* is the new black."

I laughed. "Yeah, you go ahead and do that, and see if he ever talks to me again." Our laugher melded into the cacophony of the room as he departed with a nod in my direction and a familiar wave.

By this time, I had three omelets ready, plated them and called off the names on the tickets. I served five or six more aircrew and khakis before I saw another familiar face. "Hi, Ace, how's your morning going?"

"Good. Seen Sammie—I mean Anders anywhere?" His inquiry surprised me. I knew they were hanging out more and more at work, but also knew he probably didn't hold a candle to Trigg, and now Dirk. I had a funny feeling something strong had been kindled between Dirk and Sammie this weekend. Only time would tell, but...

"Have you checked out on the flight line? I know some birds were getting back. Maybe she's out recovering them?" He smiled as though considering what I said when our bud Lucas showed up.

"Get my egg sandwich?" he asked Ace, but I already knew he hadn't, so I threw on a slab of ham and cracked an egg for Lucas's order.

"Yup, it is almost ready." I winked at Ace.

THE BREAKFAST CROWD completely tapered off by 1000, and then it was time for a little break before lunch. Since I'd taken the orders, cooked them, and run the register—efficiently by myself—I'd earned a thirty-minute break before I had to be back for the lunch crowd.

I headed out to my secret chill spot; the Line Shack. I say secret, because only a few of us were actually privy to what happened out in the Line.

I walked into the Line and Sammie, wearing her yellow Line vest, greeted me with her usual, "What's up, hooka?"

I sarcastically stuck my tongue out as I plopped down on the green vinyl couch opposite the chair she was spinning side to side in. She and the line shack runt who was saddled with training her were the only ones there. I guess the others were hanging out in their respective future shops. That or the Geedunk.

"So, you gonna tell me what your and Noah's status is? I mean, where exactly do you stand?"

I looked over at the young airman. He must have been eighteen or nineteen but looked more like fourteen with his high and tight haircut, and acne. He was busy playing the air drums to whatever CD was in the player, so I doubted he was listening. Even still, I lowered my voice and said, "Okay Sam, so *what* EXACTLY are you wondering, since you keep bringing it up?"

She rolled her beat-up, dilapidated office chair right in front of me on the couch. "So, you guys did do it, didn't you? You have to tell me… I *bet* he was good as fuck, huh?"

I just smiled back knowingly.

"I knew it!"

"Shh… we didn't do *IT*, but I did let him slide in me for just a sec, so I could feel him."

She made the strangest face at me, "Uh, hoss… you do know THAT *is* considered fucking, right?"

"Well, technically, but not really since he pulled out before he came. I mean, yeah, I know, I know… but if we ever get the chance to actually do it, I intend for him to be in longer than for just the one pump I allowed him. Ya know what I mean?" I gave Sammie my 'serious' eyes.

"Well, if you want my opinion…" Our eyes shot over to the airman in the corner, who wasn't supposed to be listening, and answered in unison, "We don't!"

Sam, the airman and I laughed.

"Maintenance to Line, come in," the Maintenance Chief crackled over the radio.

"Rodger Maintenance, it's a go from Line Shack one." Sammie silently busted up, she loved this radio shit.

"We have bird 610 ready for recovery." He was calling out for a Line Captain to recover the P-3 that had already hit the deck.

"Rodger bird 610 ready for recovery. Where do you want to park her?"

I could hear some back and forth discussion over the radio in the maintenance office while they discussed the best place to pull her into. "Take spot A-04."

"Rodger parking pig 610 on spot A-04."

The radio com went dead and the airman, acting as captain and training Sam ran out the door first with his wands. Sammie grabbed her cranial and wands and quickly followed suit.

*Typical. When a call comes in, they have to fucking hustle, since they have fewer than sixty seconds to be geared up, out the door and beating pavement. They have to get in place to recover the birds as they taxi into their spots.*

Since their departure emptied the Line Shack, I made my way back to the 'Dunk' before my thirty-minute break ended. Still fighting the emotional hangover from the weekend, compounded by the lack of sleep, suddenly, I just felt… drained. I didn't want to deal with the lunch crowd; I didn't have the energy for keeping a fake smile on my face and making meaningless conversation with each new order.

"Petty Officer Rodriguez, I feel kinda shitty this morning. Headache, you know." I looked at her with half-lidded eyes and tightened my lips, imitating hangover nausea. "Can I go lie down in my shop for a bit?"

Thankfully, in spite of Roz's reputation as a hard-ass, she and I generally hit it off. She gave me a good once over, "Christy, make yourself scarce. If Chief sees you, he'll wonder why you aren't at your assignment, and I'll have to tell him I don't know where you went off to… so either suck it up and do your job or take my one get out of jail free card and hide in your shop for the day. I'm serious. Scoot."

If we hadn't been at work, and if she wasn't the epitome of a warden at a women's correction facility in the States, I would've hugged her. Truly. "Thanks, Petty Officer Roz."

"Go. I'll tell your shipmates that you have a migraine. Don't make me regret this."

I high-tailed it out of there, my head really beginning to hurt, and found my way to the AE shop. When I walked in, Stu was just carrying his toolbox in from a repair.

"Hey, Stuie, what's up?"

"Two birds down for us; one for power supply, the other main wheel well landing gear."

"Bummer. No wonder everyone's out. Where's Ari?"

"Signing off on the four-hour wire bundle repair I just made in the 'closet' of bird 36."

I nodded, understanding that Stu was probably in no mood to visit with me after having been in the confined space. Even someone small like me had to stand sideways, completely straight, or risk a substantial 12 volt DC shock from touching the walls of wiring on either side. The last time that I went on that repair, I came out drenched in sweat.

I sat down on the red vinyl couch, and Stu plopped down next to me, tossed his ear protection onto an unoccupied chair across from us and put his feet up on the toolbox he'd just carried in. His head hit the back of the couch and his eyes closed as he reached over and patted my leg.

"I heard you had a pretty rough weekend."

"Oh?"

*Shit, I had no idea news traveled so fast.*

"Yeah, I can't remember if it was Ari who heard it from AD2, or if it was from Airman Anders…"

My ears perked when I heard Sammie's name. *I'm so gonna kill her…*

"…but I heard you and that security guy Garren rode one hell of a roller coaster this weekend."

I opened my mouth to speak, but he continued. "Which, I have to say, was quite a surprise to me. You guys seemed pretty damn chummy to me… hell, to everyone at the Lagoon on Friday."

"Well shit, Stu. You know how that goes. Speaking of, what happened to your wild and crazy night with the college girls? You know, the ones that were what? Seventeen?" I started laughing, and he leaned over and pretended to kidney punch me.

AE1 Dunnmoth and my Division Officer, Lieutenant Kupps walked in at that instant. "Petty Officer Towers? Get out on bird 218 and help Petty Officer Cai."

"Sure thing, LT." Stu rolled his eyes at me, grabbed his box and headed back out into the hangar.

"So, Petty Officer Christy," …AE1 Dunnmoth paused, hanging my name out there flapping in the wind, while he kicked back in the old office chair and threw his feet up on the desk. Lt. Kupps casually took a seat beside his feet. "Seems your name has come up quite a bit as of late. Anything you care to discuss or share with us, just shipmate to shipmate? I can't speak for LT," he nodded to where he was sitting, "but I promise not to pull the ol' supervisor card on 'ya."

Lt. Kupps shifted so he faced me more directly, "Tim's right, this is not us coming to you as your superiors, but rather as friends—so *this time* you don't need to worry about what you tell us. It's behind closed doors, so to speak."

I shifted uncomfortably on the couch. If I had known getting away from the Geedunk would turn into an interrogation, I wouldn't have even tried to take off. It really sucked, because this was my ONE get out of jail free card, and now my shop supervisors were raking me over the coals.

"Petty Officer Dunnmoth," I began.

"Tim is fine for now," he interrupted me.

"Okay, Tim," I said, nervously glancing at LT, "I'm not too sure what you've heard, but I met Petty Officer Garren from base security Thursday dancing at the club. Ari, I mean Petty Officer Benson, invited Airman Anders and me on a day trip to the Blue Lagoon Friday morning, and Petty Officer Garren also came along. Long story short, everyone but Towers and Benson spent our three day weekend together off base," I paused, fearful that I may have let too much slip since I knew we weren't authorized to take any overnight off-base trips.

"Petty Officer Christy,"

I interrupted him, "Tessa please, Sir."

LT nodded, "Tessa, please—consider us friends—there's no

need to be concerned about repercussions from this lack of judgement, just don't let me find out if you take another overnighter," he smiled and motioned for me to continue.

"Sir, AE1, with regards to Garren, I cannot even tell you what's going on. Honestly, I'm surprised you're asking me about it, 'cause parts of it were fine; parts were great; and some parts of the weekend were really fucked up, but I cannot figure how it would make news back here at the squadron."

Tim gently rocked back and forth with his feet propped up. It seemed like forever until he addressed me. "Well. Hmmm, not too sure either why we've heard about it, but it would seem some of your fellow shop shipmates are concerned about the choices you are making. Not saying they're right or wrong, but something you should know—everyone makes everyone else their business on deployment."

Lieutenant interrupted, "Tessa, you want to make sure that when you make squadron 'news' it's in the best possible light, if you catch my drift."

"Petty Officer Dunnmoth," I lowered my voice and looked into LT's mismatched eyes, "I didn't even fuck anyone. I really can't figure why it's anyone's business anyhow."

LT shifted his position on the desk and continued to eyeball me, his mismatched eyes unnerving me, "It's not, but you're a young, attractive girl who is new to the squadron. To put it delicately, lots of eager eyes are on you, Christy. Lots of speculation surrounds you."

"Yes, "AE1 chimed in, "and I'm just saying, as a friend, and if you were my daughter I'd give you the same advice, watch your Ps and Qs. Take that as you will. It is *not* actually my place to tell you what to do, and if you file a grievance," he glanced up at our Division Officer who nodded in agreement, "we'll both deny this conversation happened. You don't have a lot of friends here, and you needed to hear some sound advice from someone who's not trying to get into your pants. Understood?"

I nodded. "Yes, Sir."

"Don't address me as sir; I work for a living." With that, he stood up, grabbed his mug and left.

My eyes followed Dunnmoth as he left the shop, then returned to look at LT. I'd seen him around plenty of times but hadn't noticed how striking he looked—I mean for a superior officer that is. I'd never even allowed myself to be intrigued by anyone in a pay grade that far from mine, and I didn't intend to start now… although it was altogether unsettling how he just sat there staring at me.

"Sir."

He stood up from his perch and took the two lithe strides to reach me. "Call me Tad."

It was my turn to eyeball him. I narrowed my eyes and cocked my right eyebrow, gunning him down with my piercing, emerald green eyes. "Sir. Thank you for your sound advice. I will take it into consideration, *Sir*."

I could've sworn I saw the corners of his mouth curve up the minutest amount before he headed towards the door. Stopping just short of it he turned, "Petty Officer Christy…"

"Lieutenant Kupps?"

"I look forward to seeing what you can do on this deployment—seeing what you're made of." With that, he turned back to the door, opened it and was gone.

I breathed a sigh of relief… *What the fuck was that about?*

Before the front door of the shop had closed behind Lieutenant Kupps, the hangar door opened. As luck would have it, Petty Officer Simone Cai, aka 'Bitch-Lady' sauntered in… talk about a revolving door!

"Don't you have work you should be doing?" Cai eyed me haughtily.

"I'm doing it, holding this couch down," I answered smugly before I laid my head back and closed my eyes.

"Don't get too comfortable, sweetheart. If I were you, I'd be doing damage control. Your reputation is going up in flames."

*Fucking Bitch. Just fuck off.* "Really? Hmm…What's that saying? Oh yeah! Isn't this the pot calling the kettle black? Maybe you should open your ears to what's being said about you, Petty Officer Cai." I held my 'snark' in check. In fact, I oozed syrupy sweetness, just so she couldn't file a complaint about how I'd addressed her. She was, after all, a pay grade above me and could claim insubordination if she really wanted to push the envelope. Before she could answer, AE2 Ari Benson walked in from the hangar.

"Hey, Christy! Taking a break?" He sat down next to me and patted my thigh. I opened my eyes, smiled wearily at him and motioned at Cai with my head, giving him an exaggerated roll of my eyes.

"Ah, Tessa, you crack me up."

"Petty Officer Christy," Cai addressed me, dripping with syrupy goo; she was always less of a cunt when others were around. "I'm sure your supervisor from the Geedunk is probably looking for you, since it's about lunch-time."

"Thanks, Cai, but she's released me for the day to the shop under Benson's supervision, so I can have him sign off some of my training cards." I looked at Ari. It was total bullshit, but that bitch needed to step off my shit. She got the hint and slammed out into the hangar.

"Tessa, you don't want to make an enemy out of her. She can, well, to put it nicely…"

Before he could continue I cut in, "Ari, there is no way to put it nicely. She's a bitch and is on a witch hunt directed squarely at yours truly."

He smiled. "Yup, pretty much where I was headed with that." We both laughed.

Ari and I sat in the shop for only twenty minutes or so before the shop started to fill up with AEs and ATs for lunch.

"Hey Stu, bring me some of that over will ya," Ari motioned over to the crock pot of nacho cheese and salsa goo that had been warming for the last ten minutes or so.

"Sure thing; so, after lunch, what do we have planned?" Stu asked while dishing up a heaping pile of nachos for Ari and himself. Ari shrugged. "Tessa, want some?"

"Nah, I just called out to the Line Shack. Sammie mentioned she has a huge order out there and needs me to help her chow it down."

Just then, the hangar door slammed open and the floodgates opened. AEs and the ATs who shared our shop crowded in, dumping their toolboxes and hearing protection, and stacking their parkas in a huge pile off in a corner. The many who took off through the squadron door towards the Geedunk flooded back in with their food. Pretty soon it got way too crowded for me; uncomfortably so, since I barely knew anyone on this shift except Stu, Dunnmoth and Ari.

I leaned over close, "Ari, it's gotten crazy crowded. I'm outta here." I accidentally brushed Ari's ear with my lips. He spun his head and those eyes, those damn green eyes of his… looked at me in surprise, warmly questioning. They pulled deeply at my heart.

*Jeezus, why'd I have to fall for a guy like Noah with all of his bullshit baggage? Ari's so damn sweet.*

I patted his leg and mouthed "Sorry."

He nodded slightly before quickly looking away and pulling his leg from under my hand. *There's my cue.* I tossed out my goodbyes to the shop and received a few from those who weren't stuffing their faces, before heading out the heavy hangar door.

On the way to the flight line, I couldn't get Cai and the conversation Ari and I had just had out of my head. It didn't help that I swear I saw her throw me the finger as I passed her on my way out there.

I threw the door to the Line Shack open, "Oh my fucking word! I cannot believe what a roaring bitch she is!" Several pairs of eyes, including Sammie's, turned and focused on me. I marched over to where Sammie sat and hopped up on the desk, planting my ass on the large desk-calendar and dived in for a loaded nacho chip.

"Her again?"

I just nodded, appreciating her discretion. I hadn't really even considered if the shack would be full.

"Just let it go. Pretty much everyone knows it. The only reason some don't agree right now is 'cause she's blowing them, but they will soon enough." Sammie winked and held out the plate of nachos for me to have another.

"Oooh, this sounds juicy!" Airman Butler, 'NayNay', as we called her, was another squadron ho. In fact, she probably took lessons from Petty Officer Cai. She checked in right before me but had already left a line of married men in her wake. Trash like her was the reason I didn't use names in the shack, that way nobody could say I said shit. Loose lips like hers sank ships.

"Trust me, Butler, it's never as exciting as it sounds. It's just the same old fucking drama." I smiled at her, faking sincerity. The last thing I wanted was more bitches like AE2 Simone Cai gunning for me.

"Bummer, and here I thought the afternoon was looking up!' She shone her pearly white, bleached teeth at me and tossed her bottle blonde, shoulder length bob. She was maybe 4'10" with at least a 'C' rack. Guys thought she was cute, and I mean I guess I could see that. However, her whole better-than-me attitude made me look at her more like an obnoxious little hobbit, what with her stocky build and piggish, upturned nose. But who was I to judge?

The afternoon dragged on. Several birds were down, and those needing repairs had been bumped from both the flight and wash schedules. The Line Shack basically had a vacation day. Sammie was out with her plane captain, working on getting her fuel tests signed off, but other than that, everyone just sat around. Kids in the shack played cards, some were dancing—albeit more jokingly than seriously—and two Linemen slept against the back wall where the vests and ear-protection hung.

The shop phone rang and, after a minute, someone I didn't recognize answered it. "VP1602 Line Shack, Airman Dodge." The airman looked around as though searching for something. "I'm not sure," was followed by some Uhh-huhs and oks. "Is there a Petty Officer Christy in here?"

I'd already been following the conversation from where I stood and walked to the desk, taking the phone, "Christy here."

"Hey Tessa, it's Ari."

I interrupted him, "Hey, sorry about earlier. I didn't mean to get that close."

There was a pause. "You need to get your butt to the shop ASAP... AE1 and I want to talk to you."

"What's it about? Did I do something wrong? Is it Cai?"

"No, no… Tess, just get over here, OK?"

"Rodger that. On my way." Before hanging up I quickly added, "Sorry again OK? We're good?"

"Sure, baby girl. Aren't we always *just* fine?"

The line went dead as Sammie breezed in. *Fuck!* I looked to Sammie. "Work calls, I'm outta here."

"Adios, hooka!" Sammie blew me a kiss as I passed her.

I leaned into the heavy flight line door. When I pushed it open, a blast of icy cold air hit me in the face. I had left my jacket somewhere… maybe in the 'Dunk' or AE shop, and I definitely regretted it. The Arctic air blew through my coveralls like tissue paper.

Racing through the cold, I entered the hangar and a blast of warm air from the powerful heaters they'd set up hit me in the face. *Thank God the heater's on. Hope it's on in the shop too…*

I pushed open the doors and, there sat Ari and Dunnmoth.

Ari spoke first. "Have a seat." He was smiling, so my trepidation subsided.

"What's up? Everything okay?" I looked from Ari to Tim and back to Ari.

Dunnmoth began. "Christy, we have a squadron NATO detachment coming up, and Ari suggested you as his second for this one."

I looked at Dunnmoth, "Really? Why would I get to go? I'm not even in the shop yet."

"Well, we discussed it with your First Louie chief, and it would appear you're being transferred to the Line Shack soon. We made the argument that since First Louie and the Line Shack are both pretty well staffed, now would be the perfect time for you to get some shop sign-offs; plus, we aim to get everyone on at least one detachment per deployment. As luck would have it, Petty Officer Benson here suggested that since you guys work well together, you should be his worker on the det. to Turkey next week.

I looked at Ari and back to Tim. "I don't know what to say. That's fucking awesome!" I stood up and did my silly little happy dance. They both laughed with me. I ran out of the shop and out to the Line Shack to share with Sammie, thinking as I went that today had turned into a pretty fantastic day.

The shitty thing was that the only person other than her I wanted to share it with was MIA. I hadn't heard from Noah yet today—not that I exactly expected him to call me at work—but it was still a rough pill to swallow after everything that had happened over the weekend. I knew we weren't anything official, but felt we had become so much… *What a fucking mess.*

# Chapter Twenty-Three

"Tess?" Sammie popped her head through our open barrack-bedroom door. "Ace and Lucas are pulling out the lasagna."

"Thanks." I could actually hear them down the hall in our floor's public kitchen, shooting the shit with someone while they cooked.

"Hey, what's with you?"

I looked over at Sammie, now leaning against our door jamb. "I don't know. It's been almost a week, and I thought I'd have heard from Noah by now, that's all."

"Why? I mean, seriously? Isn't he taking off to go see his baby mama anyway?"

I shrugged, knowing full well she was right, but after the way I'd left him lying in my bed the morning after our road trip, and my 'just a feel' on the way home in the bus… I'd thought I would at least find a note when I got home from work, or a call or… *something* in the past week.

"Hey, Tess, dinner is done… they're waiting. Let's go."

I grabbed the key and pulled our door closed, heading into

the kitchen. Dirk stood there, as did Noah. I pulled up short, blinking in surprise.

I made a quiet croaking sound, cleared my throat and said, "Hey, guys," to Ace and Lucas. They nodded their hellos as they filled up our paper plates with food. Dirk smiled and greeted me. Noah just stood there drinking a beer.

*Why the fuck is he being so weird? Why am I?*

I walked up to Noah and gave him a friendly nudge with my shoulder as I looked him up and down. He was still fine as ever; my heart skipped a beat just being next to him. He wore a plain black t-shirt tucked loosely into the front of his dark and perfectly distressed jeans. He had finger-combed his hair, and a five o'clock shadow had formed on his jawline. He looked like a model for Hugo Boss. He stood there brooding, his arms crossed, holding his beer and leaning against the counter. I waited a second longer as he ignored me, and then touched his arm. "Noah?"

He pushed off the counter and set his beer down beside me. "Hey, Dirk, not really up for this. Sorry, man, but I'll catch you later." He addressed the room with a "Later." His eyes drifted to mine briefly, and then he was gone.

That was it.

I grabbed my plate and sat down, stunned, trance-like.

*What is it with me and guys? Is there something wrong with me? Did I do something the last time we were together? Maybe he's upset that I left for work Monday morning without waking him to say goodbye?*

"Tessa?" I looked up, surprised to see Dirk addressing me. I didn't respond for fear my voice would crack and I would start crying. I just shoved a large bite of Stouffer's Lasagna in my mouth.

"Tessa, don't give it another thought… about Noah, I mean."

I looked back up at him and cocked my head ever so slightly, encouraging him to go on. In spite of losing my appetite, I forced myself to take another small bite, hoping he wouldn't expect me to talk. "He's been talking to that Vi chick every day. Got his tickets earlier this week and leaves tomorrow."

I nodded.

"He's been a bear to live with… if that helps you feel any better."

I shook my head, trying to keep my eyes from watering. I didn't want him to report that I'd been crying.

"I just…" I cleared the frog from my throat. "Fuck, I just thought we were at least friends, that's all." I took another bite. *Thank God for lasagna.*

He nodded. "Let him work through this. She's really fucking with his head. So is everything that happened last weekend." He looked me in the eyes with a seriousness that conveyed he'd been informed of what transpired between us; then he looked to Sammie.

"Fuck, won't someone clue us in?" Ace blurted, and Lucas tossed his fork on his emptied plate.

"Boy, this was a fun dinner." Lucas stood to clean up and tossed his dish in the trash. He then grabbed a beer and sat down heavily.

"Seriously, Lucas?" I looked over at Ace, then Dirk, "Where do I even begin?" I laid my fork down on my half-eaten, unappetizing pile of food and took a long draw from my beer.

"If that guy from the club did anything to you…" Ace looked over at Lucas.

"If that guy did anything, you'd better let us know, cause it'll be the last time that fucker gets away with it." Lucas seethed.

"Hey, guys, you're jumping to conclusions. Noah's not even here to defend himself," Dirk proffered reasonably, taking a long slug from his beer.

"Tessa, you can start wherever you feel you want to share, or you could start with how the story ends... how you guys, well... you know, and then how he's now leaving?" Sammie offered. A kind gesture, but it irritated me that she advertised sex was involved in Noah's and my relationship... when I didn't even feel it was.

"Gee, thanks for that, Sam. Glad my secrets are safe with you. Besides, it wasn't even *sex*, sex." I rolled my eyes.

"Never mind, so long as it was consensual... I got the gist and don't care much for drama anyways." Lucas stood up, gave Ace a pat on the back, bent over to administer a friendly kiss on the top of my head, waved to Dirk and Sammie, and then disappeared out the door to his room downstairs.

I shouted, "Thanks for dinner," after him, but who knows if he heard.

Ace spoke first, "So... your weekend sounds pretty trying, huh?"

I looked up from the plate of food that I'd made an even bigger mess out of—by pushing it around with my fork incessantly. "Yeah." I sighed heavily. "You have no idea."

"Come on now, it wasn't *all* bad was it?" Dirk had his hand under the table, probably on Sammie's thigh, as he was grinning at her like a fool.

"I didn't say it was bad, but for sure it was an all-around overload—too much food, too much drinking, too much emotion, too many questions—just too much of everything." My shoulders slumped. I looked at Ace, then at Dirk and Sammie. "Why'd he leave like that? *Fuck*, Dirk! Why'd he leave me all week wondering what the fuck was going on? Don't I mean more to him than that?"

"I can tell you this, Tess: FUCK HIM! You deserve better than that, and for any guy to not see what Lucas, Ari and I see… well, fuck. They're just not worth your time." Ace paused, getting his anger under control. "Tess, you deserve better than *some guy* who's only goal was to exploit you and then toss you aside after the weekend's over. But that's just my two cents." He shrugged—almost apologetically.

Dirk's eyes caught mine, and I could tell it was taking all he had not to defend Noah to Ace—it seemed we were both in agreement that it wasn't what Ace assumed it was—but only time would tell.

With such *pleasant* conversation, I wasn't too surprised that our casual dinner party barely lasted another ten minutes.

"So, Tessa…" Sammie spoke as she and Ace stood up with their plates. "I'm gonna head back to Lucas and Ace's room and watch a movie. See ya in a bit?"

"Yeah sure, no problem. I know I am not much company right now anyways."

She smiled at Dirk and winked. He flashed her a gorgeous smile before they took off. I smiled awkwardly across the table at Dirk… can you say uncomfortable?

"So… what are you up to this weekend?" I mean what the hell else was I supposed to talk to him about?

"I have duty. Actually, Noah took this weekend off as part of his leave, since he flies out tomorrow around noon. Tonight is pretty much the only time we'll get to hang out; besides, I'm on the schedule for gate duty Saturday and Sunday nights, 2230-0630 anyhow."

"Mid-check, huh? How'd you get so lucky?" I asked,

thinking back to when I'd worked those hours in Puerto Rico. *Mid-check can be hard on some people, especially the really social ones, since life's pretty much shut down when they're up, and happening when they're sleeping.*

"It's not so bad, especially on weekends. That's when all the drunkards come through the gate. It keeps duty from being boring." He laughed. "Boy, the stories I could tell you."

I laughed. It felt good. "I know, huh? Like last weekend when Ian, Stu, Ari… all of them got dropped off by those underage chicks. I bet that made for a little fun harassment at the gate when they all had to *walk* through." I chuckled at the visual. "I'm just glad they had enough wits about them to ditch the chicks before they'd had more than a couple of beers."

"Yeah, no kidding." I was watching Dirk; he had a fair amount of charm. He was no Dax or Noah, but I could see what drew Sammie to him.

"So, I was wondering…"

"Uh oh." He laughed nervously.

"What's up with you and Sammie? She's been totally tight-lipped, I mean with the details between you two. So, what gives?"

"Who's asking? You or her?" He joked.

I shrugged, "I'm just curious, I guess."

"I dunno. We're just, well… whatever we are. We're all about keeping it easy and fun. No reason to get serious so soon." His eyes caught mine and he looked uncomfortable.

"Yeah, but I mean, you guys got pretty serious when you checked into the bunk-bed motel last weekend… *all* weekend. I mean, every time someone asked where either of you were, you were in there together."

He shrugged and laughed it off. "Why? Is Sam wondering what's up?"

"Nope. Hasn't really talked about you, actually," I commented. I figured I'd make him squirm a little; you know… having a guy a little jealous is *not* a terrible thing.

"Yeah, so why's she down there with what's his name, when I came over for dinner? You guys hang out with them a lot?"

"Almost every night, ya know, dinner and a movie and stuff." I shrugged. "I have no idea what she's up to. Maybe you should ask her or go find her. Lucas is married though, so I wouldn't worry about him."

"That's the one that she left with, then?" He watched me intently.

"Nope, that was Ace, and he's single." *Serves ya right. What's with guys not giving a shit unless another guy does?*

"What floor did she say she was going to?"

I chuckled. "Second… their door is usually open." As he stood to leave, I did too. "Hey, Dirk, say hi to Noah for me when you get a chance, okay?"

He looked back over his shoulder and said, "Sure thing."

I cleaned up the rest of the kitchen and took it upon myself to put away the last of the clean dishes my shipmates had left drying in the rack. My thoughts took me to what Dirk had said about Noah. I began having second thoughts about inciting issues between him and Sammie. Hopefully, she didn't find out I got his bees stirred, and that's why he showed up downstairs, assuming he actually found Ace's room. I left the kitchen and found myself in front of my door, which stood slightly ajar.

*That's weird. Sam must have gone back in and left it open.*

The interior was dark with the blackout curtains drawn, so I didn't notice the form on my bed.

"Tessa?"

I jumped, and a startled scream slipped out. "Who is…" I strained to see into the darkness. "Is that you, Noah? How'd you get in here?"

*What? Not only is he totally absorbed with his own life right now, but he does some breaking and entering on the side? Boy, I sure know how to pick 'em.*

"Do you have duty this weekend?" He propped himself up on his elbows, waiting for an answer. He watched me, training his intense stalker eyes on me.

"What are you doing here?" I demanded, my irritation thick enough to cut with a knife.

"What? No kiss?" Sarcasm oozed out of his perfect mouth.

I turned on the small lamp by our Blue Beast, barely rendering him visible.

He slid off the bed and moved with the ferocity of a wild beast about to take down his kill. I felt hunted, and I shivered with anticipation. I found myself backing away from him, until I reached the door. I could retreat no farther. In four lithe strides, he reached me, trapping me against the wooden structure with his body. He caught my wrists and pinned them, crossing them above my head with his strong, expert ones. I was his hostage.

*Oh, my God. He smells so good, feels so good. What is wrong with me? He's ignored me for a week! He's chosen Vi! I can't forgive him.*

He slid his free hand down my ribcage to my waist, and then lower to cup my ass.

*Oh. My. God…yes!*

*Who is this guy? Where did this animal come from?*

"Tessa, I can't go without saying goodbye." His desperate mouth descended on mine, full of intense passion to which I gladly opened. I struggled to free my hands. I wanted them in his hair, around his neck. I wanted to feel him, but he kept them locked above my head. His hand snaked around my waist and lifted me, so I rested on his hips against the door, allowing him to control our kiss as he tipped my head back and brought his free hand to my jaw. I liked how he took charge and responded by ravishing his thumb when he teased my lip with its tip. This drew a low, desire-laden hiss from him.

His mouth then continued its expert exploration of mine. My body vibrated with awareness, and my soul hummed in its proximity to his. *He's so bad for me, he's good.* I didn't want to overthink Noah and me, so I just let him dominate us.

"Why, Tessa? Why?" Noah growled out a gravelly plea; one that fell short, one I wouldn't even bother trying to answer.

I could've just as easily asked him the same question, but didn't want to waste my breath or interrupt the electricity sparking between us. When he moved his hand from my wrist and entwined it in the hair at the nape of my neck, pulling on it and driving me madder, I fisted *his* hair and caressed his face and neck. I felt like I couldn't touch him enough, couldn't taste him enough.

"I want… God, Tessa, I. Want. You." Noah's voice took on a different tone; higher, bordering on panic.

"Shhh, Noah. You have me."

That was all he needed to hear. He pulled me from the door, still holding me up with his hand under my ass as he strode deliberately to my bed. He placed his knee on it and laid me down. His body, rigid with restraint, towered over mine. My eyes caught his; jade and sapphire meeting and clashing. He brought his mouth, at last, gently to mine. The soft graze of his lips sent tingling traces down my spine.

"I've missed you this week. I've missed this. Man, beautiful, I'm going to miss you." The heartbreak in his voice devastated me to my core.

*How could I care so much for a man, feel so entwined with him, after such a short time? I'll tell you how; my soul is a traitorous bastard, not even checking in with my common sense for its input.*

Noah shifted off me and lay at my side, our energies still connected, but his no longer felt predatory. I turned toward him, entwining my legs with his, snuggling my hips into the rigid length that begged for my attention. I bit my lip and held back the desire to take it out and move things further. He brought his arms around me, and I felt the sincerity in this gesture, in his touch.

"I fly out tomorrow morning."

"I fly out Monday, for Turkey."

"It's going to be a long flight, having you on my mind the whole time." He cleared his throat, his discomfort palpable.

"I hope it will be an even longer *trip*, having me on your mind." I sighed.

Noah shifted uncomfortably.

"That's not going to happen, is it? Once you get there, I'll become a faded memory and you'll have found your family with Vi and Suri." I sighed again, more quietly, but continued. "I really am glad we've known each other, even for as short as it's been."

"Tessa," he began and stopped just as suddenly. He went still, and then cleared the emotion from his throat before he started again, "You will *never* be a faded memory. I can't explain what you do to me, or rather—how do I say this without sounding completely crazy—your *soul* completes me in ways I can't even understand. I can't ever forget you. My soul hungers for you, even if my mind and heart are at odds with it." Noah stopped, realizing he just admitted that his mind didn't think we should be together, and his heart loved another more.

I had no more words, and neither did he. We lay in each other's arms until we comfortably dozed off.

We were rudely blasted from our sleep when a party arrived in my room and the lights blared on. I glanced at the clock that hung above my bed: 0119. *Fucking great.*

"Whoa, buddy!" Sammie greeted, slurring her words.

I shifted just enough so I could see her, Kari, Ari, and Dirk, all holding beers. In fact, Ari had a mini cooler with him and confidently strode over to my bed. He ignored Noah's hand on my ass, as he grabbed my hip and pulled, rolling me out of Noah's embrace. My upper body budged, my lower did not. Noah's strong thighs held my legs captive, and his hand still draped over my hip and ass in a controlling clutch. Apparently, Noah didn't want me going anywhere.

"Why don't you join us, baby girl? Come have a beer?"

"Ari, I just woke up," I said, sounding more irritated than I intended, but he did interrupt my last night with Noah for Christ's sake.

"Okay, we just swung by to grab you. We figured you were here alone, and there's always time to sleep later."

"Yup, I'm on it."

Noah acted like he was still sleeping, though there was no way he could've been with all the noise. Moving his hand, I sat up, swinging my legs over the edge of my bed. I took in the chaos around me; Sammie and Dirk were sucking face, Ari had Kari on his back as they headed to the door.

"Kari, when'd you get back?"

"Today. Come on, I have to tell you all about it!" She motioned for me to follow as they disappeared into the hallway. They were being pretty loud for as late as it was. Sometimes, I had to remind Kari and Sammie that this was like an apartment building, not a frat house, and that people *did* occasionally sleep here. This time, however, Sammie was off the hook… she was too connected at the face to be the one making all the noise.

Noah reached up and rubbed my back under my thin t-shirt. "Are you going with them?" It startled me, and instead of it feeling wonderful, it gave me goosebumps—the weird kind. My mind immediately leapt to our exchange against the door earlier. My body responded to the memories, working my mind into a state of confusion. *My body responded to the memories of us together, and yet, it was slightly repulsed, like the wrong end of a magnet by the same touch just a minute ago. How strange. A defense mechanism maybe…*

"Hey, hooka!? Are you and Noah coming?" *Looks like Sam finally came up for air.*

I shrugged Noah's hand off my back and stood up. "Going where?"

"Ran into Trigg and Ketts, and they're having a party at their place off base tonight. They're waiting for us downstairs. We figured you should come; you know, have a good weekend before the shit hits the fan next week." She motioned her head in Noah's direction, where he now leaned against the bed with his arms crossed.

"Oh, is that all I am? Next week's shit?" He asked it sarcastically, but it came off sounding pissy instead.

Dirk laughed. "Dude, if the shoe fits…" He gave Noah the peace out sign.

I walked past Dirk, grabbed Sammie by the elbow and led her into the hall.

"Are you really taking Dirk over to Trigg's? Isn't that a conflict of interest, so to speak?"

"Nah, Trigg and Ketts were hanging out in Ace's room when I got there. Then, thanks to you, Dirk showed up, and everyone actually hit it off really well."

"Yeah, well, why shouldn't they? They have the same taste in chicks—*you*." Under my breath, I added, "…and all your intimate parts in common."

Sammie gave me a look of total disdain. She slapped my arm. "Hey, just cause I'm gettin' some and everybody's cool with it, doesn't mean you have to rain on my parade."

"I wasn't trying to start shit, but I wanted to point out the totally obvious in case later tonight you say you wish someone had told you. That's all."

"Well, in that case. Thanks, *Mom*." She took my hand and pulled me back into our room.

Dirk was facing Noah as they talked quietly. Noah glanced up when we entered and motioned to Dirk with his eyes. Dirk took a step back and said in a louder voice, "Awesome, then. All set ladies? Noah's coming too."

I looked at the clock and wondered just how long Noah had before he had to leave. Shrugging, trying to put it out of my mind, I started to primp in the mirror for whatever the next few hours had in store for me.

# Chapter Twenty-Four

We took a taxi van from the BEQ to the gate, where we said goodbye to the driver. There was no reason to take it off base; it would've just cost us some of our valuable beer money, and the walk to Trigg and Ketts's place was short.

"Hey, fuckers!" Dirk and Noah addressed some of their shipmates, who were guarding the gate.

"Look at the shitbirds the wind blew in!"

A couple of the duty gate guards walked over and slapped the two of them on the back. I could hear them bitching and moaning that they wished they could join us at the party. The testosterone was so thick you could cut it.

Sam, Kari, Ari and I were tired of the bullshit the security guys were stirring up. It seemed like they were all a little too amped up on testosterone for our liking. The four of us passed through the gate and started off, trailing behind Trigg and Ketts.

Ari spoke up first. "So, baby girl, what's up with you and Noah? I'm a little confused. Is it on again or off?"

I shrugged and glanced up at him in spite of the stiff wind that was whipping the frigid Arctic air across my already chapped lips. Trigg and Ketts had fallen back, walking with us in a tight group. They seemed especially interested in what I had to say.

"Yeah, you know… it's the weirdest thing. There was all this like heady sexual tension tonight; then we fell asleep. ASLEEP, asleep… like *nothing* happened asleep."

Ari cut me off. "Tessa, really? Is there any other kind of sleep?"

Everyone laughed at my expense, but I knew what he meant. I just wanted them to know NOTHING had happened tonight.

"So, smart ass," I lowered my voice and directed my comment towards Ari, "when you guys came in and woke us up, it was, I don't know, somehow… different."

Ari came in even closer, basically hip to hip; he looked over his shoulder. Noah and Dirk had left the base and were gaining on us. I considered the circumstances and left it at that. I didn't get into it any deeper with Ari about why a switch had been turned off in me. It was too damn cold, my voice would've been carried off anyways, and the guys were like, right there. Ari's closeness comforted me, and we all put our heads down and dug into the stiff wind.

*Why was it so different with Noah? I'd been so into him… like REALLY into him. Oh my God, how that boy can kiss… Even on the bed, I'd wanted him to hold me. So why then? Why did he give me the heebie-jeebies when he touched me? What flipped the switch? Better question,* I thought to myself, *is will the switch get flipped back?*

Ari bumped into me, and I made out his smile in the dim moonlight. "We're going to have fun on det., aren't we?"

I smiled and nodded in agreement. *Just so long as he gets that this is a Squadron work detachment, NOT a working Tessa det.*

Dirk and Noah caught up to us right as we reached the guys' house. There was no mistaking the party going on inside. Loud music pounded, a few cars clustered around the front, and from what I could see through the windows, quite a few people gathered inside. We couldn't make out if it was anyone we knew, since they had the red lights on, but at least it was a 'happening' party. *Nothing worse than getting all dressed up, doing your hair and make-up, getting somewhere, and then it being a small, dead gathering.*

When we got to the door, it was locked. Trigg pounded on it and when it opened, my jaw hit the ground. Dane. Stood. There.

Boom. In my face.

"'Ey, Tessa."

Noah put his arm around my waist as we walked in.

*Jeezus, why tonight? Drama free. Drama Free. DRAMA FREE, PLEASE.*

This thought ran through my head about a million times in the few seconds it took for Dane to notice Noah's arm draped possessively around me. He raised an eyebrow, looked at me, back at Noah and paid it no mind. "'Ey, *sæta mín.* 'Ye are looking hrífandi, absolutely stunning 'ey."

Noah backed off a bit. Dane came in for a European kiss, one on each cheek, and a tight hug.

"You're looking pretty damn good yourself. What's it been, nearly two months?"

Dane smiled. Ari hadn't moved. In fact, it was as though everyone were waiting for an invitation—everyone except Trigg and Ketts. They had long disappeared, presumably into their kitchen to get drinks. Everyone else stood there rooted to the spot, right inside the door.

"'Ey, Tess, tell 'ye mates to make themselves at home."

I looked around the group. "Well, you heard Dane. Make yourselves comfortable." I took off in the direction of the kitchen, hopefully to find a *STIFF* drink.

*Jeez, who thought this was a good idea? I'll have to remember to kill Sammie!*

I felt someone grab my arm, and it spun me around. I found myself staring right into Noah's chest. "What the fuck was that all about?"

My eyes narrowed as I took a step back. "Dane and I are friends."

"Sure looked like you were a hell of a lot more than that."

I REALLY disliked his tone. *What right do you have to go all possessive on me now, asshole?* "Keep your voice down; so what if we *were*? So WHAT?"

"Are you fucking serious right now?" Noah shoved his fists into his low-slung jeans and raked me over with his intense, stalker eyes.

It bothered the hell out of me. I couldn't believe Noah had the audacity to act like I was in the wrong. I was *not* having any of that. I grabbed his arm and jerked him into a side hallway.

"How the *fuck* do you get off asking me… no, telling me that I'm doing something wrong by saying hi to a friend?"

"It looked like it was a helluva lot more than a friendly hi to me."

"So, what if it was?" I hissed. "Noah, we've been over this fifty fucking times, if not a hundred. Yes, I feel something for you. Yes, you feel something for me. No, it's not going to work because I am not your priority and I won't be your second string girl. End of story." I went to push past him, but he caught my arm.

"Tessa, you fucked him, didn't you?"

I rolled my eyes and followed the tip of my boot as I smoothed an invisible wrinkle out of the throw rug. Looking up, I saw the lightest blue I think I had ever seen his eyes—even in the red light.

"Yes."

"You and him? Was it the same as with us?"

"Noah, we haven't even…"

He cut me off right there. "The hell we haven't. I was in you and goddamn it, you were around me; we were intimate, damn it!" His voice sounded pained.

I cleared my throat. "I'm not doing this, not now. This is neither the time nor the place."

Noah took my arm and pulled me from the hallway into a dark bedroom. A small fish tank provided the only light. He pushed the door shut and backed me up against it. His mouth came down on mine possessively, wantonly, insistent and borderline callous. His hands roamed over my ribs, up my breasts to my neck. He buried one in the hair at the nape of my neck, the other at my jaw, on my lips, touching… feeling as though he weren't sure if I were real. He kissed me deeply, tasting me, making a memory.

Between our kisses, I grasped for the words I wanted to say. "*Noah*, I can't do this. I'm really mad at you."

He tore his lips from mine; our connection immediately lost. Even though I wasn't 'feeling' it, my soul was recharging off the energy we created when we were together.

"You didn't answer my question."

I sighed and pushed him back a little, so I had some breathing room. "What's your question? I'll answer any you have, because after this weekend, you probably won't care what I have to say anyways."

Noah just shook his head. "You really think that, don't you? That even when Vi and I get back together, I won't think of you, I won't *feel* the need to be with you. I guess that's why I need to know about that half-wit Icelander. What's his name?"

"It's Dane. He's not a half-wit, and don't be cruel. You don't want me to get started on Vi." I shifted uncomfortably again. *OHHH trust me, you don't want me to get started on her…*

"You said you'd answer my questions. So, why the fuck won't you kiss me back? Don't you feel like you need to? Like your soul's alive when we kiss?"

I placed my forehead heavily on his chest. "You really want to hear this? My feelings and take on it?" My voice wavered. I drew in a long, slow, shaky breath before exhaling in a rush. "Noah, I am one hundred different kinds of mixed up—pissed off, frustrated, intrigued, confused, hurt, into you, over you, heated by you and repulsed by you."

I felt my words take the wind out of his sails; his shoulders fell and his chest, where my forehead still rested, deflated.

Finally, I looked up. "To answer your question; no, it's not like what Dane and I had. He and I had *easy*. We had incredibly hot, passionate, mind-blowing sex together. Then it was over, and we haven't talked for nearly eight weeks. He left, he's back, and it seems we're still friendly, but that's not the point. The point is that it was easy. It was exactly what it appeared to be; nothing less, nothing more. We liked one another, we liked sex with each other and that was it. When I felt drawn to him, it was purely physical, albeit strong and crazy; but it was a surface attraction. I didn't even know there were different ways of being attracted to someone until I met you."

I faltered, dragging in a labored breath of air as though it were my last, before speaking again. "My attraction to you is *difficult*, to say the least." I shook my head, not wanting to go on.

*Why do this before he leaves, before I leave for Turkey?*

*God, why can't this ever be EASY with you?* Tired of trying to make sense where none could be found, I sat down on the back of the sofa that created a sitting area in the room.

"Difficult, how so?" His soft, comforting voice made me want to open up to him.

"I knew from the beginning, or shortly thereafter, that you loved someone or rather two someones. Every cell in my brain has warned me against you, giving me every reason, telling me every step of the way not to call you, see you, kiss you or be with you, and every logical reason begins with Vi and ends with Suri. But goddamn it, every fiber of my being, every weightless ounce of my soul is drawn to you, and I cannot fathom why, especially since I knew it was over between you and me right when it started."

Noah strode deliberately to me, pulling me toward him. I found great comfort in his warmth and strength—but I obstinately pushed away.

"See? That's exactly, EXACTLY what I am talking about. I genuinely despise that you have me in here right now instead of out at the party, and I hate that you chose right now to do this instead of somewhere more private, but when you touch me or get within three feet of me, I succumb to you—*Every. Fucking. Time.* And, in case you can't tell, this mixed bag of bullshit emotions and torn feelings is NOT *easy.* It's *not* Dane. I'm not someone I want to be when I'm around you. I wonder how my spirit can yearn for someone so completely wrong for me." I ran my hands over my face and kept them there, shaking my head. I just kept coming back to the thought… *How could someone so wrong for me feel so right?*

"Tessa? I don't even know what to say."

"Don't say anything. Not five minutes ago I heard you say *when* you and Vi get back together, not *if* you get back together. So, just to make things clear—fuck what my soul is feeling toward you and has felt for you… *since forever*. Screw what you said under the stars about our attraction being some cosmic draw that is deeper than even we understand. I am trying to be as kind as I can, but still be clear when I say to you that we are O-VER. I have no room in my life for someone who has no room for me."

Noah stepped away from me like I had burned him. He had scorched me this past week, and I was ready for some healing by means of, Dr. Jack and his nurse, Coke. I opened the door, but he caught it before I went through.

"Beautiful…"

I angrily cut him off, "DON'T… just, *don't* call me that."

He sighed deeply, "Tess, I'm sorry for… everything." He shrugged lamely.

"Yeah, me too." I looked up and gave Noah the most genuine smile I could muster. "Have a good trip. I really mean it when I say you deserve someone great."

I didn't stick around to see what he'd say, and I sure as hell didn't want to get emotional, so before the room closed in on me, I stepped into the hallway, and right into Dane.

*Can't a girl get a damn break?!*

"'Ey, Tess. 'Ey was looking for 'ye. 'Ey thought all of 'ye left." Thank God for small miracles, Dane handed me an ice cold Jack and Coke.

# Chapter Twenty-Five

I can't really recall exactly how the rest of the night (or rather early morning) went. I slammed down a few stiff drinks and started to feel numb, like I was ready to party and chill out. My heart wasn't broken, but it was pretty fucking tired, so I let it rest. I kept my distance from Dane. A good roll in the hay would've distracted me further, but wouldn't have solved anything, just given me more shit to deal with.

At some point in the early morning, I went looking for Dirk, Sammie, Kari and Ari. I found Sammie & Dirk making out, *like always*; looked everywhere for Kari and finally found her in Trigg's room on the house phone talking to Dax. Finally, I liberated Ari from the unscrupulous, albeit drunkenly desired attentions of a handful of Icelandic girls.

"Hey, there you are, baby girl!" Ari said, happy to see me. He stood up and toasted me, sloshing a good wave of platinum label liquor over the side of his glass. "Here's to your freedom and our adventure, which starts in," he fumbled until he uncovered his watch. "Holy Crap, it's 0618…so that means we leave in, shit—less than forty-eight hours! Well, here's to our adventure in Turkey that begins in T-47 hours."

As the party wound down, I held onto Ari. We made our way toward the door. I hollered at Sammie, as she was STILL saying goodbye to Trigg. I waved to him and Ketts.

Dane met me at the door, and I went in for the casual, chummy 'goodbye' hug and Euro kisses. Dane had something else in mind, as he pulled me into an aggressive, tight and demanding hug. I know it couldn't have been from me, but there was an active presence in the front of his jeans that I swear gave me a tiny shudder somewhere deep inside my core.

"Þú veist, Tessa *mín*, myndi ég elska að sjá þig aftur. Bráðum."

"I love it when you talk to me in Icelandic, even if I have no clue what you're saying."

"I'll give you one fucking guess it's meaning," Noah snidely remarked as he intentionally bumped into us.

"'Ey, Tessa, call off 'ye guard dog 'ey?"

Noah angrily rounded on Dane, "Come on, FUCKER… you have something to say to me? Do ya?"

I gave Noah a disgusted warning look as I intentionally positioned myself between them. Dane reached out and pulled me back into him. Yup. His caged snake was ready to escape and make its new home between my legs. I smiled at the lewdness of my thought. Noah's proximity made it doubly inappropriate, but still humorous. Dane took it as an invitation of sorts and bent his head down so his lips rested on my neck right below my ear. I looked up at him, but he was glaring past me directly at Noah.

*Are you fucking kidding me? He's instigating a fight with Noah!*

"Just so 'ye know, 'ey had said that I'd *love* to see 'ye again. Soon." His whiskey-laden invitation, whispered in my ear, wasn't one that I was seriously considering; but right at that moment, everything about Dane sent an adrenaline spike through my body, drawing my nipples taut.

"But, what I'd really like is if 'ye stayed da night with me. Ég myndi elska að grafa mig í fullkomnu litlu kisa þinn aftur. If 'ye remember, we promised we would. 'Ey have waited long enough, *sæta mín.*"

He softly whispered his reminder that doubled as an invitation in my ear. I gave his Popeye-like bicep a squeeze. "It's not gonna happen tonight, hoss."

"Yeah, or any other... *fucker,* " I heard Noah mutter under his breath behind my back. I glanced over my shoulder and looked back at Dane. Giving him a small kiss on his cheek, I said, "I'll keep that in mind," and winked at him as my entourage left his party.

We walked back with the sun glaring in our eyes, showed our IDs to the security at the front gate and walked through... all of us. Yup, even Noah, who brought up the rear.

"Hey, Tessa, you'll keep what in mind?"

I turned and looked at my best guy buddy. A drunken, although cute version of his usual self, all untucked and looking thoroughly ridden hard, even though he hadn't been.

"What was that, Ari?"

He smiled one of his million-dollar smiles. "Baby girl, you told Dane you'd keep that in mind. Keep what?" He swayed back and forth. "Is he throwing another party? Did you get another invite?"

I smiled at the funniness of the situation. "Yeah, something like that." I didn't explain any further. I heard Noah snort behind me and growl something under his breath.

*Fucking whatever dude!*

It was such an incredibly beautiful morning; cold as fuck, but the wind wasn't blowing. We'd all been walking in silence for the past ten minutes or so of a forty minute walk that it took to get back to the BEQ, nursing the beginning stages of our hangovers.

"Hey, beautiful." Noah had shouldered up beside me, surprising me with his husky tenor. I looked up at him and his face modeled that of a man ashamed for the way that he'd behaved.

"Hey," I said flatly, still angry with him over the ridiculous way he'd behaved at the party—*I knew when he decided to go that it was a bad idea.*

"You know, I'm… I'm sorry. It's just that…"

I put my hand up to stop him. Glancing around, I noticed Dirk and Ari had grouped together in the back, bullshitting and razzing Sammie and Kari about something. Sammie and Kari looked like a scene out of *Night of the Living Dead.*

Keeping my voice down as I didn't want to really have this conversation in front of everyone else, I whispered, "You know, Noah, I just don't know what to make of you. You're acting all jealous over a guy I slept with months before you, and on the same day, you alluded to *WHEN* you get back with Vi. I mean, how am I supposed to take that?" My voice quivered from pent-up emotions: frustration, confusion, hurt, love… the whole kit and caboodle. *FUCK! This is making my head ache.*

"I know." He hung his head. "I don't know why I care about Dane either. Just the thought of his greasy hands on you, and him and you… FUCK!" He grappled for control, running both hands abrasively over his face, and then one through his unruly locks. He took a deep breath, "Even though a piece of me is torn and wants to stay; you know I have to go."

I nodded and trudged forward, not sure if my traitorous eyes or the glare off the wet pavement nearly blinded me. Renegade tears rolled down my cheeks. *At least the heat from the sun feels marvelous,* I thought, swiping at my cheeks angrily. *And he's just as fucked up as I am. What a pair. No wonder we just stay stuck in this stupid place.*

He sighed heavily. "Beautiful." He stopped, turning and holding my shoulders so I faced him. "You and I... there's just something I can't explain, and it unnerves me, upends me. *Fuck, Tessa, look at what you do to me. I can't lose you no matter what happens.*"

"Well, you should've thought of that probability long before now..." My eyes refused to meet his, hurt and angry. I was over the drama and still found myself softening at his confession. *Why can't he just see what I see? Why's he think Vi's still the one for him? Fuck!*

I looked up, and his dark sapphire eyes drew me into their depths—they always did. "I just can't find it in me to play second-fiddle. I want to be with someone who wants me..."

"But I DO!"

"...and knows it, Noah. Someone who chooses me above anyone else." I broke free from his slight hold and looked to Sammie, who had nearly caught up.

"Hey Sam," I called out buoyantly, "wanna head to the Café Barista for a strong cup of joe?"

She looked from me to the guys and jogged the few steps to catch up to me. "You bet I do!" Smiling, she wrapped her arms around my shoulders. "Come on, hooka, let's ditch these losers," she looked pointedly at Noah, "and get the best damn cup of coffee you've ever had. You deserve it after last night." She hooked her arm in mine, and we started walking, elbows linked, hands buried in our pockets, in the direction of the base coffee shop.

"Forgive me?" Noah called after me, his voice unhinged.

I shouted back without looking, "I always fucking DO," and shook my head.

WE MADE it up the flights of stairs to our room with haste; shivering in the frigid halls. All I wanted to do was climb in bed and cocoon myself in my covers. We let ourselves in—but to our chagrin, our beds weren't empty. Dirk lay in Sammie's bed. *Sammie, Sammie, Sammie...* I shook my head and mentally clucked my tongue at her. She shed her jacket, kicked off her boots and flopped onto the bed beside him, and within a minute, her breathing grew deep and even.

Undressing down to my panties and camisole, I climbed into bed. Noah nuzzled up next to me in just his boxer briefs. He stirred in his sleep and said in a tortured, sleepy, diminutive voice, "Mama, please forgive me? I didn't mean to let her get stolen away." His voice changed, and he now spoke in more of a hushed whimper. "Please, Mama NO. Don't do that. Mama, please don't do that. Dad will come home—you'll see. Please forgive me, Mama? Please?"

I shook Noah awake and his striking blue eyes opened just long enough for him to pull me into him tightly and ask me, "Should I go?"

Torn, I lay silently waging a war within myself; my carnal desires outweighing every logical argument I came up with. "No. I guess I'm kind of glad you're here," I whispered softly, not wanting to awaken Dirk.

He shifted again, stirring himself awake. "Tessa?"

"Yes, Noah?"

"I leave in a few hours."

"I know."

"I just wanted to say goodbye to you one last time. I really hope you're okay with me being here. It's just, I needed…"

I smiled at his groggy admission and interrupted him. "Yeah. You know, I truly felt the need to say a final goodbye to you too, one that wasn't so… angry." I drew his arms tightly around me and snuggled more closely into his body. His package was not nearly as asleep as the rest of him; it met me with stout resistance. An instant fire ignited in my belly, a deep burning ache that throbbed for more of him. As tired as I was, I couldn't help myself and ground my ass into his hungry, restless cock.

"Tessa…?" The question fell from Noah's mouth quietly and not without a recognizable tone of shock.

I kind of purred, my contentment bubbling up in a languid kind of hum. "Mmm Hmm?"

"Let me make love to you. I think about you *every* night when I 'm alone with my thoughts, and I pray that if I get some closure, you'll stop haunting me."

His plea moved me. My soul stirred, and my body responded by deepening the already familiar ache that threatened to consume me. When I was with him, everything else, *everyone* else faded into the scenery. My steadfast resolve eroded to nothingness; no trace left for me to dispute over.

I heard Dirk say mutter something in a sleepy voice, and Sammie responded with, "Me too."

Noah and I stilled, only our heavy, passion-laden breaths audible.

"My head," he muttered. "Need air."

"Let's go for a walk then," she replied softly. I heard Sammie and Dirk rise from the bed.

Not shockingly, her keys jingled. Soft footsteps swished across the floor, and the door clicked quietly in the jamb.

Noah's large, rough hands resumed their mission-driven exploration over my hips, flirting across my flat abdomen, and up past my ribs to my full breasts, which were already heavy with desire.

"If you don't stop me, I'm going to make love to you." His lips brushed my neck as he breathily expressed his desire against the sensitive spot below my ear. His hands continued their demanding exploration across my breasts, finding my already taut nipples before he rolled and pinched them. I sucked in a sharp breath. His other hand continued its assault on my senses as it made its way south. He slid its rough strength into my barely-there panties, his middle finger sliding through my moist valley repeatedly before it entered me. His thumb negotiated circles around my most sensitive bud.

*Oh, my fucking God. I don't want him to make love to me, I want him to fuck me now. Hard.*

My brain and body were no longer warring against each other. It was as though two opposing forces had joined the same mission, and now both fought to get me to an explosive orgasm.

The intense pleasure Noah aroused in me should've been illegal. I can't even explain how responsive my nerves were; even the air circulating by the fan from across the room tickled my skin and made my hairs stand on edge. Noah's onslaught on my breast and clitoris as he drilled me with two fingers made breathing nearly impossible.

One second, I lay writhing on my side against Noah's rigidity. One well-executed maneuver later, he'd roughly flipped me onto my back and was grinding his impressive cock between my eager thighs.

"Oh my God, Tessa. You have no idea how badly I've wanted to have you underneath me, writhing for me… and I can fucking tell you this much," he growled in a husky, passion-laden voice, "this time I'm going to give you more than a goddamn *feel*."

His mouth melded with mine… branding me. Claiming me. Our lips danced to our own beat with a fierceness that had only been matched that morning in the tour bus. His tongue teased and sparred with mine, our lips merging perfectly. I couldn't get enough of Noah. My hands in his thick hair pulled him to me, before sliding onto his powerful back, feeling his muscles bunch and flex as he moved over me. The assault he was orchestrating forced my hand, and I couldn't keep my exploration from heading to his sculpted ass. Grabbing his hips, I pulled his huge fucking dick toward me.

"Noah…"

"Mmm hmm."

"Noah, I want you to take me, fucking take me the way I want to take you."

Noah paused, pulling his mouth away from my neck. "Oh? And, my sweet Tessa," his mouth went down to my nipples and I drew in a sharp breath of air, "exactly how *would* that be?" He lifted his head and raised an eyebrow at me as the corner of his mouth turned up in a smartass smirk. Even then, the absence of his lips on my skin left a vacancy in my soul.

"This is our one and only night together, and I am not looking for sweet love." My voice dropped as I suddenly became self-conscious at how wanton I sounded.

"So, let me get this straight. You don't want me to make love to you? You want me to fuck you. HARD." His voice cracked as he said the latter.

I couldn't find my voice, so I nodded as I arched my back, sending my most private parts aggressively into his rigid and twitching cock. He responded by throwing my calves up over his ass. He drilled against my sheathed apex, grinding hard against me before nestling his cock quietly on my dripping sex.

"See, I knew it!" He growled his victory huskily into my ear. "I knew you'd be up for the kink, the lewd fucking lascivious shit I'm into. You don't know what you've asked for. I'm going to fuck you until I have to leave, and, you *will* come so hard you won't be able to walk, well into next week. You won't be able to think of anyone but me, the entire time I'm gone."

My eyes widened just before his mouth came down on mine in another soul-wrenching kiss that curled my toes. Noah grabbed the already raised hem of my camisole and rolled it into a makeshift blindfold as he pulled it up over my eyes. He reached down and, with a swift tug, tore my sheer panties off. My heart leapt into my throat, pounding like a freight train.

"God, Tessa, these are so fucking wet. I cannot get enough of you. I love the way you smell." He positioned a hard thigh between my legs and slid the other farther up the bed…I presume so he could balance, as the next thing he did was tie my hands together with my barely-there panties.

"You're so beautiful, Tessa; painfully, sinfully so. Do you have any idea the depth of my desire for you? How long I have ached to feel your hot, wet pussy around my cock? You have no idea what this means to me, or, since I've met you, how many nights I've lain awake in bed, needing to make you mine. Imagining how to make this happen; what I'd do to you. How you'd look tied up; how sweet your begging would sound; the readiness of your sex; how you'd taste. Jeezus, Tessa! What have you done to me? Will I ever be able to get over you?" His voice faltered, and was already so soft, I strained to hear him. It seemed as if he was confessing these things to himself; I wasn't so sure they were meant for me to hear. They made him sound so vulnerable, so goddamn sexy and… breakable.

*I want to break you like you've broken me…*

I felt his weight shift, and then his mouth arrived at my already over sensitized sex, merely a breath's distance away from the source of my raging need. It drove me crazier than his one hand teasing my nipples. His other hand handled my hip firmly, manipulating it in such a way that his desire surged through even the tips of his fingers.

His tongue plundered my most sensitive spot, which had already swelled and begun aching with desire. My hands clenched and fisted in their bonds, and my head tossed as I felt the momentum building toward my orgasm. He continued his assault as his ravenous tongue lashed and flicked my clit, all while two fingers drove into me, teasing my g-spot. I felt the waves cresting, and right when I felt I would surely die from the intensity, Noah rammed his enraged cock full tilt into me. His mouth covered mine to muffle the orgiastic cry that was ripped from deep within me. My salty juices provided a sweet contrast that co-mingled on our lips.

Noah ripped the blindfold off me and double banded my wrists.

"I need to see you, Tessa. I need to see your eyes when I come." His voice snarled, harsh with restraint, and his engorged cock twitched at that moment, causing my back to arch from its sheer depth.

"You feel so good. Oh my God, Noah. I just had…" I

struggled for the breath to express myself. "I had NO IDEA it would be like this with you."

"I did. I knew it from the moment our souls collided and our bodies entwined together so perfectly. I knew you would do this to me."

Vulnerable from sharing, he began to circle his hips, withdrawing and plunging deeply into me, as though he needed me to experience for myself how incredible he knew it would be. I countered each of his thrusts, time and time again.

Noah was truly beautiful to behold, his brow furled in concentration and restraint, his eyes hooded with passion, his lips parted, raking in harsh, shallow breaths. Every time he slowly and with antagonizing, deliberate measure withdrew to his turgid head, and then crammed his rigid, torrid length root-deep into me, I broke even further. I loved how he rutted with harsh ferocity, then withdrew with leisurely ease. His eyes never once left mine. Never closed. His gaze remained married to mine, always seeking, imploring, and demanding my truths. Our orgasms both built at an excruciatingly deliberate pace; Noah's experience and unfathomable restraint delayed our simultaneous climax.

"Tess—ah, …I can't any longer. I can't…" Noah sat fully upright on his knees, and with both hands, yanked my hips up so only my shoulder blades remained on the bed. The power he used to pull me onto him as he lustfully pounded into me—while his eyes bored unwavering into mine—drove me over the edge. I came undone. Wave after wave of sheer ecstasy hit me.

"Goddamn it—look at me!" He growled.

I opened my eyes in time to see him break above me. Still rippling with my own orgasm, I felt his rigid length explode inside me, pumping his hot seed into me; his cock pulsing now to my body's own rhythm. If I hadn't known before that I loved him, I certainly did now. There's no way to share such a crippling, soul-shattering climax unless hearts had become involved. He collapsed onto his forearms on either side of me, and then, with his right hand he reached up and yanked the lace bindings from my wrists. My hands enveloped him as he laid his chest on mine.

"Tessa…"

"Noah." I felt a single renegade tear escape from the corner of my eye.

"I can't even describe what you've done to me."

"I know. Me either."

Noah moved in for a sensual, languorous kiss—one that stole away what little breath I had left. Gasping, Noah sat back on his heels, still buried inside me. In sheer wonderment, I tried to wrap my brain around how, if he'd already come, and wasn't fully hard, he still remained fully buried in my pussy. *Noah has one impressive fucking cock.*

I couldn't help the ridiculous, cat-got-the-mouse, shit-eating grin from spreading across my face.

Noah chuckled. "Looks like I did something right." Winking at me, he gave me that arrogant half smirk of his. I could feel how rigid and unyielding he had become in me again.

"Maybe…" I teased, squeezing my inner muscles so that they undulated along his cock.

Noah clenched his teeth in an effort to remain in charge. "Hmm. Well, if you're not too sure, then maybe I should rectify that?" He pulled out and with lightning reflexes flipped me so I lay face down. He grabbed my hips, snapping me up to him, ass high in the air before he crammed me full to the hilt again; smacking my ass for good measure.

"I still need to make good on my promise that you'll not be able to walk or forget me while I'm gone." Noah grabbed the tendrils of hair at the base of my neck, wrapping them around his fist. He planted his other over my shoulder and began another calculated assault—one of many before we were both too spent to move.

As I finally drifted into a dream state, I heard, "I love you," fall from his lips in a sleepy confession. All I could think was that I couldn't agree more.

*I am so broken. Fucking Vi.*

LOUD KNOCKING WOKE me from my fitful slumber. I could hear it way off in the distance, but didn't want to move, to end the dreamy state I was in. *I don't want to get up. Didn't we just fucking close our eyes?* I turned my head toward Noah, taking in how confident and sweet he looked while he rested.

"Babe, there's someone at the door," I purred in Noah's ear. He held my hips captive in his strong hold, while he lazily rubbed his growing erection against my backside. "Bet if we ignore them long enough they'll go away. It's only 0945."

This earned me a thrust, as he moved more powerfully against me, and I could feel his rigid cock at my ass.

"9:45?! Oh my God, let me up!" He shifted from behind me and bounded out of bed. Grabbing his briefs, he ran to the door, tripping on discarded clothing and shoes. He reached the door and threw it open.

Dirk stood there disheveled, groggy, and looking all the worse for wear. "Oh, this is great. You have *got* to be fucking kidding me. Good thing I decided to check on your sorry ass—

you should've been on the 0935 transport to the airport! Your flight is at 1145 and you're supposed to arrive there two hours early to clear customs and get weighed in. Damnit, Noah! Don't just stand there. You're going to blow your ticket… get the fuck ready. You're already late!"

Noah left the door ajar and sprang into action. He had thrown on his sexy briefs—*oh my God they do nothing to hide his erection*—and sat on the edge of my bed tugging on his jeans.

"What can I do to help?"

"Please help me find my shirt and shoes. Fuck, I can't find *shit* in here."

I slid off the bed, grabbed my robe and began sorting through our discarded items scattered across the floor.

Noah stood, and as he brushed past me, took them items I held out and gave me a quick squeeze.

"Just breathe. The plane isn't going to leave without you, and they never leave on time anyway," I offered with a smile, trying to calm his nerves.

"Shit, Tessa, I have less than five minutes if I want to catch the 0955 bus, which is NEVER going to happen… I still have to run back to the barracks and get my shit packed." Noah's tone verged on panic. I could see he was hustling his ass off, so he could get to the airport in time, but even I felt doubtful.

He finished getting dressed, grabbed his jacket and zipped it, ran a hand through his unruly hair and looked back at me. Noah had nearly made it out the door when he paused and turned, grabbing my arm. He pulled me against his body for a heart-fluttering, pussy-clenching kiss.

"No matter what happens, you have part of my heart and soul forever. Last night meant more to me than even I could've imagined. You've done something to me. Permanently. I have A

LOT to think about. I just wanted you to know that before I leave today."

"All I have to say is—thanks for last night." My voice cracked, and I nearly lost my shit. I fought for control of my emotions and struggled to keep my mask in place. *Last night was the closure we both needed in order to move on.* "I wish you the best of luck, and the rest... how I feel just doesn't matter because you've already bought your tickets." I smiled sadly. Tears welled up again, and if he didn't leave soon, he'd see the dam break.

"Noah—now! You've got to go!" The urgency in Dirk's voice seemed to resonate with him. He broke our embrace and strode toward the still open door. Dirk had already started down the hall.

Noah turned back one last time. The vision of him standing in the middle of our hallway—wrinkled and unsure, scrubbing his hands over his face while he swiped fiercely at his traitorous eyes—burned itself into my memory. I shut the door, blocking the image.

Seconds later a knock sounded at my door. I flung it open and to my shock, there stood Noah, tears on his cheeks, and his heart on his sleeve. He was my very vision of a loveable man, a desirable partner, a sexy lover and a beautiful soul—my other half. Seeing him there, feeling what it did to my heart and how my soul swelled to new proportions, I knew he was my soul mate. I flung myself at him, and his strong arms caught me, encircling me with their strength, squeezing me to him as he grabbed a fistful of my loose locks and laid a no holds barred kiss on me that weakened my knees.

When our mouths parted, I looked into Noah's eyes and saw fear. I brushed a quick kiss on his parted lips. I smiled weakly at him one last time before I gently pushed him, encouraging him to go.

I'd nearly gotten the door closed. "Tessa!" The most grieved, insecure and wounded voice called for me—causing me to freeze in my tracks. I opened the door a crack. Noah still stood before me, wearing yesterday's unkempt clothes, but completely naked. I blew him a final kiss, my glassy emerald eyes mesmerized by his liquid pools of indigo until the closing door broke our connection. The sound of the door clicking in its jamb echoed deeply in me. I rested my forehead on its cool surface, tears of anguish fell down my cheeks, unchecked. More than one door had just closed.


The End

Look for: Veneration

An excerpt from book two of Noah & Tessa's story

at the back of this book.


Coming soon: Vexed

Noah and Vi's story in St. John, told from Noah's POV.

# Acknowledgments

First I want to thank God for instilling my love of writing and for giving me the gift of expression through writing. There were many times I wondered if I were on the right path, but I always came back to Him and when I did I became refocused and confident in my choices. Writing centers me and genuinely makes me happy.

I want to thank my rock-star of a husband for loving me unconditionally, even when I can be trying. Sometimes, getting the right words out was a struggle, and I know it stressed me out, but you remained sweet and supportive throughout the process. You are the Yin to my Yang, my balance and constant that I count on when the world is spinning. Thanks for understanding my crazy hours, long nights, for entertaining the kiddos on the weekends and in the evenings so I could get some writing in, for sleeping on the couch beside me while I stayed up writing much later than I should've, for your constant encouragement and endless support, and for so, so much more. You're my best friend, lover, and life-long partner in crime. I love you forever. More than you know.

A special thanks also to my smart, charming, wonderful, demanding, attitude-y, hugely-loving, energetic, and supportive kiddos for putting up with me often writing when I should've been joining in more. You provided me the time I needed, sometimes more than I should've taken, when you needed my attention, to let me finish the thoughts I needed to get down. I love you bigger than the Universe, and you two are the center of my Universe. My world revolves around you, even if I took a detour to write Volition. You're my daily reason why. Your unconditional love, constant support, sweet smiles, tight hugs, generous cuddles, and witty words of encouragement pushed me to finish this first book, and fulfill my dream of becoming a published author.

I'd like to thank my parents for your love and support. Your encouraging words and kindness mean more to me than you realize. I especially need to thank my mom, my first and longest best friend, for always knowing that I was a writer, and for reminding me often that I should follow my dreams. You've always told me I had the gift for writing, and have always encouraged me to do what I was good at from a very early age. Sorry, Mom it took me so long to hear what you were saying and to believe it. Thanks too, for sharing your books—*Sky O'Malley* and *Timeless Passion*—with me when I was a teenager and a voracious reader. They were sweet romances that filled my head with romantic notions that encouraged me to hold out for a true, sweet love. Mostly though, thanks for always being my constant since childhood, the one I could call any time, day or night as I traveled the world. All my love, Momma.

*I need to give credit where credit is due…to my team who put in the hours and work. You all helped make Volition happen:*

Jude. There's so much I am thankful for, the list is long. For being the first to read Volition in its raw form and even liking it then. For never losing touch. For knowing so much more than me and imparting your wisdom and know-how with this whole book publishing process. For sharing Simone with me, the best editor ever. For genuinely (which is rare), wanting my success as much as I want it. For always being quick on beta turn-around times. Without fail, I can COUNT ON YOU EVERY TIME to read something for me and get back to me quickly while I am anxiously waiting, and we both know I seriously lack patience. You have been a steadfast friend and a tremendous support when I needed feedback, ideas, or when I had writer's block and just needed a stress-free break. As time has gone on, you have never wavered through the years; your generosity with your time and friendship means the world to me. I love ya girly!

Simone. I know you came in at the photo-finish of my four-year journey with Volition, but without you I never would have made it to the finish line. You got me from the get-go, and I loved how easily we were on the same page through the entire process. Working with you was a dream. You took my raw diamond, and polished it for me. I am so grateful. Thank you for helping me un-edit my book, helping me recover my voice beneath the layers of previous edits. It was a daunting task, and when you suggested it, I wholeheartedly wanted to say no! I was concerned it was too big of a task with the challenges I face. So, I am beyond grateful for your support, boundless encouragement, selfless commitment to helping me get Noah and Tessa's story told, and for the hours upon hours you spent with me, Noah and Tessa, instead of with your family. (Thank Eddie and the kids for me!) Thanks for being so generous with your time, expertise, and self in spite of your family, other personal projects, career and crazy life. Your feedback was invaluable to this project and I cannot wait to work with you on my others. Yours has become a friendship I truly value.

Lisa. For being my mentor; my first initial contact four years ago when I reached out on a random Facebook page asking about how to write a book, get it edited, and published. You have always been by my side through the highs and lows of it all with your support, unmatched wisdom, continued encouragement, amazing ideas, late night and early morning brainstorming sessions, honest opinions, and forgiveness. When I needed a beta reader you introduced me to Jude—our amazing friend—and helped me build my remarkable team. You're friendship is authentic and I'm blessed to have met you.

Kari. You gave my book and brand a face and I cannot thank you enough for the gorgeous logo and cover you created. I get compliments on it every time I share it on social media. You listened to me, dealt with my indecisiveness and multitude of changes and never once complained. You are a true pro in every sense of the word and I cannot thank you enough for working on this project until I felt it was right.

Lastly, this book wouldn't have even made the leap from my head to the page if I hadn't read some amazing books by some pretty remarkable authors. Through your example I became so inspired and encouraged that I finally sat down to seriously write. Thank you Kristy, Sylvia, Pepper, Eva, CJ, Laurelin, Kristen, Constance, Judith, Mary, Victoria, and many others. You'll never know how much your books mean to me.

*Excerpt*

Veneration
A Uniform & Lace Romance
*Noah & Tessa's Story*
*~Book Two~*

All Rights are Reserved and Copyrighted
2018 by Tina Maurine.
*(Excerpt may change before final publication.)*

"Dirk's been telling me about Noah since he got back. I guess his trip was cut short, and then there's Ari. I mean it all just piled up—you having everyone and me feeling like I don't really have anyone. So, anyways… sorry for being all jealous and shit, and for lashing out at you." Her apology gushed from her like a breath held too long that explodes out, uncontainable and forceful. I gave her a reassuring smile and another quick hug to reassure her that all was fine between us.

*Noah's back? He got back early?!*

I peeked around the corner of the doorjamb, and Lucas's eyes connected with mine. They grew large as he rolled them, and then, giving his head a little nod, he tried to tell me to get our asses back in there.

"First of all… everyone does not want me. Secondly, YOU have got to catch me up on Trigg and you—Ketts and Dane. Thirdly," as I took a deep breath, my chest involuntarily constricted, "you need to fill me in about Dirk and Noah." I had planned on having a *fourthly*—if there is such a thing—and even a finally, but after just saying Noah's name, I couldn't get anything else out.

"Let's go rescue the guys." Sammie threw a head nod in the direction of the kitchen. "I'll catch you up later."

As we walked in, the two Aviation Technicians (ATs) who worked with the guys in the intermediate leveled shops back home stood up from their chairs and smiled as they walked past us. Lucas rose, grabbing seconds and offering to get us more, but I was having a hard time getting through all the food he'd already served me before Sammie had pulled me into the hallway.

Ace was the first to speak, after taking a long draw from his beer. "So, everything fine with you two? Is your lover's spat finally over?" He chuckled and I raised my beer to him, tipping it in a sarcastic toast.

"We're fine. It's just, this deployment can really get to ya sometimes, right, Sam?"

She nodded at me, smiling back.

"So, let me get this right. You guys worked for like three days on your detachment to Turkey—that's it, and you were gone a week?" Incredulity heavy in his tenor. "What did you guys do Friday, Saturday and Sunday?" Lucas had reseated himself at the table after grabbing us all a new, ice-cold brewski from the fridge.

"Well, the officers and aircrew still had to fly two more days with the NATO forces, so we readied the birds the first day, packed up a shit-load of parts we never used, tools and materials, so we'd be ready to jet out Monday—then we did some sightseeing." I paused to shovel another bite of calzone heaven into my mouth, washing it down with my beer, which seemed to get better and better with each swig I drew off it.

"Okay, so other than the coastline, which I'm assuming you liked, what was your favorite part you saw while you were there?"

I turned my head startled to hear a voice coming from behind me—a *very* familiar voice. My eyes connected instantly to deep pools of blue—stormy, grey-blue eyes that I had missed for too long, and yet not long enough to move on…

*…if I ever could.*

I sat paralyzed, glancing at everyone at the table and then turning to look back at Noah as he walked around to my side.

"Well, get up and come give me a hug!" His playful command came out in an emotionally laden tone, walking the line his voice took when it was full of lust and desire.

*Oh. My.*

I stood mechanically at first, and then I rushed him. My heart winning out over my mind, I threw my arms around his neck as he pulled me to him tightly for a full-body hug. Everything about me that felt skewed the last few days immediately righted themselves and our souls drew together like magnets, each recharged off of what the other offered. It was a truly carnal and nearly supernatural thing, how we connected so completely. So borderline indecently.

Noah's arms wrapped around my waist, pulling me into his already thickening desire for me. His arm shifted, crossing my back, pressing my taut nipples into his thin, t-shirt clad chest. His hand, nesting at the nape of my neck, guided my lips towards his. I could feel his breath coming in short, hot pants—mirroring my own. His lips grazed mine, eliciting a shudder from me. Then he kissed me, delicately at first, then more fully. It was a kiss that didn't just tell me things, it screamed confirmations about how much he'd missed me... and then our lips began a lascivious dance—pulling, drinking, robbing the other's senses.

"Fuck, why don't you just kiss her already?" Ace quipped, and then laughed as I heard his beer bottle tap two others behind me in a toast.

I pulled my ravished lips from Noah's skillful ones, only able to drag in ragged breaths. My emerald eyes once again connected to his gaze—now a heated cerulean hue.

*Goddamn, he's hot. I lov...* I caught myself before I admitted the depth of my feelings for him. I just couldn't go there—Vi and Suri were still swimming around in the back of my mind. *What had happened on Saint John?*

He smiled a wicked little half smile at me before placing a chaste kiss on my forehead. He spun me around and, placing either hand on my hips, pulled my ass to him. I leaned back against him in a reverse full body hug—we didn't need our arms for our bodies to connect completely. I blushed, remembering the things he had done to me the last time he'd placed his hands on my hips like this...

"So, Tessa..." Lucas cleared his throat, obviously turned on to a degree by what he'd just seen, which was understandable, seeing as how he was remaining completely faithful to his wife back home and it had been a couple weeks shy of three months since we'd left Jacksonville. "...about what Noah asked. What did you like the best while you were there?"

I pushed my ass off the substantially hard cock I'd been resting against and playfully negotiated Noah off the fridge door. "Anyone care for a beer?" I ended up pulling out a total of five, opened them and passed them around. I took a seat at the table, and Noah pulled up a chair beside me, taking my fork and shoveling a large bite from my calzone into his mouth.

"Well, one day we went to Incirlik and the other to Adana, both pretty close to the base. We actually went to Incirlik a few times with a handful of guys and gals stationed there and some guys from the Royal Airforce. The small village-town was within walking distance about twenty minutes away, and there were some local bars—dives really—that stayed open late, especially if we were there spending money."

"Yeah, I've been down Incirlik's narrow, dingy, dirt road more than a few times, coming and going from ops out of Kuwait, but Adana's markets are a whole lot more fun to get lost in, especially if you're drinking, wouldn't you agree?" Noah laughed, knowing full-well that I knew better than to get trashed and then try to sightsee and keep my bearings. I was way too much about being in control to let myself lose control in that kind of a situation.

*Any situation really... unless Tad was the one taking away my control.*

The slightest blush crept up my cheeks to my ears. I prayed no one noticed, so I quickly went on. "Yeah, I mean hanging with the crew at night was fun, and I bought a great black leather cigar jacket from Incirlik, but you're right; if I'd had more time I would've definitely gone back to Adana... after all, it was only like five or ten miles away, and *oh man,* the shopping I could've done!" I giggled and Sammie snorted. She knew I was a total shopaholic.

"Get anything good in Adana? Buy anything extra that I could buy from you and send to my wife?"

"Oh, Lucas, I'm sorry, but the best thing I picked up was a pair of leather string sandals... the soles are made from tires. Oh, and I picked up a pretty marble backgammon board for my dad, and an ornate scarf for Tulla Dean." I watched Lucas's eager, hopeful eyes turn dismal. "Oh wait, I have some Turkish Delight that you can send her!"

Lucas looked at me cautiously, "What the *fuck* is a Turkish Delight—some kind of sex toy?"

*Oh my Gawd!! Now that's too funny...*

"No, stupid," I said good naturedly, as I laughed. "Turkish Delight is a gummy, marshmallowy treat made of dried nuts, fruits, syrup, and some other shit. It's a national favorite. I personally hate the stuff, but to each his own. I bought a bunch 'cause everyone was raving about how great it was—and Kupps bargained for it and got it for a really good price. It's known as lokum in Turkish—a word also used to refer to a voluptuous woman." I giggled, "Now *that* I learned having a shot of elixir in some rug shop; Kupps actually knew where the closest pastane or souvenir shop was from there." My soliloquy died on my lips and I quickly brought the beer to my lips and took a long hard draw, giving me plenty of time to take a breath and think...

*Oh shit. Kupps...*

*Did Noah pick up on that or anyone else? FUCK! How many beers have I had? Four, maybe? Damn I should've eaten more...*

I looked over at Sammie, and she raised an eyebrow at me, then at Lucas. He looked at me and cleared his throat.

"Oh, okay so Kupps is from your shop? You work with him?" Noah's tenor hitched a bit at the end, obviously nervous about how I'd answer his questions.

"Yeah, pretty much."

Okay, so Kupps *was* basically from my shop... I mean *so what* if he was the Division Officer? Nobody sitting at the table could really go about hearing what I had to say and then throw stones. Noah didn't *REALLY* need to know all the specifics. Besides, he did just get back from seeing his baby's mama, and I am *SURE* they fucked up one side and down the other… that is, after all, what Noah does well.

I hurriedly went on so that he wouldn't continue along that line of questioning. "So, I have a few bars that you're more than welcome to; in fact, there are probably enough for all of you to have some."

I didn't have to glance at Noah to feel his heated gaze on me. He gave me a rough squeeze on my thigh. I jumped just a little, and a nervous giggle escaped. "So, what did you guys do while I was gone for the week?" I eyed the table, and then looked squarely at Noah. "How was *your* visit with Pallavi and Suri?"

Noah stood up, lifting me by my elbow. "Join me in the hall, Tessa?" His steely tone left no room for argument. As he briskly led me toward the door I tossed out a flippant, "I'll be right back, guys—don't do anything I wouldn't do!"

I heard someone shout, "That's doesn't really limit us very much!" and they all laughed.

Who is Tina Maurine?

Tina Maurine is the gal on the sidelines at the party. The gal who smiles at everyone, but rarely initiates conversation; never the center of attention, but always taking notes on those who are. She loves watching people, their authentic responses to everyday occurrences and in turn has turned years of notes into fodder for her stories, an encyclopedia of emotions and character traits that come alive on the page. She never feels more alive than when she is creating; be it stories, music, graphic art, or painting rocks and canvases with her daughter.

She is a wife, mom, best friend, secretary, teacher, cheerleader, house-straightener, chef, chauffer, video game playing, Barbie doll dressing domestic multi-tasker. She likes her French baguettes crispy, her beer dark, and her chocolate even darker. Her music tastes are eclectic, but if there's a beat, you can bet her body is moving to it… even in the car… and the louder the better.

Tina Maurine lives in Oregon with her amazing husband of twelve years, and their two beautiful children. Prior to marriage and children, she served eight years in the United States Navy and saw the world. She and her husband share their love for travel with their kids, and take as many family trips as their busy schedules allow. When they aren't hitting the road or the skies, and when she isn't teaching, Tina is content to sit at the table in their backyard with her keyboard or a good, sexy book, and watch the kiddos play.

Follow her on Twitter and Instagram @ TinaMaurineAuth
Email: tinamaurine@hotmail.com
http://facebook.com/tina.maurine.1
http://tinamaurine.com